CREATURE
STORMS

·············· ❧ ··············

CREATURE STORMS

❧

RON CLINTON SMITH

To order additional copies of this book, contact:
Xlibris Corporation
1-888-795-4274
www.Xlibris.com
Orders@Xlibris.com
110087

For Sue, Jeremiah and Sean

In time of war the loudest patriots are the greatest profiteers.

—August Bebel

Beware of the leaven of the Pharisees, which is hypocrisy. For there is nothing covered, that shall not be revealed; neither hidden, that shall not be known. Therefore, whatever ye have spoken in darkness shall be heard in the light; and that which ye have spoken in the ear in private rooms shall be proclaimed upon the housetops. And I say unto you, my friends, Be not afraid of them that kill the body, and after that have no more that they can do. But I will forewarn you whom ye shall fear: Fear him who, after he hath killed, hath power to cast into hell; yea, I say unto you, Fear him.

Luke 12: 1-5

CREATURE STORMS

Cambodia, near the Mekong Delta, 1967 —Operation Wandering Soul

The voice came first, ghostly and indecipherable like the cries of some wailing, prehistoric bird floating through the trees. When he heard the chopper the VC squad leader Lt. Chin Ghai Trang signaled his troops into the high elephant grass along the river. It was the first time he or any of them had heard a sound like that in the jungle, with or without the thrumming, and the pitch and timbre of it froze them.

Sergeant Jim "Honcho" Hawkins pushed his Huey a thousand feet off the mist-solid riverbed through cloud-cover so dense it was impossible to see any ceiling as folds of fog rolled into jungle. So far he'd been lucky on these spook missions but he wasn't crazy about them. There were pilots and crews who wouldn't fly them, gut-sure they were tempting bad luck or worse, but the missions had returned few casualties. The tapes seemed to make the Cong curious, but he knew it wouldn't last. Any day as the weather cleared they'd cease wondering and open up with their big cannons. He was nearing the end of his second tour and getting superstitious again. He swore if he didn't make it through one of these harassing gigs he was coming back with his own little harrying visit for his CO.

Parrot, a wiry-nervous blonde-haired kid from Baton Rouge hung by his monkey belt in the open door with his 70 mm. angled on the riverbank, working a fast chew. Through the voice-squalling which made him nervous as a cat he was all reflexes for a flash or the sound of rattling metal on the fuselage. Machine-gun fire killed the effect and reason for these operations, they were told, and they'd been ordered not to open up unless heavily fired upon. Two weeks ago a door-gunner had been knocked from his chopper by small arms fire, and Parrot had been jumpy ever since, peppering herons occasionally and languar monkeys in rubber trees.

Music Man crouched with his headphones by his reel-to-reel monitoring the volume and reverb with the voice's shrill pitch, a grease-smeared script in his lap. Every twenty seconds he'd boost the volume blurring it to give it a trill-like, other-worldly effect, then pull it back so that the words stood out but tremored as they reverberated. He'd rehearsed it until he could milk it like an Italian opera. It was an arcane art spooking the chinks. He figured the Air Cav was lucky to have the ear of a true Jersey sound man for this. He could plant the ethereal voice like God's own in the dreams of the Viet Cong and make them believe it.

Perelman, Honcho's copilot, a cocky, mustached MIT grad from Rhode Island, watched the mirrored snake squirrel and uncoil through the mist. He'd just passed out Cubans for his baby girl in the states and was feeling more bulletproof than usual. Joining up to fly choppers for the sport of it he viewed every mission as a day at an amusement park and these demoralization runs bored the hell out of him. He felt better when the bright-red,-white and-green tracers began to float up at them out of the trees.

The squawk boxes beneath the Huey blared as the chopper churned upriver. A shard of light slit the cockpit hitting Honcho like a bolt through his third eye, a radiant horse kick to the brow as he fumbled for his flight glasses. His cornea was light-sensitve from a Plexiglas sliver nicking it his first tour when his windshield disintegrated under 50 mm. fire. After months of heavy monsoons intense light burned his eyes like smoldering pearls. The weather was breaking finally. In a few weeks the real war would commence again. The Cong would have plenty of gun emplacements waiting for them around firebases carried in under the rains. On the Tennessee mountain farm where he'd grown up there'd be snow now, ice on those winding roads, and plenty of fog like this. He didn't miss it.

This was where he belonged. Regardless of how many lily-livered kids protested this war he would tough it out until every one of these soulless communist roaches were sent to hell. He chewed the end of his Cuban and chuckled as he hummed "This little light of mine . . ." over the shrill voice whining under his cockpit.

Chin Ghai Trang crouched in the grass listening to the shrieking voice with the rotorthuds. Two young soldiers beside him, farmer's sons from northern villages who'd joined the VC nine months ago as friends, watched him as they listened to the strange, unholy trill. They'd heard every noise in the jungle since childhood, human, animal, machine, and this sounded nothing like them.

"Man or wounded animal?" the first said.

"Man," Trang said. "A tortured one."

They could make out words now, a pleading-whining in Vietnamese changing the hairs on the backs of their necks.

"My living descendants . . . I died at your sides . . . I beseech you beyond the grave to give up this senseless struggle . . ."

"Is he speaking to us?" the second soldier said.

"What do you think?"

". . . before all our sisters and brothers are massacred, burned and buried . . . defect to a peaceful life . . . don't desecrate our deaths we beseech you . . ."

There was a short, stabbing howl as if the voice had been pierced followed by fluttering groans.

"How can the dead speak from helicopters?"

"If pushed from them to die."

"Are you joking?"

"About that I wouldn't."

"You've seen it?"

"Shut up and listen," Trang said.

". . . defect and stop fighting we implore you from the graves of all Viet Cong wasting our blood . . . We wander forever in our misery . . . Stop dying and bring us peace . . . lay down your weapons . . . save yourselves . . . tu cuu khoi . . . tu cuu . . ."

As the chopper skirted the riverbank the timbre of the voice made them flinch and squeeze their rifles. They shrunk into the speared leaves as the echoes seemed to surround them wailing mournfully, a forlorn, abandoned howling, popping blades seeming to blur with it in the jungle as if it were trapped or both were tangled up in the trees thwacking around in grappling circles. They waited, sweat dripping from their chins listening to the pattering dissolve into jungle chatter. After a while there was only the isolated voice by itself with the other animal sounds as they'd heard it before, crying back to them like some stray, aberrant creature wandering through the trees.

Eastern Tennessee, 1986

Ninety miles west of Knoxville in ozone country a near-perfect corridor runs north and south between two mountain ranges for sixty miles. Rich and mostly rocky farmland, it was far from the world until the new Air Force base was built at the north end of the valley. Not part of any game refuge or national park, being off the beaten path and flanked by natural barriers kept wildlife lush and forests unspoiled in that part of the country. The roads in and out were mostly rugged, twisted and wild, the closest towns small and made up of farm families who'd been there for generations.

Sixteen miles out of Treetorn off Highway 17 was the farmstead settled by Terrence and Irma Hawkins thirteen years before the South seceded from the Union. There had never been a slack or failing crop of tobacco, corn, cotton or soybeans on the seventy-six-hundred acre spread, if you didn't count the four years Terrence had fought with Nathan Bedford Forrest as a Lt. Major in the 3rd Tennessee Cavalry and the Army of Tennessee. It was a Hawkins code of generosity to feed neighboring farmers who weren't so lucky. The Hawkins secret to prosperity had always been keeping the code, planting by signs, rotating crops and following the teaching from *Deuteronomy* of letting fields lie fallow every seventh year. These things had worked for them. They were what "living right" meant to five generations of Hawkins and the spread had been blessed through what were hard times for the rest of the county, sometimes the state. Except for a modernizing of machinery and farming techniques little about the farm had changed in a hundred years.

On a warm, clear night in late April Deke Hawkins sat in the center of three wide picture windows of the farmhouse where his father had sat with his paper every night for thirty-nine years. There was moonlight sufficient to see the furniture was covered in bed sheets. In heat lightning everything through the picture windows, in the yard outside, beyond, and everything in the living room came alive in daylight flashes. Deke stared motionless through the glass except to itch a chigger or mosquito sting. Light on his rippling forearms showed a roadmap of briar scratches and dried blood. His hands had hardened leather calluses like alligator skin. At forty-two he had the lean, chiseled body of a twenty-year-old man, and his face was sharp, hawk-like with a pitted complexion. He more than his two brothers had always had his father's Indian strength. Deke even looked a little Indian though there was no known descent of it in his bloodline. American flag paper weights anchored the edges of sheets on tables and dressers. It wasn't lost on him that the sheets made the house seem ghoulish, as if it, or he, needed any of that. Every time he came here he felt the urge to yank all the sterile-looking things off of the furniture, pile them up in the middle of the living room and set the whole damn place on fire. Instead he stumbled in like some wayward ghost, a sleepwalker, some estranged houseguest. He sat in the same spot on the couch indented by his father having sat there for forty years and watched silently into the yard, listening.

Through the middle picture window his eyes fixed on a dozen gourds swinging from the top of bent poles like dangling heads blowing and bumping around each other. In flashes he saw the rickety, spinning windmill on the barbed wire fence and knotted strands gleaming. Corn stalks in the field behind them that'd been rotting on the ground for eighteen months. The line of tin sheds to his right beneath which his father's '48 Ford truck stood by the barns, giant pecan trees bulking suddenly in the yard like frozen dinosaurs. A half-hearted cricket sang from the kitchen to one outside in the wind. The wind chime he'd made from pipes for his mother as a kid jangled erratic tones on the porch. Everything in the yard had a dull-silver sheen from the moon.

Wearing army boots and camouflage fatigues he'd sat for most of an hour like this, chin down, a half-amused smirk on his face, listening and staring out. After a while he got up slowly, the floor gentle-creaking as he went to the wall of pictures leading into the dining room. Familiar outlines in the photos blinked back like shocked glimpses from daylight scenes as if the people in them were surprised to see anyone looking back at them. His father in overalls with Honcho and himself as kids on a tractor. Their mother in the same field bent-over in jeans, faded shirt and orange scarf, grinning at the camera. The family of five when Jason was three, Deke and Honcho fifteen and eighteen huddled together on the steps in front of the screen porch. A large aerial photo of the farmhouse showing sheds, barns and silos under the thick pecan grove, a shadow from one of the trees shaped into the field like a running dog. Pictures of himself and his brothers with beagles in high corn. A couple of the whole family fighting a mud battle in a field after a day's work, Madge hurling and getting the best of it, everyone scattering, mud-splattered. Jason about five in tears, his face mud-splotched looking pitiful.

Lightning lit the next wall with his father's face glaring off it like an engraving from Mt. Rushmore, an intense head-up shot of him over a football as center at the University of Tennessee. Standing next to his P-51 Mustang in full-leather flight-gear. With a ten-year-old Korean boy wearing a new pair of blue jeans Deke's father asked his mother to send over for the kid, boy and pilot beaming in front of the Air Force canteen in Seoul. There were photos of his father flying P-51's taken from other planes at high altitudes, a framed commendation from the President for saving the life of a mechanic struck by a propeller, several photos of his father receiving the medal. Deke stopped as he always had, staring at the low-angle photo of his father in dress uniform, high boots and staff, a still American flag behind him in high dusk light. There was a strange reverence in this picture that had haunted him as a kid making it even stranger to look at now. Getting closer to it he studied it, lightning flashing on and off it like a child toying with a light switch.

He went blind to it, turning down the hall blinking, stopping to look at the covered lazy Susan on the kitchen table. Empty hanging baskets held the sheet over it. He went into his room where dressers and tables were sheet-covered as in the rest of the house, linen curtains shifting slightly in window drafts. In the fluttering light he looked at the rugged faces of his grandparents, and Terrence and Irma, oval-shaped portraits of two couples in bubbled glass glaring back with stern pride. He slung the drop-cloth splattered with dried enamel off his chest of drawers and fished out three pairs of socks, three underwear. From the top drawer he took penlight batteries, a creek stone he'd given his father before leaving for Vietnam that his father had rubbed until he came back, a worn "UT"-embossed gold football the size of a peanut his father had given him, his father's gold Air Force wings, a pack of dental floss, an old tube of chap stick. The bottom of the drawer was covered with Cherokee arrowheads he'd found and collected on the farm since boyhood. He took a blood-red chiseled one out and rubbed its coolness on his face. With them was a Civil War Minnie ball he'd found with his father in the church parking lot after a storm when he was eleven. He stuck it in his pocket. Something thumped against the window and he turned to it. The curtains drifted. He looked back in the drawer at an old yellow clipping, reading ". . . when the Volunteers need a bone-crushing tackler behind the line they turn to young James Hawkins, a pig-iron-tough farmer's son from Treetorn. Coach Lester says he's never seen a more fearsome defensive back in his coaching career . . . Jim also snaps punts and is a crack blocker . . ." Deke shut the drawer. He threw the drop cloth over it and went to the closet. In the right corner behind hanging clothes stood his father's tarnished elephant gun. He wasn't planning to use it but he should clean it up anyway just in case, wrap it in cheese cloth and store it in his father's trunk. He found his waterproof gigging light on the floor by his rubber boots, stuck everything in a paper bag he found there and went back up the hall whistling. He stopped to look at a few more frames, one of his mother with Honcho and himself in uniforms in front of the porch with nine-year-old Jason beaming proudly. A picture of three boys and dogs swimming in the pond. A traditional print of Jesus. A copy of the Constitution. Jason's pledge of allegiance scribbled in red, white and blue crayon. Their father standing with Honcho as an Air Cav pilot next to his Huey helicopter at Fort Wolters, Texas. He went through the kitchen, stopping again to peer through the window over the sink. Mountains flashed in a pale outline, ragged corn stalks in front of them, a few half-standing like wounded soldiers refusing to die. On the counter were more hanging pots holding withered plants, above the sink a wooden plaque that read: "*Who plants a seed beneath the sod and waits to see believes in God.*"

He went on through the dining room, in the living room listening again to the streaming quiet music of the house he'd grown up in, glanced around and walked out onto the porch. A furled American flag stood in the corner on

a stick, several clumps of charcoal dust beneath it. He left the door unlocked
and strolled into the yard, threw his clothes and other things on the seat of
his old green Chevy pickup and walked toward the sheds listening to the
frogs down at the pond croaking their heads off. Perfect night to plant, he
thought. He could feel and smell a fruitful night's setting out with the warm
anticipation of kissing a fertile woman in the dark.

Lightning lit the seven huge doors with faint outlines of engines, junked
tractors, plows, harrows and other implements, equipment top-covered
with black plastic. There were rusted refrigerators, a half-dozen freezers on
blocks, cages stacked on tire rims, stacks of lumber, two feeding troughs.
On the roof loose scraps of tin flapped and hummed. He was hunting
burlap sacks to carry manure fertilizer and found a few in the back of his
father's '48 truck, glancing at the rear bumper sticker that said "DON'T
LAUGH/IT'S PAID FOR." Plastic milk cartons dangled in a line beside it,
a tangle of chains and other metal junk piled beneath them. In the corner a
flash on an old rocking chair with three large wooden spools stacked in the
seat looked like the upright torso of a man for a second, the chair swinging
easily in the wind. He threw the sacks over his shoulder and moved to
the next shed. He had twelve of them, just about enough by the time he
stepped into the small room that was part of the barn where dismantled,
hollow heads and sections of four or five standard five-hundred-pound
aircraft bombs lay in disarray on the dirt floor. His father's good collection.
He was so damn proud of the things. Under a hanging line of rakes, scythes
and shovels was the black-splattered stain on the wall with the wood
pelleted and stripped away. Everything creaked here. Deke stared at the
spot for a moment. It was a dreamed, uncharted territory. He looked at
the light flashing through cracks on the rusted bicycles leaned against the
wall. Something, the same whipping tin probably, made a banging slam
somewhere back in the sheds. He zoned for a minute listening to crickets
with the wind whistling through the buildings, the soothing, rhythmical
sounds he'd listened to as a child, forty years crisscrossing playing fields,
crop fields and battlefields, all real and imagined. Their father being a
fighter pilot he and Honcho had obsessed over flying. They'd rigged every
conceivable means to get off the ground, Honcho devising the cleverest
ideas, Deke ginny-pigging most of them; their catapults and makeshift
parachutes and the infamous launching bicycle ramp. After rehearsing a
few times Deke had come barreling down a steep slope, hit the ramp at the

top of a hill yanking with all his might on the handle bars and sailed sixty feet into a pear tree stripping most of the skin off of his neck, stomach and arms, scraping down it with the bike on top of him tangled up in chain. Amazing any of them had made it to manhood.

He turned from the haunted room through the main part of the barn, going under the hay loft across the yard to the truck tossing his sacks in the bed. One more thing. He ducked into his mother's ceramic shop, a low-ceilinged dark room with several tiny windows, shelves crowded with animals, molds, paints and chemicals. On the giant table in blinks on yellowed newspaper he saw green ceramic deer, rabbits, pigs with suckling young, fish, groundhogs, swans, all smashed and headless. He crunched ceramic pieces on the floor. Next to the kiln on a counter were a half-dozen incubators with broken eggshells spilled on concrete. It was pitch black in here except for flutters from the cramped windows. He should fetch his flashlight, he thought, but on second thought remembered he needed the darkness training. He'd need all the night vision he could get in the next nine months beginning tonight. Create light, there was always a trace of it. He was morphing into a pretty respectable owl these days, bat anyway able to hone in on things with his other senses. He felt through the cabinets laying hands on bottles of chemicals, rubbing, sniffing them. He felt a particular top and slick plastic container, smelled, looked at and caressed the B-1 transplant juice jiggling it lightly. Three-quarters full, that would do. They'd pick up a few gallons on the next supply run. He returned to the truck with it, climbed in and sat a minute watching the blue front planks of sheds and barns glinting in soft flashes. Their old rooster, Rojo, sole remaining guardian of the place, crowed once from the backyard at the brightness of the moon. It's time, he thought. Just the night to launch their forbidden flowers: full moon in Scorpio, sun in Taurus: you couldn't beat it for strength, endurance, fertility. There was so much light the song birds were singing. He started up and chugged out of the yard leaving the lights off crunching along slowly to the gate. In his side-mirror he watched the abandoned, dark-windowed house reflecting the rising moon. It hung fat and round to the east on the craggy, purple peaks of Traggert's Mountain, fireflies circling over the yellow fields. The long red drive gleamed with truck tracks out to the highway. He listened to the languorous frog chorus as he eased quietly-rumbling back toward the cabin, bumping unhurried along the weed-choked fields. It was time to pick up the Reverend and Witch Doctor and put down some redemptive roots.

Rear-heavy and camouflaged with kudzu the green pickup squeaked through the dry field grass, glass and chrome glinting in flashes. The three men jostled against each other listening to Marvin Gaye on a scratchy AM station, from a distance the truck looking like a large leaf-creature crossing the moon white fields under shadows of mountains, slogging through creek beds, water cans shifting-banging against the bed door. Deke ducked to see through the overlapping vines, reaching out now and then to tear a window that would seal up in a few bounces. The radio boomed and rattled, light from it fluttering on their yellow faces.

Barrett Harperson hunched between Deke and Deke's kid brother Jason who was twenty-seven but looked closer to twenty. Barrett was Deke's black blood brother and best friend, a year or two older than him, the only friend Deke could honestly say he trusted all the way around behind his back. Barrett had a large muscular build like a small buffalo's. His satiny arms gleamed under the radio shaking through rippling light. On his left cheek and temple he had eyelike scars from a claymore in Vietnam, in the tire flesh on his right side a bayonet gash from the same day. He and Deke'd been buddies in infantry training at Fort Gordon in 1967, surviving a tour in Vietnam including the TET offensive with more grisly, near-death experiences than they liked to talk about. Through them they'd become more like brothers than friends. After the firefight where Barrett'd caught fragments in the face from the same claymore that'd torn Deke's knee apart, saving Deke from bleeding to death using a mudpack with his open palm for three hours in a pitch-black, rain-filled hole while mortars took out trees around them, then fought off half a Viet Cong company hand-to-hand with a hunting knife, they'd concluded they were never going to get rid of each other.

When Deke sent out his SOS at Christmas Barrett didn't bat an eye. He dropped his road gig with his Memphis blues band to help Deke out. The band didn't amount to diddly next to his friend's jam. He could go back to them or hitch up with another group any time. He knew his stuff and literally broke his back for these people. After logging a million miles with the Shadow Haulers in three and a half years he was itching to get off this numbing treadmill anyway—loading equipment, unloading, setting up, breaking down, driving, crashing, unloading again . . . all the god awful food and sleep-on-the-run in ratty motels, not to mention the road women which were the most hazardous part of it all. He did the work for the music, but if his friend was jammed up he was there for him; especially when Deke wanted his help to do what he would've done every day of his life anyway if not for this government's obsessive "war on flowers." Not that that silly campaign had ever dissuaded him from doing it. Cultivating cannabis was more to his liking than anything else he'd done except playing slide guitar and singing with the bands that hired him to tote their equipment. He had some scorching licks he'd honed down on a Kay acoustic his pop'd given him when he was eight. His voice resembled Bobby Bland's, some said, magma and velvet sandpaper, but he had his own signature sound. Sometimes he held back so as not to upstage the fellas, but they'd never complained when he cut loose and torched a room. He could do it when the Visitor, his spiritual musical Host, showed up for him. Funny thing then was that *he* was the man and they were looking to *him* for the sound. One critic said he glowed on stage. He didn't know about that but whatever he did sure lit him up inside. He could've had his own gig, his own blues outfit and name anytime, but when playing turned into a business he was worried the magic would get sucked out of it. It was no sweat cutting loose on a full moon sounding like the Second Coming, but try pulling that off every night for six months on the road. He'd seen what the boys went through with traveling fatigue, squabbling like married folk, sounding like shit too many nights because of it, the hecklers, drunks and amateur critics, bar manager's asses they had to kiss in every town they rolled into. Not to mention getting ripped off by booking agents, road managers, the clubs themselves, anyone who could figure a way to do it. He didn't need all that mess. He was playing for Barrett Harperson at the moment and that's the way he liked it. He'd cut loose one day and the world would hear what he *really* had to say with an electric six string. He'd know when that was, but it wasn't quite yet.

Coming back to the states in 1969 he and Deke'd smuggled in several pounds of prime Vietnamese marijuana that'd gone for pennies in-country. It'd been a nice therapeutic souvenir, something to ease them back into the world. Sharing it with their buddies they'd watched it disappear overnight.

The herb was a communal thing in those days, not something you hid or horded away. After smoking it down to a bag of seeds they'd decided to throw them in the ground to see what they'd do. How difficult could it be to grow weeds that grew wild in jungles? They'd come up with some scraggily-looking, stunted little plants that'd gone completely to seed. There wasn't much weight to the buds but the quality was what they'd smuggled in. The potential was there. The last thing they wanted to do was let this exotic seed slip through their fingers. Keeping it alive would salvage at least one good thing that'd come out of that ungodly war, because sure as hell nothing else had.

The next two seasons they'd studied everything they could get their hands on about growing it, apprenticing with a half-mad, eccentric hermit named Alexander Christmas who lived up in the hills growing mushrooms and indicus plants in grow rooms and greenhouses. Their feeble little patches started to look like native Vietnamese gardens. Marijuana cultivation was a sacred art, the old wizard taught them, his glazed eyes sizzling as he hovered around his green children. He showed them how to grow stronger, higher-yield *sensimilla* by yanking the males and letting the females strain to be pollinated until they draped on the ground under their own flowers. Deke and Barrett grew isolated patches every year with both sexes to keep fresh seeds. They vowed to keep the Spiritchaser pure by not letting it crossbreed with other strains that would dilute and cheapen it. The seeds used to grow these hearty, woody-stemmed, six-week-old virgins in the truck bed behind them were pure-blooded as the ones they'd brought back from Saigon seventeen years ago.

Barrett had the Rastafarian grow-gift; cannabis DNA seemed to swim in his blood. Deke'd always been able to grow anything just like his old man; he swore never to plant a marijuana seed on his family's farm. The last thing he needed was to get his family in trouble or lose their homestead. He'd hike into national parks and bivouac a few days to grow it and sometimes he and Barrett grew it together. The Spiritchaser became their ritual smoke to remember their dead buddies by. When the plants stood head-high it was as if their long-dead pals were raised up in them, the smoke like a spiritual channel or line of communication to those boys. When they relaxed enough to hash out the war lying half-drunk in jungle hammocks smoking the same seed taken from peace pipes with their dead brothers years before, it was as if those beautiful, time-frozen sons of bitches, kids' hearts forever now, were sitting there in a circle with them, big grins on their dumb, innocent, sweetheart faces, killing time before they hoofed it back into the bush to die.

Though Barrett'd made some money off of their stuff, Deke'd never worried about that. He only wanted smoke he grew himself that he knew wasn't sprayed with paraquat or pissed on by some Mexican field hand. There was nothing sweeter than having your own line, especially this kind. The smell and taste were so aromatic they would've smoked it for that alone. The incense intoxicated you lighting it up. The high was buzzy-clear with a warm, orgasmic body rush. It was the only thing they could smoke after a while. After the Spiritchaser the dry-molded, seedy crap smuggled in from Mexico and Columbia just gave them a sinus headache.

Another reason Deke didn't want to grow a cash crop was that it was always greed bit you in the ass with this stuff: he didn't want to jinx it. He liked working his father's farm, in a few years he'd be running it himself. He wasn't going to jail and ruining his life because of some illegal weed no matter how exotic it was. As long as he grew a little for himself he knew the law wouldn't bother him, it was the truckload cultivators they were after. Every now and then when Barrett'd gotten out of touch he'd start thinking, he's done it now, the crazy son of a bitch's sitting in jail on a cultivation charge. When Barrett showed up with a wad of cash and some hair-raising stories, Deke just shook his head. He didn't need that stress or agitation. His friend always raved about how "fat" the money was, trying to lure him with seductive pictures of what they could do with it, and it was damn good admittedly, but Deke was okay without it. He hadn't needed any extra money and hadn't expected to, until the shot was fired sixteen months ago.

In that instant everything changed. He kicked himself for not seeing this coming, as if he could've done anything to stop it. It never occurred to him that this could even happen in his family, especially to his old man who'd been their rock. They were toast, he thought; they were good and fucked, and he was shaken to the core. There was nothing they could do to save themselves. What could they do? There were massive sums of money to come up with, it was ridiculous what they were demanding from them. He was so in shock at first it didn't matter, and when it started to he realized he was under an insurmountable mountain of shit. The IRS had declared the farm "inactive" because his father had planted fewer and fewer acres in the last five years, an absurd and arbitrary judgment, but you couldn't deal with the sons of bitches. With no warning they'd slapped his father with nine-hundred thousand dollars in back-taxes. He already had too much in FHA loans and they wouldn't extend them. The banks would only deal with Deke short-term now, lending him money to make tax payments against their land. How was he going to come up with so much money in a season to pay them back and all the other taxes? It couldn't be done. They were actually going to lose the place.

He gave up for a few weeks and drank himself into oblivion. He had moments of weakness of his own. He'd practically had to commit his mother when she'd taken an axe and started chopping down everything in the yard. He'd never considered suicide before, not at war or anyplace else, but he'd stared down some demons some nights that made all of this seem darker than hopeless. He'd drunk enough liquor in those days to kill most people anyway.

A week after his father's funeral he'd started to get angry. He'd gotten so goddamn angry he was ready to kill somebody if that would save the place. It wouldn't, of course, not by itself, and he'd sobered up and started to rethink this. It didn't take an hour to realize what he had to do. Here it was, his one and only prayer in hell. He had nothing to lose by doing it, not a thing. If he didn't do it they'd sure as hell lose every stitch and scrap and piece of dirt his family had slaved and sweated and died for for generations, and that made no sense to him. It was as ludicrous as what had brought them there.

His family had been violated by a tax law that, like his father always said, was illegal to begin with. He was not going to be a willing victim of government by the idiots, for the idiots and of the idiots. He'd done enough of that duty in that shameless little war. He couldn't undo what they'd done, but if they could arbitrarily disrupt people's lives by burying them in taxes he'd do what he had to do to shovel them out of it. He knew what prime sensimilla was going for. He wasn't going to apologize for this, why should he? Screw the bloodsucking bastards. They'd screwed his mother and father, his whole blessed, backbreaking family all the way back to Terrence and Irma, so screw them. This was his farm now, his responsibility. His father had taught him to be a damn good farmer—he could grow anything God had put on the green earth—so that's what he was going to do, *grow something*. His mother'd withdrawn into herself and was sitting in a nursing home knitting Kleenex dolls. Big brother Honcho was flying jets on the other side of the world with the Marines and didn't seem to care about the place. His younger brother didn't have a clue. *The Lord would take care of it. The Lord helps those who help themselves,* Deke reminded him. If anything was going to be done they'd have to do it; *they'd* be the ones. Wasn't it dangerous? Oh hell yes, dangerous enough, but what wasn't? What were they going to take away from them that mattered more than this place? It was a no-brainer. Risks were things you worried about when you had other choices. He wasn't worried, he really didn't give a damn. Not only was he going to make this work if it killed him, he was going to relish snubbing his nose at these land suckers, these fucking government leeches when he paid them off in full. No one was going to rob him of the few simple things he had left: his spirit, his battered peace of mind, the only livelihood he and his family had ever known, all connected to the soil they'd sweated into for a hundred and fifty years. All he cared about was protecting their place now, and on that day he'd begun to do exactly what it took to save it.

The truck eased down into a swamped, rotted patch of leaning cottonwoods, Deke touching trees with his bumper plowing and crunching over them, tires slicing through muck. Jason sprayed something on his neck and arms Barrett twisted away from.

"What the hell's that, little brother?"

"Repellent. Want some?"

"Hell no," Barrett coughed fanning it. "Get it away from me. Wait 'till we get out the motherfucking truck."

"Serious?"

"Good guerrilla keeps his animal senses clean. You wouldn't smell an army's ass wearing that shit but he'd find you."

"That's what we are, guerrillas."

"Bet your white halves, Reverend."

Deke stopped the truck under low-draping trees casting shadows down the foot of the mountain, above them grassy clearings blazing spotted with small pines. In moonlight and heat lightning they could see the lit open areas shining through the trunks. A shallow-green creek glistened on the far side of the field.

"This it?" Deke said, popping the door with the truck droning.

"Damn perfect if it ain't," Barrett said.

". . . WVOL and Smokey The Bear remind you to be careful with matches . . . lack of rain makes every spark a danger to our forests . . ."

The radio died with the engine, crickets and cicadas filling the void with a deep-shrill-running noise. They got out bending and stretching, dragging vines under the trees, untying the canvas bed-cover. Barrett folded and stuck it under the truck. They unloaded five trays of marijuana seedlings, shovels, post-hole diggers, five-gallon buckets, canvas duffel and burlap bags of manure, eight-hundred pounds of it mixed with lime, blood meal, bone meal, a small addition of chicken shit. There was an army-green canvas sack of drinking water. Barrett propped the plant trays against the trunks and fished through the music tapes.

"Tote everything halfway up that first clearing," he said. "I'll scatter the plants."

"Toten' here, boss," Deke said.

"Thought we'd work with brother James tonight. 'Popcorn' and shit. 'Git Up Offa That Thing.'" Barrett chuckled.

"Want to get every one of these in tonight. Work 'till I can't think straight or move."

"Count on it, Tar Baby. Let's get to it."

Deke tossed eighty-five pounds of manure over his shoulder and hustled up the mountain feeling the weight knotting into his neck, back and thighs. The first one was unbelievably heavy then they seemed to lighten as you realized what had to be done. Above him Jason was dropping tools and trotting back down. Barrett slid a tape into the boom box and "Licken' Stick" started and he was chuckling in his throat. He lifted a tray of plants from the bottom with one hand, boom box in the other, shuffling up through the trees passing Deke where he'd dropped his first sack.

"Keep everything near the edges," Barrett said. "Up against these little pines. We've got field-grade visibility."

"Oh yeah."

Barrett slid the boom box into brush under moon shade and kept digging to the top of the third clearing with the tray of plants shining. Lowering them gently to the ground he got to his knees checking them for breaks, his face in the leaves filling his nostrils with fragrances. The plants had that subtle-pungent sweetness, a green spicy smell.

"You're gonna love this shit, honeys," he purred. "Deep, rich cow, chicken shit, all the earth you can eat, first morning sun." He held two seedlings up to the moon singing *"People standin' . . . standin' in a trance . . . sister's out in the backyard . . . doin' her outside dance . . ."*

Deke dug yard-deep holes with a long-handle shovel, sweat dripping from his nose. He went after them like a maniac, impatiently, hungrily as if they all had to be dug at once. The season was rolling. There was a sexual sensation when the shovel slid in without hitting rock. On the next one he was jumping on his tool, plunging, throwing, scraping, twisting on stones, digging out boulders. Occasionally a spot would feel doomed and he'd abandon it but he liked to complete anything he started. He knocked each hole out quickly, took a few deep breaths and attacked the next one working with the music in a steady, seamless, straight-business-like rhythm. The key to this work was backbreaking toil, especially the way they did it. It wasn't a job for wimps. Every extra effort was worth it, another little piece of insurance. There was no better feeling than when the first hundred were in the ground and you could lay in bed listening to the rain falling on them, feeling them rising up in your dreams. Then you had momentum. Then you were rolling like a bus. You came out in a week and they were lifting up in all directions, spreading out like God-almighty, hearty, treelike, mushrooming to the clouds. Every time you dug a hole after that you felt ahead of the game. Your children were putting down roots, working for you. God had taken over and you were partners with The Man. That's what he thought about every time he broke new ground now, pulling out chunks of monkey grass, loosening it, jumping on his shovel, long-thorned briars ripping at his pants, slicing the tops of his hands. In thirty minutes he was sopping wet and getting warmed up with a dozen holes gaping in the moonlight. They were lovely. It all was. Every hole meant thousands of dollars if the season went right. This was going to be the one, he declared. This crop would put them in the black for sure. As he worked into it he felt the soil change with his shovel blade, transform with it. He felt himself breathing life into it every time he plunged in, brought up fresh ground and turned it in the air.

Jason and Barrett grunted with fertilizer bags to the upper clearings. Jason dropped his and plopped on it. "Enough up here, little brother. Don't step on the babies, they're all over the place, see 'em?"

Jason nodded, huffing.

"Why don't you go on down and dig a few holes, I'll fetch the rest of the shit. Lookin' good up here."

"Want them that far apart?"

"Got to be. Any closer they'll look like a patch. We got miles to spread 'em over, remember. We're doing good here, lookin' good."

"I hate these spider webs you can't see in the dark. Got welts all over my face."

"You'll learn to love 'em. Come out here just to get stung one day."

"Yeah, sure I will."

Jason slid down the mountain passing his brother digging furiously, grabbed a post-hole-digger and went to work. He tried hard as he could not to worry about this. He'd promised not to drive himself crazy, to rethink it too much. There was no other way to go right now, Deke'd made a pretty good case for that. This was it, what they had to do to save the place. If he was going along with Deke's plan he was putting his heart into it. He was doing it, all right, for better or worse, taking a sabbatical from seminary to grow illegal weeds with his wild-headed, well-intending brother. He couldn't believe it at moments; it felt like dream walking. He wasn't raised to break the law but he couldn't see anything else to do, for the first time in his life he had a glaring blind spot. At least Deke'd come up with some kind of plan, he was thankful for that. Everything Deke said made sense on some level, but it was what he didn't talk about, that they could go to jail as well as lose the place that worried him. He'd put in plenty of fence wire with his father using one of these things, so he tried to concentrate on that part of it, the width and depth of holes, the spaces between, the east-west line, everything Barrett had gone over with him. Midnight farming, Barrett called it. It was freedom, all right. They were on their own working all night planting "forbidden flowers." He was sewing and reaping, that's one thing he was raised to do. Occasionally the shadowing voice would ask him what he was doing, not the thundering one he'd heard as a boy when he *knew* he was doing something wrong, a little tug on the sleeve, a nudge here and there. He dug a little harder and faster as he hummed with the music, reminding himself if Deke hadn't pulled off a crop of these plants last year they wouldn't be here. His father's, old Terrence's and Irma's farm would be in the bank's hands now, the government's or someone else's, it was unthinkable, which drove and committed him to this lain-brained scheme of Deke's despite his misgivings. It's true, he said to the faint, nagging voice that wasn't even that loud anymore. It was enough to keep saying to himself, and he kept it between him and the voice as he picked up steam, listening to his brother digging and groaning like a madman, the Witch Doctor yodeling and hollering down the mountain with the wild-cat-screaming, bass-thumping music.

Barrett spread the plants over the clearings, laying the soaked containers on their sides. He tried to keep them from the main shadow lines of trees. Cannabis girls loved their sun-torture. The more you gave them the more flowers they'd give. He worked them into niches and contours, between small pines where the light wouldn't be blocked, humming and muttering as he stooped to look around at the ones he'd already placed, making sure they were raggedly-scattered, uneven-looking. It had to look like a natural, unattended landscape from the air. If anyone climbed these mountains on foot they might find them, but that was the only way they would, not from the sky. He squatted, duck walking to shift a few seedlings, rearranging them and singing, doing a little jig to the moon letting out a howl and crazy laughter down the mountain.

"Keep 'em spread out!" he hollered, cackling across the valley. "No patterns! Don't write your names with 'em!"

By midnight a hundred and twenty holes were ready to plant. Deke and Jason took turns dragging and shoveling fertilizer bed-to-bed. Barrett mixed the stuff by hand pulling out debris and rocks, feeling the manure into the soil like a potion. He checked each seedling against the moon, tapping it gently upside down from its container, whispering to it. Breathed into and kissed the roots before planting it with his face at ground level, grinning at the beauty and pleasure of it, sweat glistening in the buzzing blue light. The stench of manure and the oxygen smell of open earth excited him. He liked to get his face in it. It was all he could do not to wallow in the stuff, the breath of life that exploded these green twigs into fruit-heavy marijuana trees. He molded a small mound around each plant with a trough inside to catch rain and mulched each one with leaves and straw, restoring the ground to its natural state. White moths flapped round his face and hands. They didn't bother him, they'd always come around when he planted at night like mystically drawn spirits. They were a good omen and he talked to them as they tickled his skin. *Godspeed to the heavens*, he whispered to each fledgling plant before he slid to the next hole. *Grow strong and true and flourish*, he said, scrambling on all fours to the next one like a fair, impartial father repeating the fertility rite to each daughter.

They'd worked through a boxed set of James Brown by One A.M., breaking for peanut butter sandwiches, sardines and apples, hitting the downward stretch half-giddy, floating and working on in near-exhaustion. Low-flying bombers roared down through the fog from Jasper Air Force Base. Fireflies blinked like Christmas lights on the ground-mist. The valley felt like being on top of the clouds when heat lightning touched it. To Deke the woods were paradise at night, especially on a full moon. He'd been a night person since coming back from Vietnam, at first without choice, later finding it his magical time of day. When the world slept it was all yours, no thought-waves, psychic clutter or noise-confusion, his head was as clear as a mountain lake. He craved that brilliant night-stillness.

There were drawbacks to working in it though. His lip was swollen from burrowing into a yellow jacket's nest; a vial of Clorox and a rag countered the poison. He carried a beat-up snakebite kit that'd probably saved his life a few times, dangerous not to have poking around in the woods at night. There were moccasins, rattlesnakes, more copperheads than people in this county, not to mention an array of scorpions, spiders and ticks. He kept stumbling into these crazy flocks of geese roosting in the dark that would shoot off straight up through the trees like terrified goblins yanking his heart through his throat. About the time he'd forgotten them another flock would leap up through the shadows scaring the dog piss out of him. He'd hear Barrett chuckling: "Gotcha another one, Tar Baby? Flush 'em out Tar Baby!" as he tried to calm his heart, swearing he'd be ready for the next one.

By Three the plants were in the ground and mulched, the last twenty beaded in a spaced, crooked line on the wooded side of the creek bed. Deke was zinging with sleepless energy and could've drilled on till noon. With a full moon he felt like superman, and was for a few days, then for a few days he couldn't even get out of bed. He had to pace himself, get enough rest to do this tomorrow night, the night after that and every night for the next few weeks. There'd be weeks of marathon toil into the season. Mountain irrigation—hauling water up these slopes—they dreaded most. They had to drench the girls tonight to give them a good launching, but if this drought didn't lift and they had to carry water all summer it was going to be a brutal one.

He was relieved Jason had decided to work with them. The Reverend had been reluctant and Deke'd had to coax him some. Besides needing him for planting he felt responsible for the boy and wanted to keep an eye on him. Little brother might be doing better than he was for all he knew, but he wanted him there just in case. He'd heard suicide ran in some families. It was the first time it'd happened in his he knew anything about. Maybe that was all myth anyway, maybe it was the power of suggestion, the cryptic act of a father luring you toward what seemed inevitable anyway. It gave him the willies. As if some unseen silent predator was hovering over you waiting for the right moment to drop. Who the hell knew. It wasn't something he wanted to think about all that much, but maybe it was a good idea for them to keep an eye on each other for a while.

Jason splashed backwards into smoke-white mist in a foot of water, the bone-cold numbing his genitals.

"I'm gonna lay here for an hour," he gurgled. "I might sleep here, boys, in this streaming bed."

Barrett waded in, squatting and scoop-rinsing, pond-waders scattering round his knees as he guzzled from the stream.

"Ain't finished little brother, got to haul water yet."

"You're kiddin'."

"Ain't comin' from the heavens unless you know a damn good rain prayer. Man, I wish you did 'cause there hadn't been water in this ground in a month of Sundays."

Deke stumbled in peeling off his cammie t-shirt, wringing, wrapping it round his neck. "How about frog legs for breakfast? Anybody hungry?"

"I could deal with that. Why don't you round 'em up while I teach the Reverend to baptize."

"Damn good start to the season, fellas. Meet you at the cabin in an hour. Don't kill the poor boy, Doctor Feelgood."

Deke stumbled dripping toward the truck.

"Come on little brother," Barrett said, tugging Jason to his feet. "The babies are thirsty, and I'm 'bout to starve out here."

Deke straddled the rowboat seat on the moonlit pond in a clash of crickets and frogs. "Night Train" droned from where Barrett and Jason were watering. The air was chilled near the surface, still mist hanging in lightning flutters on the dark glass. Deke wore his straw Filipino frog-farmer's hat picked up seventeen years ago on his plane trip home from Saigon. He poled with a slight, unhurried movement along the shoreline making quirky noises, happy unearthly calls, whispering and croaking. His beam hit a frog almost at the instant the gig nailed it and he held it squirming against the gunwale, severing its legs with his hunting knife, tossing them in a five-gallon bucket.

"Thank you, my friend. Just want to borrow these."

He slapped the legless frog back on the bank staring bug-eyed from it. He drifted again croaking quietly, whispering the theme from Miss America. The light popped on and he stabbed another one, grabbing and yanking its legs. He set it on-shore with the others, shuffling leaves and grass around it to cover its condition.

"Double amputees get full benefits," he said, patting its head. "Good luck, pal."

Slowly he circled the pond, crossing it, reversing direction, skewering every frog that made a noise. Moonlight wrinkled on the black surface. His eyes were sharp as candles. He could pick out frogs from a distance and drift up on them like a floating log, whacking them blindside. He was the primordial hunter, every fucking frog's nightmare. It was like every frog on the farm was lined up here waiting for the leg-man. He was slap-happy as a goddamn goose, *rejuvenated* doing this shit. He howled and muttered to himself like a street-crazy, psycho-wino, jabbering every kind of quiet sick call he felt. It was good therapy. They'd put him away if he did this in public, he thought. He plunged his gig into one of the fattest frogs he'd ever layed eyes on, a real monster that fought like a small dog at the end of his pole.

"Meaty thighs! A big-legged woman . . ." he said, yodeling to it, singing as he whittled its legs off.

Jason and Barrett dug up the mountain, water buckets sloshing in their boots.

"Drop 'em here, little brother, in that flat spot," Barrett said, lifting a container dribbling it out. "Splash above the plant and run it around 'em, keep it uphill to make sure all the roots get watered."

"How long you been doin' this?"

"Sixteen, seventeen years on and off, since your brother and I come back from 'Nam. We agreed to keep these seeds going and pure so one of us had plants every year."

"Deke says you're as good as they get with this stuff."

"Gotta love what you do is all. I love this shit I tell ya, like I love the blues. Just as soon be in the presence of an indicus in full-flower as smoke the stuff. Ever grown it?"

"Naw, we were taught to yank 'em so daddy could burn them. Six years ago he found a mess in his corn rows, you should've seen the bonfire."

"Owee, what a sacrifice," Barrett shook his head. "People afraid of their own shadows. So afraid of the stuff they never get to the place of respecting it. It's the voice of God, but it ain't the goddamn Boogieman."

"Think it's got spiritual powers?"

"Does a fat Pope shit in the woods? It's one of the anointed green vessels, son."

"Why do you say that?"

"Why would anyone give a shit about it if it wasn't? It reveals too much, opens doors. People want 'em shut up. Most of the world's afraid to know any damn thing, afraid of themselves, the way they really think, way they *really* are instead of what people tell 'em. They're preached to it's safer, but it's the other way around. Government's got its citizens afraid of their own instincts, afraid of their own goddamn shadows. It's like that Mose Allison tune, 'How Much Truth Can The World Stand?' "... *threatened by the works of man . . . destined for the fryin' pan . . . how much truth can the world stand . . .*" he chuckled.

"You think it should be legalized?"

"Understood's the word. Respected. Every growing thing's our birthright, see. Every seed and twig's our medicine, don't belong to any government. Once you have that you look at what it's here for, its properties, and learn to respect every sprout in the plant kingdom. Anything else's just foolishness, government manipulation and control."

"If it were legal we wouldn't be able to do what we're doing."

"If it were legal we wouldn't have to. If the government let people plant what they wanted, none of this would've happened, Reverend brother."

"You don't have to call me Reverend."

"Thought that's what you were studying to be."

"Yeah, but I'm not yet. Got another few years if that's what I'm gonna do. I want to make sure we hold onto this place."

"There you go. You're a young man."

"Just curious, did Deke promise you something here or are you doing this for other reasons?"

"Deke said I'd have a home here but that's not why I'm doing it, if that's what you're askin'."

"He told me a long time ago you saved him in Vietnam. Asked him about it the other day and he looked like he wanted to kill me."

"I don't know that I did. I took care of him and he made it. You should know better than to ask him about that shit."

"They gave you a medal, didn't they?"

"Oh yeah. The same bastards flushed my generation down the slaughterhouse toilet. You think I give a shit about some piece of tin?"

"You're bitter as Deke."

"Not half as bitter as I used to be, brother. Naw, see, I love your man Christ, He's my man too. He got me through a lot of that shit and helped me when I came back from over there. But you listen to me now, and I'm dead serious about this. Every night you should get down on your knees and thank God you were too young to get sucked into that meat grinder. Thank Him you didn't have to see one man's legs blown off, buddy's faces shredded with incendiaries, boys shot in the back by their own choppers for no goddamn reason. For freedom? Whose freedom? For a bunch of lying bureaucrats who wouldn't admit their fuck-ups. If you really love Jesus Christ you should thank Him you were spared that shit, 'cause I'm tellin' ya, Reverend, you've been blessed."

"Weren't we fighting communism?"

"*Communism*? Ha. You know what karma is?"

"Reaping what you sew?"

"Same thing. He said we'll be judged by how we treat the least among us."

"Yeah."

"A country's no different than a person, is it? It's made up of 'em and everything it does comes back on it. Don't matter if you're American or Yugoslavian, the universe don't care. We're filling out our karma card every second with the decisions our leaders make. If they wrong some other people on our behalf, we're gonna pay for it, simple as that. If you do wrong you suffer for it. We'll be paying for that goddamn war for a hundred years, don't matter how they spin it. Don't matter what you say or what kinds of tricks politicians play to get power, it's what they do and why that makes this place a living heaven or hell. We still hadn't lived down what we did to the Indians, or slavery, shit. We go slaughtering villages of people in Indochina, fucking with other people's governments, you don't think there's a spiritual price to pay? Like I said, America don't get a pass just because it's America. We killed all the people we were supposed to be helping over there. Communism my ass. Hate to break it to you little brother, but Jesus Christ taught communal living. You call it whatever you want, but he told the rich to give what they had to the poor, remember? If a man asks for your cloak give him your shirt too, right? He comes back talking that shit they'll string his ass up. This ain't no Christian nation, it's an Old Testament nation. You say 'blessed are the peacemakers' and you'll get your ass shot off quicker than anything. People don't know Jesus Christ in this country. They like to pretend they do so they can club you to death with Him. Pride's an awfully evil thing, little brother."

From his knees Deke stretched over the gunwale trying to retrieve his swimming gig. He'd hooked another world class frog just enough to piss it off, it hit the water and the wet gig slipped from his hand. Now the frog was swimming frantically, dragging the gig along the bottom into deeper water. With the light held high in his left hand he paddled and lunged with the other, cursing, giggling in frustration as it plunged a little deeper every time he reached for it. The frog was coming up on a rise, the pole coming with him, Deke stretching deeper hanging off the boat to his shoulder feeling the cold water tickling his chest. As he touched the pole with his fingertips the boat flipped on top of him spilling him headfirst. Going down he felt the pole brush his face and grabbed it, looking up at his waterproof light rocking on the surface. He caught it coming up, slapped the gigged runaway unconscious on the capsized boat, put his hat, the gig and frog on top of it and went down with the light for the sinking bucket of legs. They floated around him like a school of short elbows. He dived, stuffing them in the bucket. With his own splashing and cursing he didn't hear the two military choppers coming across Traggert's Mountain. He heard the rotorthuds at the same time he saw a rusted cricket bucket and half an ancient oar light up on the mud floor twelve feet below. Cutting his light he hung a few seconds feeling the searchlights making passes on the rippling surface. He looked for the bulked outline of the rowboat under the light and made for it coming up under it in variegated shades of green. He listened to the choppers hovering, one making slow, thumping circles around the pond. Maybe with their own lights they hadn't noticed his. They seemed to be interested in his boat though. Not that being seen here was any crime, he had every right to be, it was his place; but he and Barrett had decided to keep themselves invisible and the place dark-abandoned-looking until every flower was harvested and sold. If it seemed abandoned a couple of lights might draw more attention than if the place was blazing with them.

The two Air Force recon H-57 Rangers piloted by Major Webb and Lt. Jacobsen in the lead ship, Lts. Morris and Dravagio in the stern, combed the small dark piece of wrinkled water. Morris ran his beam along the shoreline and swung out from it looking for land vehicles. Webb hovered over the capsized rowboat rotating his chopper beams in a widening circle. They knew every speck and shack in this quadrant and hadn't expected to see anyone. There were sections of ground that had been dark a year now where they never saw a soul. They'd flown this alley a hundred nights and the only lights they'd seen within half a mile of this property were from a shack across the highway they knew was inhabited.

"Sure I saw a light," Jacobsen said to Webb. "Couldn't tell you what it was."

"Maybe lightning on the water?"

"Seemed localized, concentrated."

"Probably some skinny-dipping party in progress. Which quadrant we on?"

Jacobsen unsnapped the black classified notebook with the large irregular-shaped rectangles of lettered sections labeled (S) and (US).

"Q for Quicksand. *Unsecured.*"

"Muskrat, could've sworn I saw something or someone in the water when you put on your lights," Dravagio growled from the rear chopper.

"Roger, Weasel."

"Maybe a flicker round that turned over crate."

"Vehicles?"

"Negative. Nothing out here."

"Don't think it's worth hanging around for. Looked like a couple of kids, maybe a drunken farmer fishing. Let's shuffle west to quadrant Y and zigzag down the alley."

"Roger, Muskrat, turning with you."

Barrett and Jason stood in the open with a bucket in each hand listening to the rotorthuds grinding toward them. Barrett dumped his water and slid down the mountain to the nearest clump of trees. They'd heard the choppers and were keeping their ears open but Barrett figured they'd turned and were backtracking away from them.

"Take cover, little brother! Grab those buckets!"

Jason followed dragging two cans and a manure sack, snagging in his boots as he shuffled down. They slid feet-first to the center of low-hanging branches, Barrett stacking the buckets scooping leaves, straw, dirt, anything he could find concealing them. He tossed straw over their feet and balled up with his face toward the trunks, hugging the manure sack in a fetal position.

"Tuck in. Bury your face, don't look up . . ."

His voice was drowned by popping blades, their bodies blowing white under the searchlights seeming to linger a second, percussive flutters suctioning the air. It hadn't sunk in to Jason until then they'd actually be hiding out on their own property. Eyes down he saw darkness, lifting them watching the bright lights drag off across the patches without seeming to hang on anything, rotor blades fading behind the mountains.

"Damn those bastards," Barrett said, brushing off. "Bringin' searchlights and shit."

"Think they saw us?"

"I doubt it. They're lookin' though; they're *damn* sure lookin'." Barrett strung vines over the buckets until they were covered up. "Hope your brother didn't show his ass over there 'cause that's where they came from. Help me remember where we left these buckets. Hell now, son, it's chow time, ain't it? I've had more than my share of this shit tonight."

Dripping wet, still cursing under his breath, Deke dragged the rowboat on shore flipping it under the trees. What you had to do for a little dinner, he thought, sliding the gig and pole under the boat masking it with fresh poplar branches. A few feet away the leaf-covered pickup was camouflaged in a garage of scuppernong vines. With the truck already draped in kudzu he just plowed into them and you'd never see the damn thing if you didn't know it was there. He dug his way into the passenger door, tossed the bucket of legs, light and frog-farmer's hat on the floor, slid under the wheel and backed out under moonlight raking off half his kudzu. He listened a second for choppers, shoved the truck in gear and headed up the mountain winding past the empty cattle fields. Unused, rotting hay bales were eerie in the moonlight, fat black lumps like giant armadillos crouching in the grass. He dipped into the shallow creek at the bottom of the trail, got a running start and hit the mountain in third gear digging up hard avoiding canyon ruts. A quarter way up he dropped into second and bumped up the rest of the way until the hairpin, stopped again, shoved into first and crawled up the last rocky grade.

He squeaked into the yard next to the low-flat, kudzu-cloaked cabin. Constructed of railroad ties it sat at the edge of a large kudzu field surrounded by giant pines. The rusted tin roof was buried in vines. In a few months the runners would be snaking through the floor and walls. Deke's grandfather had built the shack on top of the mountain sixty years ago for housing hands. Friends and relatives came here to hunt and on holidays when the farm was overrun with houseguests. It was rugged but comfortable, a perfect headquarters. Even when the kudzu died back the vines were so thick it couldn't be seen from the air. As long as they kept the place darked-out and no one noticed them coming and going they were never here.

He cut the engine and listened to Muddy Waters singing "Voodoo Chile" in the cabin. Pencil-thin light sliced from the blacked-out windows. He pulled a burlap sack off the floor, dumped the legs in it and carried it to the side of the house tossing it in the kudzu. This would be fun, he thought. Who knew when he'd be in the mood again. With a hangdog expression he opened the door slowly and slumped in with the light and empty bucket. Barrett and Jason sat at the round mahogany table eating boiled peanuts, watching the weather on television with the radio on. Barrett sipped a Red Stripe with his feet on the table.

"Something's messin' up our weather patterns," he said.

"You don't get a single inch of rain in April something's screwed up. Get those legs in the skillet, buddy, I'm gettin' weak here."

"Didn't find any," Deke said, dejected. "No frogs."

He took a beer from the squat Frigidaire and plopped across the table. Barrett stared at him incredulous. "No frogs?"

"Strange, isn't it? Guess it's too dry for 'em. Had to hit the pond too when those choppers came over, sons of bitches."

"That's funny," Jason said. "I've heard tons of frogs tonight."

Not taking his eyes off Deke Barrett turned off the radio. "Uh huh. I can hear 'em right now matter of fact. Sounds like a goddamn convention out there."

"Oh, you can hear 'em but you can't find 'em," Deke said.

"Don't understand it. *Very* weird."

"Goddamn right it's weird. Goddamn right. Didn't see no frogs?"

"Not one."

"On a fucking full moon night. Didn't see no fucking frogs!"

"That's what I said, Br'er Rabbit. You think you can do any better the gig's under the boat."

"Gimme that goddamn bucket," Barrett said, snatching it, grabbing another beer from the fridge. Slamming it he glared at Deke and stomped to the door. "This damn light work at all?" he said, shaking it. "Come on, little brother. Got to do every damn thing 'round here, goddamit. While I'm scarin' up your dinner put your ears up, see can you find what the hell those choppers are up to. Try not to fuck *this* up." He stormed out slinging the screen door. ". . . Didn't see no fucking frogs . . . on a fucking full moon night . . . didn't see one lousy frog . . ."

Barrett stood in the rowboat stern poling himself and Jason toward the shadows where most of the croaking was coming from, Jason seated holding the light and gig.

"I've never heard so many frogs in my whole goddamn life," Barrett said. "Am I crazy or is your brother losing his shit? Is he stone-blind?"

"I don't know, but look," Jason pointed.

In silhouette and flutters they saw a half-dozen frogs sitting motionless on the partially-lit bank. Down shore one leaped slapping the surface.

"All right now, you shine 'em, I'll stick 'em, we'll throw 'em in whole. When we get enough we'll clean 'em, show your brother how it's done, son. Didn't see no frogs."

Jason handed him the gig as they swung parallel to the bank, Barrett hitting the first one, dropping it in the bucket. Nothing moved. Jason shined the next one and Barrett hit it quickly, nervously shaking it off the barb. Down the shore another leaped, its strokes like liquid mercury swimming toward the moon at the center of the pond. Four frogs sat stolidly like statues and Barrett nailed them before they could budge.

"This is takin' candy from a baby," he whispered. "They ain't even flinchin'. I see half a dozen waitin' on that point."

"What was Deke doin' out here?"

"Playing with himself I guess. Got me." For twenty minutes they worked down the shore like an assembly line, Jason poling, shining, Barrett gigging them, tossing them behind him. Every now and then one broke the surface; nine out of ten were sitting ducks. They looked moonstruck, in some kind of sluggish, dead-eyed trance. Maybe it was the mating season knocked them out like this. He'd never seen them so languid and sleepy. It was kind of funny really. A honeysuckle breeze was backing off the mosquitoes. Barrett grinned and hummed at the ease of it. Usually you didn't breathe slipping up on them, but they were so oblivious he tried to warn them, make it interesting by heckling them a little, singing a bar or two just before he stuck them.

"Come on, baby! Meet papa's gig . . . nowhere to run . . . see that . . . *Gotcha!* See that, little brother? The master bwana. The breadwinner, baby."

"How many should we get?"

"Couple-hundred. Freeze 'em if we have to. They come this easy you take all you find."

"Look how close those three are sittin' over there. Never seen that before."

"Shhhhh. Drift right up on 'em. Here we come. Hello, honeys. Hello you sweet luscious mothers . . ."

Barrett stabbed them hard one on top of the other, giggling as he shook the dead weight into the pile.

"See any frogs tonight?" he said.

"A few."

"Don't see what the goddamn problem is. Don't believe your brother was even out here. The boy's worthless."

Jason shined the light down shore. They'd worked three-quarters around the pond and were coming back to the dam, they could hear the rushing sound of falling water behind it. Where the bank made a protruding red lip beneath the moon an odd green shape stood a few inches from the water's edge. Without knowing what it was they knew there was something funny about it. Drifting closer they saw it was one frog squatting on another's head, two facing in opposite directions.

"What the hell?" Jason said. "What're they doing?"

"What you think?" Barrett said, plunging the gig through the dead weight, shaking them off.

"Mating?"

"Reckon so. Dinner now."

Around the next corner the light fell on something that froze them. Seven or eight frogs were stacked neatly on top of each other like a totem pole. Barrett stared in spooked consternation. Neither of them spoke for a moment.

"How in the . . ." Jason said. ". . . How did . . . ?"

They drifted past it, the light hanging back on them. In a flicker something caught Jason's eye and he jerked the light to a mass of green meat and eyes staring goofy-eyed in front of them. As the boat grounded there was a light lapping with the buzzing of cicadas. Barrett dropped to his seat. They sat motionless staring at a pyramid of stacked frogs, eyes of the bottom ones skewed and bugged-out under the weight. Jason counted thirty-two frogs mounted in perfect symmetry. It was one of the most horrifying sights Barrett had ever seen. He smelled something in the breeze, sniffing it.

"What is it?" Jason said.

"Something cookin' goddamit."

"I don't smell anything," Jason said, turning his head. "Wait a second, yeah . . ."

Barrett yanked the light out of his hand, shining it into the fifty legless frogs overflowing the bucket piled and sprawled across the floor. He spotted ten or twelve, lifting one up by its tiny front leg, dangling it in the light. He shined where its legs had been severed and back into the bottom of the boat on the mountain of legless frog flesh.

"Son of a bitch," he said. "No frogs my ass. The goddamn son of a bitch."

At the cabin the table was set with three plates, beers, salads, two bottles of Texas Pete on newspaper. A large platter of steaming legs took up the rest of the table. Deke dumped sauce on a mound of them and spoke nonchalantly without looking up.

"How'd you do out there?"

Barrett waited by the door watching him. Jason went to the sink and splashed his face and hands.

"Son of a bitch," Barrett said, his voice tight and quiet. "I owe you one all right."

"Right after you boys left I came across a whole sack of legs out there in the kudzu so I decided to fry 'em up for you. Sit down, fellas, a Brando picture's on."

Jason dug in, raking legs on his plate, gnawing them ravenously. He was used to these pranks, his father loved practical jokes, always played them on college and Air Force buddies and on them as kids. Deke and Honcho had turned them into an art form, fabricating every imaginable stunt on each other. Every now and then Deke had been seriously incensed at Honcho's pranks. He remembered fistfights breaking out, one about a girl Deke liked, and after that Deke's jokes became downright dangerous. Pranks were bread and butter in their family. He knew Deke and Barrett had gotten into them but he was too famished now to care or be amused. Barrett stood silently at the sink, emotion bowed in his back and shoulders. He set the water, gazing at it, resoaping and scrubbing his hands, a scene from *The Missouri Breaks* droning on television.

"Swear to God I'll get you for that one," he muttered with his back to them.

"Which one's that old son?" Deke said, raising his beer. "You know I've heard frogs can get damned ingenious with configurations they'll get into, heard they'll kick their legs right off on certain full moon nights. *Amazing* creatures. I was watching a show—"

"Fuck you, Deke. Fuck you goddamit. All right?"

He tossed the towel on the counter, biting his lip, his back humped over. His shoulders bounced as he laughed back tears.

"You crazy motherfucker," he said. "Can't believe I fell for that motherfuckin' shit. I saw that goddamn pyramid, I thought, I'm working with the craziest son of a bitch in Tennessee, what'd I expect?'"

He turned and sunk to the table, blinking, stuffed a towel in his shirt and started eating. Without pausing Jason cleaned off legs, tossing them in a paper bag.

"Look out," Barrett said, chuckling with exhaustion and the miraculous taste of fried meat, tears dripping in his food. "The Avenger shows up when you least expect him and he's got no mercy; not a drop."

"Forewarned," Deke said. "You gotta admit . . ."

"*God*," Barrett said. "I feel like I been smokin' our shit I'm so goddamned hungry and tired. Pick up anything on the scanner?"

"Busted a field in Pinyard County, sounded like a large outfit. Watering trucks, the whole shebang."

"No shit. How far?"

"Twenty, twenty-five miles. Wasn't no guerrilla operation."

"Those are the ones," Barrett pounded the table. "Don't know why people don't use the brains God gave 'em."

Jason looked back and forth at them and down at his plate. "What's the schedule tomorrow?"

"Yeah, what's on tomorrow's agenda straw boss?"

"Plant another crop on that western slope," Barrett said. "Have to tote water with us on the truck. Almost out of lime, somebody's gotta make a run."

"I'll hit Brinkers before noon," Deke said.

"You been buyin' too much supplies from them the last few weeks, let's not attract attention we don't have to. Let Jason drive out to where nobody knows him and pick it up."

"Take my jeep," Jason said.

"Sure you can handle it?" Deke mussed his hair.

"Maybe I should go," Barrett said. "Reverend might mistake the DEA for God and turn state's evidence to the Lord."

Jason glanced embarrassed at them as he chewed. He nodded, looking at his plate. "Assholes," he said. "Forgive me," he swallowed and burped. "Yeah, sure, I think I can handle it."

Eighteen years ago he'd made this trip with his father in their two-tone '57 Ford. He remembered that bright-cloud-torn day, his father's leathery face and voice and these gritty, curling back roads. The carton of Kents on the seat, a box of Dixie Crystals sugar cubes for his father's diabetic emergencies and "Honeycomb" playing on the radio as his father told him "the problem with asphalt was it was butt-trouble," chuckling with his elbow on the door as he flicked ashes through the half-opened glass. His old man had a booming baritone voice he'd warm up Sunday mornings singing "How Great Thou Art" and "Go Tell It On The Mountain," waking Jason and his brothers. If they didn't get up they'd get a face-full of ice water. He remembered them bolting up in bed shivering-wet cursing as his father strolled down the hall belting out "Love Lifted Me." He could be a tough son of a bitch but there was always wisdom in it. He challenged Jason to sit in the front pews of the church and grinned at him from the choir through services as if he'd seen something in him he hadn't and wanted him to have the best seat to know it. In the middle of the sermon he'd glance over and his father'd be beaming at him. His old man had a faith he lived instead of talked about, would do anything for anybody, was humble to God, but didn't give a damn about making pious appearances. Every now and then he'd say or do something a little wild and suggestive, tell an off-color joke for instance, just to loosen up churchgoers and let them know he had an inside joke with the Lord. Loving God didn't mean you had to be dull, boring or dead; laughter was a reward of faith, it freed you up to smile through this misery-strewn, beaten-down world, to get off of your sanctimonious ass and make some joyful noise. Watching his old man he saw where he found his power and off-the-wall, irreverent joy, and followed it.

He remembered rumbling along in their blue and white Ford that day telling a joke that'd cracked his father up. It was the Roman Emperor's birthday and The Great One had planned the goriest celebration of all time. He'd brought in all his gladiators and lions and Christians, starting with gladiators battling each other, a hundred or so chopping each other to pieces. He was thrilled by this display of bloodletting but it just wetted his appetite. He threw all his Christians in, hundreds of them, and the gladiators sliced them up while they fought each other for hours. It was such a glorious, bloody mess the Emperor couldn't contain himself and ordered his lions let loose on everyone standing, dozens of beasts, and the Christians and gladiators and lions tore each other to pieces, and heads and body parts were everywhere, blood spurting all over the place and the Emperor was beside himself; he couldn't sit still. It was the most perfect birthday he'd ever had, the fattest blood-fest he'd ever known. He jumped from his seat with his sword charging into the bloody floor of the coliseum screaming and cackling, hacking away at anything standing or moving. When nothing was left he kept chopping heads, arms, legs, anything chopable. Across the room he heard a faint, raspy voice. Covered in blood he stumbled over dozens of bodies to get to it, the voice coming from a bloody, decapitated head on the floor, its mouth barely moving, which seemed to be trying to say something. The Emperor stuck his ear down to it and after a minute he could barely make out what it was saying. In a feeble, broken whisper the voice groaned: "*Happy birthday . . . to you . . . happy birthday to you . . .*"

Jason remembered their old Ford weaving across the road with his father's bouncing laughter, and how he hadn't stopped laughing the rest of the afternoon. He seemed to get as big a kick out of him knowing the joke as the joke itself. He remembered how it felt making his old man laugh like that and that it was the first day they'd spent together as two men. His father reached across the seat ruffling his hair with his big, powerful hand, chuckling through his nose: "*happy birthday . . . to you . . .*" he said again, eyes sparkling as if seeing his son for the first time.

Seven miles from Karaville he turned off Highway 26 and climbed the steep hairpins over Paris Mountain, listening to a backwoods gospel group picking and singing some spiritual stuff. The preacher came on and started huffing about repentance and damnation, and Jason flipped around until he found Eartha Kitt purring on a Nashville blues station.

There was more Holy Spirit in her broken-down love song than whatever that man was doing. He was one reason Jason couldn't step into a church right now, because listening to that sound robbed you of something. God *was* sound and you could tell how much He was in the world by flipping through radio stations. Most of it was awful, grating noise people adapted to like drinking half-bad water. The music was beautifully eerie, but the preacher's voice was fear-based ranting. Love and freedom from fear were what Christ was about, not being driven by some spiritual cattle prod. Anyone who loved God was protected and didn't need to worry what the devil was up to or God either. If you led them to the water of life you didn't need to scare them, but you had to have love in your heart to do it, you couldn't just rant and bludgeon them to death with scriptures. God was Sound, the Sound was love and the soul would gravitate to it if you gave it half a chance. Maybe it would be more complicated than that in time, but that's what his ministry would be about today.

It was freakishly dry for April. Farmers plowing fields stirred dust-trails over the road. With little rain the pollen smothered everything. His molar abscess was flaring up like it had the last two springs. He stuck his bottle of well water between his legs, raising it now and then to wash down the gagging powder. You had to have faith in *something* to harrow that hard-parched ground, he thought, watching a farmer make a turn at the end of a field in a dust-cloud. An atheist farmer was a contradiction in terms. At the foot of the mountain he passed a Walmart, Burger King and Auto Zone where a horse farm had once stood, mountain shadows stretching across acres of vacant blacktop. He could see the sea of green pastures on his right running up the mountainside, animals grazing around hurdles, white fences and horse trailers not there anymore.

Crossing Highway 238 to Nashville he wound past shops and antique stores, Indian mounds, shacks crumbling in weeds, the old Pure station where he and his father had stopped that day for orange Nehis. He passed the sign that said "Looney's Trenching" they'd made jokes about. There were dozens of catfish and trout farms. A few farmers burned ground cover and insects in the woods. He was behind a slow Ford tractor, the overalled old farmer bobbing along the twisting curves. This canyon of clay and granite cliffs had seemed higher to him as a kid. The farmer signaled, turning off, lifting his straw hat with a wag, half a mile ahead *Harbeson's Feed and Fertilizer* coming up on the flattened crest, the supplies store notched into the wall of the mountain, its red rusty sign wobbling across the road. Trucks filled the gravel lot lining the docks, two men stacking feed on a flatbed. A half-dozen farmers stood in the center of the lot gabbing and chewing, turning to stare at him from a haze of blue smoke. All he was doing was buying lime, he thought, relax. He parked near the steps, nodding to them as he went in.

The high-ceilinged warehouse smelled of meal and fertilizer and was palely-lit from the loading dock, a dozen overhead fans creaking. Exhaust fans roared in the wired windows with "Behind Closed Doors" blaring, overalled farmers turning to him as he passed the wide aisles.

"Hope it didn't rain till Christmas," one said. "It'll make my mind up for me."

"Bob Jenkins said he had to have a big one or he was finished," said a little man in striped coveralls. "His best or his last the bank told him."

"Still he has his cows . . ."

"Help ya?" someone said from the floor. Jason made out a hugely stout man on a knee in plaid shirt and jeans with a head the size of a watermelon pushing up feed sacks.

"Need three-hundred pounds of lime if you've got it."

"All right," the man rose slowly. "Whatcha need it for?"

The bluntness of the question startled him. He couldn't see the man's face.

"What difference does it make?"

"We've got three brands, some like one more for one thing than another. Powdered or pelleted?"

"Powdered. *Broccoli*. Any brand'll do. Scotts if you've got it."

"By the shipload," the clerk said, waddling to the register. "Four thirty-two a twenty-five pound bag. You said three-hundred pounds?"

He felt someone watching him. In a narrow space over a desk of paperwork old Harbeson was sitting in his wheelchair. He remembered that day his father and Harbeson greeted each other making jokes about feed and stock prices. He was like a wild old wiry-thin rooster, his sharp voice piercing the high-ceilinged noise as he led them to a warehouse to show them a combine. Leaning back in his chair smoking a pipe, the old man stared at him as if trying to place him. Jason turned his back, then thought, why'd I do that?

"Fifty-four forty-three," the clerk said. "You don't look too familiar."

"I'm not . . . from around here."

Jason handed him three twenty's.

"Where from?"

"Little town eighty miles north."

"Which is that?"

"Tazewell."

"Tazewell," the clerk nodded with his chin out. "Got a helper from up there. Own a farm or hirin' out?"

"Hirin'," Jason said, feeling stranger all the time. He didn't like white lies and wished he hadn't started, but they'd wonder why he was so far from his farm buying lime and he'd have to make up something anyway. *Don't tell anyone anything,* Barrett and Deke'd told him. "Need to get back with this."

"You betcha. Who's your boss over there?"

Jason felt Harbeson listening.

"Harper Paterson. In Drake County."

"Don't believe I know him. I'll ask my helper Dave if he does, he's related to everybody in the state. Pull up to the dock and we'll load you."

Keeping his back to the old man Jason stumbled down the steps. He felt self-conscious as if someone were watching him; entities besides the gallery in the parking lot turning again to glare at him. One made a joke and they laughed out loud. Palms sweating he got in his jeep and felt his Bible on the seat and said a prayer, apologizing. He started up and backed to the loading dock. A man chewing tobacco wearing a Fu Man Chu in a dirty, sleeveless t-shirt waited with his lime on a dolly, Jason unzipping the rear window as the man watched him handing down the bags.

"Say you're from Tazewell?"

Oh boy, Jason thought, here we go.

"Born there," Jason said. "Moved when I was a baby."

"Work for Harper Paterson do ya?"

"Yep."

"Saw Harper at the Drake fair a week ago. Married my wife's second cousin when his wife passed."

"That right," Jason said, looking up to see if he was serious. He was not only serious but probing.

"Said he'd laid off his help. Could barely keep his sons around."

"Tell the truth I'm workin' part-time, going back to seminary late-fall."

The man was silent. Jason could feel him listening the way country people do sensing you.

"Be a preacher will ya?"

"Hope to. I better run. Appreciate it."

As he slid into the jeep an orange Chevrolet truck pulled up and a man in his late-sixties limped out extending his palsied hand. It was Mr. Rutledge whose daughter he'd gone to school with and whose family he'd known since he was eight or nine. What was he doing ninety miles from his farm? Jason felt himself tensing and tried to relax. The fact he felt nervous made him more nervous.

"Jason Hawkins? How you doin', son?"

"Not bad, sir. How're you?"

"Well for an old man. Workin' your daddy's farm?"

"No . . ." Jason glanced at the clerk and helper listening from the shadows. Old man Harbeson rolled up beside them in his wheelchair. What *was* this? He knew they sensed something, he felt it whether they did or not. "Workin' part-time between quarters at the Moody Bible Institute. Going back when I save some money."

"That old nigger in the shack up the road from you says he sees you and your brother comin' out of there, figured ya'll were plantin' . . ."

"No sir, not farmin' this year."

"Just livin' there," Mr. Rutledge peered into his jeep.

"Limin' a field?"

"Garden, yessir."

Suddenly he was panicky. Why was everybody so friggin' interested in what he was doing? He have a flag around his neck or something? He had to get out of there.

"How's your mom?"

"Holdin' up I guess."

He glanced at the helper on the dock boring holes through him with an aggravating smirk, climbed in the jeep and cranked up while Mr. Rutledge was saying something about his mother being an angel and a remarkable woman. He was sure any second he'd blab something that'd blow his whole silly, pathetic story. Everyone in the place knew he was up to something because they sensed he himself felt he was and they all knew what the lime was for.

"Mr. Rutledge, I'm runnin' late. Good to see you." As he shut the door the old man stepped in trying to say something but Jason cut him off. "Say hello to Mrs. Rutledge and Janie—"

"Janie's not married. You ought to drop by . . ."

He'd almost slammed the door on the old man's hand and as he swung into the lot he could see Mr. Rutledge still trying to talk to him but yanked off, spewing gravel on the old man's shoes, tailgate and tires, glancing at the slack jawed faces in his rearview mirror watching him gunning it, skidding and sliding sideways out of the parking lot. He felt like he was in slow motion and something was after him; *something* or somebody. He pushed it around the first turns, watching his mirrors. He felt runnish as if he were fleeing some scene in a dream, praying and mumbling as he hit the banked, chute-winding curves faster and faster, tires squalling as he leaned side to side, not slowing down until he reached the foot of the mountain ten minutes later.

In a Brazier parking lot he munched on a fish sandwich watching lunch traffic with the radio droning. A jacked-up seventy-two Malibu with a foot-high yellow decal that said "Bad Boy" rumbled in. Carloads of girls shuffled by giggling and hitting their brakes, a crusty-looking sheriff cruised in at crawling speed staring at him behind his mirrors. Jason stopped chewing, watching him. The cop prowled the lot, sitting a while at the end of it, easing out with excruciating slowness. What was that about? Maybe Harbeson'd reported a man acting funny giving conflicting answers had purchased three-hundred pounds of lime. He was sure that's what it was. Any minute they'd close in on him, drag him from his jeep and wrestle him face-down to the pavement for his crime.

He watched a ten ton box truck back over a twenty-foot sapling, the tree crumpled under the truck's bumper when it stopped. The driver slid out oblivious to it, loosened his belt and tucked in his shirt. The side of the truck said "The Big Green." Jason kept chewing, watching the truck broadside with the tree mashed under it, the driver combing his hair in his side-mirror getting it perfect. He heard something on the radio about

a marijuana bust and turned it up, accidentally blasting it into the parking
lot.

> . . . Last night in Pinyard County the DEA assisted by state
> militia confiscated twenty-two acres of marijuana seedlings and
> made twelve arrests. The growers were spotted by helicopter
> shortly after 2 A.M . . . Estimated street value of the illegal weed
> was six million dollars . . . Sheriff Leroy Jenkins said it was the
> largest confiscation in his district . . . The trial of accused mercy
> killer Adam Lemslaw resumes . . .

The truck driver had disappeared and Jason stared at the skinned,
doubled-over tree as he thought about those choppers last night. How close
had they come? He wasn't keen on going to jail and making the news for
growing illegal weeds before he ever reached the pulpit. What a way to start
a ministry. When he returned to the farm now they could be sitting there,
every squad car in the county and half the state militia waiting for him,
Hawkins Boys Busted in tomorrow's paper. He started to panic, rocking
a little praying and sweating, caught himself and thought, all right, stop
it, *beware of sudden fear,* what good is it? You can't run out on Deke, you
agreed to help him, remember. You've got to stand and fight. Maybe it *is* a
righteous effort. He hated dishonesty and breaking the law but maybe this
was different. He could dig up scripture to justify it, but he didn't trust that.
There were dozens of verses dealing with persecution, losses and injustice
people were always abusing, lying to themselves about, using to excuse
all manner of corruption. He'd ask for simple guidance. He said a prayer
for clarity as he'd done every day since that hellacious Sunday morning,
knowing God knew what was in his heart anyway, and started out of the
jeep to tell the driver about the tree, when the sheriff's car reappeared,
prowling in slower than before as if he wanted to look at somebody and
wouldn't be noticed creeping in at this ridiculous speed. Staring at Jason,
he stopped in front of him, blocking him, picked up something and started
writing. What's he doing? Jason thought. Am I putting out some kind of
scent today? He was leaving, the frigging tree could make it on its own,
if the sheriff was trying to rattle him it was working. As he cranked up
the lawman turned and glowered at him. Give me a break, he thought,
nodding at the man who looked down and kept on scribbling. Jason cut

his wheels back and forth and worked past the squad car's bumper. When he reached the end of the lot and was pulling out he glanced back and the sheriff was glaring at him over his shoulder.

Shirtless in sweat-soaked khakis, Deke crunched through the brittle field-straw, powder lifting from his unlaced boots. There were rumbles behind the mountains. The cacophony of cicadas had put him in a trance under the dying sun. Every now and then he'd stoop to feel the dry-cracked earth with his palm, flicking up layers with his fingers. The largest field on the farm heat-blurred with flies into a blue, shapeless horizon. This was his Holy Ground. Skirmished over in the Civil War, cleared by hand by his great great grandfather, sweated and bled and prayed into over a hundred and thirty planting seasons. They'd grown corn here mostly; sometimes tobacco. He could see rows plowed until the soil was a foot deep soft as sand disappearing into the edge of the earth. He remembered sunup to sun-down tobacco croppings here, the pungent-fresh smell of tobacco leaves curing in barns, Cokes so cold they made your hand ache at the end of a row you guzzled before you started down the next one. He'd seen mirages and spirits out here in the dizzying sun he'd never talked about. When he was twelve he saw a Cherokee Indian chieftain standing in full headdress, his rugged, raised face proudly staring back at him. He wondered later if he'd dreamed that. In a Vietnamese rice paddy after he hadn't slept for three days he'd seen his old man striding toward him and believed he was stumbling across this field. A farmer's son kicked out of his head on hashish sleepwalking to his father's spirit across an endless garden of war.

As he walked he picked hollow-dry reeds with his fingers, squeezing them for moisture. There wasn't a drop of water out here. A crow cawed from the edge of the woods near the farmhouse, flapping sluggishly, crying to its echoes in the tree line. He kicked mounds and rock clods, muttering to himself:

". . . A little bit dry . . . just a bit . . . it's goddamn Saharaville out here . . . peas wouldn't make it . . . peanuts maybe. Get the harrow out and turn it, boys . . . Beat water outta the sky. First thing in the morning we'll dig in here," he said, planting, dust from his boots swirling in the wind. "Can't tell what the Lord'll send. He'll send something though, hell yeah, he'll send something." He shuffled ahead. "Try cotton. Cactus maybe.

Might be dry for cactus. Look at this place, it's a fucking moonscape. Might as well be under water, daddy, let's flood it and grow catfish." He stooped to touch a set of panther prints leading toward the pond from the woods, following them as he spoke. "Creeks are dryin' up. Little dry to plant. Tell Honcho to call the hands? We aren't worried, are we? Set out tobacco next week, corn on the big twelve-hundred. Hung in there a long time. *Long* time, dammit. Had to feed half our neighbors that year, remember? Remember that dinner mama set out Sunday mornings? Family we never saw, ate while we were at church and we never knew who they were? Who were they? Starving farmers? God's hungry," he chuckled, kicking a rock skipping across the dirt. "Took care of them, didn't He? He'll take care of us. Always has. Due now boys and girls. Climb the corn to the clouds this year . . ."

He stopped suddenly, shutting his eyes, swaying in the wind. He plopped on the ground with his head hung forward, rocking rhythmically; eyes clenched humming with the wind and flies. His father was *there* all right. Sinking to his back he felt the heat baking his skin. There was a subtle rumbling through the ground as he lay on it, listening to it as if it were some cryptic coded message. It ceased, starting up way down again, and he sat up gazing across the long white fields. The farmhouse was in the rumbling's path; he couldn't see the house but knew where it was behind the weeds waving along the fence line. The thunder came from there. He felt another groan through his feet and watched five or six vultures tipping above the house, circling lazily toward the highway.

"Wait a second," he said. "You were here it'd rain, wouldn't it? Did you take it with you?" he laughed, feeling the grumbling trembling back, listening through the dry-rustlling straw, got up slowly, staring across the three fields to the abandoned house shimmering in a parched blue blur. He felt that presence like the breeze at his back with the static music in the wind, the faint-tinkling wind chimes on the porch, the myriad, chirping, racketing creatures tied to the soil. There was a strong music here, spirits of his family's voices moving, they were all here with answers whether you liked them or not. As he listened a boom like cannon-fire interrupted it, and he frowned at the horizon, a few wavy specks like toy structures standing in the green splotch of trees.

He turned toward the cabin walking faster. What was he doing out here? He had to mix compost, fertilizer, lime, fill the duffle bags, load water cans, check tools and work lights. He flushed a rabbit and in a reflex was chasing, hollering after it, lunging like a starving man clawing for a meal. Diving on his stomach, cutting it off hooting at it, slapping the ground. In a few seconds he was laughing so hard he couldn't move. Rolling to his side he coughed, flopping to his back howling at the buzzing sun burning down through his eyelids.

Late-day sun trickled through the grape arbor where Barrett Duck walked around the last marijuana seedlings. Checking for males and hermaphrodites he hummed a Little Walter tune as he circled the trays, picking through the delicate leaves. There was good camouflage here with light enough to break them in as he went over them. He parted the top blanket of interlaced foliage, eyeing the stalks and stem for male pollen sacks. They were rugged, fragrant beauties ready to hit the earth and transform into trees.

In March he'd sexed out the plants by shortening the days under artificial lights from sixteen to eight hours, simulating the end of summer. This triggered flowering. Anything with a male bloom was jerked, then he'd marked every plant with only female flowers until there were nothing but females, shocked them back into vegetating with twenty-four hours of light for three days, then put them back on their regular sixteen. Some still showed the lacey-white hairs that would be arm-size colas in October. There were always fence-jumpers, females popping up with male pollen sacks. You had to be damned vigilant because one or two would litter a patch with seeds. Nature would pull a fast one to insure them and you stayed a step ahead going for all the flowers you could get. Usually she'd slip a few past you. A female turned hermaphrodite would not only seed every plant in the patch, cutting yield, but weaken the strain. Hermaphrodites were a pain in the ass.

When he finished this rooting out, trimming dead bottom-foliage as he went along, he picked the tiny top-center-clusters of each plant, dropping them on a screen to dry. This made the plants bush out and turned them into fatter, heavier trees. There was a bonus to these pinchings. Next to them were curling leaves he rubbed between his fingers he'd make something sweet out of with these tiny buds, a special little ritual surprise for the wrap party.

It'd been a smooth setting out for having to dig into baked ground and haul a river of water. They'd not only had to soak every plant as they put them in but go back every other night and water every seedling planted in the last three weeks. It'd driven them into all-nighters, doubling the labor they'd have expended with one or two showers a week. But the goal was giving them a healthy start and they'd done that. No one had been seriously injured, thank God. Jason'd had an allergic reaction to a sting on his left ankle, spider poison probably, eating a patch of skin off the size of a silver dollar. They'd soaked the ankle in Epsom salt and he was okay. A thorn'd caught Barrett in the center of his left pupil. He'd known better than to breeze down that trail in the dark without shielding his eyes, no moon, pitch blackness, then the electric shock and flash on his pupil like an explosion when the briar stalk popped it. He was blinking a few days before he stuck a patch on it. Lucky it wasn't worse. Besides scaring up goblin geese in the dark and getting stung by bees Deke'd had no mishaps. They'd done well considering the overtime put in hustling around these dark slopes, and kept themselves out of sight. No one had seen them except on supply runs to several towns with distance between them. The only unseeing faces they'd seen had peered down from military choppers. Two years ago Barrett'd bought a few powerful scanners at a military surplus auction, some modification handbooks and secret frequency lists from a former RTO in Vietnam. He'd learned to eavesdrop on military jets and choppers as well as law enforcement. Knowing who was in your airspace could spare you all manner of unwanted surprises. It'd saved his ass more than once. The ships were alternating days and nights now, and with live camou, using the scanner and radio and very little light they'd kept the place a veritable ghost farm. They'd wrap planting tonight if everything went as it should, two weeks before Memorial Day. It'd taken a month to get these in but there were a hell of a lot of them. The patches were well-spaced and wild-looking. Ground cover appeared natural around them, or they around it. Some of the finest midnight farming Barrett had been associated with.

He could feel Deke getting higher and a little lighter every day and the Reverend seemed to be handling things. Jason was a bit naive but not afraid to work, a good, sensitive kid and tougher than he seemed. Like Deke he was caught up in this mission and passionate about it. They were on one, all right, struggling with their family's dismal fortune and still in shock about it. This was the doctor's orders, raw-edged, gut-expending work to get it out of your system. When they finished this season and the money reins loosened up it'd make better sense to the Reverend. Amazing what that evil green cash could do for the troubled soul. It was how and why you made it refreshed or beat it down, and no man or government could tell you you were wrong when you knew damn well you weren't, especially when you were up against a wall the government itself had pitched in your path. He'd always been amused by what was considered clean and dirty money in this backasswards world.

Since coming here he'd started to rethink his own father's fatal "accident," the steel mill fall in Atlanta that'd killed him three years before Barrett had been sent to Vietnam. He'd decided not to dwell on the circumstances years ago, had to to keep from going bonkers over it since there was no way to know for sure, but since coming here it'd started to eat at him again. He'd start to burn with it, wondering what he could do after twenty-one years, reopen the investigation maybe, hire a motherfucker of a lawyer, talk to everyone around the vats that day; then he'd go, Oh God, fuck it, it's gone, it's dead, he's dead, and if anyone did anything they'll pay. Sure they will or they've paid already. Stick to business at hand. Take care of these boys, help save their homestead. Which is when he realized his deeper need to be a part of Deke's mission. Deke's father getting pushed over the edge had delivered him here, and the possibility his own had been shoved into a vat of molten steel twenty-one years ago fueled him to see that Deke's family were vindicated in some commensurate way, not pushed out of here or over some other godforsaken edge. Redemption, it was. Like the Epsom salts in hot water drawing the poison out of Jason's leg, it drew something out of him he hadn't realized was still festering so strong.

He was glad to be here anyway, working with these plants on this lush, heavenly spread. If they could just get some rain and not have to beat the world every day toting water to them. Ideally you slipped in occasionally just to pinch and feed the ladies, check for bugs and fungus, but they were having to go in every day now which put the project at risk. Wearing down trails, trampling patches; another bad side-effect of drought. With the dryness there were wildfires popping up around them, he tried not to worry about them but they gave him nightmares. The vegetation was so crispy the sun could touch it off and getting zapped by short, violent

electrical storms with a few elephant tears, not enough to dampen the
surface. You felt like a straw man at a flamethrower's convention.

He was frustrated not getting to play his guitar much. He couldn't play
shit in daylight, it had to be night when the Voice and Visitor showed up.
Mornings he couldn't even think about it. It'd take an hour a day jamming
to rebuild his finger calluses. He missed the soul and sound that soothed
the savage beast. He'd get his chance again when the rains came in, he'd
pick up and play that sweet-necked mother like she was his baby girl he
hadn't held in a month or so.

He heard thunder booming out of the northeast. It turned into a pair
of F-16's soaring in low practicing close-cover ground support. He watched
them flickering through the trees, tremoring along the valley walls, glanced
down and saw something under his nose concealed in a blanket of foliage:
a shining bandit. He touched the male sacks with his fingertips and yanked
the whole plant, holding it up in the failing twilight. You had to admire the
way it masked its male flowers, the slippery little cross dresser.

"No swingin' dicks on this hooch farm," he said to it. "Who you think
you're foolin', pal?" He started to toss it, then thought better of it. Breaking
it off at the root he popped it in his mouth chewing it.

When a wheel dropped the chassis rocked on its heels and floated. From
a quarter-mile away Deke could hear John Lee Hooker wailing down
the mountain. It sounded like a lawn party up there. If they were using
headlamps he hoped their ears and eyes were open for choppers. Lightning
stabbed long-speared shadows through the trees. He'd veered off his
original trail but that was better really, he was forging a new one toward
the growling voice reverberating off the mountains. He was nervous about
his tires with all this weight on them, having to change one on a forty-five
degree angle, worse having to haul all this water up by hand. Hearing
thunder he shut off his engine and listened to it simmering. Lightning
blinked on the side of the mountain, he could see every ripple and leaf on
it. There was a steady breeze and he could almost smell the moisture. He
heard Hooker break into "The Motor City Is Burnin'," cranked up and
pushed on up through the narrow-laned trunks, working to keep his nose
straight. Flashes underlit limbs behind a rounded rim through a mesh of

pines and brush. He gunned it, tearing a new rough opening under the clearing, jerry cans slamming the bed walls. Two headsets turned to him; Barrett and Jason were on their knees mulching the last planted patch. One started down he could tell was Barrett by his heavier gait. Deke pushed the door against the kudzu to check his camou, cut the engine and it coughed a few times.

"What took you so long?" Barrett said.

"Couldn't find a stream deep enough to fill the tanks so I had to run back to the pond. We selling tickets up here? Maybe we should set up Tiki torches."

"I can hear a chopper from the other side of the world, Kimasabe."

"Yeah, well, we've been blindsided before. One of these cowboys ambushes us we've had it, buddy."

"You're right. Didn't want anyone else getting his eye poked is all."

They watched the sky illuminating and churning.

"Looks like we might get some."

"Don't trust it," Barrett said. "It's the dry heaves. We'll soak 'em, if it comes it comes."

Deke dragged handfuls of kudzu from the hood across his windshield as Barrett lifted the cooler from the truck bed, dropping it, slapping his arm.

"Bloodsuckers?"

"Big enough to stand flat-footed and fuck a turkey."

"They're meaner in this weather. Thirsty I reckon."

Barrett reached under the seat pulling out a package the size of a banana wrapped in foil. He took three beers from the cooler, tossing one to Deke.

"Come get it, little brother. Time to start the wrap party."

Jason stumbled toward them with his headlights beaming.

"You guys are worthless. Aren't we gonna water first?"

"Look what I made for the occasion," Barrett said, holding an eight-inch cigar of marijuana leaves bound together by stems.

"What's that?" Jason said.

"I call it The First Reward. All those little tops I pruned to make the plants bush out are in the center of this mama."

"Will she smoke?"

"Naw," Barrett said, lighting it, puffing until the head glowed red, handing it to Jason. Jason drew on it and blew out hacking.

"This is what it's all about, little brother."

"He's never done this," Deke said.

"Tried it a couple of times. Nothing happened."

"*Goddamn* the pusher man," Barrett chuckled.

Backs against the truck fender they sat sipping beers, passing the cigar. Barrett guzzled the first one tossing the can in the bed.

"Can't get addicted to this, can you?"

"Oh yeah, if that's what you want to do. Otherwise it's good medicine. Hey, we got to have the right music for this."

Barrett brought the boom box, propping it against the truck wheel. "Riders on the Storm" played as they watched the sky moiling and shuddering.

"Oh man," he said. "This is good, brothers. Got 'em in, didn't we? One thousand ninety-two."

"I smell rain?" Deke said.

"Naw. This is the spookiest fucking weather I've ever seen."

"It's a drought, Br'er Rabbit, don't make a thing out of it."

"More than that I tell ya."

"Thank you, oh prophet of mystery."

"Who's that?" Jason said.

"The Witch Doctor. Don't get him started unless you want to hear the weirdest fucking hoaxes of all time."

"Like what?"

"Spontaneous human combustion. Ice blocks from the sky. Vanishing people. All that circus shit. Unknown beasts and wild children."

"You're a blockheaded motherfucker, you know that?"

"I've heard of some of those things," Jason said.

"There's things out there we've got no idea of."

"Then why do we have to worry about them?" Deke said. "Day-to-day shit's weird enough without worrying about people vanishing and exploding."

He slapped a mosquito, watched it lift up and crushed it.

"Because we need to look below the surface of things, see what's *really* going on in this freakish world. There's spirit life in the plant kingdom most people got no knowledge of."

"Spirit life?" Jason said.

"The Ojibway tribe believe trees possess souls. Don't like to cut 'em for fear they'll make 'em suffer. The Iroquois believe spirits in corn, squash and beans take the form of three beautiful maidens."

"Sure they do."

"No kiddin'. There's this tribe in Borneo believes there's a spirit in rice, so they have ritual feasts every year to keep it from leaving so their crops don't decay."

"Can't seem to get on the same page, can they?" Deke said. "That's all myth and legend, none of it's scientific."

"Science can't explain the spirit world. This is what Alexander Christmas was talking about."

"Alexander Christmas was fried out of his mind."

"So why does every culture have these plant beliefs? Gotta be based on something, sensed, dreamed, maybe seen."

"The European water lily's supposed to be St. Peter's helper judging souls," Jason said.

"There you go, Rev. We've got a learned man here."

"In the Old Testament there're talking trees. The burning bush spoke to Moses. David was told by the mulberry trees when to attack the Philistines."

"See that, Tar Baby? Those beliefs and stories are in every religion and culture. The Greeks believed the goddess Artemis lived in cedars and willows. They believed some trees were oracles 'cause their roots reached way down into the underworld."

"Maybe they're just trees with tree souls," Deke said. "Maybe their only life's chlorophyll and all that spirit shit's superstitious crap. Beautiful maidens, my ass."

"He believes it," Barrett said, leaning to Jason. "Your brother's been spooked; doesn't like to deal with the other world."

Deke stared at the clouds lighting up the colors of an oyster shell.

"And you're not, huh?"

"Course I am but I deal with it differently. Don't run from it; I run *to* it."

"You used to run *from* it as I remember. You used to have a few problems with it."

"Talking about Vietnam?" Jason said.

"*No*," Deke said, flattening his can with a grunt, flicking it in the truck bed. Barrett nudged Jason who was watching Deke and handed him the cigar.

"Oh yeah," Barrett said. "There was shit over there weird as the Bermuda Triangle. What was that crazy Colonel's name lifted thirty dead VC in a helicopter sling, dumped them from two-thousand feet into a village we knew was harborin' and supplyin' VC?"

"Purser," Deke said, handing beers. "Colonel Mavin Purser."

"That was a sick motherfucker, man. Can you imagine those papas and sons raining out of the clouds like that? Smashing through hooch tops, crushing old people, goats, chickens and children."

"It makes you *proud*," Deke sighed, crossing his legs.

"The good colonel had his shit blown away. Somebody booby-trapped his personal latrine."

"Who told you that?"

"That geeky Lieutenant from St. Louis, Mitnick, the Corvette freak. Ran into him a couple years ago in a blues bar in Texas."

They listened to the rumbling.

"Here come our boys," Barrett said.

A military jet knifed through the ceiling, flying slower than it sounded. As it banked east everything in the truck shimmied and rattled.

"Bombers must have played hell with your daddy's livestock."

"Three and a half years like this," Jason said.

"Sons of bitches," Deke said. "I think they're harassing people round here. Heard a couple of old boys at Brinkers talking about some big government buyout."

"There're always rumors around Air Force bases," Barrett said. "They own every fucking clod anyway, what they need to buy it for?"

"*The guuuvmint!*" Jason said, squirming up slowly with his back against the fender. He weaved to the beer cooler, laughing as he raked through ice.

"How you feeling little brother?"

"*Different*. Might become a guuuvmint man. Put on a guuuvmint uniform. Work for the goddamn guuuvmint for a change."

Barrett puffed the half-burned cigar, turning and admiring it.

"A woman's just a woman, but a good cigar's a smoke."

"Who said that?"

"Kipling, I think. My old man used to take off on him. *'Gunga Din Din Din, where the hellavyoubean? Piss me some water, nigger, water get it, hitherooo . . .'"*

"Your old man was a trip."

"I dug yours too, Tar Baby. One reason I'm humpin' these hills instead of chasin' pussy around Memphis right now. Free enterprise and the American way."

They clanked cans and drained them.

"We'll have a hell of a crop if we have to water it ourselves," Deke said, knee-walking to the cooler.

"We can pull it off but I hope we don't have to. It's like making love to a woman with artificial lubricant."

"What is?" Jason spoke up groggily. ". . . Did you say . . ."

"Earth's exactly like a woman, see. Got to be fertile to bring anything to bear. To grow good fruit she needs rain that's like a slow, quiet foreplay, gets her wet and workin' way deep inside. She'll give it to you then, give you anything you want. Like this we're just finger-fuckin' her."

"She'll get off," Deke said.

"Rain's magic shit, Tar Baby; don't underestimate it. We ought to be setting out drums to catch it. We don't get good showers soon we better start warmin' spring water in the sun or we'll send every one of these girls into shock."

"We've got stacks of empty barrels at the house."

"The *guuuvmint's* done it," Jason said, breaking into convulsive laughter. "Son, I work for the *guuuvmint*. How you want your weather, poached, fried or over easy?"

"Wish you'd get in a better mood, little brother."

"I'm in a goddamn *guuuvmint* mood."

"We kind've figured that," Deke said.

"I think he took to the Green Lady. He's talkin' more like the common man than a man of the cloth."

"I've never felt this good in my whole fucking life," Jason said, giggling, taking another draw.

"Got to get this water off and on these plants by sunup," Barrett said.

"No hurry. Do it in our sleep."

"You and I can. Little brother's busy."

"Let the guuuvmint shower blessings on the hills of Tennessee!" Jason said as he blew out a lung-full, bending and coughing.

"The Reverend's talkin'," Barrett said, nudging Deke.

"Talk to us, Reverend. *Say it.*"

Jason stood unsteadily, tipped his beer and poured it in a circle in the leaves, staggered back a little and took another sip, looking up.

"Let the guuuvmint shatter the eardrums of the weak to fill the coffers of the mighty!" he said.

"Go ahead, little brother. Go ahead."

"Let all those who own and till land give up their land that they might walk the streets impaled on the guuuvmint's beneficent finger!"

"You got it," Barrett laughed. "Go ahead. Talk to us."

Deke watched Jason stumble downhill, leaning up it with his beer in one hand, the short-burnt cigar dangling from his fingers. His face and mouth twitched as if it were tickled. Maybe getting him like this wasn't a great idea, he thought. Barrett was grinning, shaking his head as he went to the back of the truck loosening ropes through the jerry cans. Jason swayed with his eyes shut, raising one arm at a time in some private, delirious rhythm. The tape finished and he was chanting quietly to himself, nodding-singing it. He sipped his beer and held it over his head, dousing himself, sipping as he gazed up through the trees.

"Let the blessings fall into the pastures like huge heaps of cow dung rained from great heights into the faces of the humble!" he yelled, staggering back; catching himself on a bent sapling, opening his palm to the tiny humble people on the ground, he hung a few seconds glaring at them.

"Man's talkin' righteous!" Barrett said.

Jason looked up. "Let the guuuvmint do ya right every time! Do I hear an amen?"

"Amen," Deke said quietly, pushing up.

"*Amen*, brother man."

Deke and Barrett unloaded water cans lining them by the truck.

"Let the guuuvmint take over the farms," Jason said, his voice cracking, "so that it controls the food prices of its sheep and all the souls therein!"

"Yeah," Barrett said. "There you go. Tell the truth."

"Let the long lip of the law suck every independent farmer out of the crevices of the earth where he would take a country crap without asking the guuuvmint's permission, 'cause the law will not have it!"

"Go tell it, little brother. Shout it for us."

Jason leaned against the tree, puffing the cigar. He doubled to the ground in a coughing spasm and fell against the trunk with his eyes shut, face flushed.

"The law will tell you what to plant, who to sell it to, and how much you'll get for it. Because this is the law! Listen to the *laaawww*, brothers and sisters!"

"Listenin'," Barrett said, nudging Deke.

"I can't tell you how happy I am to see these shining faces tonight ground down under the laaawww's magnificent wheels!" Jason said, grinning up at them like a cheap car salesman. "I can't tell you, brothers and sisters, how happy this makes me . . . tonight . . . I'm just so happy . . ."

Deke had a hard time watching him. It was amusing but a little strange. Jason stumbled back barely keeping his feet, turning and twisting, waving his beer and cigar in the air. He hung bent-over, shuffling sideways making rough, throaty noises, eyes watered.

"He all right?" Barrett said.

"Don't know who he is," Deke said, lifting water cans.

"Now I see the Great Thresher turning toward us!" Jason bolted up straight. ". . . separate the wheat from the chaff . . . salt from the earth . . . man from his property . . . *the husband* . . ." He was falling and running downhill, tripping sideways into a bed of briars. He rolled on his back blathering and cackling. ". . . I'm just so pleased to see each and every one of you fall down on your knees tonight! Before the guuuvmint's gleaming teeth I'm grateful to see you offer up the fruits of your labors to a bunch of official fools and highway robbers . . . you're the salt of the earth, but if the earth loses its salt who inherits the salt mine, you sons of bitches! . . . Who do you think! Who do you think you are! . . ."

They heard thunder as they watched Jason's head drift back and he started to shake convulsively. Dropping their water cans they slid down the embankment to him. When Barrett heard what was coming out of him he felt a chill up his spine. He'd seen this once as a boy in an evangelist's tent and it'd had the same effect on him. Jason's mouth was chattering, his jaw jumping like he was having a febrile seizure, his whole body twitching and trembling. He made a guttural stream of unintelligible words like some backwards, garbled language.

"What's wrong with him?" Deke said.

"Never heard tongues?"

"Never seen this."

"Holy Spirit's speakin' through him. Boy's a conductor. Never seen this before?"

Deke shook his head as he stared at Jason's eyes plugged under their lids. His head jerked as the whites wobbled and danced. Three jets roared over the treetops as they watched him convulsing, his chest heaving and sinking. He was whispering in a strange monotone but they couldn't make out what it was. Barrett pried the cigar from his fist.

"Ow, shit!" he said, slinging it in the leaves. He pulled Jason's fingers apart and there were no burns on his calluses. The beer can dropped from his other hand as his head slid to the side and he went limp, twitching a little as Barrett felt his neck-pulse.

"Heart's racin'. Skin's clammy. Let's lift him to the truck."

They carried him up the embankment, laying him in the bed. Barrett ripped a towel in strips soaking them in water, placing one on Jason's beaded forehead, wrapping his wrists.

"He's coming down," Barrett said, taking his pulse again. "Hell of a cherry for him. He's sleepin' like a baby."

Deke watched his brother's pale, reposed face, his slight-twitching childlike smile.

"We got an hour and a half before daylight," Barrett said. "He'll be all right now, I wouldn't worry. Be a little hungover when he wakes up. You comin' Tar Baby?"

"Yeah, I'll be there in a minute. Go ahead, I'm right behind you."

Deke soaked another cloth strip, patting his brother's lips, cheek and neck with it. He stood a few more minutes watching his face in heat-lightning.

Jason's brown-on-white Appaloosa Shawnee stepped gingerly down the piled yellow creek stones to drink from the tiny stream. His withers flinched with the sound of the storm that had woken him. It was moments before dawn. In the fog lightning lit the bright, dry creek bed that several months ago had flowed three feet deep and twelve feet wide. The horse twitched nervously with cracks of thunder, his tail flicking, working fast. He climbed up out of the creek bed and stood listening, trying to figure it out, tossing his head toward the wind rushing down in the trees. Surrounding mountains were hidden in the ground-clouds that broke and swirled across the pasture. A few crickets droned. The sky was beginning to pale with the first sounds of birds waking.

Three-hundred yards away at the base of the mountain a pair of raccoons sniffed the garden of buried human and animal scent. One by one they went to the dew-heavy plants, digging and scratching the ground beneath them. The fresh manure intrigued them. After clawing into it for a while it was all they found. They left each plant uprooted next to a hollowed-out hole. When they'd dug up most of the patch without finding anything else they decided to check out the fifty gallon drum at the edge of the clearing. The top was covered with a square of screen mesh camouflaged with straw and leaves. They yanked on the screen until it slid off the barrel. One leaped up on the open edge, pulled himself over the top and peered inside, sniffing. Nothing here either. All this scent spread around and nothing to eat. One of them picked up the human scent and followed it down into the field, down the red banks into a thick briar patch. It ended at a half-dozen five-gallon water cans in a tangle of vines. They pushed the cans over, opening the lids, touching the gurgling water.

It was daylight and the wind was whipping violently in the trees. Light changed quickly across the fields. The two scavenging raccoons listened to the sound coming fast through the leaves, like a waterfall rushing and the air building up and popping, limbs cracking. In a few minutes it was dark as it had been an hour ago and they scurried back into the woods for cover. Water cans clanged with hail chunks. The rushing sound was still coming, white rocks bouncing along the red bare banks at the edge of the woods, small, white-bellied frogs pelting with them slapping the ground, sprawling open-mouthed, laying stunned beneath the trees. The thick hail-rain was white as fog, a static kind of mothball snow, raining frogs knifing through the trunks onto the leaved floor, bouncing belly-up, a few hopping-crippled and dragging. Ones that were alive were being pummeled by others. They fell and lodged in tree branches and vines and made muffled smacks as they hit the ground and each other.

Shawnee had taken cover under a canopy of trees above the creek bank. He listened to the rattling-hissing pouring across the field and felt the solid objects thudding around his hooves. He was jumpy and wired. There was a loud electric pop and he broke for the stable in full gallop, feeling a shock as the tall poplar over the creek was clapped by lightning and he was running before the ear-splitting crack brought it crashing into the woods. He'd felt hail before but something else was hitting him as he ran. Fleshy objects were slapping and clinging to his back and haunches. Already pumping with adrenaline from the close strike, he sprinted with renewed panic into the stable, swinging and reeling to shake off the flesh, rubbing against the stall gates. The high tin roof of the shelter made a loud, racketing-drumming like a thousand feet running across it. He looked out at the black sky lighting up with this storm. At the open door he bent over to sniff dead animals laying at the edge of the straw. Then suddenly it was quiet. That was a noise in itself. It was as if a faucet had shut off. The horse backpedaled slowly toward the middle of the stable and stood against a wall, nodding and waiting, listening. He could hear flies buzzing around a corner stall. Thunder rattled the walls and tin against the planks. Mixed with large hailstones the egg-white stomachs of frogs speckled the yard and lay on top of each other, a few attempting to crawl or drag themselves. The sky swirled with light. Low pink clouds lay like smoke on the sides of mountains. A breeze blew through the tall field grass. Dead frogs hung from stumps, vines and limbs, in the crotches of trees, lay sprawled along banks as if washed up in a tide. There were a few more rumbles as the bright light glistened on the scattered bodies. Some hung onto labored breaths, in dead-eyed trances, egg-like stomachs pumping. In a few minutes they were still.

They dozed as the plane droned over the cabin, Jason snoring on his back, breathing irregularly, his right leg dangling from the bed. Barrett slept naked with a beatific smile, hands folded on his chest like a happy dead man's. Deke lay in a fetal position nodding in a fitful dream, every now and then rolling to his back as if trying to break out of it, his face and neck soaked with sweat.

From the shades thin rays crept with dust motes across the floorboards. The refrigerator hum was part of another droning none of them were aware of. They were aching-tired. After Deke and Barrett had put Jason to bed they'd set out two truckloads of barrels near their patches to catch rainwater. So exhausted he couldn't relax, Deke listened to Jason mumbling in his sleep while he downed a few more beers. He'd heard the storm pass through the back of the farm, blowing through so quickly he doubted it did any good, and now the nearby plane's engine was an unplaceable appendage to his dream.

As the plane moaned over the mountain and stalled Barrett screwed his face up, rolling to his side. Deke froze from fitfullness as if listening to the empty space. A cricket chirped under the floor as the refrigerator's monotone seemed lower, kudzu washing against the cabin in the breeze. The engine started up close to the mountain farther from where it'd stalled, purring quietly, wound louder and drifted down stalling again, the vacuum of sound filled with the same hanging stillness. With a break in his snoring Jason made a monosyllabic grunt and coughed, his left hand flopping on his cheek where a fly had landed. Barrett was listening but he had no idea to what or why. When the plane's engine moaned up again it was five-hundred feet above the cabin. Deke gaped to the ceiling as if watching it with his eyes shut as Barrett scratched his nose, rolling to his back to listen better, refolding his hands. Before the plane was out of earshot it stalled again, its silence suspended down the mountain a half-mile away, purring and droning fainter.

Deke sat up with a beer can clanking to the floor, listening to the buzzing, the refrigerator humming. Turning to slivers of light he groaned, rubbing his eyes, squinting around the room trying to remember something. Some god awful, obstacle-ridden dream he couldn't pull back left him jumble-brained. He felt like he had the goddamn flu. Why'd he woken then? He listened to the Frigidaire shut off, the tin roof lifting-pattering in the wind, kudzu brushing timbers with a hushing sound like children whispering through the walls.

In cammie t-shirt with pants rolled to his knees Barrett dug in the deep mud of the shallow streambed. He'd been at it for an hour damming the creek with three-quarter-inch plywood braced by two-by-fours. He'd hauled stout rocks against the wall and shoveled mud and sand from the natural pool on the dammed side, driving two-by-four stakes every yard along the wall as base supports. When he'd finished the top of the wall was starting to bow, so he drove a couple more stakes in the middle and yanked the release plug. It might not hold in a gully washer but they should be so lucky. They needed several more downstream to pool reservoirs deep enough to fill jerry cans. The creeks were so wizened you couldn't fill a cup. He stood on either side eyeing the wall. A damn sight better than government work. Splashing his face in the clear-opened stream he let it pour and trickle over his head. It was breezy and not humid but he'd been working hard and the cold water felt good on his neck. Might as well wash while I'm down here, he thought, humming as he stripped.

Movements caught his eye through the thick layers of leaves. Flecks across the valley the creek flowed through and beyond on the other side of the mountain. He knew what they were but there were so many they looked like something huge seen in pieces through the compressed limbs. Wrapping his pants round his neck he scrambled up the bank to get a better view, through a window in the trees watching hundreds of vultures circling along the crest of the mountain. There were so many they were flying into each other, five-hundred or so spread out into the valley, drifting toward him with sentinels around the kettle fringes, a few making lazy circles at high altitudes. Most were concentrated behind the mountain, flapping and sinking down. He'd seen fifty or sixty at a time but never this many. Jason's horse was over there, he thought; but the birds were distributed in a half-mile radius around the valley. Squatting and taking a knee, he watched several drift over him, picking up his scent, wide specter-like shadows rippling through the trees along the mountain flank. He watched them scrapping beyond the long line of saddles and tree-knobs across the field, dozens flapping up and disappearing behind the pine ridge.

Deke signed in with the flirtatious silver-haired lady at the front desk and took the slow elevator to the third floor, clomping down the Lysol-washed linoleum past huddled people in wheelchairs staring through their televisions. He felt like an intruder. The smell nauseated him. It didn't take long to realize these places were elderly asylums. A woman playing solitaire spit into a bowl. A rail of a man faced a wall, laughing, stopped and turned gumless wrinkling his face at him. Within five or six people watching a war documentary one man was saluting and rambling some crazy narration as the others stared catatonically at the screen.

Deke carried yellow roses from his mother's bushes and a white chocolate rabbit. She was crazy about chocolate. As a boy the first thing she'd taught him to make was fudge. They'd bake a batch and sit out on the porch at night listening to the whippoorwills, eating it with cold milk. They'd do it again as soon as he rescued her from this loony bin.

He stopped by the door at the end of the corridor holding his head in his hands, staring glassy-eyed at the floor. Looking up he saw a bath robed man in an alcove stammering, screwing his face up, shooing him in like a dog.

Half-sitting his mother was silhouetted against the flowered drapes, a soap opera droning through bad reception. Around the room on sills, chairs, tables and floor were small white dolls made of Kleenex. She didn't seem to notice him as he watched her gnarled fingers knitting one, twisting and molding it, tying the soft paper with monofilament line.

"Mama?" he said, stepping in. "You've got company, girl."

Her fingers stopped working. She looked at them as if waiting for something. He lay the roses and candy on the sidetable, touching her shoulder.

"Mama, it's Deke. What you working on? Looks like our old mule, Bullthroat."

Suspiciously she raised her eyes with her head down, a hint of a smile, a secret sideways look. She went back to work on her doll as if she were alone. Deke looked at the circle on the floor holding hands, angels with mindless faces made of buttons and threads.

"You've got a lot of friends here, mama," he said. "Brought you some chocolate."

"Not hungry, young man, take the tray away."

"It's Deke, mama."

She looked at the crackling screen.

"If Sarah marries that imbecile he'll kill her. She's been through this before, Charlie. She doesn't need a man, I've told her a dozen times."

"I'm Deke, mama. Look at me, please."

She looked at her doll. He watched the fierce determination and pride in her hawk like face as she made every thread and wrinkle right. When he opened the drapes she paid no attention, her fingers kneading feverishly. He turned and stared out the window. An elderly couple hobbled down the lane toward the wisteria-covered trees.

"Why do I come here?" he said.

She glanced with an uncomprehending smile.

"You're not sitting in this godforsaken place the rest of your life, so don't get used to it."

"I said I wasn't hungry; take it away."

"Get past this, Madge."

"I'll throw it on the floor if you don't. Leave it and see if I don't. I don't want to smell the rubbish."

He turned and leaned into her.

"I've found a way to save us, mama. I've been trying to tell you this for a year now. I wish to God you'd let me know you understand anything I've told you."

She kept knitting without looking at him.

"Listen to me. Do you understand?"

"Just kiss him you old fool," she said to the television. "Don't listen to your friends."

He sat on the bed gripping her shoulders, squaring up to her. Her muscles felt like tightly-wired cords as she maneuvered the needle through the paper head.

"Mama, please, listen to what I'm tellin' you, we didn't lose the farm. Soon there won't be any liens on it and we'll bring you home, get you a nurse; we'll work in the garden together."

"I don't need an enema, Charlie."

"Mama, goddamit, it's me!" he said, shaking her. "Don't you know me? Look at me. You *know* me. Who am I?"

Her eyes lifted, slowly taking him in. She seemed to ponder as she recognized something. She sat back as if it dawned on her, scanning his face and up and down and back to his eyes.

"Where've you been all day, child? You've worried me to death disappearing like that."

"Sorry, mama. This place gets to me."

"Don't give me any excuses. Run off again I'll sic the hounds on you."

"I'll try to come every week from now on."

"We've got to get you a haircut, Honcho. And fresh school clothes. You can't wear those rags another year. I'll pry your daddy's wallet open and we'll go shopping Tuesday."

Deke dropped his head, running his hands through his hair.

"I'm Deke, mama."

"You'll wear those corrective shoes another year then we'll buy you the shoes you wanted."

"Mama . . ."

"If you shoot one more of my robins you'll wear corrective shoes from now on. I don't know what possesses you to do that, Honcho."

"Please say two words to me . . ."

"You're too young to have that pellet rifle in the first place, I wish your daddy—"

"Honcho's a pilot in the U.S. Marines, mama. He's halfway around the world in Lebanon. This is 1986 and I'm your second son, Deke, remember?"

She paused a second, looking snarled.

"Who wants to know?" she said, frowning.

"Keep looking at me. If you remember Honcho you can remember me, I'm Deke." He cradled her cheeks, peering into her eyes. "I'm Deke, mama, your *second* son. Your grown-up son, remember me?"

She shrunk back, shaking her head. She frowned as if she didn't believe it or was scared to. Her eyes slowly filled with tears as she nodded, looking at his hands, panicked.

"You're not him," she said, pushing his hand away, rubbing her arms.

"Yes I am, see me? I'm here, mama."

"You're not dead?"

"'Course not," he laughed.

"We got a letter. They said you were missing. You're dead, Deke."

"That was a mistake, remember? I'm right here, see me? You're touching me, Madge."

"You're alive? *My son's alive.*"

"Damn right I am. We're survivors, Madge. Nobody's gettin' rid of us."

Suddenly she was choking him, pinning him with a trembling grip, burying tears in his neck.

"Of course I'm alive. Come on, Madge."

She rocked side to side, clenching him. "Why you! You prankster. You should be ashamed of yourself. When's you get home, Deke? Why didn't you phone us?" She leaned back, shaking her head in disbelief, squeezing him again moaning with relief. "Your father's worried sick, son. He's been crazy-sick. We've been so beside ourselves . . ."

"Come on, mama. Daddy's dead, you know that."

Her grip relaxed as if the strength went out of her arms; she smiled as if she knew no such thing. Sitting back without looking at him, picking up her Kleenex doll perusing it, she knitted again gazing at the television.

"I've got everything worked out, Madge. Hang on a little longer and we'll make our break at Christmas, we'll get you outta here, girl."

"I'd like my tray now, Charlie," she said, nodding with a peevish smile. "And don't forget my sweetener this time, you ought to be able to remember that by now. Oh that's just fine, girl, kiss him again, he'll break your heart like he did before. Don't say I didn't warn you you hardheaded nincompoop."

Deke sat in the corner cabin recliner pulling beers from a cooler on the floor, the television flickering. He hadn't bothered turning on a light and the shadows in the room had gradually met until he was sitting in near-darkness. The fishing gear was gone; he figured Jason and Barrett were catching dinner. He'd been sitting in this morose coma for about an hour, chuckling at nothing, mumbling pieces of songs, jabbering to himself. He'd guzzled five or six beers before the President started pontificating on television; now he was listening to him with a half-drunken, fascinated curiosity. *His* man, he thought. Old Ronnie boy. He was nuts about The Great Communicator. He popped another one and toasted him, sucking off the cool foam. He listened, then started mumbling over him as he laughed and sipped, wagging his head like him.

"'*Yes and there are those who say . . .*'" he muttered over and over again, paying no attention to him.

"'*I saw war protesters the other day carrying signs that said, 'Make Love, Not War,' but from the looks of them it's unlikely they could've done either one,*'" he quoted him from the sixties. "Remember that one, Ronnie? That's my boy. That's my Ray-gun. Fantastic." What a man, he thought, using coward and manhood jokes to shame American kids into committing genocide on a bunch of third world farmers. "You're the one, Ronnie. You're the boy. That takes heart and wisdom," he toasted him. "Good old fucking Ronnie boy."

He listened to the wind vibrating the roof. He listened to the swaggering man again, cringing as he studied his prune-like prudishness. He would never understand why anyone bought this guy. Maybe he'd overestimated them. His parents had voted for him twice. He remembered the sallow expression on his father's face every time Reagan spoke those last couple of months, the way all color left his face before he'd get up as if physically driven out of the house to walk the fields at dusk. His father had never said another word about Reagan or mentioned his name.

He sat in silence listening to him, mumbling over the old kidder, swinging his head with that good old and honest fella condescension. When the word farmers came out of the President's mouth he reared and hurled his beer across the room splatting it off his face. Foam streamed and evaporated, blurring the black-dyed hair. He took another one from the cooler. "Do it Ronnie," he said. "*Do it* baby. Now Rennie. Now Rennie." He leaned to the nodding face, tilting his beer to it, yodeling and singing to him. "*Goddamit, do it, Ronnie! Come on baby. Bring it on home to us.*" He drank and stood up and stared at him and started doing a soft shoe. He was in the groove with him, working with him, feeding off his *Me* attitude. "It's all about you, Ronnie. It's you, baby. Tell 'em now."

When the President started his spiel about "the Evil Empire" Deke flung one arm forward at a time sloshing beer in his face. The President droned behind the dripping screen. Deke flicked on the boom box on the table in the middle of "Get on the Good Foot," turned down the TV shuffling close to the screen doing a belly dance. He watched the President playing the crowd, nodding and bullying, patronizing them, and did some funky chicken for him. He hunched the TV a few times. He jumped back, doing a hand-whammy on him. He watched Ron wagging at those evildoers, those despicable disagreers. "Yeah. *Yeah! You know the long-haired hippies and the Afro-blacks . . . they all get together across the tracks . . . and they party! . . . they get on the good foot . . . you know they dancin' on the good foot . . . dancin' on the good foot . . .*"

Deke put his face to the screen and grunted, pursing his lips, scratching like an ape. He shuffled around the television, crouching, darting like a crab all over the room running over chairs, knocking things over, screeching and huffing. He shuffled up close to the screen, his ape face close to it howling at him, giving the old man a smooch on the lips. He backed to the door with his arms dangling to the floor, grunting and hooting out it. Behind the screen he hooted a few more times, howled, and slammed the door.

Barrett slid feet-first down the slick pine straw, pausing to catch his breath and listen for choppers. He'd heard one minutes ago that might've been five miles away but sounded closer in the saturated air. He'd kept off his paths and trails to give them a rest, slipping into each patch through a virginal opening. A light-blue mist refracted through the trees pooled into the pastures. The short rain before sundown dampened the soil and the air was fragrant, the leaves and straw having that rich decaying smell of fecund earth. Woods after a shower reminded him of a woman. He'd love to be with one now in this blue-soaked forest, rolling around like a couple of kids in the musk-slippery leaves.

Through gaps in the trees he made out a fence line along the shallow creek bed across the field. As the mist changed he could see a few features on the opposite slopes. He listened to the rain frogs croaking as he worked down to the patch, a long, sprawling opening set against the sky several-hundred feet from the foot of the mountain. The treetops were good clearing markers, especially at night. There were outcroppings of rock all over these banks you had to be careful not to bust your ass on, little and large tongues jutting, protruding everywhere. When the clouds shifted they appeared in front of you suddenly like statues crouching at your feet.

As he slid into the patch he saw plants lying on their sides. Pulling his penlight he studied the clawed scratches from the holes, a few half-dug-up, eight or nine torn from the ground with their roots cleaned.

He heard stray chopper blades north of where he'd heard the others. He was sure they were far enough away, but they could run up on you like a bird's shadow even at night. Cutting his light, he went to work in the dark feeling the root systems, locating the soft-center-depths with his fingertips. The plants gave off that translucent glow making them easy to pick up. If sixteen plants were uprooted here who knew how many were in other patches. Once the varmints started scavenging they could do some damage and you had to check them frequently to keep from losing plants.

"All right, all right!" he yelled out around him. "Real fucking cute but I don't need your help! This happens again we'll go rounds, you hear me? I'm not bullshitin'! I won't have this foolishness!"

He listened as if expecting a reply, scowling along the tree line. "*Nosey* motherfuckers," he muttered, working again. "If there was something to eat it'd be different. I won't have this bullshit! I don't want to have to get heavy here, fellas!"

Holding a joint in his lips he scrambled hole-to-hole, fluffing and redressing the ground. Another shower and you wouldn't know he'd been there. He had a feeling the choppers had vacated the neighborhood. Woods sounds were rising to one of those monumental compositions, a deep-trancing rhythm as the chorus reinforced itself. He'd done enough of this work tonight, hustling around to thirteen of their forty-two patches. It was muggy as hell and he was bushed. He guzzled his canteen and strolled down from the plants to keep his smoke away from them. Few things were worse for marijuana plants than their own smoke. He found an alley where he could lay back and look across the valley, lighting a doobie from their infant pinchings, inhaling and holding it, releasing it as he looked at the stars. Wisps of clouds drifted, fireflies blowing through the trees like flying embers as he let the damp ground soak into his back and shoulders.

"Yes, yes," he said, crossing his legs. "Thank you, Lord, I love this shit. The sweet smell of mountain laurel. Give me the city and I'll sit my ass right here, thank you. *Thank you*," he said, meaning it.

He toked and listened to the overlapping waves of cicadas and thought about Marsha. ". . . Only thing is—it ain't like you to do this unless you're pissed at somebody—I hope we haven't messed up your irrigation system 'cause these boys need a good season. I'll do what I can if you'll give up more of the wet stuff. Thank you," he said.

He took another hit and held it as he hummed. At least the plants got a dousing tonight. He pushed up and stretched, popping the roach in his mouth, chewing it. An owl dipped inches from his head startling him, weaving down the mountain with quick, tight wing beats. He watched it glide across the pasture into the trees.

A fog-like mist was settling in the valley up to the same level where he stood, on the opposite mountain. On the top edge of it he saw a file of people wearing leaf-camouflage threading through the trees. They faced straight ahead, moving quickly, evenly-spaced along the mountain flank.

He looked away, rubbing his eyes. When he looked back they were there, the whole path seeming to move with them like a stream of black ants feeding through the leaves. There were thirty or forty of them. He blinked and looked at the ground. The moon behind him made wet needles glisten like fire. A beetle crawled through them under shining beads weighting the speared tips. He saw this at a glance as he listened to the chant-like ocean of thrumming, narrowing his eyes as he raised them again. He watched the figures fade into the landscape and mist like flowing apparitions, simply dissolve into it.

He blinked and squinted at where he'd seen them. More mist had accumulated in the trees, a few fireflies swinging lazily up the mountainside. His heart pounded. Blood in his ears washed over the woods sounds. He looked up through the rising light-strands breaking through the trunks, everything vibrating with that sizzling chatter through grainy moonlight. He was stoned out of his mind. Hell yes he was. It still amazed him how everything could change in an instant smoking this stuff. What the hell was that over there? What did he *think* it was? Nothing like that'd ever happened before, nothing close to it. He'd had some stoned experiences, weird hallucinations, but never seen anything like *that*. Oh shit, he thought. Lord almighty.

He stood watching the side of the mountain with moonlight reflected off the bluish-silver. The moon was over the trees now and everything was bathed, drenched with light. He didn't see anything over there but the vertical trunks and a few trails gleaming with fog, lichen-covered rocks.

"Uh huh," he nodded, looking around. "All right, I gotcha." As he waited the fog kept rising obscuring his view of everything around him. He shook his head, loping down into it, chuckling, sure he'd just hallucinated his ass off. "Strong stuff," he said. "Remember where you are, Dr. Feelgood. Thought you'd lost it for a minute there, didn't you?"

Something rustled in the thicket and he shined his penlight on it, a raccoon's eyes reflecting at him with that soft otherworldly glow.

"It's you, is it? Hope you heard what I said. I'll make coon stew out of your ass you fuck with my babies again, you hear me? Try me, go ahead."

The raccoon stood on its hind legs patting and waving its paws, black eyes gleaming.

"Yeah, now. Don't even start that shit with me. That don't cut no mustard with me, pal."

Deke and Jason jostled up the steep trail with loose gear jangling in the truck bed, Jason groping at the radio tuning in a scratchy country station.

> . . . Scorching weather continues to wreak havoc over Tennessee and most of the southern states. Severe drought has hit Georgia's peanut and peach farmers. In the Volunteer state soybeans and tobacco are expected to suffer. Without solid drenching in the next couple of weeks corn yields could be down thirty per cent . . .

A flicker caught Jason's eye on the ridgeline as the truck dipped and jolted.

"Deke, hold it a second," he said. "Think I see something up there."

Deke planted the brake, rocking.

"Yeah?" Deke said, bobbing until it glinted in the sun.

"Yeah, I see it."

He pulled the truck against the mountain, popping his field glasses, studying the vertical tip with shaded-grey metal.

"Looks like one."

They hiked up through the moist leaves, the night's rain leaving a thick fresh stickiness.

"See that hornet's nest at three o'clock?"

"How many patches we have on the other side?"

"Eight or nine small ones grouped into three's."

They saw the intact metal body as they came up on it. Deke studied the black walnut tree it had careened through, smashed limbs carpeting the ground and the maple from which it'd stripped a long yellow swath. It had fallen down the mountain and tumbled before lodging nose-up against two catalpas.

"Another one for daddy's collection," Jason said.

Deke squatted, feeling the rotted leaves on a piece of limb under it.

"Dropped in the last month. Maybe three weeks from the looks of this foliage."

He rubbed the dull-reflecting titanium, wetting his fingers wiping one of the dried bark-marks off a tailfin.

"Daddy ever tell you about the pissing contest he had with Frank Joiner?"

"Pissing contest?"

"Yep. He and Drake Lewis were helping Frank repair a barbed wire fence one of Frank's bulls had torn up. They were finished and havin' a few beers so Frank challenged them to a pissin' contest and stuck ten dollars on a wire strand. Said he'd stand back three paces from where they stood and piss higher on the tree than either of them. Finally he ragged them so they said what the hell, and stuck a ten each on top of his. Daddy pissed about twenty inches up. Drake pissed about four inches lower. Old Frank decided to make it fair so he stands back five steps, unzips his pants, pulls out this catheter bag he hadn't mentioned and was knockin' leaves out of the top of that saplin'."

"Frank always had an ace in the hole," Jason laughed. "What made you think of that?"

"Daddy told me that story the last time we found one of these walking fence line along the north fields. About two months . . ."

Deke stopped, feeling it again. He stared at the aircraft bomb a few seconds. In the silence he knew Jason could feel it with him, the presence palpable, neither of them moving. They didn't look at each other or make a sound. Deke gazed off across the mountains. A towhee was singing in the breeze. After a minute he stood up and cleared his throat. Jason was looking up the mountain behind him. Deke took five steps back from the dug-in bomb, planting and unzipping his pants.

"Bet you can't hit it from here."

"Standing uphill?" Jason said. "That's easy."

"Naaaaw," Deke said, already urinating on it. "Try holding on the nose for fifteen seconds, an uninterrupted flow like this."

"We're grown men, Deke," Jason said, raining on the bomb.

"I christen this hallowed fireball from the fire-raining gods of war," Deke said. "Let's leave it up here as a monument and official pissing place."

"Mt. Pissmore," Jason said.

"That's terrible," Deke said, zipping up. "All right, you're showing off now. What, damn, son, you been training for this? I never knew you were so talented."

The horse ignored him until he heard oats spilling into the feeding trough. Shawnee took a couple of steps toward the stable from the edge of the yard, glancing through the double doors, leaning to munch another stubble of field grass. When he heard the machete chopping apples he loped across the yard to the barn. He'd wondered what was taking his friend so long. He wasn't enjoying living off of parched, brittle straw while swarms of vultures invaded his grazing grounds. More shyly than begrudgingly, some of both, he moseyed up to Jason, head nodding, stopping to nuzzle his armpit. Jason knew his horse was peeved but just as relieved to see him. He hugged the Appaloosa, stroking his muzzle and cheeks, whispering as to a child. The horse leaned and scoffed up mouthfuls of oats as he eyed the wet-cut apple on the chopping board.

"Good to see you, boy. Brought you some fruit from mama's trees, got a freezer full of 'em." Shawnee sniffed and chomped the apples from his hand. "Juicy fellas. Mama used to bake the best pies in the state with 'em." He lined six halves on the stall rail for the horse and stooped to inspect his shoes. They were in fair shape but his knees were bruised with nasty-looking scrapes like he'd walked on them or slid down on rocks, stumbled badly.

Jason'd seen the rotting frog carcasses on his way through the woods and a hell of a lot more around the stables and yard. The hot dead smell drifted across the field. They explained the vultures Barrett'd seen over here a few days ago. A dozen or so birds circled aimlessly over the far side of the briar field. Something besides a plague of frogs had spooked his horse, a panther or mountain lion, pack of dogs, for him to bang himself up like this. Drought made animals edgy, especially humans, you never knew what'd set them off. He should've looked in on him and felt like hell he hadn't. What if he'd broken his leg and been unable to eat or drink?

He could tell how the horse felt about it. He'd doctor these stone bruises and scratches or they'd get infected. He took the yellow brush and worked beggar lice and briars out of the horse's breast, stifles, flanks and thighs.

"What's going on, Shawnee? Looks like you had some excitement over here. Been chasin' that wild unicorn lady up the mountain again?" he said, brushing snags from his piebald rump. "Hey, got an idea. Wanna take a swim later? After lunch we could take a dip, what you think? Ride back to the shady pond and cool off a while. I hadn't forgotten you, fella, you know that, don't you?"

He could tell by the horse's eyes Shawnee knew exactly what he was saying. He faced him, scratching the sides of his muzzle with both hands.

"We don't get a shower today I'll be watering all night again; my legs and back are killing me. This is boot camp, I'm tellin' ya. Got one more apple, want it? What you say we split it?"

He lay it on the cutting board, slicing it, munching half from one hand as he fed the horse with the other.

Barrett slept on his right side mumbling against the thrumming, twisting to his back, swallowing; the skin under his left eye twitched. The spasm was like a draft or mild electric flutter. When he scratched it quit and he felt it start again. There were voices distinctly Vietnamese with the chopper blades, a low cacophony slipping in and out of earshot. He knew he was in-country as Drake his second CO jogged by barking something smartass to him, grinning stupidly. So crazy Drake was alive, he thought. He felt the noises getting closer; he could smell the steaming paddies, munitions, the burning chopper fuel. He saw Vietnamese farmers scattering across a rice paddy as the line of choppers lifted and circled. He heard the chattering scurrying in all directions, the line of Huey slicks going up like a string of helium balloons. Soldiers shouted and a two-way radio blared. Three prop planes roared low over the paddy as if they were going to scoop up something with their bellies. Fifty or sixty Vietnamese farmers were scuttling along under them, the frightened people looking over their shoulders as they crawled, tripped, hobbled and fled in a wavy, fanning line. The planes that had dropped out of nowhere were making cumbersome, slow-moving shadows down the fields like sinking metal clouds.

*There was a sound like a heavy metal door slamming. He didn't know
what it was but he knew he was in one of the planes looking down at the people
hurtling across this paddy like a herd of fleeing animals. Everything seemed to
slow suddenly, grinding down. There was a tremendous leaden hum in his ears,
aching in his molars, cheeks and eyes. When he yelled out he couldn't hear his
voice. The two pilots sitting forward of him stared straight ahead. He was a
goddamn ghost, he thought. What was he doing there? He knew what was going
to happen to these people when liquid fire dropped from the belly of this plane.
He could see it as if it'd already happened, flesh melting and dripping from
bones like burning plastic from toy soldiers he'd set on fire as a kid . . . He was a
few feet from their faces, they were beneath him and the lead-heavy, stulterous
humming. He was closer than he could've been, but there anyway, flying and
crawling into their wide-opened screams . . .*

He bolted up into blackness, groping to hold onto anything; gripping
wads of an army blanket. Swimming to an oily surface he fanned the
darkness. He could see the line of bunks and smell the war in the jungle
firebase, making out Deke dead-asleep on the other side of the cabin. What
were they doing there? Had they knocked them out and dragged them
back there? He was panicked for a minute, nauseated, realizing he was in a
tight, enclosed space, a small barracks, still believing he was in-country. He
heard Jason snoring in the front room with the refrigerator buzzing, cicadas
outside. He started to recognize things. Wait a second, he thought. Lord
God. Lord help me. *Thank you Lord*; he knew where he was. Thank God,
oh shit. He clawed his face, giggling with his forehead in his hands, his
breathing settling. He hadn't had one of those in years, not like that. This
shit was nearly twenty years old, why was it fucking with him now? He'd
been kicking the war around with Deke and Jason. Which was likely why
he'd hallucinated those black pajama people on the side of the mountain
the other night. Yeah, well, maybe he should stop doing that.

He took a 16 oz. Tecate from the refrigerator, standing in the screen
door sipping it, listening to the night. Thank God for cold beer at four in the
morning, he thought, listening to Deke and Jason snoring. He wondered
what Marsha was up to, if she even thought about him now. Who knows.
Who the hell knows. If he thought about her she probably thought about
him. A rain frog was screaming up on the hillside with that bladder-like,
desperate shrillness, like something being strangled or tortured, a soul in

distress. Maybe it was happy as a lark. He listened to it a while, sipping and swallowing. Every now and then a firefly streaked up into the darkness.

Deke sat alone in the dimly-lit room surrounded by dismantled bombs at his feet, his father had collected after the first one which he'd reported to the Air Force and they'd sent munitions specialists out in two trucks to retrieve. After several jet-fuel spills had drenched a corn and then a tobacco field, his father had started taking the things apart himself, dumping them here.

To the side of the small bench where he sat was the dark stain on the wall. Every time he started to wash it something kept him from it. It was in the wood like some irretrievable map. One day when he figured it out he'd pressure-wash it, but it'd still be there. Nothing was going to get rid of it. Hanging over and around it were rakes, scythes, chains and pitchforks. The tiny shed room was half-lit through cracks and from a square open window at his right softly lighting his upper body and face as he rocked the bench on its front legs, listening. It was windy, damp-warm; storm weather building. He listened to the creaking wood, corrugated tin thumping and banging, janglings from the wind chime on the porch, baby finches twittering in the rafters. Sitting in the room where his father had taken his own life, he wasn't thinking about it. He leaned over and scraped up handfuls of soft dirt, sifting pebbles, dinging them off the nosepiece of the junked bomb at his feet. He turned to the square window, his face in yellow light, listening to the quiet rumbling, head bobbing as he mouthed a tune. He looked at the overcast sky and kept humming as the jets roared close to the trees, rattling everything.

Memorial Day tomorrow. A big commemorative bash in town with parades, bands, a fair, people pouring in from all over the state. Usually he avoided these scenes, but he needed to get away for a day, get his mind off things. If he wasn't working on the goddamn plants he was obsessing over them.

He turned and tossed a few pebbles at a nosepiece in the corner, listening to the finches chattering in the rafters, excited by jet thunder that faded suddenly like a silencing toilet flush. Clasping his hands he looked at the shadows on dirt from the pecan trees blowing through light-shafts, turning to the window, staring out at the sun breaking through the fluctuating sky, listening to the wind chime pausing, then heavy-jangling like church bells.

Standing, he pulled the gold football with UT and his father's name engraved on it and his father's Air Force wings from his pocket, moistening them with his breath, polishing them, squatting under the wall-stain burying them in the soft-powder dirt, smoothing it flat with his palm. He drew an American flag with his finger, pointing the stars with a sharp stick. He sat on the bench, scooping handfuls of pebbles, humming a little, feeling the quiet boom in the walls, pitching a few stones out the window. Tossing one up he caught it in his mouth, spitting it clanging off of a nosepiece at his feet.

He barreled along his property line for a mile on the paved country road. It wound through deep-wooded frontage without dirt roads or signs, buzzing over the radio and his engine rumbling. Sipping a Red Rock ginger ale he blotted his neck with a towel. He hadn't cleaned up this much in months, put on a starched shirt, shaved; he felt practically normal. He waved to Lucas March rocking on his porch on the other side of Hawkins Road, the old black man who'd lived there thirty-nine years, fifteen alone since his wife Elsa died, on a disability earned from stepping on a mine in the Ardennes, Germany. With a heavy limp on an artificial leg, Lucas'd been his father's haying foreman. Half of what he'd learned about sex as a boy he'd gotten from Lucas. The old man lived for his music and vintage records. He had stuff you'd never heard of and could tell more than you wanted to know about recording artists in America since the Twenties. A tattered American flag he'd brought back from Germany draped from a knotted pine-pole, a saxophone played, Lucas was smoking a pipe and rocking with his dog next to him.

He passed the marker at the end of his property which was where Mosely's started. You couldn't see the change, just a creosote-posted barbed-wire fence disappearing into dense underbrush, the road winding and rolling through mountain bottomland for another nine miles. At the end of Hawkins Road he turned on the main highway, waving to Martin Burgess plowing up dust in a field of wilted silage. There were smaller farms along state route 37 where flags flew from porches and mailboxes, fence posts and trailers. The radio harangued with Memorial Day ads on mattresses and above-ground pools with patriotic country songs. A horse trotted along the shoulder, the rider wearing an American flag suit with a white western hat he tipped once with a nod.

Over planted fields crane-sprinklers jetted water, cows bunched in shaded puddles that had been ponds six months ago. He took off his sunglasses, digging out his War tape, passing motor homes and truckloads of people flying streamers and flags, blowing horns. A Model-T rattled by with an *Oga-Oga*. Several miles from town there were red, white and blue banners across the road: MEMORIAL DAY PARADE MAY 28TH and HONOR OUR WAR DEAD TODAY.

On the outskirts traffic crawled with crowds filing along in the grass, children waving stick-flags. Booths were set up with canning and quilts and country arts in the fields. Striped tents with signs for American Legion barbecues, Kiwanis catfish fries, hordes of people around long tables with babies and kids, fat, jowly men sweating over grills. Three hot-air balloons floated up and some idiot was dangling from a rope from one they were hauling back down. He listened to "Low Rider" and took a Tampa Blunt from the glove box. It'd been a while and would be again, so he was going to make the most of this.

Crowds flooded the streets, blocking traffic, twenty horns blaring at once. From a side street a high school marching band turned toward the center of town with twirling batons. Behind them were lines of Shriners in miniature sports cars, doing wheelies on motor cycles as firecrackers popped and crackled around them. A few in burgundy jackets and tasseled hats were smoking banana-sized cigars, their sweat-shining faces beet-red as they zigzagged from one side of the road to the other. The leader wore sunglasses ten times normal size and did a ridiculous, bouncing jig. A bottle rocket zipped past his face and he froze, glaring into the crowd with mock indignation, his lip turned up like a swollen boxer's. In a few seconds he threw up his arms and jumped back into his happy jig.

Deke's passenger door flew open and a tiny, bearded man in a coonskin cap flopped across the seat with a half-gallon flask under his arm.

"*Killed me a baar when I was only three . . .*" he snarled.

"Davey? Davey Crocket? Where the hell you been, swamp rat?"

"Trackin' baars, goddamit! Baars tall as these goddamn poles. Jack Daniels, Hawkman? Fruit of the fucking vine?"

"Let me park this thing," Deke said, spying a hole in the gravel lot across the road. Davey jumped in and immediately began to shout obscenities at cars blocking them. A mortified group of women in a station wagon let them through. Deke wedged into the space as a loaded van shot up, jamming on brakes, the driver glaring at them as if he'd stolen their spot.

"What the hell do *you* want!" Davey stuck his head out the window. "My fist up your ass?"

The van scratched off in the gravel.

"Same old Davey," Deke said, slapping him. "Same old warrior death wish."

"You got that right," Davey said, yanking off his fur cap, swiping his face on Deke's towel. "I'm one of those sons of bitches don't die though. I'm like a goddamn roach, I'll outlive *everybody*. If I don't starve sittin' here in your piece-of-shit truck. I got no money to eat, boss."

"Hey, I'm hungry. What you want, tunnel man?"

"Barbecued baar and fruit of the vine," Davey growled, swigging from his flask, shoving it to Deke as he dabbed his beard.

They stood in an American Legion line loading their plates with ribs, beans, potato salad, slaw and biscuits. Growling, stogie-smoking World War II vets in dirty aprons served them.

"More meat," Davey said to a tattooed ex-Marine who piled blackened ribs on a second plate.

"I'll give you the whole damn bull if you'll eat 'em, chief."

"*Gimme back . . . gimme back my bullets . . .*" Davey chanted. "Don't you love this patriotic shit? I love this patriotic shit. I try to re-up every year but they won't take me, goddamit. Can't figure it out, Hawkman."

"What for?"

"Kill me some baars! Get back to the *real* life."

They sat under an open-sided canopy table with checkered cloth gorging and passing the flask. It wasn't crowded and there was a warm breeze. Deke glanced at Davey's forearms.

"Hip bracelet, huh? Woman wore this POW thing two years for me, believe that shit?"

"How'd you get it?"

"Tracked me down and mailed it to me. Asked her to marry me but she's hitched. Most devotion a woman's ever shown me."

"I was looking at your tracks, asshole."

"These? Oh, naw. Been in clinics for years now, Hawk, I'm offa that shit. I'm an alcoholic now," he said proudly, guzzling from the flask. "Stand for something or you'll fall for anything, you fucking Hawkman. Goddamn, it's good to see your sorry ass, buddy."

After second helpings they smoked cigars and walked through the center of town. Crowds were moiling heavily around the decorated square. American flags waved and danced along parade street. The PA announced marching bands, American Legion posts, military columns over blaring music and singing. Confetti rained from rooftops on Main Street. An Uncle Sam on stilts wielded a wobbly cardboard limb that said BIG STICK. He was bopping people on the head with it and the crowd was rocking him so he was having a hard time keeping his hat and beard on. Davey nodded and slid into a tight alley, pulling wadded newspaper and a half-gallon bottle of bourbon out of a hole in the bricks.

"What you doing?"

"Refill time," Davey said, spilling the bourbon over his hands, licking it as he dribbled it in the flask. "It ain't Jack Daniels but that'd be a pitiful waste at this point. *Gimme back . . . gimme back my bullets . . .* goddamit, son, this ain't half bad . . ."

They pushed back into the throng to the edge of the square where booths were set up selling pennants, pins and hats. A short, black-haired woman leaned over one looking at something on one of the racks. In her tight, raised denim skirt her turned-up bottom was perfectly heart-shaped. Deke saw it, turned, then started to grab Davey. *"Oh, don't do that!"* Davey cried, stumbling up behind her, patting between her thighs. The woman spun, exploding fists into him as she screeched and berated him, Davey ducking to the ground covering his face, burying his head. She kept hitting him with little yelps and furious, whipping screams as Davey curled up tighter, going *hey hey hey* stop it *hey* . . . She stepped back, panting and scowling, her black hair spread across her face. She was drop-dead gorgeous, probably full-Cherokee, and wouldn't have been more ravishing without that chilling fury. She wore a grey bone necklace with white feathers she ran her hand across in an odd, insinuating way, staring at Davey, her lips moving in some silent incantation.

"He's blind and apologizes," Deke said, giving her a look to let her know it was over.

She hooked her dagger-like finger in Davey's face: "You . . . you're a dead-rotting dog," she hissed, and disappeared into the crowd.

"My goodness," Davey said, lifting his wobbling head, leaning on his elbow swilling from the flask. "That was worth it. Where the hell are we? Tai Won? Let's tie one on, Hawkman."

"Smooth move, buddy. She was impressed."

"Hey, I thought so. Where'd she go?"

Deke picked up his coonskin cap, dusting it off. He was more aware of the women and young girls brushing by now. He'd sworn off women until Christmas and Davey had to do something like that. He took a few swigs to get their scent out of his head. He was getting a little ripped, he thought. Another high school drill team pranced by with tom toms and bass drums pounding. Thirty girls in gold-sequined suits strutted by kicking their perfect brown legs over their heads, pert-raised bottoms jutting, flexing and bouncing. My God, he'd have to break his solemn vow. How couldn't he? The liquor's loosened you up too much. Remember what you have to do and what women can do to you now. He saw his plants swaying in the sun and thought, there's too much at stake here, be true to *these* girls, look after their interests. Hard as it was in one way it was life and death in another. When the crop was done he'd run down to Mardi Gras and have all the women he wanted.

They staggered along the parade route against the walls of bannered buildings, watching a bagpipe corps march by playing "The Battlefield of the Republic." Davey had a fresh scrape over his eye. He wetted his hand with bourbon, dabbing it.

"Remember that Cuban Sergeant Lopez at Quang Tri?" he said, squinching his face in a Latin smirk. 'Let me tell you fucking people something. If you fucking think you can fucking fuck around with me, you've got another fucking thing coming. I'll fucking fuck up any one of you fucking guys gets out of line with me, 'cause you're fucking with the wrong fucking person, you understand me you bunch of fucking fuckers? I'll fuck you up if you fuck with me . . .'"

"We filled his boots with buffalo shit didn't we?"

"Fucked him up real good as I remember it," Davey laughed, looking up at wagging arms and flags on the fourth floor roof-top, a chant floating down to the street. "Let's go up there, buddy. Come on, maniac."

They climbed to the flat gravel roof where a party of kids lined a chest-high wall over the parade, a local college glee club. The women behaved like ten-year-old girls and were amused by Davey's coonskin cap. They huddled, pointing and making faces at him, one strolled over and asked if he was really who they thought he was.

"King of the Wild Frontier," he said, yanking his hat off with a flourish.

"What do you do, Mr. King?"

"I help young women."

"Exactly how?"

"Well, any one of you girls wants to get liberated, come on home with me, *I'll* liberate you."

"Oh yeah?" said the cocky, short-haired blonde, the ringleader. Seven or eight girls were gathered around him. "And how would you do that?"

"Give 'em a break, Davey," Deke said, patting his arm. The one who'd asked questions grabbed Davey's hat, laughing, flinging it to another girl. Davey pretended not to be bothered but Deke could see he was getting irritated as the cap kept flitting over his head. Finally he snatched it back, his face crimson-red as he grinned at them.

"All right, ladies, what fun. And now I have a little riddle for you." He lowered his voice dramatically as they leaned to him. "How many feminists does it take to change a light bulb? There's a nice reward for the answer."

"We don't know," they said in unison, innocently sipping their fruit-colored drinks.

"Three, exactly. Two to screw it in and one to suck my dick! Now how many takers do we have! Come on, girls, pucker up!" he said, opening his zipper.

Their faces turned white as they stumbled and tripped over each other to the far edge of the roof behind their boyfriends. A few peeked back as they huddled and whispered.

"Snotty little bitches," Davey grumbled, leaning on the wall sipping his flask.

The boys beside them were lighting and tossing bottle rockets over the street.

"Plenty of beer in the keg," one said.

"We're good," Davey said, handing Deke the flask. Someone tossed a pack of firecrackers close to the wall and everyone jumped, girls screaming as they fell into each other sloshing drinks on themselves and the crowd below. The kids threw confetti and streamers as they broke into "This Is My Country" with a wailing black band with twirling trumpets and tubas dipping. Davey leaned down the wall, teetering, reading the draped banner.

"GOD BLESS OUR MEMORIAL HEROES," he said, slapping the plastic with his hand. "I mean this goddamn chokes me up. Don't it choke you up? Makes me want to die for my county. Don't it make you want to die for your county?"

"Hell yes," Deke said. "What county're we in?"

He looked out over the ground activity. He could see for miles in every direction. There were people and flags bouncing everywhere, rockets going up from side streets and rooftops. Some kids on a rooftop a building over were having a rocket battle with the boys on their roof. Every so often a streamer would come spewing in and chase around the wall like a smoke-crazy snake. Below the sidewalks were crammed so thick you couldn't see anything but heads, arms and flags. A chant of "USA . . . USA . . ." went up from the street as Uncle Sam and Lady Liberty bumped by on a float holding hands followed by some crowned beauty queens in convertibles.

"Makes me want to wrap myself in an American flag and take a big leap right into the middle of that tuba section!" Davey shouted over the music, leaning off the wall. "Yeah! You tell 'em!" he yelled, gut-screaming furiously. "This . . . is . . . my . . . country! . . ."

"Davey, lighten' up, buddy."

The USA chant on the street hit the rooftop. It felt like the whole town was singing in staggered waves. The kids pushed their flags in each other's faces as they chanted, and someone was waving and sticking them into Davey's. Davey jerked the flags out of their hands and shoved into the middle of them. "Murder women and children! . . ." he shouted. "Burn women and children! . . . Murder women and children! . . ."

By the time Deke got to him Davey had climbed up on the wall with handfuls of crumpled flags. He staggered over the chanting crowd on the roof who had no idea what he was yelling at them. He waved his arms like a symphony conductor. They thought he was performing some death-defying act of patriotic bravery. They pointed their flags at him and kept chanting.

A few of them were getting it and backing away. Deke grabbed Davey by his calves and tried to yank him onto the roof. Fighting Deke's hold on him, acting like his feet were stuck in glue, Davey wobbled then toppled backwards. Holding Davey's ankles, Deke braced himself as much as he could, clutching the wall with his own elbows and knees. Davey's head slammed against the banner and building like a coconut hitting concrete, bouncing, dangling upside down over the screaming, jammed-together crowd. Am I really doing this? Deke thought, half-hanging himself, looking down at the stirring mass of people as he squeezed Davey's ankles. The jerk from Davey's fall had just about slingshotted him off the roof and his heart was going ninety miles an hour. Arms around his thighs anchored him, people were shuffling and groping, girls screeching, he couldn't hear anything they were saying there was so much screaming around him. He couldn't get a solid grip with his right hand, he clutched a wad of jeans that were slipping.

Davey hung limp with his cap in one hand, a flag in the other, moaning drunkenly. He pulled the cap on slowly as he looked up, cackling upside down, grabbing the end of the banner. He hoisted himself up, still chanting. The end of the banner snapped as he put his full weight on it and he kicked furiously against Deke's grip.

"What're you doing!" he yelled at him. "I'm trying to save you asshole! . . . stop kicking me . . ."

"Let go me you son of a bitch!" Davey yelled back red-faced, snarling and squirming. "Why the hell'd you do that? Let go or I'll whack your ass!"

As Deke tried to lift him back onto the roof Davey kicked him squarely in the jaw. It was one of the strangest sensations he'd ever felt. He didn't know whether to laugh or sling the bastard against the wall. Stunned a few seconds with his head ringing, he felt the ache in his ear as he held one of Davey's ankles, then a sharp, blinding kick to his temple. He saw white and his arm was raked loose.

Davey twisted free and swung down the building like Tarzan on a vine, dangling thirty feet over the street by the banner, howling and screaming. Everyone on the roof pushed to the wall to see the crazy little man swinging out over the crowd on the sidewalk. Along the street heads turned to see what everyone was looking at. With the banner between his legs Davey hung by one hand waving a flag in his other, rocking and pushing along the brick building, screaming: "I died for my county, you motherfuckers! Give me back my goddamn bullets and let's go back to Cambodia . . . There're still women and children with their heads connected . . . fuck you, assholes! . . . fuck you! . . ."

Deke heard an announcement for a twenty-one gun salute to be performed by the Tennessee 76th National Guard Unit. The procession and music stopped. There was a faint rumble and whiney trill from a march song at the front of the parade. Davey's shrill voice cut through the quiet. The crowd murmured up and down the street, trying to figure out what the commotion was. The rifle squad halted in front of the building Davey dangled from and he was shouting at them. Leaning over the wall Deke was trying to work his hand under the other end of the banner to get a grip on it as he could see it straining. The volley shots cracked and hovered between the buildings. They seemed to particularly piss Davey off, sending him into an even more apoplectic rage. He pointed and cursed and screamed at the rifle squad, wriggling furiously. Deke got his right hand around the top banner cord. Under him Davey looked like a man in a straight jacket, writhing over a flame.

As the last shots rang out the banner ripped in half. Davey dropped into the crowd on the sidewalk, knocking down half a dozen people. The first one to get up was Davey, slinging the banner off, screaming and fighting to the street, slugging people in the head. The firing squad marched with the Army band playing "Hooray For The Red, White and Blue," the voice on the PA making another announcement and the crowd cheered, waving flags and streamers.

Davey elbowed through them, pushing over anyone in his way, crawled over the barrier and ran out in front of the National Guard columns. He shoved ahead of them, strutting ludicrously, throwing his arms up like a stiff baton erection. Leaning back in his coonskin cap he was shooting a bird with his baton finger, goose-stepping ahead of the military ranks. Deke watched him with a sick feeling going along the parade. He saw the military personnel and state troopers closing around him. Davey weaved up the middle of the columns, tripping and plowing into them. They caught and wrestled him down in the middle of the street, the columns stepping and splitting around him.

He couldn't watch it. He had to. Goddamn it, he thought. The stupid crazy son of a bitch. Looking up he saw Davey being dragged off in handcuffs, snarling back at him spitting. They pushed him into an unmarked, navy-blue van. Deke picked up the flask and took a hit. His head was still ringing from when Davey kicked him. Below two injured people were being treated on the sidewalk, one woman appeared half-conscious; they were cradling her neck, bracing it with a board. People were craning and pointing up at him.

The PA announced a salute from the 3rd Tactical Wing from Jasper Air Force Base. Four FA-16's roared over the crowds, drowning the music and noise in the streets. One peeled off, signifying the missing soldier. It hit him as he watched the lone fighter disappear into the blurred horizon, exactly why he was there today. He'd tried never to think about it, about any of it, it was too goddamned painful and pissed him off too much; he'd done everything in his power to rid his mind of it and suddenly it was all he could think about. He had to get out of there, he thought, watching the sea of contorted faces reveling and cheering around him. Another military band marched by with a hundred American flags standing stiffly in the breeze.

He started out of town stone-faced, sipping Davey's metal flask listening to a reenactment of Pearl Harbor on the radio. In the mirror he watched fireworks lofting up along the parade that was still going on, sparkling-popping on the pale-orange sky. There was plenty of traffic heading out and coming in. They were packing up booths, breaking down tents in the fields. For fun somebody had smeared a cheeseburger on his windshield, just for kicks. He'd wiped most of it off but remnants fluttered on his driver's vent window.

A white-haired woman in an American flag apron waved to someone from her mailbox. An evangelist's trailer looking like Ringling Brothers Circus blew by in a blur of music and noise. He felt so god awful bad all he could do was laugh occasionally with his head against the window. He felt the alcohol in his sinuses, he had a dull, drunken headache, but he wasn't going home yet, he was heading to the place he should've gone in the first place today. He felt so goddamn shitty it was funny and kept shaking his head at it with dry little laughs, driving for a while with the radio off listening to the sound of his truck in the wind, staring at the back of a

Winnebago that said REAL MEN LOVE JESUS as he tried not to swerve off the road.

He remembered a shortcut and left the main highway, taking back roads along miles of run down, abandoned shacks and overgrown crop fields. Passing a ghost town with empty storefronts boarded up and a dilapidated mill, a half-dozen skinny black children playing in an empty gas station with a starved-looking dog.

He hit the four-lane toward Knoxville passing unincorporated little towns that weren't on the map, trailer parks, tractor dealerships, mountain diners. Turning on the radio, laughing at it, getting completely sick of it and shutting it off, getting more cross-eyed as he drove. Damn near polishing off Davey's Memorial Day "baar-killer." The crazy son of a bitch, he thought. He didn't want to think about it, it was too goddamn sad. There was nothing he could do about it anyway. He understood it, felt for it and was sick to death of it at the same time. He wasn't going to be anybody's victim because of that stupid goddamn war.

He started to chuckle again. In a few minutes he was hooting and moaning, yodeling and howling, singing with the redneck songs as he drank and drove. There was nothing funnier than a good hillbilly tune about how proud you were to be a fool. He sang along, sounding as degenerate as possible, making up his own moronic words. Boy, you *are* in a state, he thought.

The next car he passed had its lights on and he flashed his, tooting his horn, waving and hollering. He did the same to the next one, laughing giddily, and they honked back at him. He was laughing some about Davey. He was laughing about his father blowing his head off. He was laughing about Jason's pure heart, his mother sitting half-crazy in a sterile hospital as alien from a farm as you could get, about Honcho's weird detachment and Barrett's wise, backbreaking, simple loyalty—good old spooked, superstitious Barrett, his Rastafarian grow master, his adopted brother.

There was the farm that was the only solid thing he had left. It hurt to imagine losing it, and what if he did? He had to laugh. It would hurt so goddamn much he'd probably die. It would be like having his family's soul gutted out of him. He'd like that. It was incomprehensible, hilarious. What if he did lose it? He supposed he would still have a family but not enough. The good was as absurd as the bad; the good was made unbearably sad and painful by the rest of it. The most beautiful things were excruciating, especially the memories which he wouldn't trade for ten farms. The good hurt more now because you knew you'd lose it eventually, tragically probably, and it all started to seem like the same fucking thing, the same bad and cruel and dirty joke. He didn't trust any of it. He knew something had happened to him to make him think like this. Damn right it had. He'd been tricked by happiness and wouldn't be again; he'd laugh at all of it no matter what it was, laugh around the clock if he had to. He was laughing because thousands of people being honored today—and he was damn close to being one of them—had landed on beaches and crawled through jungles to be shredded to death by bullets and incendiaries. It wasn't funny, hell no; it was *way* beyond funny. It was like some wicked trap, the hilarious tragedy of the stupidity of the race, the sacred and the profane, the good and the bad, the whole fucking human nightmare drama, and he could laugh at absurdity better than anyone. He was the king of that fucking shit. Everything was so fucking screwed up. No matter how trite it was to know it. No matter how trite it was to say it and write songs and books and speeches about it, it was still stupid enough in a purely ridiculous way if you saw it just right to make you laugh your fool fucking head off. He was cackling like someone on laughing gas, thinking about a joke that kept getting funnier and funnier. He couldn't stand this, but he was getting to the heart of *something*. Yes, it was right in here somewhere. He kept wiping tears, thinking that was the end of it, but it wasn't; it wasn't the end of it; he wouldn't stop, goddamit; he didn't care if he laughed himself to goddamn death. He goddamned hoped he would.

He passed two local police having a conversation car-to-car at a Tasti-Freeze, waving to them, one of them lifting his hand off the door. There was something so good about it he laughed until he couldn't see straight. Then he had to stop; he was losing his goddamn mind. He'd lost it way back there.

He drove along shaded streets of an old-town section of big homes with wide porches, giggling, drying his eyes, convulsing again as he drained the last drop from the flask. He kept licking the lip of it, suctioning it with his tongue to get another taste. He could see people looking at him from cars and street corners and when they did he went off again. He was laughing himself sick. It was getting harder and harder to steer.

It was dusk when he turned down the long straight entrance and saw the American flag the size of a house wafting above the trees, wrinkling at half-mast against the grey-purple horizon. The iron gates were shut. NATIONAL VETERAN'S CEMETERY stood above it in wrought-iron letters. He didn't see anyone or any cars as he crawled up to it. Getting closer he wondered what it would feel like just to bang into it. At a couple of miles an hour he slammed into it in first gear, jangling hard, the truck coughing, spitting and stalling. Dropping his head, laughing drunkenly with tears rolling down his face, he tried to milk one more drop from the flask. He got one and pitched it to the floor.

He gazed through the gate. It settled on him then like the end of the day sinking down. He tried to say something, but it came out feebly, a slurred, painful groan. He was trying to say he was sorry; he wasn't sure why he needed to, though he *was* sorry. Very sorry. Tears bumped the seat between his legs. Oh goddamn, he thought. Oh fucking goddamn to hell. He was staring at the sun's shadow line along the trees and the rows of white markers on the slope near the gate, rocking a little with his mouth open. He started laughing again, in a falsetto, crazy giggle. He was crying against the wheel, hugging it with his face against it.

"*Daddy* . . ." he said, ". . . *goddamit* . . . why'd you do this? Why'd you do it? . . . Huh? . . . We were gonna make it . . . we always fucking made it . . . You let us down . . . You let *me* down, goddamit . . . It's . . ." He yanked himself violently against the wheel. "*You didn't owe them this!* Hell no! You didn't owe them a goddamn thing! They owed you, for Christ sake! Why'd you let them do this to you! You didn't even tell me what was going on! You didn't give us a chance to do shit. Shit!" He jerked himself against the wheel, swinging the truck, grabbing the dash tearing upholstery off it, slugging the windows, flailing and kicking the doors. He broke the passenger window out with his heel and kept kicking it. "Shit!" he said. "Shit! *Shiiiiiiiiiiiiit!*" he screamed, snapping the window handle, kicking the door apart, lying on his back with sweat dripping on the seat, squeezing his temples. After a minute he kicked the door open and fell out, dragging himself up on the handle, panting against it.

He staggered to the gate. It was locked. He shook the bars, rattling them. "Open up! I gotta get in here, goddamit! Hey, you cocksuckers!" He yanked it with all his strength and weight, shaking it, thinking he could tear the goddamn thing down, but it wouldn't budge. "Open up you sons of bitches! You can't keep me outta here! I gotta get in here!" He lowered his head, banging his fists.

He looked up. He could get over this motherfucker, he thought, and started to hoist himself, getting his feet lodged in the bars. He wriggled out and hung by his arms, hand-over-handing, slipping on the slick paint and sweat; he hooked his hand on the top one and fought his way over the spear-tipped iron, six or seven inches apart between his crotch, gasping, resting a second. Even loaded it hit him how dangerous this was. He didn't want to end his life impaled drunk on a cemetery fence. He caught his breath, grabbed a spear in each hand and slid off the other side, hung a second and hit the ground hard, uppercutting his jaw with his knee like a loose string-puppet. He readjusted his lower face with both hands. That felt good. It was already crackly from high school football days. The climb had winded him and he sat a minute waiting for the ground to level out.

He got up and weaved up the narrow drive, huffing and wheezing, humming "This Is My Country," stumbling past rows of white and grey tombstones. To his right was a hillside covered with small, identical crosses. As he lifted his head to the left he saw a large black Nazi swastika painted on a white stone, other marked stones moving behind it coming out from behind each other as he moved up. Behind more rows were stones with words written in rough black letters, one word on each stone, DIE NIGGER JEW LOVERS. He stumbled up between them, swaying and turning, slipping down, getting up and looking around. What the hell? he thought. Was this some kind of joke? It was hard to grasp through his alcohol haze. He swayed and stumbled, looking for someone to explain this. How could this happen in a veteran's cemetery? Didn't anybody watch this place? Did security take the day off for Memorial Day? What a crock. Another good government fuckup. He had to take a knee to keep from hyperventilating. This wasn't what he'd come here for.

He got up and staggered onto the drive. As he went up there were more swastikas the size of cars blackened on pavement, rows of swastikas on each side. At the top of the hill was a large one on the obelisk monument with the insignias of military units. There were small swastikas on each insignia and PRAISE ADOLPH HITLER scribbled across them. He rocked and swallowed, rubbing his forehead, looking around. If he got his hands on the cretins that did this . . . but they were never around . . .

At the obelisk the drive split off in seven directions and he stumbled across the grass toward his father's grave. Almost everything he passed had a swastika or something defamatory on it. Stones were kicked over and smashed, rows of crosses were piled up with a big deformed swastika rippled across them in the grass. Seventy yards down he stopped in front of the white marble marker that said *James T. Hawkins*. A black swastika was painted on the engraving covering the name. He let out a sick groan and slid to his knees. On all-fours he vomited to the side of the grave.

He sat for a while with his eyes shut, dripping dry-mouthed, his head feeling like a mush-filled bowling ball. He looked at the desecrated markers trailing out of sight down the hill and threw up again, coughing up bile. Crawling away he lay on the ground on his side, licking the grass. He kept hearing a clickety-jangling and some other muted noises. It sounded like a mockingbird. Some of it was like a metallic ratcheting accompanied by rattles and other funny noises. Of course this was part of it, being sick-drunk in hell, you had to listen to strange, cryptic sounds and try to figure them out.

He heard something like snickering. Another sound that wasn't birdlike. He raised up, listening again, hearing that clickety-rattling noise. That wasn't any bird. He heard something he knew was human, a whistle-like yelp, and with it other clicking jangles. When he stood his head wasn't reeling. He'd puked and sweated it out. Except for a nasty case of cottonmouth he didn't feel that awful.

He climbed the hill with his pulse and brain thumping, crossing the top of the drive where a ten-foot swastika was painted with the words HITLER LIVES HERE, listening to the snickering and rattling getting closer. He felt his temper rising. There was a snatch of song with the rapid clickety-clicking. The tombstones were older grey markers, some massive, and he was sliding in and out of them with a view like a stalking animal's, opening his mouth to quiet his breath.

In seams between rocks he saw the crouched back of a wiry man with a shaved head except for a bone-white ponytail. Getting closer he saw the earring and cut-off leather jacket with some kind of dragon on the back and spindly arms solid with tattoos. He was rangy, thin but tall. His body reminded Deke of an upright lizard's the way he swung it and leaned back as if he were sitting in a sling. He was spraying a swastika on a tombstone. In his other hand was a black plastic garbage bag jangling cans as he went

stone-to-stone making queer little flicking noises and whistles with his
teeth.

Deke was twenty feet behind him. He watched him, wondering if he
was just some grotesque dream. He felt surprisingly sober, the adrenaline
sharpening his senses. He waited for the man's face to lean in as close as
possible to the stone he was working on, then sprinted toward him, leaping
and slamming into the back of his neck with both feet. The front of the
man's head hit the tombstone hard, and he collapsed with cans rolling
around him, blood trickling from his nose and forehead. Deke picked him
up by his jacket collar with a handful of chains and hit him so hard he felt
his fist go down his throat with a few teeth. The man coughed on his side,
bleeding in the grass, kicking feebly away from him on his back. Deke
picked him up again and was about to take his head off when someone
dropped on him out of the sky, from the top of a large stone, and he felt
a cold-heavy chain across his Adam's apple. He was on his back on top of
the man who was growling in his ear. Pinned and choking, looking up at
the curved silhouettes of five or six tombstones against patchy-grey sky,
thinking, this is the way it ends? The man was some kind of beast, Deke
felt the heavy flesh and muscle-bulk of his body and couldn't get a finger
between the chain and his neck that was cutting his skin as he choked him.
He was trying to flip over and get the man on his back so he could lift and
bash him into a rock, ram his head into anything, but he was two-hundred
and fifty pounds at least, strong as hell, and had the leverage of the slope
and probably a stone behind him. Deke could feel the wiry bristles of beard
on his neck and smell his dog breath as he kicked and twisted.

"Whas' a matta, Uncle Sam?" the man growled. "Don't like our
decorations? Come to the right place to die, you and your fuckin'
Jew-lovers . . ."

For a few seconds Deke was blacking out and didn't realize it, sinking
into an oxygen-deprived painless place with this steel collar lulling him.
The man's voice roused him and he kicked wildly, grabbing and clawing for
anything, getting a handful of the man's greasy hair, jerking and heaving
on it as hard as he could as the man hissed and grunted. Deke felt the
chain clamp tighter and clawed the ground. Reaching to his right he felt
a can of spray paint, brought it up and sprayed it into the man's face.
The man screamed like a castrated bull. The chain loosened enough for
Deke to get his hands underneath it, he wriggled out of it, elbowing him

in the head several times as he rolled over. Dog breath was digging at his eyes with both hands, flailing in agony. Deke stood over him with two paint cans, spraying and kicking him, blackening him, pressing the nozzles into his eyes; slugging him sideways with the bottoms of the containers, backhanding him with his fists, laughing and screaming out of his mind. "Whas' a matta, boss! Be the first hand-painted Nazi nigger in history! Whadda you think, you stupid worthless motherfucker! How you like it! Don't let me miss a spot, you disgusting piece of shit! . . ."

He'd forgotten the first man who came down on him now with a large ceramic vase, smashing it full of water and flowers over his shoulder. He felt a spasm in his arm as he fell, rolling over, seeing the chain swinging like a straight whip at his head; it grazed his face and nicked him. Deke yanked him down by his arm using the man's momentum. The man sailed and glanced off a few rocks and was up quickly swinging the chain as they faced off. It was the first time Deke'd looked at him straight on. He had a serpentine face with piercing eyes, large scar under the left one, gold tongue-ring. He alternated odd little yelps with working his tongue in and out like a snake with a flicking noise. Blood ran over a swastika on his forehead, and there was some kind of dragon tattoo wrapped round his neck with blood on it from his mouth. He used yelps and tongue noises as a distraction before swinging the chain. Holding a can of spray paint in each hand, Deke nailed him in the chin with one and lunged inside the chain to take a swing, when he felt something stab his leg. The other man had crawled up behind him on his stomach and plunged a bowie knife into his calf. He felt a pain like a vising muscle cramp. As he grabbed to yank it out the first man grazed him again with the chain near his eye. The knife had slid out, he must've thrown it himself, he hoped so because he didn't know where it was and didn't have time to find it, as he caught the chain coming back down, pulled the snake man into him and kicked him with a sixty yard punt into the groin. He turned and kicked the other man squarely under his blackened face, lifting him a few feet off the ground in a dead roll. He turned and got the first man by the collar and started to slug him mercilessly. He kept hitting him, twelve, fifteen times at least until he was completely limp.

"You picked the wrong *fucking day* . . . and the wrong . . . *fucking place* . . . and the wrong . . . *fucking guy* . . . to be doing this with slime ball . . . motherfucker . . . whatever the hell you are . . ."

As he reared back to hit him again he saw the battered, unconscious face slathered in blood. He heard a motorcycle rev up, then roar off. The bearded man was gone. Listening to it fade he stared at the snake-faced man he held by his jacket on the ground, realizing to hit him again would be a pointless waste of energy. He started to laugh again, holding and shaking him, looking up at the sky. Slumping, he dropped him, turning and staggering uphill toward his father's grave using stones like steps to hold himself up. When he reached the marker he swayed over it with his head cocked. He slid to one knee, touching the stab wound on the back of his calf. He took his shirt off and tied it around it to slow the bleeding. He leaned his head on his father's gravestone, mumbling a half-conscious, rambling apology. He thanked everyone there for what they'd done for him. He thanked his father for his service and for everything he'd taught him. He kept losing his train as he rambled, realizing he didn't know what the hell he was saying anymore, that he wasn't making any sense or able to remember what he'd just said, and passed out with his face against the stone.

Lucas March rocked on his front porch listening to Mahalia sing gospel. Two whippoorwills made a steady accompaniment on the side of the mountain across the road. He and Rashan had just polished off a batch of Orville Redenbacher popcorn and Lucas smoked some homegrown tobacco from his hand carved pipe. Fireflies swayed on the dark mountainside. Lightning showed purple storm clouds behind distant peaks. It was pretty but didn't amount to anything, another ghost of a rain which was all they'd had in a month. He hummed with the gospel singer and got up and hobbled down the steps with his cane, peering over the rooftop to the east. It was all sitting to the northwest, brilliant silhouettes and flashes with long rumblings, then the sky went black as coal again.

"What you think, Rashan? Think we'll get a drop?"

Rashan took a break from tonguing buttered cheddar from his forepaws and sat up, studying the flickering sky. Tilting his head he whined once and licked his chops, shuffling his forefeet.

"Yeah, I'm with you. Don't think we will either."

Rashan trotted down the steps next to Lucas and looked up the road, whining again. A warm breeze struck Lucas in the face as he made out the truck engine Rashan'd heard first. He was pretty sure who it'd be as he recognized Deke's truck misfiring a half-mile before he saw the lights and raised his pipe as Deke blew by, not wearing a shirt he noticed, watching his hand go up as a reflex. He could feel the boy's emotion and his heart went out to him. Sometimes he recognized it more than others, on certain days, not really expecting it or thinking about it, he could read people as they drove by the way others could read palms or signs. Especially if he knew them and had a pretty good sense of where they were. Deke was a wild-spirited boy but always treated him with respect. You knew where you stood with Deke and Jason. Not so with Honcho, but none of them had ever been jackasses to him, and their daddy was one of the finest men he'd ever known and a trusted friend. Lucas had a feeling these boys were going to lose their place, though Deke said it wouldn't happen. He hoped he had a genie in a bottle somewhere because he'd seen it happen too many times. Unless Deke knew something he didn't he was resigned to having new neighbors in a year or so. He listened to the truck downshift at the end of the drive, hitting third, continue past the farmhouse and after a few minutes the faint downshifting-grinding up the mountain. He turned, listening to the final shift into first going up the last grade. Why they were in the old mountain cabin he couldn't guess. Maybe the farmhouse held too much, and it was none of his business anyway. He leaned down scratching Rashan's head, shut his eyes and thought about his Elsa. Warm air brushed his face as Mahalia's voice pulled the Spirit from the sky and he swayed in it, moaning and humming, feeling Elsa standing in front of him in that green-flowered dress he'd bought her in Memphis sixteen years ago.

Deke lay on his stomach wincing as Barrett doctored the knife-wound under a Roy Rodgers lamp. The stab throbbed like a son of a bitch and every time Barrett poured peroxide on it, prying it apart with a Q-tip, Deke gulped from the bottle of Cuervo on the floor. That and some painkillers took the edge off but it hurt like hell. He dabbed chain-nicks on his face with alcohol glancing in a hand mirror, keeping his mind on the Braves-Padres going into the twelfth. Jason leaned on the table with a bag of chips monitoring frequencies on the scanner. Every now and then snipped voices bit through the swirling static.

"This is all we need," Barrett grumbled. "Got over a thousand children out there and it ain't exactly a picnic with all of us humpin' it."

"I can haul water, boss, no problem. He's throwing you junk, Murph, wait him out."

"Hell no you won't. You'll get gangrene 'cause you can't keep it dry. Three days of penicillin before you do any damn thing, you hear me?"

"Ahhhhhhhh!" Deke gritted. "*Son* of a bitch."

"I'm stitchin' now. Drink some more of that to-kill-ya. Keep your leg still, dammit. You're lucky the blade missed any veins. You're sure about the shots?"

"Yeah," Deke gulped. "Daddy made tetanus shots a ritual since we were babies. We were triple-redundant with that stuff, weren't we?"

"Absolutely," Jason said.

". . . Roger, Weasel. Tell me when you locate landmark Q . . ."

The voice inside the military chopper sounded in the room with them.

"Believe I locate it a half-mile ahead, dead on. Begin your perimeter at two miles working in, Muskrat."

"Roger. Do we have this one unsecured? Looks like it's on the burn-list."

For thirty seconds there was churning air from one of the choppers.

"Uh . . . Roger," the second voice said in a changed tone. "That's affirmative."

"Nobody home. It was like this a month ago. Wonder what the problem is."

Barrett's eyes rolled to the ceiling as the scanner blades synchronized with the humming roof. He dropped the stitching-needle.

"*Blackout* little brother."

Jason leaped to the door, flipping the wall-switch. Everything in the cabin shut down as the choppers hovered over the mountain. The ground and everything attached to it vibrated as white light knifed through the window cracks.

"Yeah, Muskrat," the second voice said. "Breaking up here . . . switch to first security frequency . . ."

After another droning pause, very clearly, without any static the first voice said: "That's a Roger."

For a moment the three men watched each other's silhouettes as searchlights swung through the rooms. Voiceless static hissed on the scanner. As the lights and thrumming pulled off they listened to the scanner hopping.

"Did you catch that shit?" Barrett said.

"He said something about a burn-list," Jason said.

"Wasn't supposed to say whatever he did over the waves. Other man shut him up, did you hear that? Find their frequency little brother, hurry up."

"Trying. Might be a blocked channel."

"Shit man, they were talking about something there. What the fuck were they saying?"

"Who cares?" Deke said, squeezing his Cuervo bottle. "They're trying to drive everybody crazy in this fucking valley. Long as they don't see us I don't give a damn what they do . . . piss on 'em . . ." He took two gulps and pointed his bottle to the ceiling. "Here's to the valiant whirlybirds and their war on flowers . . . I salute you . . . *I piss on you* . . . sons of bitches . . ."

"Yeah, I reckon," Barrett said. "Couldn't have meant nothing, could it?"

He sat slumped in silence at the end of the bed, light fluttering in the room from the searchlights backtracking a mile away. The scanner locked on a clear transmission.

". . . That's a negatory, Weasel. Like to drop a wet-fly in that river we just crossed."

"Roger that, let's track our southeast vector, pinpoint R for Road hog. Copy that."

"Yeah, that's a Roger. Ought to be on it in about two minutes . . ."

The three of them sat motionless except for Deke raising and sloshing his tequila bottle in the dark. After a while the scanner voices turned into garbled snips and static.

In the tiny government conference room the three men sat at the table under a suspended light. Wearing Marine dress blues with medals, Honcho sat with his face slightly shadowed, sensing the room. The Air Force General sat cater cornered across the table smoking his pipe, silently observing the Major's eyes and body language for clues as to his sanity. Major Hawkins was either a veritable nutcase or had more guts than sense, he thought. His scores were high as an Army Air Cav pilot, he had a strong war record in Vietnam. Four purple hearts and the Distinguished Flying Cross through three tours and recommended twice for the Medal of Honor, which he never received due to incidents of insubordination under battle conditions. A hardheaded hotshot who'd gotten the job done with flagrant displays of bravery, but always seemed to shoot himself in the foot. He'd left the Army at the end of the war, enlisting straight into jet fighter training with the Marines where he'd distinguished himself in his class. His flight record in Germany, Korea and the Mideast was impressive, exemplary. He'd been a loose cannon in the early days, and maybe that was still in him, but sitting with him now the General couldn't detect any particular psychosis.

Colonel Hood, the General's assistant, leaned into the light, his bald head glistening, shuffling notebooks, plates and charts as he rambled about his fishing weekend on the Chesapeake. He was loosening up the Major as he cased him out, figuring contingencies and options he was about to deal with. The Colonel had said something both he and the General chuckled at to break the tension in the room, and Honcho smiled reservedly, more amused at them than at what was said. He wouldn't be patronized by these bureaucratic cutthroats. He knew every ruse and flanking maneuver, and their predictability annoyed him. He noticed the more detached he was the more intent they were on him, until there was a deathlike silence in the room. As he exchanged a long stare with the General he realized he'd never seen eyes so pale-blue before; glassy-nuclear-clear like transparent ice. It was like looking at a fixed ghost you got nothing back from.

Colonel Hood cleared his throat, glancing at notes.

"Now we're to understand, Major, that you're executor of a sizeable tract of land you believe the Air Force might be interested in."

"Affirmative."

"Might we ask how you came by this information," the General said.

"I have a few friends in the Pentagon."

"I see," the Colonel said impatiently. "And did these 'friends' suggest their information might be classified?"

"More or less."

"Uh huh," Hood said, studying his notes, his moist scalp shining. "Now Major Hawkins, regardless of what you may think we want any property for, will you swear here and now that whatever you were told by these 'friends' and what we say today won't be confided beyond this room?"

Honcho waited, looking at both of them.

"That depends on what's said in this room, Colonel."

"Major Hawkins, this is highly confidential military business, we'll need your word before we can go any further. I'm sure you understand that."

"My word," Honcho nodded. "I like that. *My* word. All right."

"Exactly what is the deal you want to make with us, Major?" the General said abruptly.

Honcho waited; there was a decided rhythm he wanted to this, he wasn't going to say anything too quickly.

"In exchange for my upgrade to Lt. Colonel," he said finally. "Along with double current market value for my land . . ." He paused long enough for this to sink in: "I'll transfer my seventy-six hundred acre tract to the Air Force uncontested."

Colonel Hood chuckled and leaned back, tossing his pen on the table. "What a deal," he said. "And what makes you think we can't acquire this property without you, Major?"

"Well, it's my land," Honcho said. "So that would be stealing on your part, wouldn't it? Another is the sensitive nature of the project proposed there. I happen to know you'll have it one way or another."

He felt Craig's humorless gaze as the Colonel continued to smile.

"You may have overestimated both the nature of the project and what we're willing to do to make it happen," Hood said.

"Well, judging by what a little birdie told me, and your confirmation of it a minute ago, I doubt that, Colonel. My sources are unmistakable. I've made personal confirmations as well."

The Colonel licked his lips, sniffling, flicking through jumbles of papers and acetate-covered maps.

"We have information foreclosure began on your farm over a year ago. Why wouldn't we wait until the process was complete and take it then?"

"Because foreclosure was held up by substantial cash payments, and very likely will be cancelled by a few more. I'm sure you have all that before you, gentlemen."

"Someone in your family made these payments," the General said. "A brother?"

"That's correct," Honcho said. ". . . sir."

"Where would he have come up with such a sum of money in the twelfth hour of a major foreclosure?" the Colonel asked.

"I suppose daddy told him where the money was buried. Wouldn't tell me."

General Craig leaned forward, glancing at a page of notes and leaning back. "I see your father passed away a year and a half ago. You have our condolences."

"Thank you. Self-inflicted, yes sir."

He saw a flinch from the General, a recognition in his eyes.

"Terrible thing," the General said, glancing down. "I'm sorry."

Colonel Hood leaned into the light with a wan smile. "We can still acquire this property without you, Major. Have you heard of something called eminent domain?"

"I'm sure you can do many things, Colonel," Honcho said evenly. "And I'm sure I can make this little project and your means of achieving it such common knowledge it shrivels like shit in the sun, or at least falls under a very uncomfortable light."

He felt the Colonel bristle.

"Did you not just swear to General Craig and myself to keep this classified?"

"You're mistaken," Honcho said.

"You gave us your word," the Colonel said lividly.

"Yes, but I haven't decided what word that should be, Colonel. How about *usurp*? *Evacuate*? *Steal's* a good one. *Murder's* not even out of the question, is it, gentlemen?" He waited, sensing his power, leaning into the light. "I know exactly what you're doing to acquire this farmland, gentlemen; and exactly why you're doing it. I know exactly who you're doing it to and what it's doing to them, so my oath's contingent on whoever's side you're on in this matter. If the United States Air Force isn't on my side, I don't owe you or it the sweat off my ass, do you copy that?"

After a few seconds he sat back, and the Colonel sighed, shaking his head as he shuffled notes. The General smoked and watched Honcho like an old poker player who'd just been raised. Hood flipped methodically through a stack of numbered, coated plates, finding the one he wanted, laying it face-up under the table-light. He pointed to an area with his pen.

"All right, Major Hawkins, for the record, for verification purposes only, we're not promising anything here. Would you confirm that this is the tract of land you're sole executor of and willing to turn over to the United States Air Force under your proposed conditions."

Honcho's eyes dropped to the map. Well, what do you know, he thought. Maybe he was going to get what he wanted or close to it. He felt a twinge as he recognized the familiar, hard lined, t-bone shape of his daddy's property. He glanced up at the General's poker glare boring through him. They exchanged searing looks for a moment, broken only by the General's barely perceptible nod.

With blackout shades strung up for air the windows blinked white blocks in flashes. In an explosive streak Barrett jerked awake, fumbling for his alarm clock on the sidetable. He held the collapsible face close reading 4:22 A.M. Another near strike with thunder rippled across the mountains. It was coming down somewhere out there. He turned to the window with a frown as the wind lifted Jason's hair beside him, and sat up stretching the soreness from his back and shoulders. Pulling on his pants and boots he leaned over Jason with a whisper: "The Man answers prayers, little brother," he said. Jason rolled to the window with a groan and kept sleeping.

Barrett crept to the refrigerator, quietly easing it open, guzzling from a gallon of milk, took a joint from a jelly jar, lighting and holding it in his lips, finding his camouflage parka by the door. The door went cobalt-white as he opened it. He turned to see the same shock of light freezing on Deke sleeping soundly in the corner with a pillow between his knees, clicked the door shut and strolled into the yard to take a leak. The rain-charged air smelled of laurel and the wet-fresh manure pile under the shed. He got in the truck and creaked down the mountain, puffing his spliff listening to "Heat Wave" on the radio through fidgeting static. Elephant tears thunked the windshield.

"Shit now," he said. "I can piss harder than this. Come on, baby, give up the good stuff."

The woods lit up four or five times, shuddering, waves of rain lashing the windows. He squinted and ducked to see through the camouflage vines.

"Something happening over there," he said. "Water that patch for me anyway."

He found the flattened weeds at the edge of the turn-off, steering into the soft-carpeting needles, leveling as he braked down. Through the passenger window Deke had kicked out rain slapped his thigh. He shook the joint ashes and took a final suck on it, pinched and chewed it. Beneath a cluster of dogwoods seventy or eighty yards from the patch, he turned around and parked. The fog was thick down here, the terrain tricky, he was better off hoofing it in.

He lifted his parka hood, got out and started down through the dripping trees. He felt good this morning. Some grasses made you stuporish and sluggish, not the Spiritchaser. She buzzed and focused you into whatever you were doing.

Rain spattered his jacket. The sky felt pregnant and like the bottom was about to drop out. He coaxed water from the clouds as he strolled down through the low-prickly branches, listening to a woodpecker riveting behind magnified pops and drippings. Lichen lit the faces of trees. He stopped to let a few flutters give him a better view. Even with the lightning nothing looked familiar down here. He'd left his flashlight in the truck. Maybe he should go back and get it. The problem with darkness and fog was, you could be fifty feet and three degrees off and suddenly feel like you were in another country. Forty-five minutes to daylight, he thought.

He glanced to his right as the woods lit up in a thunder-clap. He could've sworn he saw a handful of people standing on a raised clearing behind some spindly pines. A breeze caught his hood snatching it off his head, and it was ink-black again. He waited for more flashes that didn't come immediately as he blinked and looked around. What the hell was *that?* A mirage of body-like outlines? Wood forms, shadows and fog, you could see anything in them he guessed.

He turned, chuckling. It was raining harder as he watched flashes light up the tops of trees, the sky whitening behind a filigree of trunks and branches. He loved this shit: God's fireworks show. He glanced toward the clearing and felt the hair rise on the back of his neck. *He couldn't have seen that.* What the hell was that? He fumbled in his pocket for his Case knife, clutching it in his fist as he squinted into the darkness. Just in case, he thought. In case what? There was a crowd of people standing over there? *He couldn't have seen that.* He was awfully damn high, but goddamn, he'd been high thousands of times and never seen anything like that. Being high's no excuse, he used to rib Marsha when she was paranoid on the stuff. Hell yeah, take your own advice. He wondered if she was still in the clubs. Why was he thinking about her now? He waited for lightning to show him beyond ten feet and the lichen suspended on trees around him like day glow eyes.

In a flash he saw a dozen NVA soldiers in the same clearing less than forty yards away. They stood in a semicircle, seeming at ease, leaning on their weapons or checking them, a few smoking cigarettes. Several were on a knee. In that half-second he saw their wet faces and black muslin pajamas covered with leaf-camouflage. One was speaking to the rest with a raised hand-gesture.

He hit the ground with the air piling out of his lungs, chin dug into the needles. He lay flat-hugging them with his heart thumping, trying not to make a sound, rain dripping from his eyelids. His hand trembled in the straw.

"*What?*" he mouthed. "What in hell . . . NVA? Why would they be here? What the hell is this?"

He didn't move except for his smothered panting, listening to the taps and rumbles. There were claps of thunder like something tearing out of the sky. No he wasn't, he thought; he *wasn't* in a war zone and he wasn't having flashbacks. He'd seen some weird as hell shit out there he couldn't explain, but whatever it was he knew where he was.

He flinched as he licked his lips, listening to the woods sounds. No voices, clicks or clanks, nothing human. The woodpecker was rapping behind him, pecking, stopping and rapping again. Did he actually believe there were people out there? NVA soldiers in the backwoods of Tennessee? What would they be doing there in 1986, or any other year? They wouldn't, that's what. There was nobody out here no matter what he'd seen. Then why was he lying on the ground like this?

He batted away gnats, scratching his face as he peered through the weeds. The floor rippled with mounds and humps of straw. He must've had some kind of dream last night. He'd gotten very high and come out here with these people in his head. He'd done the same thing on the side of the mountain a few weeks ago. What the hell else could it be?

Daylight was breaking slowly with the storm. Ground-fog drifted like wood smoke. The woods flashed again with a chain of flutters and he could see there was no one out there. Of course there wasn't, but he kept watching the spot as lightning illuminated it three or four more times, the trees and floor irradiating and flickering. He rose to his elbows, looking around. There was no one. He got up, brushing off his pants, picking snails from his knees. "All right, shit," he said, rubbing his eyes. He was beginning to see dim outlines on the sky. He started toward the clearing, crouching every few steps to see if there were any tracks or bent branches, fighting the impulse to look for trip-wires.

Reaching the spot where he'd seen the soldiers, he squatted and duck walked around it, looking for cigarettes and ashes, but there weren't any. NVA wouldn't leave their butts anyway. There was no burned smell. The ground was pristine, needles fluffed, no branches cuffed or broken. There wasn't a damn thing here. What'd he expect? He dropped his head. You've got an imagination, he thought. Rein it in for Christ sake.

He studied the lichen on the trees and from the direction it faced found true north, making another reckoning toward the patch. The fog had risen to neck-level and he couldn't see his hands as he stumbled down in it, it was like floating through clouds that dissipated then suddenly swallowed you like a bowl. Behind him a limb or the top of a tree cracked and tumbled through the branches, jarring the ground. He stopped and listened a few seconds; he shook his head and kept going.

Stepping over logs he saw movements on his left periphery. When he turned there were mottled leaves, objects on the ground, rocks, flowers, stumps. Gradually they were catching light. The woods lit up with sustained lightning, rain falling like an avalanche, popping on his parka hood. Trees and ground flashed and crackled. He was walking straight into it. Fine, he thought, let it come, whatever it took to bring it was okay with him: rain like hell, baby. He lowered his head, shielding his eyes. He remembered the deep ravine to his left and had a pretty good idea where he was unless it was the wrong one. If he could find another landmark he'd know if he was below or above the patch. He found three fallen trees uprooted across it, remembering the way they lay across each other, probably felled in an ice storm. He should've brought his damn flashlight.

As he stumbled down he got a feeling of things pulling into brush, just a sensation at first, leaves like upright human branches snatched into fog.

He stopped and looked back, frowning and grinning at the bobbing leaves. This was silly. As he walked it started again, short, deft flicks, twitch like movements, nothing to see when he turned but the light-dancing shifting of rain and wind shaking branches. It's nothing, he thought. Some game your mind's playing. He'd play along, why not? If you thought something was strange in fog it would become so, especially when you were stoned out of your mind. Head-straight he'd hallucinated squads of VC in rain and fog in-country and sometimes when he thought he'd hallucinated them they'd start shooting back. Remember that time you nearly got your ass shot off thinking you were hallucinating those sappers? Yeah, and again, maybe that's your problem, remembering too damn much.

He could see pale outlines of slender trees for a distance now. Something huge flew across a window at the end of a corridor of trunks, a real and damn big bird, pilated woodpecker probably. He turned to see the same darting movements behind him. He blinked and wiped his eyes, gazing at the ground, listening to rain spattering his jacket; stumbling ahead again, feeling peculiarly agitated, rolling his eyes into the trees. Squirrels leaped limb-to-limb above him. When he looked down movements scattered like roaches in ground-fog. He saw something else, something clearly leaf like pull into it, a foot or hand.

"What?" he mumbled out loud, palming his eyes. "Come on, *come on,* quit this crazy shit."

All he could see was the rain pattering leaves. He had to be getting close to the patch, maybe he'd walked right by it in the fog. Lightning hit something nearby, beginning with a thin-sizzling pop in the treetops exploding to the forest floor like a mortar shell. He swallowed, looking around uncomfortably, feeling his pulse thumping, his heart shuddering like the flickering light.

Something darted ahead of him. The rain was coming down so hard he was half-blinded, but he saw that. What was it? It looked like leaves. Leaves? He didn't see what it was but he took a step toward it as something to his right yanked into foliage and he jerked a look toward a high wall of swaying-leaved branches. He stopped again, clenching his eyes, concentrating, fighting to clear his head, his eye beginning to twitch. "You're not here," he pointed to it. "I *smoked* your ass. Get the fuck away from me . . ." He opened his eyes, shooing them: "Get . . . *Get away* . . . get . . . get . . . get . . ."

Stumbling ahead he slipped in the mushy straw. Ignore this shit, he thought. It wasn't real. You know what's real. He felt the movements around him again but didn't react to them. Screw them, he thought. He heard something like whispers. He was sure at first they were leaves brushing, rustling, sussurant sounds, but as he crunched ahead he was sure they were something else. Whether they were or not he was hearing them. He felt the hair rise on the back of his neck again. This was insane. He wasn't imagining them like the soldiers he'd imagined a few minutes ago. "*Beware from the air,*" it said. Yes. "*Than trong tu . . .*" No. Hell no. Maybe he'd dreamed that too, huh? Have you lost your ever-loving mind? Are you hearing it or just saying it to yourself like a song you can't stop repeating, thinking, humming in your head. Come on now, come on. He kept walking. It wasn't getting any quieter. This is fine, he thought. This was the weirdest fucking shit he'd seen in his life. The movements seemed to increase as the foliage nodded and swayed ahead of him.

"I hear ya," he said. "What the fuck? You ain't here, you don't think I know that? *Fuck you, goddamit.*"

He was giggling, his eyes watered. He was getting spooked and a little sugar-weak. He hadn't eaten enough and his hypoglycemia was acting up, he was lost as hell, he didn't know which way to walk. How'd that happened? Rain peppered his cheeks. He slipped into a hole in the spongy straw, plunging his right leg up to his hip. Goddamit, he said, as he pushed up, thinking about bunji pits. Don't start that now. Quit. You're making yourself loco, buddy. This was what schizophrenics did, wasn't it? They started hearing, seeing, and thinking nonexistent shit? Come on, think about it, you were fine until you smoked the joint and came out here. It's something in the smoke. Something's going on here. In your head, yes, but it ain't just you.

The voices were getting more convoluted and insistent. After a minute he was sure they were talking to him. He realized how strange this was, which was a good thing, he guessed. He felt like he was walking a gauntlet. Things seemed to be flicking and darting in all directions like bugs leaping from rocks. He thought he'd lose his mind if he hadn't already. But nothing had touched him. Nothing yet anyway. He stopped and stared at the shimmering air.

"You're in the goddamn smoke!" he said. "You ain't here worth a shit! I know where you come from. Get the fuck away from me. Get the fuck away!"

He stumbled ahead, keeping his eyes on the fogged foreground, gulping, watching leaves and movements flicking on his periphery. They blossomed ahead and withdrew. He tried to ignore them but he was fucking scared; he felt runnish and panicky, giggling like a little girl. Stopping gave him the feeling of being surrounded. He kept moving, hobbling over stumps and limbs, hanging his cuff on a strand of barbed wire tearing his pants up his side.

He heard clattering on his parka and saw white pebbles pelting like mothballs. It was hailing like crazy, the woods whiting out with chain-lightning. He'd be able to see now if not for the fog, and he held a hand in front of his eyes to keep from getting jabbed. In the hissing, crackling racket the voices seemed to whisper incessantly. Something snatched into the fog to his right, and he grabbed for it, watching leaves attached to dark-clothed appendages leap away, swinging like a closing fist through the pelting white stuff. Now he'd done it. He turned and lunged at something else, fog swirling around it. He stumbled and fell on his knees, sliding and rolling down a long embankment skinning his shoulder against a rock, patting the ground ahead of him with white marbles bouncing off his arms. Where the hell was he? As he got up he saw leaf-covered figures slipping into mist. There was someone there, he thought. He wasn't crazy. He stepped blindly after them, calling out.

"What do you want?" he said. "Why're you doing this?"

He saw leaf-covered legs running just out of reach as he jogged behind them. Four or five steps ahead he heard hurried, nervous breathing, crisp hail pattering his feet. Voices were joined together like a number of people jabbering at once. They were chattering as he jostled after them, bouncing off trees, scraping his face on limbs, zigzagging as the movements reversed and changed direction. He was following shoes and calves running three or four steps ahead of him.

He pushed faster, picking up speed. He thought he was gaining on them until he realized he was losing ground the harder he ran. Weeds and trees pulled and slingshotted. When he tore his hand through a patch of briars and felt the needles lacerate his skin, he thought, this is goddamn crazy. How many times was he going to say that? Why was he doing this?

He was chasing something, that's what he was doing. The ground was crunching half-white with hail beating down ahead of him, popping like rocks on his parka as he ran along through it. He couldn't see his hand in front of his face, but he was missing trees somehow, glancing and grazing off them. No matter how fast he ran he couldn't get closer to the scurrying, leaf-covered legs. He saw half-bodies swallowed by fog now and then when he lunged faster.

"Wait a second!" he screamed. "*Hold on goddamit*! . . ."

In a radiating flash he saw three full leaf-covered figures vanish into fog. With his own panting he heard breathy voices. It sounded like they were behind him, chasing *him*. He could hear the same rapid breaths over his shoulder. He wasn't turning. They were following him now? He wasn't letting go of these leaf-covered legs striding ahead of him. He could almost feel the breath on the back of his neck. Ignore them, he thought; ignore this, then he wheeled on them, watching leaves suck and scatter in the grainy air. The movements turned into the disembodied branches of real trees he plowed into, grabbing and stripping handfuls of leaves.

Wherever he turned they seemed to appear. They seemed to be everywhere, heckling and frightened at the same time. "Wait a minute!" he shouted. ". . . Wait! *WAIT*!" He fell and shoved himself up, seeing three or four scattered, waist-high leaf-movements yanked into mist as if they grew out of wherever he sat or stood. He couldn't stop chasing them. He thrashed after them through trees that came up quickly in his face. As he picked up speed the leaf-covered legs scurried ahead again at the same infuriating distance. He sprinted faster and faster, ready to tackle them, pounce on them, get his hands on any damn piece of whatever was there. A step or two closer; the voices sounded purely frantic; he was close enough to touch one of them. He felt a bright, flattening shock as he slammed into a trunk with the right side of his face spinning him down on his back with hail peppering his eyes. He heard wild, bitten laughter, more chittering noise. Getting up gripping the trunk, tearing the bark, staring at it to be sure it was real. He touched the scrape on his face, feeling raw flesh, his hand wet with blood. He heard Vietnamese voices singing around him like a ritual war-chant.

"Who are you?" he cried. "Wha's goin' on! *Ca gi se xay ra*?"

Something darted to his right and he lunged hard at it, panting and raking through fog. He stumbled bent-over at a jog with his arms ahead, hand-over-handing off trunks, disembodied feet pulling away again. He saw the bottoms of soles and the strands of battered leaves. He couldn't run anymore, his legs were given out. He clung to trees, fighting for breath. He was half-falling, staggering forward, his brain whiting-out in waves. Leaf-covered movements seemed to multiply just ahead of him as he walked and started to jog again, his leaning weight dragging him forward. This was a bad dream. He wasn't even here. This was some godforsaken hallucination, every bit of it; he was not in his own head, he was somewhere else. He had no starch in his legs. *God help me, he thought; make this crazy shit . . . stop . . . please . . .*

He stopped and rested with his hands on his knees. It didn't matter which direction he turned, the voices and leaf-covered bodies were in front of him. The hail was slackening. The sounds in the woods changed suddenly like a vacuum sucking everything into it, voices echoing behind it at a trickling distance. They were picking up speed again, it was no use, he couldn't keep up with them. Give up, he thought. He was making himself jog through the mist as he saw the leaf-bodies fading into it. He thought he was passing out, then realized they were thinning into the leaves, as if they were just absorbed by them. As he stumbled ahead they accelerated and turned into mist themselves, leaving him groping on the ground on all-fours. He heard reverberating, chiding screams with muffled thunder, staggered up and lunged out, slapping at trunks, caroming off them, moaning hoarsely as he crawled a ways. He hugged a tree with his face against it, his mouth so dry he couldn't swallow, licking moisture from the leaves as he grunted in Vietnamese:

"*Where's your village? Lang cua ban o dau? Why're you in this province? Tai sao ban song o dia phan nay? . . .*"

He heard a voice, his own he realized, and stopped to listen to the quiet around him. It was as if he'd woken or fallen there out of the sky on his knees. He heard myriad drippings, a groan-like rumbling. The storm had passed and there was grey light around him. How long'd he been kneeling like this? It couldn't have been that long because he was still sucking air. He heard cicadas winding up and birds chirping. Blue, red and yellow guitar picks speckled the floor. He stared at them for a minute, realizing they'd fallen from his broken pick case on the ground. Through the mist he saw a patch of marijuana plants, believing he was hallucinating *them*. Couldn't be. It was the the patch he'd come down for, the stout bushes floating in the white air like alien shrubs. All over the hillside dead frogs lay in hail drifts, green-white bodies carpeting the ground. What was this? He'd been in it while it was going on, hurtling through it like some delirious madman, but something had *happened* for sure.

He pushed up weak-kneed, pasted with mud and leaves, gazing into the woods behind him. Yellow light shone where the hill rolled off into a thicket of circling vines. He stood a minute leaning on a sapling, listening to the waking sounds, stumbling down into the marijuana patch, the leaved floor smothered with frogs. The waist-high plants were storm-beaten, frogs dangling and twisted up in the branches. He slid to his knees, looking at them shining belly-white in the breeze, lodged and disfigured against the sky. It looked like some errant frog air force had crashed there. He lifted one from a plant, studying its broken, sticky-limp body, standing again, stumbling into them. As far as he could see the ground was grey-white with them, frogs crawling over hundreds more lying belly-up in every contorted position. The breeze picked up and light shone on the plants and mottled floor. A small frog bounced through the limbs, splatting to his feet, lay gazing up at him from a twisted angle, its stomach pumping hard against the cool raw air.

When he found his legs he trudged up through the woods to find the truck. The last thing he expected to do was walk right to it, but there it was: he could've hit the patch with a rock from it. No, he wasn't even going to try to figure this out. He felt like one of those hangovers from those partial blackout drunks he used to have, where most of what he remembered was sick-rolling and banging his head. The clouds had blown off and it was a clear-balmy day. He found two packs of peanut butter crackers in the glove box and ate them ravenously, munching them with hail cubes as he listened to Roy Orbison on the radio. His arms were a spider web of scrapes and gashes. He had a puffed bruise under his right eye where that tree had leveled him. He wasn't going to tell Deke and Jason about this one, fucking Deke would have a field day with it. He was going to pretend this never happened. He started the truck and eased down the makeshift trail crunching over frogs, hailstones and blown debris, parking below the patch where he could get a downhill roll with a load. He retraced on foot his route up to the trail, clearing limbs, then started filling the bed with frogs, humming a Buddy Guy tune as he pitched them in like beanbags. By the time he'd cleared from the truck he had a cushion for the rest to land on, under handing three or four at a time off the bumper. Small as they were they could live off these legs if they had to.

A single-engine plane circled the back of the farm sounding like that misfiring Grumman he'd heard last week. He took a breather in the shade, sucking on hailstones, listening to it sputtering-stalling toward the highway. Damn, he was dehydrated. He needed a piece of meat with horseradish sauce. A plate of these legs smothered in Texas Pete wouldn't be too bad.

When the plane drifted over the farmhouse he went back to work, filling the bed until frogs were even with the sides. Stepping into the patch he pinched the plants surgically, what he'd come down to do in the first place, dropping the delicate shoots in his parka pocket. Pruning damaged limbs with his knife, he braced a few with vines and rough stakes. He checked them for root-rot and bugs, they looked pretty healthy, already breaking out of their droop after the battering storm. He climbed in the truck and nudged it back and forth, feeling it sway but stiff enough to make it out of there. Gunning it up through the woods shooting over weeds and small trees, grinding up keeping his momentum, dragging the muffler. Glancing at the load of hand-size meat bouncing in a wet heap in his rearview mirror.

In the parking lot of the Holiness Lighthouse Church Jason read the New Testament by the yellow maritime lanterns strung along the roped gangway. He listened to the voices as he watched the ushers greet late arrivals, mumbling with his face down, the rotating lighthouse beam catching his eyes each time it swung around. He'd come as usual to listen to the singing that made him feel closer to his father, but since "the accident" he hadn't walked up that creaking plank or stepped through the port holed doors.

The songs ended which meant the service had started. He said a prayer for his family and was flipping to the Sermon on the Mount when a navy Trans Am pulled up with its radio blaring. If he didn't acknowledge them maybe they'd leave him alone. It was a trick he used when he wanted to be invisible.

"Better get in there and turn some heads," a female voice chimed at him. Not today, he thought, turning to the girl with short blonde hair in a white sundress and wire-rims, her pale arm draped down the car door. "Tell them how you used to throw a defenseless little girl's books out her school bus windows."

"I'll never live you down I guess."

"Hell no you won't. What you doing, Jason Hawkins?"

"Going in in a minute."

"Go ahead, I'll watch."

"You have grown up, haven't you?"

"Bought a boat. Wanna see it?"

"What kind of boat?"

"Have to see it. Redoing her myself. Come on, you're not going in there."

"How would you know that?"

"The look on your face. You do this all the time?"

"Why do you think I threw your books out the school bus windows, kid? I always felt naked around you."

"Words are cheap, Mr. Hawkins. God, you're mopey. You just gonna hang around here moping all night?"

"Maybe. Where's this boat?"

"Twenty minute drive. Give you a ride in her, she needs a christening, you could say a prayer or something."

Might as well, he thought. She watched him climb out with his Bible, strapping in beside her. She cruised slowly from the parking lot, humming with the tape going, flooring it punching a loud, screeching, rubber-burning wheel up the road in a cloud of white smoke. He watched tiny figures run out of the church, light around them receding to a dot in his passenger window.

"Like Johnny Rivers?" she said, rattling tapes in the console.

"You always do that?"

"Only when I'm nervous." She popped a tape in in the middle of "Seventh Son." "What *were* you doing out there anyway?"

"Reading my Bible, moping some. Could we slow down?"

He watched the speedometer slide back to fifty.

"Still gonna be a preacher? Dad said he ran into you and you were still going to Moody."

"In between things right now."

"Wouldn't mind being a preacher's wife if he didn't treat me like one. Like moonshine, Mr. Hawkins?"

"Never had it."

"You're kidding. You *do* lead a sheltered life, don't you?"

She tore off the paved highway, rocketing down a flat-narrow gravel drive, headlights catching vultures flapping into the trees. Rocks pelted underneath, weeds slapping and separating off the windshield. Jason gripped the door handle, bracing against the ceiling glancing at her. She was cupped over the wheel, face between her hands, nodding a little dancing in her seat, fingering strands of blonde hair from her eyes as they barreled down what looked more like a graded creek bed than a road; twisting and shooting through a maze of powdery trails overgrown with spruce and laurel. He saw a deer dart by a couple of ruined shacks as they climbed, then they were dropping again, dipping and rolling faster. He smelled the river and felt the temperature change. She shuffled handfuls of tapes in the console, finding one she wanted slipping it between her legs.

"See if there's a blindfold in the glove compartment," she said, patting his thigh.

He pulled out a black cloth band. "What's this for?"

"You need to put it on."

"*What?*"

"Trust me. These people will as long as you're wearing it. Come on, Jason, it's worth it."

She cut her eyes at him, humming. He giggled, holding it up, looking at her to see if she was serious.

"When?"

"Any minute. Almost there."

He pulled on the tied stretch-blindfold, staring straight ahead, feeling ludicrous. Minutes ago he was reading the Sermon on the Mount and now he was driving seventy miles an hour down a dirt road to a firing squad. He held his Bible with both hands damp with perspiration. Since her father'd run into him she'd been searching for him, and here he was blindfolded in her car on a deserted back road. He had muscular healing hands like a good doctor's. Beads of moisture popped on his lips as he bit them and swallowed. He seemed to trust her even if he was nervous as a cat. She'd never get to watch him like this without the blindfold.

She eased the car in a tight circle in a soft-dirt turn-around and cut the engine and lights. He heard a waterfall and could tell by other sounds they were miles from anywhere. A mosquito buzzed in his ear. She blew the horn in a series of shorts and longs.

"We'll be out of here in five minutes," she said.

A tall man in dark clothes and ragged felt hat hobbled out of the woods.

"Evening, Estridge. Anything cooking?"

"You know it, sister. Who's your friend?"

"Cousin from Mississippi. He's a good boy, don't worry," she slapped Jason's thigh. He swallowed, staring straight ahead. "Got any wine tonight?"

"Shore do. Ready yesterday. Shine's fresh, too. Yore cousin smoke? Got a little last year's crop."

"Cous'?" she turned to Jason. He nodded no, facing forward. "Cous' is gonna be a preacher. How 'bout two figs and one shine."

"You got it, Miss Blondie."

Jason heard footsteps brushing into the woods. In a minute they rustled back with bottles clinking in a paper bag.

"Same price?" Janie said.

"Yes ma'am. Can't beat it."

"Thankyou, Estridge," she said, handing the bills as she cranked the engine. "You're an artist and a gentleman."

"Any time, young lady. Ya'll settle in out of there before you start on that stuff."

Janie hit the lights and roared up the trail floating with dust. Jason sighed and sat back with the perspiration cold on his neck. She slipped his Bible from his hands and slid it under her seat, grabbing handfuls of newspaper from the rear floor mat.

"What you doing?" he said. "Can I take this off?"

"Go ahead."

She slung the newspapers out the window, smiling innocently as he tore off the blindfold.

"Where's my Bible?"

"Where you think? Turnabout's fair play."

She cranked up Johnny Rivers singing "Midnight Special."

Jason craned behind them. "You didn't . . . *did you*? My grandmother gave me that Bible. Are you crazy?"

"My school books were in shreds when I went back for them." She shrugged.

"I was ten years old, Janie! Come on, stop the car, you've gotta go back. *Please*."

"What'll you give me?"

"What do you want!" he said, turning frantically.

"Oh, I'll have to think about that," she said, pulling the Bible from under her seat, tossing it in his lap.

By the mirrored lake she unlatched the padlock on the gate of Sagget And Sons Boatyard. A single yellow bulb lit the pole near the entrance. Rows of docked boats sat motionless under the overcast sky. Janie refastened the padlock, squeezing her fingers through the metal links. They went up into the vessel-crowded yard stretching into darkness, Jason carrying the bottles in the ruffled bag.

"Haven't seen her in a while. She's gotta be wondering about me."

"I remember this place," Jason said. "We had church retreats at the Saunders cabin when I was a kid. Skied my first time on this lake."

They strolled up through an alley of weathered, refurbished, stripped-down and nearly new sailboats, speed boats, cabin cruisers on blocks in shelters and under tarps. Canoes stacked on racks next to a high hangar with boats shelved on four tiers. Near the top of the hill Janie pointed her flashlight at a wooden cruiser jutting bow-first out of the honey locust trees, a plank sided thirty-eight foot inboard painted white with blue trim and sashes on blocks.

"That's her," she said. "Haven't renamed her. She's bare without her rub rails and platform. I want to give her more coats before I fix all that that back on."

She dragged a canvas cover off the stern where a rope-ladder dangled from the cockpit, climbing it. She leaned over the gunwale, Jason handing up the bottle-bag.

"This is pretty huge," he said at the top of the ladder. "What made you want something like this?"

"Ever since I read about Noah and the Ark I've wanted a boat I could live on. Is she a beauty?"

She fished through the live-bait well, rummaging through tools and paint, coming up with a wax-covered candle-holder; flame flared on their cheeks.

"Original mahogany," she said. "She was put together in the forties. I had to replace some of the flooring, part of the siding, that was the hardest part. She's solid now though. Seaworthy lady."

"I like it, her. Looks like you made a good choice."

They stared at each other; she nodded.

"We'll see," she said, looking around.

They sat cross-legged over the candle drinking fig wine from mason jars, Janie with a plaid blanket on her shoulders warming her hands on the flame. Soft light wavered in the recessed cabin on the built-in cot surrounding them on three sides, old wood smelling of fresh varnish. Static fidgeted on the radio with grumbles outside. She found a station with "It's A Miracle" playing and poured more wine.

"Never knew you were such a boat freak," Jason said. "Guess I never knew that part of you."

"The closest thing I've got to a calling. I'm not a college type and farming's too hard these days; daddy taught me that."

"Tell me about it," Jason said.

They stared at the candle popping.

"You'd do well in college. You were always smarter than anybody I knew."

"Yeah, but I hated classrooms. Rather apprentice with someone and learn a skill, be a master boat builder. Fill my ark with kids and sail the world."

Jason stretched opposite her leaning on his elbow.

"Sounds like fun. Let me know when you finish, maybe I'll go with you."

"Yeah?"

"I've thought about founding a mission. Wouldn't mind having a floating church."

"Don't know if I'd be any good at mission work, Jason; probably lead everyone astray. I'd captain your boat though, what would we call our mission?"

She opened the moonshine, pouring a shooter, offering it to him.

"You first," he said. "How 'bout 'The Alcoholic's Crusade.'"

"Your health," she said, drinking it, puckering and gasping, her eyes watering. She smiled blearily.

"*Yes!* Your turn."

She poured a shot and Jason downed it quickly, his mouth dropping open, eyes bugging out. He gulped fig wine. Janie giggled, patting him on the back.

"That's clear stuff isn't it?" he said hoarsely. "Think I'll stick to the wine."

"Do you really feel a calling to be a preacher or is that all bullshit?"

"No, it's not bullshit," he said, laying on his back staring at the ceiling. "Doesn't leave you, either. It's like Jeremiah with these words burning out of his soul—one way or another you're gonna say them."

"Nothing changes it?"

"It's not like I'd want it to; it's who I am."

"Since when?"

"Since I had a vision in church when I was seven or eight I guess."

"A vision?"

"I guess that's what it was. I was on the front row of the balcony just before benediction one Sunday night when the lights were dimming down, and saw this haloed face on the heads of the congregation under me."

"What sort of face?"

"It was soft-gold, peaceful, perfectly wise, looking up at me, twenty feet tall. I knew who it was. I wasn't *trying* to see Him or anything, I just saw Him there, shining out of those bowed women's hats and bald-headed men, all those believers. I heard this voice say, '*Because you have simple faith you can see Me.*' When I asked everybody later if they'd seen what I had, they laughed, like I was making it up or something, imagining it like some crazy kid, so I dropped it. If He'd done all those miracles the Bible and everyone talked about, what was so strange about that? I wondered. I knew something was up."

"Ooooo."

"What?"

"Goose bumps. Did you have simple faith then?"

"Yeah, I mean I didn't have anything to compare it to. Most kids had imaginary friends, I'd talk to Jesus."

Janie stretched out on one arm sipping her wine. They listened to the toneless rumbling.

"That's wild, Jason. Why didn't you want to go in there tonight?"

"Kind of conflicted right now. The things that happened to my family changed me, I guess. I just want to go in there and shake everybody. People believe they're righteous but they look in the wrong direction; you see it in their eyes, the way they watch you, like they're 'spies for God' or something. They don't look at Jesus, they don't look at themselves, they look at *you* to see what sins you're into. This isn't some morality contest with a book of rules and everybody's the sin police. Don't know what I'll do when I go in there."

"That's gotta be hard for someone's gonna be a preacher."

"Yeah, it'll work out though. I have faith in a purpose.

What were you doing there tonight?"

She poured the rest of the wine dripping over his glass.

"I'll never tell," she said.

Rain pattered around them, the wind making the canvas shift and stir against the bow. "Little Darlin'" played on the radio with crackling static.

"There's my imaginary friend," she said. "He shows up when it rains. I call him Rainfall."

"Hasn't been around much lately."

"Let's see if he's out here," she said, taking the wine jar. Jason followed her to the deck. "Rainfall . . . you out here? . . . *Rainfall* . . ."

The canopy of leaves around the cockpit made it feel like a floating tree house. Wind swayed shadows on the deck from the sagging sky. He could feel their presence together, the sound of the two of them like some warm euphoric music as he watched her listening into the darkness. She was the same girl he'd teased fifteen years ago because she'd seemed to know too much about him. As if they'd been together before, another time he didn't remember but she did. Thunder groaned through the floor. Gusts swished around them in the honey locust trees.

When she turned they were a foot apart with silver drops on their faces.

"Don't know where he is," she said.

"Maybe it needs to rain harder."

"That's an idea."

"Not much harder."

"Isn't the fig wine good?" she said.

He kissed her and there was a blinding-warm shock mixed with her wine breath. He was dizzy and felt a static glow around them. He forgot where he was and remembered as the wind lifted his hair. It felt like they were rising and rolling on a swell. She tossed her jar over the side, digging into his scalp with her fingers, touching his skin with her lips as she grinned.

"Want a boat ride, Mister?"

"Never understood why I picked on you so much."

"Always wondered why you *stopped*," she said, slapping his shoulder. "Why *did* you, Mr. Hawkins?"

Suddenly it was pouring and they ducked into the cabin, giggling. Feeling it beat and clatter on the portholes, washing and sweeping over the bow and roof, the canvas cover flapping like a sail. He kissed her on her back feeling the boat and candlelight rocking. Wind nudging and gusting them in the thunder. The two loose cabin doors bumping in it.

Deke woke with a gnawing feeling seeing Jason wasn't in yet. It wasn't like he had a curfew on the boy, he knew Jason could take care of himself, but it wasn't like Jason not to be in bed reading scripture by ten o'clock unless they were working late. He sat under the grape arbor guzzling Tecates listening to the National Weather Band issue tornado warnings. Choppers weren't flying tonight. The sky shuddered like a shorting light-bulb; it was dead-quiet-still.

Barrett'd collapsed after dinner and Deke didn't have the heart to wake him, though he could have used his company. He was anxious as hell and would've given anything to listen to him play, to gab, drink and cut up with him, but he had to let the poor man rest. He'd picked up Deke's slack the last week as Deke's calf healed. The quirkiness of the weather and Jason not showing made him more aware of his losses. How would he feel if he lost one of these fellas? It wasn't the kind of mood he let himself get into much. He dozed off in his lounge chair, and just before dawn was shaken by one of the loudest booms he'd ever heard, the vibration carrying underground, rolling and tremoring. The wind picked up and rain slashed sideways in it. He dragged to bed listening to hail battering the roof, clanking on the windows as he polished off his last warm beer, and was dead again.

Usually Rashan slept on the worn oriental next to Lucas March's bed, but tonight he was pressed against the wall under Lucas' mattress, whining to rouse him. When Lucas didn't stir he started to growl and yelp. Lucas sat up groggily, calming his friend as he watched the light wavering fast through the porch windows, plastic on the bare panes rattling in the stickiness. He could feel air sucking the cracks in the floor as wind whipped the corners of his shack. Hail nailed it like raining pea gravel mixed with heavier muffled thuds like fisted pine cones. Rashan was trembling looking up at him as he nuzzled under his arm. After thirty minutes the storm passed and there was a raw smell of fish as the blinds seesawed in the breeze.

When Deke woke there was a note Barrett'd hoofed out to check the seven patches a quarter-mile through the kudzu. Unless they had to carry supplies these were easier tended on foot. Jason hadn't come in yet. Deke'd give him a few more hours before he started to worry seriously.

Tornado damage was reported all over the valley, mostly small stuff, but three people were dead and a school and trailer park torn up in the next county. A mountain ten miles away looked like a surface of toothpicks and a forest fire was burning south of it. A lot of livestock had been lost. One of the haunted-looking farmers who'd lost cows called it the most peculiar blow he'd ever seen. Looking shell-shocked when a reporter asked what was different about it, he gazed into the culvert where his cows lay on top of each other and shook his head disconsolately.

Deke climbed Hawkins Mountain to survey the damage. Swarms of vultures rocked in swimming circles over the farmhouse and fields. It was hard to take them in there were so many, numbers Barrett had talked about at the back of the farm a few weeks ago. He watched them diving into the fields, snatching at shards in the high grass, around the house, barns and drive. A large shadow swung through them and he watched the manned glider wheeling up in the sun. He tried to get a serial number but the characters were whited-out or too pale to read against the glare. After a while it slid out of sight over Traggert's Mountain.

He drove down to see what the vultures were after. Trees were uprooted all over the farm, massive oaks scattered around like twigs. Debris was strewn through the pastures, shreds of corrugated tin snagged in fence lines. Near the foot of the mountain were three-finger-sized fish in the woods, trees, impaled along barbed wire fences, thousands of them in the grass.

A creepy mass of birds loitered around the pond, treating him like an intruder, their linked shadows like a partial eclipse making silent, drifting passes. The pond was white with fish, feeding turtles bobbing for them. In the fields near the house funnels of birds swirled and scrapped. He saw Jason crawl in, sitting in his jeep looking at it. They strolled through the floating shadows to the farmhouse, listening to the wind chimes.

"What *is* this?" Jason said.

Deke nuzzled a fish with his toe.

"This is bizarre."

"Pretty damn strange."

"One of those freak-of-nature things?"

"Guess so. Nice bait-saver you got to admit."

"Yeah," Jason laughed nervously, scanning the fields.

Birds lifted from the straw with their beaks straining-full.

"Been looking for a sign about what we're doing."

"Think this is it?"

"It looks like . . . *whoa* . . . don't know what this says . . ."

Deke picked up one of the rigid little fishes, working its mouth like a puppeteer. "We'll take anything we can get, little brother," the bug-eyed fish said in a mock-Cagney voice. "Stay out all night again without warning your big brother there'll be hell to pay, see. We're sendin' out Sharkey and the boys next time, the fun police. Got it fella?"

"Yeah," Jason said, squinting through the grass. "I'll be sure to notify you next time, Mr. Dead Fish in the field. Thanks for your concern."

A few days later the rains came in. Gully washers swept the dams away, the creeks and riverbanks overflowed, fields and lower clearings turned to swamps. With standing water in every bottom patch they went to work digging drainage ditches. On slopes where roots washed out they remulched a plant at a time, packing the root balls with soil mounds mixed with pea gravel. Barrett wouldn't let anyone touch this, he was the Doctor

Of Immaculate Redressing. He'd tiptoe around the patches fluffing and restoring the foliage to how they'd found it.

They worked mornings under cover of fog, in visibility so bad they might as well have been under a blanket. If a storm was brewing they'd wait for it to start to dig in. Barrett had a healthy respect for lightning in the fields, but didn't sweat it in the woods. He and Deke'd slept through monsoons in Cambodian jungle foxholes under nothing but a poncho; their odds in the woods were no worse than in the cabin, but Jason said he'd take his chances there. Deke believed he was lightning-proof; he'd been zapped years ago and was immune to it. He'd run through fields with it clapping and popping around him, howling at flashes and crackles as he did his little leprechaun lightning dance. He did it just to worry the hell out of them, Barrett said.

Having the plants watered and a cloak of weather to work under was a Godsend. The air dropped twenty degrees and fresh oxygen breathed from the wet trees and ground. They didn't dog out as fast and could get more done. Without having to burrow under weeds and briars for choppers, the work went faster, and rain cleared their footpaths, erasing their tracks. Their reservoir barrels filled up and they could drink and wash from them as they moved from patch to patch.

In steady drizzles they carried the boom box under a poncho, clowned around and played pranks on each other. It reminded Jason of when his brothers and cousins played hide-and-seek and had mud battles in the fields, danced around bonfires and washed off naked in the creeks. A few of his uncles had stills and would break out their fat acoustic guitars, yelping and buck dancing with moonshine jugs and hog-wild mountain music. The argument Deke and Barrett had over whether or not to spray with a fungicide was like tiffs he'd heard between his uncles. Barrett said there was no way they were going to poison this crop with chemicals. Deke swore the solution would wash off before the plants flowered. You don't know that, Barrett said, it's risky; *immoral.* They'd save the plants by aerating the soil, he'd done it a hundred times: *Deke wasn't poisoning this goddamn smoke.* Deke said, yeah, well, it wasn't Barrett's farm, was it? And the risk of contamination, which wasn't likely, was less important than losing his goddamn spread. It wasn't Barrett's decision, and Jason stood in the rain, thinking, a year and a half ago he was studying for the ministry and his parents ran this place. Now he was slogging through the mud with illegal plants like some horticultural fugitive while two hardheaded men squabbled over a fungicide.

They were simple outlaws when it came down to it, but he felt less guilty about it every day. Credit the plants for that, Barrett said. They were a cryptic glimmer from God's eye. *The seeds will be your medicine*, the Good Book said, then some dead-souled old white men went, yeah, and we'll put you in jail if you grow them. It was as strange that people wanted these weeds so badly as that others wanted to keep them from having them, but either way they were our birthright.

The rains had a dramatic effect on the bushes. They grew into tough little battle hardened Christmas trees overnight. Stepping into a patch they'd look around, not seeing them, look up and find these transformed beauties waving at eye-level. A deeper glowing green against the rest of the vegetation like nesting extraterrestrials. On full moons they seemed to be humming with the insects. You had a feeling they were watching and hearing you, especially if you'd taken a hit or two before coming out there; you were part of their esoteric chlorophyll communion. If enough people spent some time out there listening to them, they'd be protected by law instead of the other way around, Barrett said.

A week after the first fish storm Jason came across a field of burnt-looking snakes riding Shawnee along Mosely's southern property line. He'd crossed the Little River swollen and muddied with rain, and was hit by that reeking stench. He got up-wind fast as he could but it didn't help. They looked like black licorice sticks shining in the sun. Shawnee was spooked and wouldn't go in there. He tethered the horse at the edge of the woods and waded in. There were as many snakes as there'd been fish the other morning. The flies were as bad as the smell, a sickening effluvium you could cut with a knife. Their eyes had been hollowed out by the death birds scavenging over them. He lost his breakfast. The stink was with him when he crossed Parker's Ridge a half-mile away. He smelled it on his clothes back at the cabin and had to scrub with peppermint soap to get it out of his head.

A few days later Barrett found an accumulation of frogs on Sauter Mountain. As the moon crested he saw the small, white, piled-up bodies scattered along the slopes in the leaves, silhouettes like ghostly pin-ups in the trees. Some were pollywogs, not fully-developed frogs, and there were odd little four-toed salamanders. He followed them with his penlight over the mountain into a valley of hardwoods and laurel. They were plastered like a silver sea-bottom into the swamp on the far side of the river, thousands glistening like radioactive material in the moonlight.

A week later Deke found more fish in the tree line behind the big twelve-hundred. They were different from the first ones, flatter, nearly twice that size. The others were torpedo-shaped like saltwater scones, these looked more like gizzard or American lake shad. They'd been there a night or two from the looks of them, and he watched the birds gathering as he aerated with a hoe in a bottom patch behind Old Pete's Mountain. Riding through the boggy pass, leaving the truck at the edge of the field, he trudged into the moss-covered trees smothered with honeysuckle, the woods smelling like bream beds, the big birds leaping awkward and hump-hooded as he startled them.

There was no reason fish should've been so far from water. A few might've been dropped by birds carrying them from somewhere else, but it would've taken every bird in the state to drop these. It was like a town sized fish market had rained there. It was baffling as hell finding the rest of it too, and there was plenty of it. Every two or three days they'd come across another shitload floating in ponds, damming creeks, dangling from limbs and power lines, accumulations mud-spattered over twenty or thirty acres. At first they found one or the other, then they stumbled over a whole collection of them twisted up in clumps and piles in the leaves. Occasionally there were tiny mice and rabbits. It wasn't likely they'd crawled out there and died like that, especially the fish. Hundreds of shad on roofs of barns, corn cribs and silos, snagged along fifty-foot-high electrical cables? How'd they gotten there?

Barrett had a sixth sense about them. After a storm he'd feel them out there like some queer presence had landed. Jumping in the truck, in a few minutes he'd pick up their scent, and start walking until he came across them scattered in the mist, a few still twitching if he'd gotten there fast enough. Sometimes he'd find rotting carcasses he'd missed a day or two before, the birds showing up overnight like some frenzied vulture's convention, five- or six-hundred wings blacking the sky. Droves of dark visitors roosted in dead trees between storms waiting for another feast, gorged and half-dead-looking themselves. Shoulders hunched like parkaed football players on benches, their red-naked heads gazing down in the rain.

After his last episode in the woods, Barrett hadn't been out there stoned. He knew it was the Green Lady'd opened some door for him that morning, but he wasn't going to go stumbling back through it. He wasn't into hallucinating wild goose chases and playing grabass with his own brain in the woods. If he smoked one in the cabin he stayed put. He hadn't said anything to Deke and Jason about it, thinking maybe they'd seen some things themselves, but when he asked them about it they looked at him funny and said, like what? All right, he thought, so it's just him seeing these spirits or whatever the hell they were. Everything's hunky-dory with them. What's going on here? It wasn't like he was the only one seeing strange things here, they were all seeing fish, frogs and snakes raining from the sky, which was the only explanation they could come up with; none of them had actually seen them falling. But he was the only one seeing these smoked-up visitors, unless they were hiding it better than he was.

Whatever he was seeing and these storms had to be connected. They were too goddamn aberrant to be going on at the same time and have nothing to do with each other. If he'd been straight that morning maybe he'd have found all those frogs in the woods, but he wouldn't've been chasing leaf-tied apparitions all over the place, he was pretty sure of that. The Green Lady's machinations. If he toked one in the cabin with lights and TV on he didn't see anything. He'd had some weird as hell dreams, surreal, bright-lit yellow scenes with Vietnamese faces in them. There was a super real feeling to them, as if he could touch and smell the people in the cabin. He bolted awake three times one night, dead-sure Vietnamese farmers were standing there by him, men, women and children, elderly huddled around him as if they were in some over lit hospital room. He sat in the dark wide-awake, listening to the sounds around the cabin, a screech owl circling them for hours.

He hoped he wasn't turning into some nerve-wracked wimp in his middle years. One of those pitiful, delusional druggies you saw grabbing at phantom butterflies in the streets. He'd heard of guys having post-traumatic stress ten, fifteen years after coming back from over there. He'd paid his dues with that head-stuff, and smoke'd been the remedy for it. When Deke saw he wasn't burning his usual before heading into the woods he questioned him about it. What's wrong, Rasta man? Kimasabe couldn't handle the Spiritchaser anymore? Barrett said he was clearing his head to be better focused on the plants. Sure he was, Deke said, since when did he need his head cleared to do anything? Witch Doctor worked better stoned than most people did straight. It made Deke nervous hearing him talk like that.

One night Barrett had a vivid dream about the fish they were finding. They needed to collect them in burlap sacks for fertilizer, he said, like no one had thought of it before. He sliced thin holes in the soil a foot from the plants with a shovel or posthole digger, mashing handfuls of the stiff little things into the root tips. To keep raccoons and other varmints from digging them up, he wrapped the plants with chicken wire pegged-down in a yard radius around the trunks. The instructions were in his dream. He covered the wire with leaves and straw and set decoy fish piles outside the patches to distract scavengers—there was plenty to go around. The fish-fed bushes took off like Jack's beanstalk, like some extra hormone gave them a female hard-on. They were more fragrant, sturdier, more resistant to insects. They hauled truckloads of fish to the patches, treating all of them with the heavenly emulsion, getting nitrogen-deep-green bursts from the crop in a day or two. The Good Lord's miracle-gro was falling in their laps, it seemed.

When the raining stuff was fit to eat they gathered it in sacks to freeze. The frog legs Barrett'd brought back in the truck that morning were as eatable as the pond ones. It was all okay if they got to it fast enough. Deke pulled his mother's uprights out of dry-dock and loaded them with fish under the main sheds. He rebuilt compressors of two ancient Frigidaire freezers that'd been his grandmother's, in a few weeks they had frog legs and mini-fish filets coming out of their ears. They were eating like kings with fresh garden tomatoes, cucumbers and beans, greens, okra, red bell peppers and butternut squash, watermelons and honeydews. They planted guerrilla-style so that man-mad patterns wouldn't be seen from the sky. Barrett concocted a mean frog leg spaghetti with onions, fried green tomatoes with basil and zucchini, wild cilantro salsa. Deke grilled mesquite fish under the grape arbor that was overgrown with new grapes. They drank the tart fig and elderberry wines from Janie's moonshiner, and Jason baked ginger apple cobbler from his mother's fruit trees.

The crop was on schedule and the work was letting up. There was plenty to do, the bulk of it really, but for the time being they could let the ladies go on their own. Now came the real test, the hardest part: watching the crop, and waiting for it.

Jason spent his free days with Janie. They saw a rodeo and horse show in Lebanon and a boat show on Center Hill Lake. They spent a day at a county fair in Crossville where she won him a stuffed orange brontosaurus pitching baseballs. They spent days picnicking and skinny-dipping at a secluded place on the Cumberland River. There was a waterfall that plunged seventy feet giving them a hard-pounding shower, a spa-like foaming bowl sliced into the falls they could climb up in cooling off from the heat, sipping wine. There was an overhang beneath the falls they crawled into, dozing on a quilt after making love with the echoing sound of water slapping the rocks. They hiked a half-mile upriver to the cable put up by the power company where a pulley was attached to a double seat they could ride back and forth on above the river, watching the sun sink into the fog and trees.

June was steamy and hot. Dry days they worked on her boat adding coats of paint, doing final touches, rebuilding the platform and rub rails. They had a joke about her first mate and her mating rituals with him. He had to earn his mating rights on a daily basis. After knocking off for a swim they'd catch a movie or pick up pizza or Chinese and spend the night on her boat watching old flicks on her thirteen inch black-and-white, eating Jiffy Pop from a hotplate. They talked about God and Jesus and Janie got him to read his favorite scriptures. He confessed his first orgasms had brought him closer to God. It was the kind of thing people shamed in children, but since Jesus said children were innocent how could they be judged for their sexual sensations? As he'd shinnied up that swing pole in the churchyard after service one night, the pleasure trickling into his genitals, he'd thanked God for it, and gone back to it again and again. He didn't know what it was, but he didn't need to be told if it was good or bad. He knew what the preacher meant by "your blessings overflowing."

They talked about God mixed with man in the person of Jesus and how he'd wept for Lazarus, in the next minute raising him from the dead. She liked when Jesus got ticked at the disciples for waking Him in the storm at sea, calming the waters, walking on them testing their faith by daring them to walk to Him.

She wondered why so many people rejected Him. *Pride*, Jason said. People didn't want to give up that much, and if they did they became puffed up because they were in The Country Club Of The Chosen Few. They believed they were better than their neighbors, judged them and played God themselves. When people saw these hypocrites they bolted for the hills. It was hard to watch "Christians" twist His words around like a slinky to justify their prejudices and vindictiveness. Some didn't like themselves either, she said. *I'll pass on that eternal life you got there; I don't want any of that fulfillingness stuff. Stick your peace and abundance, buddy, I'd rather be lost and stumbling around in the dark like some fatheaded fool.* She wondered if she would've had faith enough to walk to Him that night on the Sea of Galilee. Jason said he'd had dreams about that after his father died, like he was stepping off a cliff in a road-runner cartoon. He'd start to sink and wake up thrashing like Wylie Coyote before hitting the ground with the anvil flattening him. She liked the lusty business in *Proverbs* about going to the "strange woman." For all you knew there was no such thing as a "strange man." Who stoned the adulterous man? You never heard about that although female-stoning was a popular sport in those days. The secret to being a successful wife was outstranging the strange woman. If you didn't want her horning in on your man, you made damn sure you were stranger than she was.

After midnight they'd swim at a deserted beach down the road, kick out to the wooden raft watching the moon on the mountain water, and tell childhood and family stories. She never brought up his father's suicide, and when he did she'd get moist palms and clam up. He could see it hurt her too much and she didn't know what to say. She worried about corrupting him. He was Mr. Purity, all right, she'd be sorry when she botched up his rookie sainthood. He felt guilty being so happy with her, as if he didn't deserve it, as if he was supposed to remain miserable because his father had suffered and died like that. But Jesus had suffered and died for him too. Being with her gave him the eerily bittersweet feeling of the Holy Spirit shuffling things around, compensating him whether he liked it or not.

When Deke saw his brother was getting serious, he and Barrett sat down to have a talk with him. Knowing Jason would want to confide in his girl, Deke had to let him know why he couldn't. Letting anyone know you had a pot crop was how most of them were busted or stolen. People didn't realize it was critical to keep their mouths shut, and before you knew it all manner of zealots and thieves were breathing down your neck. The rule was simple: you didn't tell a soul. There was a bona fide fortune sitting out there, and plenty of self-righteous fools believing they could be moral heroes by stomping out some "devil's weed." The devil showed up, all right, once they found out about it. Trust aside, telling her made her an accomplice, and Jason didn't want that. He might as well wrap a weight around her neck and ask her to swim with it. Even if she was willing to help them, it was selfish to let her, dangerous for her, and could get them all killed.

So he had to lie to her, he thought; until the crop was harvested, cured and sold he couldn't bring her out to the farm. He didn't have much choice. He trusted her, but it was her he needed to protect like Deke said. He'd pick her up in town, and when she mentioned driving to him he made up another excuse to go to her, an errand to run on the way. Little lies were becoming second nature—*that* was a nice development. He couldn't tell her about it and she was involved anyway. That was great. He knew she sensed something—she was a woman after all—but figuring it his personal business, he hoped she wouldn't ask for a while.

On his way in he'd drop by the Holiness Lighthouse Church as usual and sit in the parking lot, listening to the voices drift out through the open doors if there was a service on. Watching the people file in, he'd slip away before they started out again.

Once a week Barrett declared a meeting of the Midnight Growers Club. They'd get a little stewed, cook up some exotic dish and play poker for nickels. They watched baseball and smoked Cuban-seeded cigars Barrett'd brought back from Costa Rica. Barrett and Deke told war stories if they were loose enough, and they'd hash out the crop and the latest abnormal storms. Deke said maybe there was something wrong that these critters didn't rain all the time. In a perfect world maybe the wild stuff fell in every storm for food, fertilizer, general repopulation. We viewed them as a "freak of nature" because we'd screwed up our environment, but in the Garden of Eden that's the way it was, the sublime state of things. I see, Barrett said, chuckling as he rolled one. You don't get the service you used to get from the friendly skies. In the old days you built a fire and hoped something good was on the menu, hustled out after a downpour and raked up a feast of fish or foul. He was sure that's the way it was. *The wise one had spoken! Deke was his goddamn prophet now, the Hawk man!* he said, holding his stomach laughing tears. *The Enlightened One Of The Flesh eating Pot fields!* Only the Hawk man could come up with that off-the-wall crazy theory. Deke needed to take some more hits from the Chaser to be sure his psychic telemeter was fully receptive to that shit, Barrett said, bowing as he handed him the smoking spliff.

Once or twice a night they were warned by the scanner and blacked-out for flyovers. They tried charting chopper patterns from what they learned on the radio, aircraft vectors crossing the farm, busts they picked up on or read about in the papers, but found the rotorheads would pop in from anywhere day or night. There was one scheduled crossing every night over Traggert's Mountain at ten o'clock. They'd hear a couple of crop confiscations a week on average. The heinous criminals usually elderly folk with loans out the ying-yang who'd had a few dismal years and were making a last-ditch effort to stay alive, cultivating a barn full of cannabis under halides or growing a crop between their corn rows. They'd see white-haired old people being stuffed into sheriff's and DEA vehicles in handcuffs on the nightly news. Deke and Jason knew most of the families, had grown up or gone to school and church with their kids. Along with this would be another report of some dispossessed farmer blowing his head off, followed by Nancy Reagan reading a letter from a ten-year-old heroin addict. Don't do drugs unless they're our drugs, Barrett said. Either Nancy and Ronnie didn't know they were the problem or believed they were fooling somebody. People ate up that sappy stuff with a spoon though. Deke couldn't bare to hear their voices for thirty seconds. Listening to either of them was like having his teeth drilled without Novocain.

One night they heard a chopper go down twelve miles east in the middle of what sounded like intensified combing. Suddenly there were whirlers swarming wide perimeters as they crouched in the dark listening to war-tones and the continuous rumbling back over the cabin. The crash was reported as some unknown mechanical failure, and a few days later a lightning fire burned thousands of acres in the same location. The networks showed planes and rotorheads dropping flame retardants on it from Jasper Air Force Base. The military said spilled fuel from the chopper had ignited in an electrical storm that hit the area a day or two after the crash.

On full moons they played homerun derby in a field with a metal bat and Deke's bucket of ragged balls. The Braves on the boom box for background, announcer and crowd and organ music echoing into the cornfields with the chatter of cicadas and whippoorwills. Homeruns were a dollar each charged to the pitcher. Usually it came down to Deke's snake ball and Barrett's big stick with Barrett driving his second and third buckets into the trees.

An hour or two a night Barrett played his guitar as they worked up blues tunes. He played slide with a socket wrench or half-inch pipe, sometimes an old butter knife or thin glass jar. He liked John Lee Hooker's chicken-talk-picking, snapping and popping the strings against the neck and frets with his bare fingers. He liked to make the flat-top scratch and squawk, bending the hell out of the strings, scat-singing with it. He had an old dobro he'd pull out for a change and they'd get slaphappy, singing off tensions built up babysitting the crop around the clock. Barrett called himself "Hardcoat Watson." Deke was "Stingray Hooper;" Jason "Jaywalk Hutchins." They taped themselves on the boom box and had offbeat originals that were different every time they played them. When they coaxed Jason into taking a few hits from the Chaser his lyrics put theirs to shame. Barrett swore Jason was a reincarnated blues man, which was why the Holy Spirit was working so strong through him this go-round. It was where his real prophecy came from; he'd passed the blues pain and paid his dues for redemption. After Jason ran in to see Janie, the two of them rode out to visit the plants, lay hands on them and rub their faces on them. Barrett sang Bob Marley, and they stumbled through them laughing their asses off, flopping on their backs in the fresh dew with cold beers, howling at the moon and squadrons of Fighting Falcons shaking down the night air. They'd talk about their women and what they'd do after the crop was sold. Deke said they should run down to Belize to check out the competition. Barrett said he was spending a week in bed with his girl before he did any damn thing, then he'd see about it.

Barrett dropped in on Lucas March to get him high and pick for him. They listened to Lucas' old records and talked about the artists, which had humped which and who'd stolen the most from the others. He picked some tunes Lucas hadn't heard, obscure delta stuff Barrett'd picked up on Mississippi tenant farmers' porches, and they talked about their best people, Little Walter, John Lee Hooker, Mckinley Morganfield, Blind Lemon Mellon, Elmore James. Their favorite Tennessee man was "Sonny Boy" Williamson, "Memphis" Minnie was their girl. They listened to Ellington and Mingus and Trane too, Roland Kirk. Lucas defied Barrett to come up with one white man who could play or sing as well as a black one. When Barrett played cuts of a Texas blues kid named Stevie Ray Vaughn, Lucas admitted there might be one mismatched soul out there. When he played Tony Joe White doing "Did Somebody Make A Fool Out Of You?" Lucas admitted the white boy had snakes in his guitar, but swore somebody'd jumped the fence in his bloodline. No certified white man could play like that, he said.

Restless nights Barrett rode his Harley into the mountains looking for honky tonk music. He didn't care what it was as long as their hearts were in it. He stumbled across a hot blues joint in the middle of nowhere, a veritable oasis called *The Fever* where he sat in a couple of nights with the house band. They had a white harp player as raw as anyone he'd heard who'd worked with Muddy in the seventies. A freckle-faced mulatto waitress took some interest, and he had a brief fling with her, but when her husband she hadn't mentioned showed up one night fresh out of prison, he was a little relieved and didn't go back. He had somebody else on his mind anyway. After he and Deke'd lectured Jason about his woman, Barrett didn't need some green-eyed, thirsty-for-blood ex-con tracking him back to the Hawkins place. He'd drink a few cold ones and ride at night, wringing his nerves. The speed and mountain chlorophyll cleared his head and helped him sleep better.

On back roads some nights he'd get a head full of somebody else's indicus plants. It was that or a skunk giving off, but he could tell the difference. There was nothing quite like that stinkweed smell. He could've parked his bike and hiked in in fifteen minutes, slipped back in October and snatched them before the owners did, but stealing cannabis made you no different than any other thief. It was breaking into a man's house, stealing food from his table, taking shoes off his children's feet. The best way to know something would go wrong with your own was to take somebody else's: something would *always* get you. He believed in working hard, living clean, respecting another man's sweat and property. It was what his daddy'd taught him, and he'd never wavered from it.

He felt good about the crop so far, visualizing it to fruition in his head: sticky bundles of sagging colas strung up in bundles in the barns. There was nothing quite so beautiful in the physical world, except a woman's bare derriere. He told Deke he wouldn't take a third share this season, it wasn't right when they were under the gun like this. They'd firm up with the banks and next year he'd see about it. He was going to make some good money anyway from the looks of things.

He couldn't stop wondering what'd happened to him in the woods a few weeks ago. He'd tried to blow off both incidents to being blitzed-high, but his chemical state didn't explain what he'd chased through the fog that morning. It was like something bewildering you'd done drunk at a party, remembering only enough later to know you'd probably done more. He was still having Technicolor dreams with Vietnamese people in them; not nightmares exactly, but he couldn't shake them either. He guessed certain spirits kept showing up in your head as long as the brain could conjure them. Who knew why these mystery faces stalked you all your life, like a tireless parade of itinerant ghosts: long-dead enemies, forgotten lovers, a stranger you'd glimpsed in a crowd twenty years ago. God only knew what they wanted and why they hung around you. You were finished with them maybe, but maybe they weren't done with you yet.

He'd noticed the ravaging little bugs on a few plants the week before. Tiny red specks so minute you had to squint at them to be sure they moved. Spider mites lived in his nightmares with fungus, root-rot and lightning fires. He'd brewed up twenty gallons of a special organic insecticide from chrysanthemums, garlic cloves and marigolds, that wouldn't kill the little bastards but would make them so stomach-sick they couldn't do any damage. You could safely smoke the flowers after putting it on them, and all traces of it disappeared in a week or so. After Barrett'd proved his point with the fungicide Deke trusted him with this solution, but if it didn't work he'd want to use some lung-lethal poison. Deke'd say odds were no one would get hurt, but Barrett'd promised to walk if he sprayed malathion or anything like it on their crop. They shouldn't use anything they wouldn't let their own mothers breathe. If they saved the farm selling a poisoned crop they'd lose it anyway. He was trying to teach Deke about karma and looking after their customers; you know, those blindly trusting saps who were saving his unappreciative ass by buying his wares? He'd seen his organic juice knock them down pretty well. It would do the job.

He carried a notebook with maps to mark bugged patches, a magnifying glass so he didn't miss a spider, four two-gallon hand-pump sprayers of the solution, and two five-gallon containers to refill them. He'd treat every patch whether there were bugs or not, drenching the leaves and trunks top to bottom. He packed a lunch, filled the igloo with water, and rolled out at first light, leaving Deke and Jason to cook up another batch.

After treating a fourth of the patches he was about to run out with an hour of daylight left. The good news was, only one in six patches had bugs and they'd caught them early enough. He wore a towel round his neck tucked into his t-shirt, pausing now and then to wring them out. Soaked with the pest-sickener, flies and gnats didn't bother him. He was working on a patch that had been a pear orchard, remnants of trees scattered along a valley about the size of a football field, where they'd sculpted and notched plants into the tree line and sprinkled them in the open twenty yards apart. After finding spiders and whiteflies on a few plants he'd jogged back to the truck to refill his canteen and grab an apple. Looking for his penlight he came across two joints in the glove box wrapped in foil. Deke must've left them. It was their pinchings, it had that unmistakable spicy smell. He stared at them, rewrapped and tossed them in the glove box, stuck his penlight in his pocket, clenching an apple in his teeth, over-flowed the canteen and jogged back to the field.

He had butterflies as he crunched along, a queasy throat-thick rush. Blue jays haggled in the trees. Insects chattered and birds seemed noisier. The crunch of his feet sounded like someone walking with him, he froze a minute listening to the cicadas building with that circular-winding, sawing sound. They *were* getting louder, it wasn't his imagination. His pulse had bumped up and he had that head-buzz he got from sugar-lows, but he wasn't that hungry. All he'd done was hold the damn joints in his hand, it'd be a hell of a feat to get contact high from that, wouldn't it?

He looked back to the truck bathed in five or six shades of green, daylight fading with that soft-yellow glow that seemed to radiate from the leaves. Everything seemed to hang in the air this time of day as if your whole life was cradled in it.

He thought about the first girl he'd had sex with. He'd met her in the woods this time of day when he was fourteen. She was childishly game and he remembered his pulse bumping through his chest and the butterflies when he went out to see her, his anticipation of a fragrant-raw female with unknown gifts and secrets she wasn't even aware of. Waiting in the shadows with the bugs revving, hearing that light treading-crackling down the bank as she came to him, that innocent little whistle that would stiffen him like the throbbing trees. There was something so nasty-delicious about what she'd do and show him, a primally forbidden, girlhood fever, and the woods held a female mystique for him ever since, especially the Vietnamese jungles. They were beautiful, mysterious, treacherous and deadly. An imaginary woman waited for you every time you went into them, sometimes a real one carrying an AK-47, smelling of sex, birth, death, eternity.

The morning he'd found those frogs his imagination had gotten the best of him. He'd hallucinated into panic overdrive. He didn't know what'd happened, maybe he never would, but the woods had been his home as long as he could remember. How many times had he laid out here buzzing his brains out, thanking God he was alive? He'd be damned if he'd let some crazy phobia take hold of him because of some silly hallucinations.

He jogged back to the truck. The insects were whirring up like a buzz saw. He stuck the foil-wrapper and lighter in his pocket and headed back to the field with a little of that excitement he got every time he met Doris Greenwell. He had no idea what'd happened to him in the fog that morning, but he wasn't going to dwell on it anymore. He'd prove there was nothing going on here. If he'd seen Vietnamese soldiers out here, let's see them again, he thought.

There was light from a waning half-moon and the pearl-clouded sky. He could taste the moisture from the trees as he carried the pump-cans and canteen up the sloping trail, finding a clearing knobbed with car-sized rocks, climbing the largest lichen-covered one looking down on the field. Guzzling from his canteen, he tossed it on the ground by the spray-cans. As he lit the joint he heard shrieks. A hawk was having it out with five or six martins overhead, the predator turning and reversing, drifting and lumbering as the smaller attackers circled and dived around him. He watched them and felt the relaxed, launched entry into the smoke, the body-high, deep intensification into the noises, elements and smells. God, it felt good, that pure rush-sensation. That sweet-fucking immersion as she crawled over you with her hair draped in your face like a silk blanket. The smell in the air was musk-warm like a fertile vagina. He unsnapped his fatigues, and using saliva masturbated with the syncopated woods sounds, feeling Marsha there with him, talking to her. When he finished he wiped his hand on the rock and lay back listening to the crickets. They were high-thin bells under the brilliant-ratcheting cicadas. He felt fine, relaxed, tired as hell. He was at a circus with his pop when he dozed off, watching the lion show with the fiery hoops, eating cotton candy from a paper cone.

He woke with something lapping at his side, tongue-like nipping at his skin. Jerking up he held his shirt bottom flapping in the breeze. A strong wind was gusting over the mountains, rushing, rattling in the trees. The moon was bright-orange at ten o'clock behind some deep-purple clouds beside its companion star. There were faint flashes and rumblings from the west. He was tight and sore as hell from working, then napping up on this uneven rock.

He saw something down in the field. First a few, two at once, then several more luminous figures stirring around. They were bent-over as if they were crawling. He saw a dozen or so, then a couple more, children mixed with men and women. He could tell what they were by their sizes and dress, the way their figures plodded and crept or skipped ahead. Finally twenty or so were scattered along the long, yellow field, but he couldn't make out all of it. From that distance in the filtered light they looked like Vietnamese farmers working a rice paddy. He realized whether he was seeing them or not, this was the third time he *believed* he was seeing something like this.

His next thought was that he couldn't be alive or awake. This had to be happening somewhere else. Be ready to be dead, or what maybe? Was he dreaming he was in-country again? If he wasn't alive, why would he be seeing this? Why would he be seeing it anyway? He felt his body, legs and hands, the tears in both knees from walking on them in the grass, his shirt sweat-starched. The canteen and spray-cans reflected in the weeds.

He rose to a squat on top of the rock and he was there, all right, sore in his legs, buttocks and back, disoriented from waking up here in the first place, not completely awake yet. He was buzzing-high. His back hair itched. He scratched it as he looked down at this. Every now and then a figure bobbed up and stepped forward, bending over again. Smaller figures flitted up the field. This was too fucking bizarre. There was a bed of mist down there; none at all where he was with the wind sifting through the trees.

He slid off his rock, keeping his eyes on the figures, scooped the cans and shuffled down the pebbly grade, short-stepping, ducking limbs and vines. He tripped on a raised root, skidding on his hands and knees, got up and kept galloping down without taking his eyes off the bright field he could see in snatches through the trees. The moon glittered on the red trail. He sucked something into his throat, snagging it on his windpipe choking on it, gagging-coughing trying to hack it up, clawing at it with his fingers. The clenching made him retch and he vomited it on the ground, something sour. A large winged beetle wriggled on its back in the moonlight. *Goddamit*, he thought.

He kept going down, at the bottom in a dried branch sliding to a stop. The field was blanketed with more mist than he'd seen from up there; white with it. He crouched, looking for the bent-over figures. There were sinewy lines of trees, winding paths, it was damned eerie-looking, but there was no one out there. He picked a blade from his teeth, a reed-like piece of wing, blinking at it. Fireflies swung up in circles on the breeze. When the moon slipped behind the clouds everything went black again.

He listened to a pack of dogs howling in the distance. What just happened? He wasn't chasing anyone through these goddamn woods tonight. He stood stock-still, listening, took out his penlight and pressed through the brittle straw with the spray cans clanking. The vapor dissipated like smoke after a fireworks show. He crossed and recrossed his paths over every inch of the field on his knees, and every imprint was his. A winged shadow drifted through him like a spear. That old hawk was swinging around the field against the moon, hunting and rocking against it. Once it came back carrying a snake in its claws, its silhouette wriggling against the clouds; he heard its batting wing-beats. Suddenly there were ladybugs everywhere, swarms of them landing on tips of straw grass, dotting it like snow in the moonlight. He'd never seen anything like it before. Maybe the juice had drawn ladybugs instead of repelled them. Every now and then the hawk drifted back empty-clawed, its shadow wrinkling down the trampled grass.

He guessed he was seeing them for a reason now, that he wasn't losing his mind. Maybe he wasn't. When he heard the dogs picking up his scent he decided to get back to the truck. He could think this out just as well without getting his ass chewed off. But he almost stood there too long, listening to the yelps getting louder. They were almost on him by the time he got in the truck, rolled the windows, and saw the six sets of glowing eyes circling him in the trees.

At the cabin he downed a half-quart of Cuervo to steady his nerves. He ate Deke's fish kabobs and listened to them prattle on about some farm news. Hunger gave him an excuse not to talk, but he thought he was going to lose it if they didn't shut the fuck up. He couldn't make himself speak. He was seeing Vietnamese people out there, did he know that? Was he gonna tell them that? That'd go over beautifully. He knew what he'd just seen had to be written all over him, which made him want to say anything to distract them from it, but he couldn't get the damn words out, about the weather, the plants, the goddamn mites. Who cared about spiders when he was seeing *this* shit out there? He knew if he had to talk about anything else for five minutes he'd lose his fucking mind.

Staring at the TV, he kept stumbling outside for air. When Deke asked what was eating at him he nearly blurted it out, then thought, are you out of your mind? He'd shot his wad and hit the wall, he said. His eyes looked weak, Jason said, peaked like he was coming down with something. Maybe he'd gotten a little heat-exhaustion out there, he felt dehydrated. He was taking four aspirin and turning in.

He covered his head with pillows to muffle the television, but he couldn't have slept anyway, he was too wired. When he drifted off occasionally he felt these people around him. Their silhouettes floated against the changed ceiling. After a while there was a roomful of them and he wasn't sure if he was awake or not. Farmers with children stood by his bed. There were looks in the old peoples' sun-wrinkled faces, glints from the corners of their eyes, flashes of children smirking at him as if he and they were in on some joke. They *knew* him. He spent the whole night asking how, where from? Had he wasted some of these people in firefights, on military missions? They looked at him like he knew, inscrutably, with wry, conspiratorial looks. There was one young woman who was devastatingly pretty, who was she? The Green Lady, he kept thinking. She was doing all this. He sat up in the dark, listening as he'd done a lot lately, the brothers snoring quietly in the next room. He was physically there with them, but what in God's name was happening to him? He was alone with these "visitors." He could tell Deke and Jason whatever he wanted to, pour it out to them right now, but then what? Maybe he was twice as alone.

He woke at first light and tried not to rouse them. He had a dull groggy headache, and felt like he'd been running full-throttle all night, but he couldn't lay there anymore. He took a Goodies powder, made a thermos of coffee, and while they slept put five tins of mustard sardines, a box of soda crackers and three apples in his tool bag, went out and found the fresh bug-sickener and refilled the dew-covered spray-cans under the grape arbor. He was going back out there. He couldn't be paralyzed by this even if it was the spookiest shit he'd ever seen. Not knowing *why* it was happening worried him more than whatever it was. If you walked around a problem and examined it, exposed and demystified it, it couldn't hurt you nearly as much as it could if you hid from it. The sleep of reason produces monsters, a man said, and he liked to avoid those fellas.

It was sure as hell something. He was sure the smoke was bringing it now, the Spiritchaser was a vehicle or had become one. These fish, frog and snake storms weren't coincidental, they were falling from the same atmospheric juice as the plants themselves, and linked to them. Something was being let out of the bag here. He hadn't wanted to know what, to tell the truth. The morning he found those frogs he knew something was up, but hadn't wanted to let Deke and Jason in on it, his way of keeping it under a lid. He wouldn't acknowledge any omens in case he got a bad one. While the storms and whatever he was seeing gnawed at him, he'd played dumb and tried to hide it, which was stupid as hell. He knew better. You had to follow your gut regardless of how ridiculous it seemed or what you had to do because of it. If this crop was life and death for the brothers, finding out what was going on might be what saved it, and their asses with it.

He drove back to the field where he'd seen the figures the night before, sniffing and listening for dogs. They were long gone, no doubt, but he'd spent a sleepless night up a tree a few years ago over a pack of rabid mongrels, so he carried his nickel-plated .38 just in case. He smelled the garlic as he came up on the grass, with his glasses picking out plants dripping in the morning sun. They were covered with some kind of specks. He saw them in the grass at a distance, in the foreground at his feet, white down floating over the field like dandelion seeds. He followed his trails through the grass from the night before, checking patches, shaking feathers from leaves. They were only in the field that he could see. Maybe there'd been a storm with birds and some other animals had devoured them, the dogs maybe. Where the hell were the carcasses? There should've been more than feathers if that'd happened, smears of blood or something. On the plants where he'd found bugs the night before there weren't any. With his magnifying glass he pored over stems and leaves that'd been smothered with mites and didn't find a spider. The swarms of ladybugs might've taken care of the mites, but where were the ladybugs? The plants were clean as a whistle. He stood there a while mesmerized, listening to the hardwoods creaking, watching the down attaching itself to his skin and clothes.

He hiked up the trail he'd taken the night before, coming across the beetle he'd almost choked on on its back buried in ants. So *it* was real. He climbed to the rock he'd napped on, crouching on it, looking down at the field as he had the night before. Wind parted the yellow grass like a picked-over cotton patch, waves of feathers lifting in the breeze. All right, what did he think was going to happen here? He was head-straight for one thing. It was a bright-clear, sunny day. Something had changed it though, God only knew what. He'd keep his ears and eyes open, do his work and try not to obsess over this.

At noon he lunched by the Little River watching a swarm of vultures feed over Mosely's wetlands. Several-hundred birds circled in a wide-ranging funnel. It was a cinch they weren't dog fighting over a single piece of meat out there. Feeling rank and sick of smelling himself, he bathed in the clear cold river, scrubbing with sand and sage leaves. He rinsed yesterday's work clothes he'd slept in, drying them in the sun. As he floated in a pool, resting with his eyes shut, three choppers thrummed fast overhead, wind milling blades down washing through the trees. He didn't believe they'd seen him under the leaning cypresses. His clothes were camou and the kudzu-covered truck was well-hidden in weeds and honeysuckle. He slid under brush, watching for moccasins, listening to the turbos roaring across the front of the farm. They were getting more earnest now, coming in triangles instead of pairs. You felt the searching intensify as plants reached visible tree-size the past few weeks. There'd been a rash of major busts. It was always like this heading into July, everything heated up and began to boil. It was when the tedious, backbreaking spacing-out of plants in the spring paid off, and you thanked God you'd had the sense to do it.

He emptied his insecticide near the old slave quarters at the back of the farm. Hundreds of acres of pines were planted back here for pulpwood. A straight dirt road cut through the perfect tall tree-rows from the dilapidated shacks slammed full of junk and useless, rusted equipment. The woods reeked of decaying fish as he sprayed the little patches disguised between stands of smaller pine seedlings.

He parked the truck in the forest alley, took a joint from the glove box and sat on the tailgate. Eighty yards down the road a herd of raccoons scampered across it, dragging something in their mouths. He lit the joint and toked it. The air sizzled with sounds. The darkness was electric and buzzing. He started to giggle, happy but nervous, drinking until his stomach felt like a water bag as he waited, leaning back in the bed now and then to watch a meteorite blink into the darkness. There were sporadic woods sounds, but he didn't see anything. He heard rustling in the straw. As his eyes adjusted he could see flying squirrels diving and soaring down the narrow tree-corridor against the sky. He listened to them scratching and chattering as they climbed and landed on the brittle pine bark.

After an hour he decided to head back to the cabin. Nothing was going to happen here, this was it. He could wait all night, but his chow was gone and he was getting lunchy, especially with his belly so waterlogged. Now he was trying to see them he never would, he thought.

He slammed the tailgate and started up, listening to Little Feat's "Feets Don't Fail Me Now." Going down the flat narrow road his headlights caught a straggled group of figures walking ahead of him. They were as bright as the reflection on the trees and didn't turn to face or seem to notice him. He stopped the truck and cut the music; watching them less than a hundred yards ahead. Barefoot or sandaled, wearing conical hats and faded rags, they carried baskets on bamboo poles. There were a half-dozen children, maybe more. They kind of darted in and out of each other. A few adults were stooped over, one very feeble-looking man hobbled on a cane to the side.

He cut his lights and slid out of the truck, leaving the door ajar. The road was black except for starlight shaded through the trail in the sky. The figures were dully-luminous, like the ones he'd seen the night before. He called to them, his voice sounding hollow in the darkness. The insects became suddenly shrill. The figures seemed oblivious to him. He didn't want to move and kept his eyes on them. He could feel himself shaking. Shaking like he'd stumbled into some phantasmic, other world reality. Shaking like his brain could barely contain this. It's a trance, he thought. I'm stoned as hell, but they're there, goddamit. He called out in Vietnamese. *Ban dang lam gi o day? What are you doing here? Why've you come to this province?* They ambled along steadily, hobbling away without turning. He kept calling to them as he watched them getting smaller in the distance. He was straining to make them out against the double lines of receding dirt tracks.

He jumped in the truck and hit the headlights. They weren't in the beams. There was a bend a few-hundred yards down the road, he knew, just before it dipped and started to roll back up. He started again, watching the fartherest point at the end of the lights. They were flooded with moths suddenly. They filled the road ahead, beating toward him in frantic, black, swarming waves, whacking and blanketing the glass. There were so many they made an obstructing cloud in his beams. A few flew in his face he swatted. He should've been on them in a few seconds. He ducked and moved to the center of the windshield trying to see through this mass of black, flailing things. He crept around the wide turn, stopping a few times, cutting his lights and engine. Where the hell were they? He should've been on them way back there. His right eye quivered again; his shaking hands were soaked. Moths stuck to the windshield, flapped and hung to the seat as he swiped them from his arms, listening to the flying squirrels scratching and chattering. It was ink-dark again and he could barely make out the lines of trees. He sat for a while listening, watching up and down the road. He didn't see another movement on it, or anything at all.

At the cabin there was a note from Deke they'd run in to see their mother at the nursing home. There was baked lasagna in the fridge with fresh antipasto, banana pudding. Jason was staying the night with Janie, Deke was hanging in town to catch a movie, having a few beers, seeing if he couldn't get into serious trouble. Just kidding, he said, the Low Rider was a well-behaved dog. He was on Barrett's Harley and would be back by midnight or one at the latest.

Barrett went to work rolling as many joints as he had pinchings. His hands trembled, he had a hell of a time steadying them. He scissored the tiny buds on a wooden cutting board, filling the bowl with gummy sticks as his mind kept dragging him in opposite directions. *This couldn't be happening. But it was. It was happening. But it couldn't be. But it was. But it couldn't. It was, goddamit.* He felt like a child who'd stumbled into some miraculous place or time warp no one would believe. Who would believe this unless they'd seen it with their own eyes, unless they'd been with him tonight? Would they've seen it if they had? Who knows? He knew Deke and Jason hadn't seen this, they were behaving too normally. He'd seen it three times and wasn't sure if he believed it himself, but he was still a nervous wreck. Watching the eleven o'clock news he'd blurt out every few seconds, *yes, all right*, he'd seen them again, what was he supposed to do about it? Was there a reason for it? If he kept going out there maybe he'd figure out what it was.

They carried pictures of Qadaffi's U.S.-bombed compound back in April. The French President was quoted saying he didn't think you stopped terrorism by killing 150 Libyans who hadn't done anything. Barrett didn't know about that. If you killed enough kids you were bound to hit a terrorist eventually, or maybe keep a few kids from turning into them. Reagan didn't seem like such a bad egg, he was just a big-headed white gangster with more toys than any other gangster in the world. Gangsters made fine presidents because they were good at beating up other country's gangsters. Libya's gangster didn't stand a chance with our gangster, he'd always get his ass burned.

Deke wasn't too keen on old Ray-Gun. In Deke's place he would've probably felt the same. It wasn't that he didn't agree with Deke, it was just that since the Kennedys he'd never trusted any of these dead old white men in their liar's suits. They'd all seemed the same to him, out for their own little club and no one else, except maybe Jimmy. He'd never been one to blame a man for his blindnesses, and this old fool couldn't see shit in a handbag with a microscope. They were talking about preparations for the Liberty Fourth of July weekend Reagan was hosting in New York harbor. A big gala flag-waving affair with Frank Sinatra and Liz Taylor topping the bill.

He stuck two jars of fresh joints in the back of the fridge, put a half-dozen spliffs in a pill case in the glove box, and headed out the next morning early with a third batch of spider juice. The mites were the last thing on his mind now. Fortunately he could do his work on automatic pilot, practically in his sleep. He felt ridiculous doing anything normal with what was going on here, but he knew that was half of why he needed to be doing it.

The next week he went out alone everyday at first light. The guys couldn't blame him for getting a jump on the day. An hour or two before twilight, after finishing his chores, he'd smoke another joint from their pinchings, each time seeing the figures in the fields and woods again. It was the weirdest routine he'd ever been on, and there was nothing routine about it.

That night he lay in a kudzu patch itching with mosquitoes whizzing in his ears, watching the same village of farmers working another field. Since when he saw them he was never straight and everything was magnified ten times, he couldn't gauge the strangeness of this, as if he needed to. These were the weirdest moments of his life, stranger than anything he'd seen in

Vietnam, but with his brain blistering and rushing and the woods humming around him, they were too far off the scale to compare to anything.

It was mesmerizing; a surreal and creepy wonderland. He didn't feel threatened by it, which was strange in itself. It didn't feel like bad ju ju. Watching the farmers was calming in an unexpected, hypnotic way, at first anyway. He'd zone into this daydream and have to remind himself he wasn't in the Mekong Delta or Ashau Valley. You're here, he'd say, in the backwoods of Tennessee; would you look at this? He'd check where he was, pinch himself and yank his nose hair to be sure this was even happening to him.

Every night he'd experiment in a different terrain and regardless of where he was, he'd see them. The first nights he still didn't believe it. This would cease, he thought, he'd be sitting out here in a stupor holding his dick and that'd be the end of it. It'd seem like some ridiculous drug dream, and maybe it would've been. The following morning he wasn't sure he'd seen what he thought he had. Was he psychotic or had he actually *seen* them again? He'd set up in a fresh spot and after three or four hits be obliterated with the woods throbbing around him. He'd watch them appear a couple at a time, squatting, crouching, bent-over working away as if they'd been there all the time. He'd observe them for hours or until the light was gone.

On the fourth dusk he saw a file of NVA in leaf-camouflage saunter down a mountain and cross a field with their weapons slung. They toted AK's, Chinese stein guns and three grenade launchers, looking like they'd come from a firefight. They were sweating, shuffling heavily, some blood-bandaged. He flattened and hugged the ground with his heart on fire. They didn't make a sound, but the insects whirred like some wild machinery. He had chills with the hair rising on the back of his neck, like it had at first, his guts churning. He watched their movements and gestures, everything exactly as he remembered it. *Unbelieveable,* he thought. Fucking spooks out here. It was nothing like watching the farmers. The soldiers left him wired and runnish. It brought back *too* much was what it did. Apparitions or not, he wasn't going to stroll out there and shake hands with the fellas. He'd never get used to this, he thought, as he slithered through the leaves and the stench of rotting snakes in drizzling dusk light, the sky swimming with vultures, themselves like some silent dark specters. He wracked his brain to get a grip again. There had to be a reason for this, it wasn't happening in a vacuum. He wasn't sure what was stranger now, the shock of what he'd seen at first, or *knowing* he was going to see it every time he took this smoke into his lungs.

A tribe of Montagnards appeared one night above the stables where Jason's horse was kept. He watched the skittish animal between himself and the odd little figures up in the trees. He was sure the horse saw or sensed them. Acting drugged or mentally impaired, he made the strangest noises Barrett'd heard from a horse, neighing with a growl-like, whining moan. He kept jutting his neck out, swinging his head like it was coming off its swivel, stomping and rubbing the ground, snorting. Nostrils flared, he galloped away and glared back at them, muscles in his neck twitching, staring at the strange-walking figures fanning off up into the trees.

Four out of five times it was farmers he watched. Thirty in the mud-caked swamp by the Little River. A fifth and sixth time forty or so along the dry streambed near the big twelve-hundred and Petri Pass. The woods went still except for the insects vibrating manic. There were so many gnats once the fields blurred blue in the late-afternoon shadows. Another time a thousand monarch butterflies floated over the high grass around the figures bent-over in it. There was never any evidence anyone had been there. No Ho Chi Minh sandal tracks, nothing on the ground. No paths or grass or twigs mashed or broken.

Something occurred to him. What price was he going to pay for lighting up a joint and seeing these figures? No telling. It felt like rubbing a genie from a bottle or getting a blank check for nothing, but nothing came free. Making love, taking a drug, even eating a piece of chocolate cake cost you something, what was it going to be with this?

He lay two hours one night watching them behind some charred stumps on a brier-covered knoll. They toiled like they were in their own country, like they had no idea where they weren't. He started to walk out to them but thought better of it, less from fear than not wanting to disturb this. Who knew what'd happen if he strolled out there. He called to them a couple of times as they picked up supplies on bamboo poles to leave, but they seemed as oblivious as before. He wasn't sure if they wouldn't answer or actually didn't know he was there.

Either way the rules were different in the dreams he was having. In that bright-lit, surreal no-man's-land they were in his face, crowding and railing around, shoving to get to him. They seemed to be trying to tell him something; his Vietnamese was rusty enough without them wrangling over each other. It was a chaotic conversation of questions and accusations, and when he asked a question they seemed deaf to it, which was a little like watching them awake. His helplessness seemed to invite this. He had no control here, like a coma patient having his brain picked over on an operating table. These weren't the dreams he'd had years ago where he resweated firefights and every other kind of soldier's nightmare, these were visitations. These people were *here*; he could *feel* them standing beside him; he had a relationship with them whether he liked it or not. He didn't have a choice as long as he was smoking this stuff, it was their territory—of course it always had been—but they were making themselves known now for some reason. After he lay sweating-buzzing in the woods, they appeared to him as if he were some kind of bait or dream-magnet and badgered the hell out of him, needling, cross-examining, harrying him. If they didn't acknowledge him in the fields, they knew he was there. The dreams were the price he was paying to smoke and watch them awake, he guessed. An odd theory, but what was not odd about this; it was the only plausible hypothesis. He'd get a feeling like he was crawling across crackling ice, and they'd say, "Look what's happening around you, don't you see it? Don't you have eyes?" they'd say, pointing to theirs. "Look, for Godsakes, what's wrong with you?" But every time he woke it eluded him again, like vapor fading into the cabin rooms. A rope slipping through his brain into the leaves.

He wasn't handling the guys very well. They weren't doing anything wrong, but everything they did seemed to drive him up the wall. Listening to their everyday chatter made him more aware of how strange this was, and him crazier with it. The sound of their voices grated on him: that wasn't a good sign. There wasn't a hell of a lot he could do about it, they'd been in different places since he'd seen those soldiers on the mountainside. He could feel this change coming over him, a gradual, subtle warping of his psyche. Not the usual marijuana effects, something more soul-altering, unsettling. He couldn't put his finger on it but he knew something was changing. All of the sudden he wished to God he'd never seen any of this. It was doing something to him, all right, making him loony as a fruitcake. Watching these people was frying his brain. What'd he expect, to light up a doobie and spy on apparitions in a field, then slide back into his everyday normal life? He knew damn well there'd be residual effects to this. He felt detached from everything, especially himself. He had a guilty conscience, he wasn't sure why. He hadn't wronged anybody since coming back from over there, but maybe he was dealing with old guilt from that war, unredeemed baggage. Plenty of guys carried that around. No matter your code you had to do some shameful shit over there, and he'd done his share. Maybe he was dredging that up with the rest of it.

The toothpaste was out of the tube. He wasn't squeezing the damn thing to begin with, but he was damn sure carrying it. He was growing and smoking the stuff that was doing it, how much more squeezing did it need? Okay, so he was squeezing it. But he was the only one being squeezed here, he didn't like that. Even if it wasn't Deke's or Jason's fault this wouldn't've happened if he hadn't come here. Yes, and that's bullshit too, you know it is, it was your choice to be here, nobody forced you. Don't blame them for being chosen, that was in the stars. They had nothing to do with that or you delving into it like some dime store shaman. You're not equipped for this and you know it. You've decided to take it on anyway, so don't be blaming them for it.

At dinner he'd feel like he was going to lose it. They'd be talking about lightning damage, drainage problems, some other insignificant tripe, and he'd start giggling and couldn't stop. They'd ask what it was and he'd be crying in his food with his face on the plate. He'd quit a few minutes, hold it in as long as he could, then burst out again like some babbling idiot. They looked at him like he was bonkers. He was headed that way. He couldn't cover this anymore. It was taking a herculean effort just to behave half-normal around them.

He hated to admit he was avoiding them, then he knew he was. It was a hell of a lot easier than pretending normalcy when he was with them. Where he was when he wasn't was a good question too. He'd leave a note he'd gone pruning, watering, bugging or whatever, and wouldn't tell them where he'd be. Sometimes he'd say where he was going and went somewhere else. The last thing he wanted was them stumbling up on him stone-blind in the leaves gazing at these stalking figures. Or was he the stalker? He'd disappear for a day, for days on end, and as long as he was busting ass for them—and he was in spite of this business—how could they blame him? He wasn't being very sociable but he was getting more work done than they were. He'd stagger in for dinner after a few days with his head reeling, bracing for small talk, trying not to break up when it started, downing three or four beers with shots of tequila to addle his brain. He'd never used alcohol like this before. Pot he'd used in quantity after the war to block his nightmares, now he was using firewater to deal with these squatters in his head.

He started diluting what he was seeing by getting drunk and more or less losing his mind. He was acting more like Deke than Deke in his manic moods, trying to get them to laugh and lose themselves with him. He'd done some off-the-wall standup between sets with the Shadowhaulers, he could be funny when he needed to be, when his woman flipped out or the world seemed to be coming off its wheels. Instead of getting depressed or into a bar fight he'd turn to the slaphappy, broken-hearted release into joy, the crazy cure of mindless laughter. Converting a drunken crowd into howling maniacs was strong medicine. It'd work for him here, he hoped, not that he had any choice in it. He was blowing a goddamn safety valve. The shit was spewing out of him like an over shaken beer. He was trying to keep himself together by getting rid of it as fast as he could.

He'd put on Roland Kirk's "Case of the Three-Sided Dream" and flop around the cabin floor, babbling like a drunken two-year-old. He'd come screaming in from the yard wrapped in kudzu, writhing on the floor like it was eating him alive. He'd come up with some new eccentric quirk every day. Uncanny how funny it was watching someone come apart at the seams. He'd lapse into a cross-eyed Irish brogue with drool and leaves on his face, dribbling beer like a black Irish madman, or wear a bed sheet and do a hair lip KKK impression, staggering around the cabin preaching "the peril of the dusky races." Whatever comically-crazed entity hit him he'd grab onto, and the boys'd be laughing their asses off. He was entertaining the goddamn troops, which was fine for several weeks, until one night he noticed they weren't smiling. Feeling the drop in temperature, he knew they'd been talking about it and went, oh shit, oh well, well, good then, fuck it. They'd seen it anyway; it was out there. At least they were with him in that now. He was probably more obvious than he realized. He considered telling them again, then decided against it. If they weren't seeing these things they'd think he was delusional and might even try to commit him. Deke calling *him* crazy, that was a good one.

He started waiting until they were asleep to drag in. He'd slip into the cabin, grab a sandwich, a six-pack and a bottle of tequila, and lay in the truck or under the arbor juicing his head until he couldn't think straight. Sometimes he'd see the figures palely-lit up in the trees he'd seen an hour before, lying there groggily toasting and mumbling to them. He wasn't sure what he was seeing in these states, but he knew they were there. He'd drink until they disappeared or he was too cross-eyed to make out anything, stumble into bed and pass out.

The first night it happened they said he'd shrieked like a castrated hog. He'd crashed around the cabin scaring them half to death, shattering a lamp and porcelain candleholder, banging his head on the kitchen sink, nearly wrecking the place. Deke thought a bear was in the cabin and was fumbling for his shotgun when Barrett floundered on top of him, growling and mewling, raving out of his mind. When he came to he had a knot the size of a lemon and could've sworn somebody hit him with a baseball bat.

The second time they found him grunting under Jason's bed, rooting it with his shoulders, his body half-lodged under it. When Jason shook him Barrett yanked him to the floor, screaming some Vietnamese gibberish. They wrestled around the cabin in a crazy sleepwalker's rugby scrummage, collapsing the kitchen table, smashing jars and window panes. He was in a maniacal trance, Deke said. What was all that yelling about them getting out of there? It'd taken a 16 oz. jar of ice water to bring him around, and he didn't remember any of it.

Every night he'd shake awake, trying to escape these badgering arguments, like he didn't want to hear anymore from the yellow-lit faces. They swam around him in this wildly disorienting place. He'd try to sweep his brain to get back to sleep, nod off twitching with his own ghost floating around him, and it'd start up again. A record shut off kept switching back on before he could get any rest. Suddenly it was dawn and he hadn't slept at all. He hadn't had a decent night's sleep in two or three weeks. It was grinding on him mentally and physically.

After belly walking one night through swamp muck watching a bivouacked company of NVA in the woods, he studied his face in the mirror. What was he doing? There were petal-like bags under his eyes. He had a deranged, withdrawn look like some jungle madman, someone staring out of a cave. Seeing it made his eye quiver; it was going half the time now, this involuntary twitch. He'd press it, feeling his pulse jittering. This ordeal was eating his nerves alive. Maybe if he backed away it'd stop. Maybe, but he didn't have a clue what was going on yet, which was why he was doing this. Even if they didn't need to know, which they did, it was obsessing him that he was able to do it at all; it'd become as addictive as a woman you couldn't stop lusting after, that you weren't even sure you wanted to be with. You didn't understand why you kept running back to her, but no matter how many times you did you didn't get enough. He was delving into it because of *and* in spite of what the Green Lady was dishing him.

He'd always been bullheaded, his mama said, his strength and curse. It'd worked for him mostly, but he wasn't sure if it was an asset here. He couldn't back up and the farther he went in the stranger it was getting. He hadn't ridden out on his Harley or had a wholesome chuckle in weeks, picked up his guitar. He'd laughed, but it wasn't the happy kind of laughter. His precious mama, he could feel what she was saying. *What you expect messin' with that wacky weed, son? You're invitin' the devil, don't you see? It's what he's givin' you. What you expect from him but confusion? It ain't that, mama,* he'd say. *Something's goin' on I know, but I've got to understand what, that's why I'm doin' this. You're right, I'm in a perplexed place, I need your help, so pray for me. But I've got ears and eyes and I've got to look at this. Gotta walk my walk and know my knowledge if it kills me. Pray for me mama, but you can't protect me from where I've got to go. Oh son,* she'd say, shaking her head, *dear hardheaded child* . . .

Jason didn't know him well enough to know what to think, but Deke knew something was going on. In a few weeks they were on different planets. When he desperately needed his friend now, Deke was the last person he could turn to. He wouldn't answer half the time Barrett spoke to him, and Barrett knew he was getting sore. Deke must've thought he was acting up for amusement, didn't really want to be there, or was going nuts for real. Barrett wasn't that mischievous, he should've known, but Deke took everything at face-value, he didn't care who you were or why you were acting strange, if you were an asshole you were an asshole. He wouldn't blurt it out, that wasn't his style. He'd look at Barrett with these wide-eyed, fuck you looks, like what the hell you trying to pull here pal? and burn off.

They didn't say a word when he dragged in from the woods. It was awkward, laughable, excruciating. These were his *boys*. While they hustled their illegal crop together, he was dodging around behind their backs, holding out on them, and lying about it. That wasn't his style and he felt like hell about it. When he got to the bottom of it he'd sit down and lay it out to them, but in the meantime he had to worry about the plants *and* these visitors while his friends looked at him like he was some alien madman. The weight of the crop was enough without this freakish menagerie.

The situation became a surreal bad dream, literally after they found him naked on the truck seat that morning. He'd stumbled through the woods bare-assed was all they could figure. Cut up, lathered with mud and leaves, sticks in his hair, he was dripping sweat like he'd broken a fever, flies and gnats all over him. He was squeezing that damn pillbox like it was the Holy Grail. The glove box was scattered around the yard like someone had just hurled it. What was he doing, chasing ghosts? He could've killed himself, broken his neck, slipped off a ledge or down some hole and they'd have never found him. He felt like a ghost himself, like he *was* turning into some disembodied alien entity.

In the middle of these visitations he'd have reeling dreams where he watched himself running through the woods as he was calling to himself. He'd run tree to tree like some lost observer, chasing his own beleaguered ghost, naked-blue-skinned sprinting along a palely-lit ridgeline. When he called out he'd look back at himself running ahead as he ran faster to catch himself, but as with the leaf-people in the fog, he'd never catch himself. Maybe that's what he was doing when they found him in the truck that morning. He realized he'd better rein this in, get his frazzled soul together before something worse happened.

Thank God Jason was there. Being near the boy made him feel better somehow. He'd watched the Reverend slip into tongues in the woods, the Spirit was all over him. He never imagined being close to him would feel like some spiritual insurance against getting his own ghost snatched into the wind, but that's what it was. On watering runs he talked to him about the storms. They were worrying the Reverend too, though he'd wanted to believe they were a good sign. When Jason started talking about plagues of frogs and snakes in the Bible, Barrett knew he wasn't alone. Of course the Reverend would've picked up on it, but he couldn't tell Jason what was happening to him. Everything would change drastically when he did, as if things weren't drastically different now.

He asked Jason to pray for them and the crop, meaning himself really. They got on their knees in the leaves and Jason asked for the Lord's protection. His voice changed timbre and Barrett felt a little more at ease. Maybe he could lead into it with Jason and break it to Deke, he thought. My God, you're neurotic. How can you gradually tell Deke you're seeing military units and villages of Vietnamese in the woods? It was like getting a little bit pregnant, wasn't it? He could stop smoking the Spiritchaser or go on with this by himself. Nobody could help him anyway except The Man Himself, and only if he was right with Him.

He got on his knees alone and started praying. He was at that point, all right, the breaking one. Jason told him to pray for strength and clarity if he was troubled; he asked for it every day now from the time he woke up until he shut his eyes, sometimes in the middle of the night. He'd stir half-awake from his night-visits and stumble under the grape arbor to pray a few minutes on his knees, stagger back to bed. He knew these spirits weren't demonic or trying to hurt him. He'd been around unclean spirits before: that was a *whole* different hellstorm. This was some kind of warning they'd been giving him for a month at least. *Beware from the air* he'd hear every time he surfaced into that no-man's-land between sleeping and waking. Being busted from the air was the obvious meaning, but he had a feeling it was more than that.

He carried his little red-lettered New Testament his granny'd given him, the worn one with the picture of Jesus at the well with the woman of Samaria. He kept it in a plastic baggie to keep the sweat and mud off, reading it like a shield before going into the woods, and when he was alone he'd lay hands on it. *Put on the whole armor of God*, it said; Lord, he was trying. He'd decide not to go any further, to work all day and come back without smoking anything, clean up and go out for a steak. Take a breather from this or drop it altogether. Maybe it wasn't his cross. Maybe none of it meant a damn thing, he thought, and then this craving curiosity, wanting to feel it again, wanting to grab it by the throat and wring its neck, would take over again, and he'd be digging out the joint nervously lighting it, his hands quivering so he could barely manage it. He was chasing the proverbial rabbit down the hole. He felt like he'd been lying in the woods watching these visitors for a year now, but it'd only been six or seven weeks since he'd chased those leaf-people through the fog. His hands shook most of the time now, this nice little aggravating tremor. He could see Deke and Jason catching it with the rest of it. He must've looked like some regular junkie with all these symptoms. He wished it was that simple. A nice chemical drug problem would've been duck soup compared to this.

A few days before the Fourth of July everything unraveled. The dreams he was having, these sleep visitations, became garden-variety nightmares. One night the faces that came to him were covered with burns. Third-degree disfiguring scalds with whole sides of flesh seared off, eyes and hair missing, burns he'd seen napalm do to Vietnamese civilians, the enemy, and some of his buddies. Jellied bodies. There were children with ghoulish, swollen heads, necks burned off, blackened stumps for hands and arms. These people he'd gotten to know were shouting and pointing at him, the ones who could, gesticulating, angry, hysterical. They were furious. He was railing back at them, saying, *I didn't do this to you, it wasn't me. What do you want from me? I did my penance years ago, my harried aftermath time, get off my back, goddamit. What are you doing here? Just spit it out and make it clear to me. I didn't order this done to you, I was a pawn back then, don't you know that? What could I do about it? What do you want from me? Tell me or leave me alone. We're trying to save our own selves here. We're trying to save ourselves . . .*

Which turned a key in his sleep again, but he never knew why it did. Something he knew or thought or did, something in his head clicked or activated it like a punishment, a Godforsaken remedial course. It was like the same nightmarish movie was being run for him again against his will because he wasn't getting it. Ranting back at them must've turned it this time; pulled a bullet into the chamber, loaded and triggered it; that recurring dream he'd started having when he came here in February. *The vault door slammed and he was soaring over miles and miles of rice paddies on top of scurrying farmers and water buffalo. In his dream he was cackling in a kind of dragged-along, helpless horror, the aircraft he was in bearing down on the same farmers he'd been watching in the fields until he was impossibly close to their terrified faces, flying into their frenzied eyes and screams . . .*

He woke in a violent seizure, hanging on the edge of darkness. He was half-delirious and couldn't tell up from down, swimming in this miasma that scared the living shit out of him. He was barely clinging there, ready to slip off and slide down from it and feel his soul disappear. Lord God, here was his answer, he'd asked for it. He looked at what he was doing now and thought, this is insane, you're losing it, buddy, look at yourself. If you're not crazy you're about to be. You're asking for protection but you've crossed the line. Asking Jesus to save you while you tempt madness? You can't do that,

Witch Doctor. You better know it and get straight with it, get some kind of grip on this and let go. Stop getting dragged along by it *today now.*

That morning he rode to Chatsworth to get away from the farm. He remembered a public library being built the last time he was over there. He ate breakfast at the Smokerise and spent the morning poring over texts on unusual occurrences and strange phenomenon. There were plenty of surreal subjects to bone up on. The universe was stranger than anyone wanted to know about. It was weird enough driving back into the world of glass and steel, banks and fast food restaurants. Everything seemed peculiar now. The library was pristine as a new church. He watched some teenagers studying and flirting, fooling around with each other. God, did he envy them. He'd tear up now and then, he wasn't sure why. He was alien from that innocence; he'd seen too goddamn much. How much truth can the world stand? You got that right, Mose. He wanted to go back to where they were, back before the war; back to the goddamn sand pile. Maybe he was having a nervous breakdown, it felt like it. A young, dark-haired librarian named Andrea with a plump figure and fat calves brought him stacks of books. He told her he wanted information on anything unexplained in nature, anything she had. As he listened to her voice and watched her walk on the new-smelling carpet, he wished to God he could disappear into her wholesome, simple life, fuck her every night and forget about this.

In an oversized, illustrated volume called "Anomalies" he stumbled across the words *creature storms.* He couldn't believe it: they were written about. He studied the calendar of documented dates and locations. He was giddy discovering anyone knew about these things. He studied the photos and rough renderings. There were incidents of raining creatures listed over hundreds of years, mostly in England and the United States. He was curious about the Biblical ones, the plagues of frogs and snakes Jason talked about. Not so much to know how they happened, but what coincided with them: *why* they did. In every case they seemed to have been signs, warnings or omens. There'd been documented "creature storms" in Tennessee in the 1880's. There was no other information about them. There were a few descriptions with eyewitness accounts of fish falling in a town in England, grainy black and white photographs of a bewildered old couple standing in a suburban street covered with whiting. There was no scientific explanation for any of these events. There were several odd and farfetched theories, but no one had proven them.

They wouldn't let him check this book out, it said *research material* on the cover. All right, he had to show this to the guys, but they weren't going to be dragged back here to look at it. He didn't need to be stealing the book either, he needed all the good karma he could get. He'd have to borrow it and bring it back, he thought. Yeah, that was going to happen. He sat a minute trying to think of another way to do it. Smuggling books out of libraries now, he thought, what's next? Stealing Girl Scout cookies? He slid the oversized hardback into his pants, and hobbled out with it like a man wearing a stiff girdle.

The smell of cooked meat made him queasy when he opened the door. Bracing himself, he stepped inside, the scanner whishing quietly in the corner. The brothers were eating and watching the six o'clock news.

> . . . One of the worst forest fires in Tennessee history swept over thousands of acres of forest and farmland last week twelve miles from Jasper Air Force Base. Air Force firefighting units chipped in with Ranger units to bring the blazes under control but were unable to until flames decimated a ten mile strip of land within the Tullahoma Valley. As there were no electrical storms in the area the fire's believed to have been started by negligence or arson . . .
> . . . President Reagan said this morning . . .

Barrett washed his face and arms at the sink as Reagan droned on. He sat and looked at the little fish on the platter, taking a couple and some fresh slaw with bread, drowning the fish in Texas Pete sauce. Watching the President he felt his skin crawl.

"That's close," Deke said.

"North or south of the base, I wonder," Jason said. "South could be twenty miles from here."

Crows congregated over the cabin and haggled.

"Rabbit's tender. Glad we got it before the vultures did. We've got meat for three winters, brothers."

"Rabbit's gamey," Jason said. "I can't eat any more frog legs."

Barrett stopped chewing and watched the wrinkled face on the screen. The cooked smell and taste of it made the prune-like face more grotesque. He was sweating, and realized he was breathing harder.

"I'm frog-legged out," Deke said. "How's that sole, straw boss, whatever the fuck those little fish are."

Barrett gagged, coughing the fish on his plate. He bolted out the door heaving in the kudzu, vomiting until his stomach was hollow, retching and spitting up bile. Sweat dripped from his nose as he rested with his hands on his knees staring at the saffron-colored mush in the leaves. He went inside, rewashing his face and hands, rinsing his mouth with the clear metallic well-water, the smell making him retch again.

"All right, buddy?"

"Ain't eaten' nothing else rains out of the fuckin' sky. Keep it away from me."

"All right, Hoss," Deke said, smirking.

"Fish that bad?" Jason said.

"It's *all* bad little brother. Regardless of how it tastes it ain't normal and we *damn* sure shouldn't be eaten' it."

"Look who's spooked now," Deke said. "Lighten' up, Witch Doctor, maybe you got a bad piece of fish there. Try this rabbit," he pushed the platter to him.

"You're not listenin', Deke. Something's going on here. This ain't no blessed fucking buffet. This is weird, unnatural shit."

"Could've fooled me. Every good and perfect gift cometh from above, right Rev? Try this rabbit and tell me I'm wrong."

He stabbed a sliver onto Barrett's plate.

"This ain't funny, Deke."

"I ain't laughin'."

Jason looked at his food as Barrett unbuckled his satchel.

"Either of you seein' anything out there?"

". . . matter of fact . . ."

"Besides the storms . . . spirits, apparitions, anything like that?"

"I think I see you flippin' out on me," Deke said, raking more rabbit on his plate.

"*Goddamit*," Barrett said.

"What kind . . . like what are you talking about?"

"Lately when I smoke this stuff—and nothing like this ever happened to me before, little brother—I'm seein' people out there I've tried to forget, some I never saw. I'm having the weirdest fucking dreams, fellas. I'm being *visited* here."

Deke glanced at Jason: no kidding.

"Flashbacks?"

"I never took acid. And if it was just me seeing this it'd be one thing, frogs and snakes raining from the sky with it's another. I've never had visions on grass, and I've never seen weather like this, you?"

Deke picked at his food. "All right, Witch Doctor."

"Neither of you seein' anything strange?"

They chewed without looking at him.

"I'm picked I suppose."

"You've always been the man, man."

"You wanna make a joke out of it you know you can fuck off, Deke."

"I don't give a shit if you want to know the truth, pardner."

"Come on, Deke, let him tell it; I want to hear it."

"He never learns, Reverend. Nothing happens for no reason. If you don't pay attention to everything going on, *especially* these kinds of things, you're blind as a dead stone in the universe. Tell your blockheaded brother what you told me about those plagues and all."

"Yeah," Jason cleared his throat. "I was telling him about these plagues in the Bible before the Pharaoh set the Israelite slaves free. There was a rain of frogs and an ancient Greek writing called *The Deipnosophists* talks about fish falling for three solid days in a place called Chersonesus, frogs raining in other places."

"So I visited the library," Barrett said, opening the book. "Look at this, will you, been going on thousands of years. Lists places and dates all over the world. In 1877 snakes rained in Memphis, Tennessee, three hours from here. In 1882 in a snowstorm in Iowa frogs fell in large blocks of ice."

"So this stuff's not uncommon?"

"Ain't common at all. Don't happen that often."

"What causes it?"

"No one knows, but I'm tellin' you, weather like this ain't haphazard."

"So our personal witch doctor says. What's this got to do with your flashbacks?"

"They're not flashbacks."

"Right . . ."

"They're happening *now*. I'm seeing people out there, they know me somehow. I don't know how, or exactly why, but they're here."

"They're here," Deke nodded. "What kind of people?"

"Kind you and I were sent to burn. Viet Cong, peasant farmers, women, children, dozens of farmers working in fields. NVA and Viet Cong on patrols, bivouacked in the woods."

Deke's expression changed. His face went white as he swallowed, cheek muscles flexing as he stared at his plate. He pitched a glance to Jason.

"Sure they're Vietnamese?"

"Bone-sure, just like the seed we brought back from Saigon and kept pure, right? You know how heavy tea is to me. It *is* heavy and everybody knows it, especially the fools outlawing it. I've always called it the Anointed Green Vessel 'cause I see it at the top of the plant hierarchy. I believe whatever she sees and feels and hears, she remembers, stores in chemical memory in her seed with her taste, high, resin, smell. Each seed's a receptacle for its place, a witness; *a sentient thing*. The plant's intelligent life with knowledge of what's going on around it. It probably knows more than we do, hell. As pure a form of the Godhead in nature as there is, that's what she gives back when we smoke her flowers."

"You don't mean she *speaks* to us?" Jason said.

"That's exactly what I mean. The Indians were all over this, little brother. They respected the spirits, listened to them, went to the smokes for answers and got them. They didn't hide from anything God grew, hallucinogenic or otherwise, they wanted to *know*. And this seed's got plenty to tell. Look at the history of these people, the invaders they've had to deal with, Portuguese, Chinese, Japanese, French, Americans. These saps've been saturated by resource grabbing conquerors for centuries, greedy power mongerers fighting over their country like it was a kid in a custody battle, ripping its arms and legs off. The French colonized them in the 1800's. The Japs raped them in World War II. The French fought them again and when the French gave up we invaded their asses. Every time they turned around a new predator was at their door. This seed we're growing, this soul bearing flower, was soaked in her people's shit for thousands of years; absorbed wars and bad blood in the jungles, heard the spirits of the dead. She carries them with her in her DNA and has the power to communicate with us when she needs to. I know this sounds crazy, but I'm seein' her faces when I smoke this stuff, hearing their voices."

"Not crazy at all," Deke coughed with a grin.

Jason stopped eating. "Why would they want you to see them? What do they want?"

"Oh God," Deke shook his head, munching a biscuit.

"At first they were just hanging around like a tribe of homeless people, loitering where I slept. Then they started talking to me and getting damned urgent with it. Suddenly they seemed pissed off, upset about something. What've I done? I thought, and as I was trying to figure that out I knew you guys would think I was off my rocker, so I tried to keep it to myself, which didn't work worth a damn since you could see me coming apart at the seams. Hell, I haven't been with you guys for weeks now, you know that; I've been *out there*, baby. This shit's nearly killed me. When I started praying earnestly, asking the Main Information Center, it came to me. *Seek and you'll find; ask and it'll be given to you.* He ain't giving us a stone if we ask for a loaf of bread, is he, Rev? I'm a witness here, an interpreter, and I know we're being warned now. The last few days they've been burned and smothered with blood, messed up like resurrected corpses: limbs melted off, mutilated and shit . . . If I wasn't here it'd be one of you seeing it, they'd show and tell somebody. This business raining out of the sky's connected to it. If what we're growing's not making these creatures rain, it damn sure knows why they do."

"Why hadn't this happened in fifteen years we've been growing it?"

"You and I never told each other everything at once. Had to have a reason, *and* a time."

"Why do you think this did?" Jason said.

"I don't know, little brother, but something's comin' down. I know neither of you want to hear what I'm about to say, but the warning I'm gettin' is for us to get the hell out of here . . ."

"Oh God," Deke snapped, slapping his napkin on the table, getting up for a beer. He slammed the refrigerator. "You're paranoid, Barrett. You're smoking too damn much. Chill the fuck out and let your head clear. You're THC toxic, pal."

"It ain't the marijuana, Deke. It's what this seed *knows*. These spirits are trying to warn us."

"Warn us of what?" Deke laughed. "Are you outta your fuckin' mind?"

"I know this sounds crazy, but I'm clear as a bell and I've never been wrong about this gut-shit. You think I'm looking for an excuse to jump ship on you?"

"I don't know what you're doin', Kimasabe, but nothing's gonna spook me outta here. Leave if you want, you don't have to come up with some doomsday fairytale to do it."

"I didn't say I was leaving. I'm trying to tell you what I'm gettin' here. If I didn't give a damn why would I bother?"

"You're nuts?" Deke shrugged, raising his eyebrows.

"Why do you always flip this around?"

"You can split anytime you like, Hoss."

"You don't think I know that!" Barrett pounded the table, slapping over bottles, raking fish to the floor. Deke clenched his beer with his jaw flexing. "I'm trying to save you asshole! Did I not sense those claymores at the foot of that tunnel complex? If you'd listened to me your goddamn leg wouldn't pain you so much in wet weather."

"That was a war."

"You don't think this is? Hell, you've said so yourself. There're more mysterious things floating around here than claymore mines, making it goddamn rain snakes, frogs and lizards? You kidding me? You gonna tell me you haven't wondered what's going on here?"

For a second Deke saw something in Barrett's eyes; they were two black holes of fear, the left one twitching. He felt a twinge and looked down.

"No ball and chain on you, bro."

"No Shit!" Barrett said, cackling out loud. He circled the room with his face to the ceiling, stopping with his arms by his side, giggling with his eyes shut. The Rev stared at his plate like he had a gun to his head. Poor bastard, Barrett thought; Jason knew Deke'd lay into him if he even *thought* about taking this seriously. If he wanted any peace he had to sit there and swallow it. "What was I thinking?" Barrett said. "I should've known better, shouldn't I? Than to tell some blockheaded idiot anything's going on beneath his blindered little world? I should've known better, because I'm one dumbass crazy nigger, right? When your best buddy sees something you don't and tries to warn you of it, call him a lunatic, there you go. Especially when it's jeopardizing your little holy agenda. What was I thinking?" he bopped himself on the forehead. "I'd've done better sticking a goddamn V-8 up my ass, wouldn't I? I'm making this crazy shit up for my health, I suppose, because I'm one nutcase nigger witch doctor jabbering on about wild children, people exploding, all that crazy circus shit. Write everything off to that, Deke, go ahead, takes care of everything you don't understand or don't want to believe. Tidies up those unsightly little messes. *Very* absorbent shit," he giggled, leaning into the wall with his splayed palms. "That's it, brother, go ahead, that explains it . . . All of this is happening because I'm smoking too much. Who's the real lunatic, huh? What the hell am I doing here?" He glared into a corner by the door wobbling his head like a windshield doll's, humming "Mellow Down Easy." "Ahhhhhhhh!" he screamed. "*Fuuuuuuuuk me!*"

Jason stared at the table. The tension was so thick he could barely turn his head. After a while he squatted and scraped the fish back on the platter, set it on the table and tried to eat again. He wasn't sure what worried him more, Barrett's interpretation of what was going on here or Deke's nonchalant dismissal of it. Deke kept eating as if nothing had happened. The scanner picked up bitten voice-scraps. After a while Barrett stumbled back over, plopping in his chair, slumping with his face in his hands.

"You're not gonna listen to me, are you, Deke?"

"Heard you, Witch Doctor."

"Yeah, but you didn't *listen*," Barrett sighed, shaking his head, listening to the chewing with the scanner hopping. He dragged a kudzu runner through the floor stripping the leaves and skin into briny strings. Maybe he should vacate, he thought; get the hell out of there before something happened. Because something was going to happen, he was very damn sure of that. Fuck it, he thought. Fuck me. Who was he fooling? This was worse than a goddamn woman. Friendship, brothers in arms. Each time he started to speak he'd shake his head, chuckling to himself. Shit, he thought. There was no answer; that was it. There was no answer and *that* was his answer. "All right," he said. "Maybe I'm crazy, I don't know. I love you guys though, you better know that. I wouldn't leave you in a lurch for all the tea in China. I came here to help you, and that's what I'm gonna do. If you're not going to believe what I'm telling you, I got no recourse. I'm crazy enough to see this through regardless of what I'm picking up . . ." Are you? he thought. Think about it, come on, a promise is a promise. This may be your last best chance to bug out of here and follow your gut to safe ground.

Going once . . . twice . . . Why'd he know he was going to regret this? "I'm that crazy," he said, his voice sounding like someone else's. "So God help us, I hope I'm wrong. Right now I've gotta get out of here before I lose my mind. I'll be back, I promise, but if I'm gonna be worth a damn the rest of the season I need some R and R immediately."

"Hell yeah," Deke said. "You don't have to ask for that, brother. Take all the time you need."

"Right," Barrett said, staring at a supply line of carpenter ants skittering under the table. It didn't take a soothsayer to predict this. Would he've believed what he'd told them if he hadn't seen it himself? He should've known better than to try to pry Deke away from his sacred ground anyway, he'd rather die than leave it. Even if they thought he was harebrained he couldn't leave them with this mess hanging over them, the same impulse that made him want to run and drag them with him forced him to stay and protect their stubborn asses. My God, was he fucked or what? The mother in him. If any of what he was feeling was true, they were sure as hell going to need him to finish this job, and a lot more than that.

"All right," he said. "I'm gonna run over to Memphis and track down Miss Marsha. Haven't seen her since Thanksgiving. Spend the Fourth with her and try to clear my head like you said."

"That's all you need, Br'er Rabbit. All we're doing's maintenance now, we can handle this, can't we?"

Jason shrugged, "Sure, no problem," he said, feeling uneasy. He'd known something was going on with Barrett, but hadn't imagined anything like *this*. He could tell Barrett believed every word of his story, which worried him. He remembered Barrett asking him to pray in the woods that day, and the scared feeling he'd picked up from him that made him *want* to say a prayer. Maybe Barrett was smoking too much like Deke said; maybe he *was* seeing God knew what out there; maybe both and he was cracking up because of it. Between the storms and Barrett being off his rocker he hadn't had a good feeling; now this. He needed to do some more serious praying on his own.

"I'll head out in the morning," Barrett said, remembering one physical miracle he had to look forward to. "Ever had any black lovin', Rev?"

"No," Jason said, looking at his hands.

"Shit, son, a sister's attention and a Coca Cola'd knock you out cold. Come over with me, Marsha's got plenty of friends."

"Better stick around here," Jason said. "You know how I love running jerry cans up these mountains."

"He's got a white girl," Deke said. "Don't ruin the poor boy."

"You sure about this?"

"We're fine, straw boss. Lap it up for all of us."

"I'll eat enough for us all I promise you; might even get into some food over there, but I ain't going to make it a priority."

They chuckled without looking at each other. There was a strained silence like somebody had died.

"You think I've lost my mind, don't you Deke? Think I'm stark-ravin'."

Deke clamped his friend's thick shoulder, squeezing and shaking him.

"Lighten' up, Br'er Rabbit. Get out of here for a few days and see how you feel. Get some love for me, love-child; *you nasty beast.*"

"Yeah, yeah," Barrett sighed, staring at the dust in the floorboards. "Couldn't hurt anything, could it?"

From the top of Hawkins Mountain Deke and Jason watched the red-violet puffs and muffled bursts explode and drift over the Maysville fairgrounds twelve miles away. They sat in a pair of beat-up oak rockers, Deke pulling beers from a cooler on the ground between them feeling painless and relishing this drunk he'd begun at sundown. He was getting good and trashed tonight, the Fourth of July crossing of the midsummer hump. He felt bullet-proof and battle-hardened, despite his old buddy and partner and local Rastafarian wigging out on him. He wasn't sure what that was about, black paranoia probably, Barrett's own brand of post-traumatic stress. What could he do? He couldn't control his friend's delusions. He'd dealt with plenty of trauma in his life and was still dealing with it, but he wasn't going to let it bugger him. He hated seeing Barrett like this, but he wasn't going to let it slow him down or put a damper on this night. There was too much to feel good about after all the shit he'd been through the last year and a half. He felt nearly goddamn wonderful and was going to enjoy it.

Behind the mountain horizon they watched faint glows from distant fireworks in other towns. They reminded Deke of the arch lights from

B-52's and the heavy shellings. Every ten or twenty seconds the closer rockets lofted up making quiet, delayed booms and flashes, their faces softly lit from faraway flickers.

"What a night," Deke said. "Kind of night makes you wanna find a woman. Where's your girl?"

"Meeting her in town later. She had a family get-together."

"Good for you. You may just be normal after all."

"Don't worry about that."

They rocked, watching the fanning colored lights.

"Sometimes I feel like daddy's still around, ever feel that?"

"All the time."

"Followed a guy in a two-tone '57 Ford that looked just like him the other day. Felt pretty strange. It wasn't him."

"I've seen him in unexpected places."

"You know what I believe," Jason said. "It feels unreal when we lose a loved one, because they're really not gone, so you keep expecting them to show up. The spirit senses the spirit so you keep looking for them."

"They're there?"

"Just not in the way we expect. We know they're around so part of us keeps expecting them to drive by."

"I thought I was the only one felt that."

"Are you sure Honcho could've come home for the funeral if he wanted to?"

"Oh hell yes, unless he was in some full-scale alert. Who knows what that mysterious motherfucker feels."

"He loved daddy as much as you or me, Deke, they would've done anything for each other."

"Ain't it the truth."

"Didn't you get that?"

"I used to think so. I'll never understand why he didn't make it to the funeral. Think it's 'cause his real father's the military now."

"We don't know why he didn't, and you're both my brothers, so I wish you wouldn't talk that way."

"You asked me, little brother."

They watched the rose-colored sky lit-up in silence.

"You really resent him, don't you?"

"You ask me not to talk about him and then ask me that?"

"All right, what is it? Other than not making the funeral, what'd he do so awful you have to slam him every time he comes up?"

Deke groaned, fishing for a beer.

"You really wanna know? All right. Honcho was daddy's model son, that's what I got anyway. First in everything. Followed in daddy's footsteps as a hot shot pilot, flyin' chopper missions in 'Nam before I'm out of high school. I hated the goddamn military and sure as hell didn't know what we were getting into over there, but I try to follow in daddy's footsteps so I can be like good old Honcho. But they won't let me fly 'cause my blood pressure's too high. Airborne's the next best thing, I think. I'm naive enough to wangle myself into the army so as not to look like a failure in daddy's eyes. I wind up swimming through swamps in Cambodia and nearly get my leg blown off while Honcho's awarded the Distinguished Flying Cross." Deke paused with a toast to the clouds and guzzled. "If he hadn't been such a bad boy he might've gotten the goddamn Medal of Honor. I come back with my mind and nerves shot to hell, seared off, feeling I murdered people for nothing, feeling we all did. I can't hold a job. Can't hold a marriage together. That night I almost died in the jungle when Barrett kept me from it, mortified me. I didn't sleep nights for years, sat up staring at the TV or walls until I heard birds waking. Remember that time? All I'd hear about was Honcho. Look what Honcho did. Honcho got another medal. Honcho got a promotion. He's always the hero in daddy's eyes, the professional flyboy killer. Leaves the army and becomes a jet fighter pilot in the goddamn Marines. Germany, Iran, Beirut, Granada, wherever they need a hot shot ace Honcho's there. I haven't trusted this government or our military since that sham they sent us into, it wasn't a slip-up or oversight, it was goddamn criminal as far as I'm concerned, toward all countries involved. Defense is one thing, that was genocide. We don't mind sacrificing another country's population for our ideals. So Honcho marries the imbeciles, becomes them. He knew we'd raped those people for ten years, taken our turn in the rotating gangbang, and he builds a vocation on it, sells his soul to them. Not only did he follow in daddy's footsteps, he made a career of it and it's all I've heard about from daddy for twenty years. Guess I built up some resentment from that. Then this funeral shit. The favorite son doesn't fly home to pay his respects to his adoring father, comfort his grief-crazed mother. What's that about? That's pretty weird, isn't it? I still don't know what he said when he talked to her, she never made it clear. She kept mumbling he'd be home when he could, he was doing "classified work." So maybe that's true, but it seems he could've just fucking gotten here. He sends flowers and promises we'll understand, well, I don't, I never will. Which brings us to the present state. A few weeks before daddy died he reminded me Honcho was the executor of the estate. Of course he was, but where is he to execute it? We're going down the tubes and can't even get in touch with the maniac. He's married to the bastards, that's what it is, they're his home. He's got to be in Nirvana with this comatose old hawk's military obsession. We're in the middle of the biggest military buildup in American history, and I guarantee Honcho's riding the glorious crest of it. One thing really gets me is, Honcho was a renegade, always pulling this shit, playing pranks on everybody, the big kidder, which is one reason he and daddy were so close; they were two of a kind. Now he's doing his mysterious antics around daddy's death. I don't care what he does, Jason. He can't give much of a shit about this place and I don't need his help to save it. Guess I've gotten pretty cynical about big brother lately."

"You got some of what he got, Deke; got it honestly."

"Yeah, I guess."

"Look what we're doing here. Daddy never was a follower, like you said."

"Daddy always had both feet on the ground until lately."

They watched the fireworks and a plane's lights skirting them, to the east lifting sparkles glittered behind a dark-spined ridge sprinkled with lights.

"God, doesn't life take some bizarre turns," Jason said. "You grow up thinking it's simple, predictable. I couldn't've imagined any of this, it's like somebody else's life. When daddy pulled that trigger it became somebody else's."

"Tell me about it. I've felt that for a long time, before any of this happened. I mean, when we were growing up we believed in our country one-hundred per cent, in the peopled running it. We trusted them like our mothers and fathers because they were wise and honest, like the founding fathers, we thought, *they were us.* Why would we doubt them? I revered this country and its leaders, I'd do any damn thing for it because I believed what I was taught about it. Little by little I saw it was different than it was supposed to be, than we were told it was. The country was the same but the people leading it changed before our eyes. Starting with Kennedy's murder, I think, that's when the rot set in. They covered up that shit and everybody knew it and didn't want to. Then that shitty fucking war Johnson dragged us all the way into. I didn't think my country was capable of that deceit and stupidity, which is why they could pull it off, nobody did. A corporate business deal when it came down to it, a way to test American weaponry; money for lives and to make sure a couple of blind presidents didn't lose face. Then all of the leaders with vision and heart were systematically killed off so that Dick Nixon could take a big steaming crap in our soul. All our worst impulses were followed. You pull a few strings here, kill a few leaders there, and gradually the country's taken from you, stolen, and most of us don't even realize it. It's a slight of hand no one wants to imagine. If they do they see such large evil forces behind it they just look the other way or go back to sleep. What can anybody do with so much power and money working behind the scenes in smoky backrooms? Money and power protect themselves, so gradually everything's bought off, and everyone with it. It's so insidious you can't see it, who'd want to believe it? This is America, right? We have to believe we're goddamn wonderful, beyond reproach, so pretty soon the heartless, soul-dead people are running the country, like right now, and no one even *wants* to know what's going on in the shadows. The Indians have a saying, 'Whatever you do, follow a path with heart.' Well, heart is the opposite of warmongering for money. Heart is the opposite of deception and blind bullheaded pride, opportunism, and the heart is being stomped on right now. This guy we have in office has no real heart, he's pompous, soulless, he has no conscience connected to anything but the elitist power he represents. He was bought and paid for years ago to bully people around, and his head is ten times bigger than his heart. He'll cram moral laws down your throat while ignoring the poor, sick, young and old, weak and broken. Somehow the lessons Jesus spent most of his time talking about don't hold much water with these good old Godly folk."

Jason listened to Deke's alcohol-breathing, watching his profile as he raised his beer.

"Look what's happening to the farmers now, the people who've broken their backs to feed us. A man risks his neck for his country in World War II and Korea, risks two sons in a prefab, millionaire-maker's war, trusts the government to run his farm all his life, tell him what to grow and how much he'll get for it, then they foreclose on his fucking life. It's uncanny Barrett said he's seeing Vietnamese farmers around here, because at moments I feel just like those poor saps. Barrett's not seeing them, he's crazy as hell, but it's kind of reminiscent with this repressive old mobster in office. He was perfectly willing to commit genocide on those people in the sixties, he's president in the eighties and look what we've got, a suicidal 'war on drugs,' which is all political crap to control the masses, to show us what a good and moral leader he is. Fuck these goddamn hypocrites. You want to know why people are killing themselves with hard drugs, cocaine, smack, pills? Shooting each other in the streets? There's no heart or vision anymore. It was heisted from us by self worshipping, sanctimonious blowhards like this actor-phony good guy, and we're not even close to the country we could've been. I'd do anything for my country, Jason. For my country, do you understand?"

Jason nodded.

"These people are not my country, they represent the worst of who we are. I don't know where it went but this ain't it. It's out there in the dark somewhere, wondering where *we* went. I sit here looking at us hypnotized by this arrogance and puffed-up vanity, this self-centered materialism, and I have no idea. The country I knew growing up is a hell of a lot more real than this one."

"You can steal a country?"

"Oh come on, sure, and make it look like an accident. If you kill the soul of the country, it ain't the country anymore, it's a goddamn fake run by fakes and profiteers. But who gives a damn? Everyone goes on in a trance as if it's tragically normal. We'll just put this sad event behind us, this assasination, and this one and this one; but it ain't behind us. It's us now. It's who we are. We're the property of liars and thieves. I miss my country, Jason. We had something going on. What great-principled people we were. We've deteriorated into a syndicate of gangsters, money-grubbing conmen and schemers, but by God we're *proud* of it. Don't tell anyone otherwise, they'll get pissed off for bursting their little patriotic bubble, part of our blind covenant to worship ourselves. They'd rather believe in a charade than realize their old man's a thief and phony."

They watched more lights flickering behind the ridgelines.

"What do you make of that stuff Barrett said last night? Is he off his rocker?"

Deke thought a minute as he sipped his beer and nodded, leaning forward.

"Yeah, nothing permanent. You're seeing what happens when someone smokes too much. I've seen him like this a couple of times. Once a few years ago we were working in a field covered with fog in the early morning, and he said it was gas and someone was trying to burn us. Got really upset, freaked-out, I mean, so we left. Came back after the fog lifted and he never said another word about it. I never asked where the gas came from, never knew what he was talking about."

"He seemed pretty spooked."

"He gets that way; he'll get over it. Even a Rastafarian needs to flush out now and then. Hey, check this out."

Their faces glowed as the sky filled with splashing, sputtering lights that bloomed and seemed to leap toward them.

"*Finale*," Jason said. "Oh man. Oh yeah."

"Check out this flag," Deke said as the sky blew up, popped and boomed with explosions like echoing bass drums. "*Yeah*! Yeowww!" he whooped, slinging his arm like a bull rider, clapping and whistling. "I love this fucking shit! This calls for another cold beer and a fat hecho a mano. Ice cold American drug? Budweiser? Cigar?"

"Just a beer," Jason said, popping and holding it in his lap as he watched the sky sink into darkness. Dots of planes crawled in the smoky distance. "I hope we're doing the right thing, Deke."

"Nothing else *to* do. Got to protect what's ours."

"Daddy'd kick our asses if he knew what we were doing."

"Would that make him right?" Deke turned. "If daddy was so goddamned perfect we wouldn't be going through this."

"So now it's his fault."

"I didn't say that. He had his own way of doing things is all, and I've got mine. I've got just as much right in the cosmic scheme of things to save this farm my way behind the government's back, as he had to let the vultures destroy him and take it from us. This government's laws aren't sacred. I wish to God they were. Don't confuse them with God's laws, Jason. His laws are sacred, they protect you if you follow them. Even in a country this righteous manmade laws don't work that way. If we'd let them come in and take the place I'd've never forgiven myself. I'll save it the only way I know how and settle up with daddy later. He'll have to understand."

"Maybe he already does."

Deke upended his beer, crushing the can, unzipping one of Barrett's Costa Rican's.

"I think he will in time."

"I just wish Honcho'd come home and we could've figured another way to do this."

"We've seen how much we can depend on Honcho, forget it. At the end of the season we'll be out of hot water, don't worry," he ruffled Jason's hair. "Go see your woman, pray for rain and leave the rest to me."

"Guess I'll head out," Jason said, getting up. "Love you brother Hawk."

"Jaywalk Hutchins . . ."

He took a few steps and looked back at his brother looking at him with a solemn, alone drunkenness, soft flashes glinting on the side of his face. The solitary General with the mission on his shoulders, fatalistically accepting his role.

"You all right, Deke?"

"'Course I am," he slurred, chin lowered as if a weight clung to it.

"I could stick around, or call Janie and tell her I'll see her tomorrow. Come with us if you want."

Deke smirked and swung up his beer, head bobbing.

"Happy Fourth, little brother. Drink the night with your woman and have a good time, don't worry about me; this is my province. I *like* this place."

Jason nodded, watching his brother's grizzled half-smile against the mountain ridges, and turned into the darkness.

From his porch where he listened to a scratchy record of Ray Charles singing "America" Lucas March heard the jeep changing gears from the end of Hawkins drive. He and Rashan had just finished a mushroom calzone with peppermint ice cream and Lucas smoked a pinch of the strong herb Barrett'd given him. He was eating a Butterfinger with a glass of valpolicella as he listened to distant pops and shrieks and gazed at the ribbed sky that looked like the sand bottom shallows of an ocean surf.

Ten seconds after Jason blew by with a white palm and clipped beep Lucas heard the shrill whistles and saw rockets flare up over Hawkins Mountain. He watched the sky as three more shot off in opposite directions, one trailing horizontally through the treetops splintering into red, white and blue particles. He and Rashan watched the blue line of smoke drifting, Rashan shifting on his haunches, perking his ears. Lucas noticed him listening in another direction as more missiles lofted over the Hawkins place, a couple so low only a few flickers were visible above the tree line. Tiny red and blue parachutes from the high ones silhouetted against the clouds, falling like a miniature invasion from heaven through the breeze.

Behind the music and flares Lucas heard the low-crawling drone of a small plane. It seemed to hang somewhere behind the cacophony of whistles, dive-bombing pops and bangs. Pushing up with his cane he hobbled to the front of the porch, leaning over the rail; he couldn't see anything. It sounded like an engine running against a wall, then fell silent. It'd been there so long he wondered if the sound hadn't been thrown back until it was sucked out of earshot.

As he watched more parachutes sinking across the Hawkins place he could've sworn he saw something bigger, a full-sized chute, or maybe two, something huge-winged or -pouched dropping quickly through the little floating things and smoke. Lord almighty, he thought. This wildflower Barrett had given him was too potent for his needs. The seedless stuff the kids were growing was a whole new bag from the rabbit tobacco he used to mix with his raspberry tea. He could tell Rashan had a contact high from the look in his eyes. In a few seconds they turned in the same direction as the engine started again with a whirring grinding a half-mile downwind, listening to it fade behind incendiaries screaming across the road, showering the sky with peppering lights.

On the bald, flat crest of Hawkins Mountain Deke danced like a crazed shaman inside a burning ring of red ground flares. He set up and fired his arsenal using five artillery shells for launches. The red flare he carried colored and lit his wet face and bare chest. He was giddily out of his gourd with manic energy, dancing his ritual version of an Indian-African exorcist, pumping his chin and neck to "Oye Como Va" on the boom box. He set up rockets pointed randomly, ran over and tossed up his beer, dousing himself, lighting the fuses in perfect quick succession, hollering: "*This . . . is . . . my fucking country! land that I love! . . . this . . . is . . . my fucking country . . ."* He ducked one whizzing past his ear, feeling with his hand to be sure it was intact. Another grazed his thigh side winding out of sight into the lower limbs. He staggered to his back with his legs bent beneath him, cackling at the sky, watching the streams overhead pouring, crisscrossing, spiraling and exploding with dripping umbrellas. He got up and danced and yodeled, cha-chaing to set more, ooing and ahing his work under a rain of debris. He crawled on the ground pouring out flares, planting them in the circle, hooting and howling rebel yells. Jumping up he stumbled to light a wizard's hat dark-blue cone covered with yellow moons and stars. It spewed yellows, purples and greens, fountaining like a volcano as he danced around, crying: "... more champagne, Martha! ... look at the lovely daffodils, goddamit ... More floating little men? More floating little fucking guys? Send in more of the fucking little floating men sinking and floating and fucking for you tonight! Go you fucking Airborne! Here they come now! You've got it, people! You've got it, goddamit!" On his knees he shuffled and ripped open boxes in the ring, relishing the heat, color and sulfur on his face, the cardboard gunpowder coating his chest and stomach. He felt ten years old, giggling as he arranged another arsenal in the shells. "... *This land is your land, this land is my land, from California, to the New York Island, from the red wood forests, to the gulf stream waters . . . this land was made for . . .* Hey, you, get off my land! . . . You people are too fucking beautiful! . . ."

Before Honcho had lost visual of his camouflage drop pack in the columns of smoke, he'd seen it sinking toward the narrow, terraced onion-field he had a dead-bead on himself, aiming for the mountain-shadows at the far end of it. At two-thousand feet a gust from nowhere yanked and carried him toward the treetops. As he dangled over them a rocket screamed under his legs he kicked at furiously, dancing-cursing as he checked his lines and chute for flames. Another exploded on his left and he watched a dozen miniature parachutes pop out, swinging beside him. He tilted hard from them, yanking and rattling his lines. He couldn't believe this shit. There was so much blue smoke he couldn't see the trees before he hit them, his lines buckling as the canopy deflated, dropping and catching him, slipping and snagging again, twisting and yanking him around so that he was straddling his wires. His weight pulled hard at a cramping angle so he couldn't maneuver either arm to pull his knife from his right calf pocket. As he hung cursing, another rocket shot over and lodged smoldering a few limbs from his head, him lying on his right side with his feet over his head watching it spew. Goddamn boy scouts, he thought. Didn't they know there was a drought on? He hadn't expected a pyromaniac's reception, Deke must be pickled out of his brain. He figured he was sixty, seventy feet off the ground where he was webbed, cradled at a precarious angle to slip from. He could hit the ground like a dart. He was in a giant white oak with small brittle leaves shimmering in his face. Chattering came from a squirrel's nest ten feet below in the trunk-split. As he tried to release from his harness everything slipped again, straightening him, his blackened face and camou-jumpsuited body dangling in the rippling light of roman candles shushing above him. Screw the chute, he thought. He'd get out of this shrub, secure the supplies, and come back after it, use his hook to grapple it down. Suddenly the problem was solved as he was tumbling with the chute wrapped round his thighs and neck, scraping his cheek on a half-dozen branches, hitting the ground with the brunt of his weight on his right knee. "*Goddamit!*" he grunted, writhing and rolling around on leaves and acorns. What a miserably sloppy piece of work. He pushed himself up on his good leg, tugging the top of the chute from low limbs where it was snagged, wrapping and tying it in a tight ball. He limped through the trees to find his supplies, listening to Deke's drunken wailing up on the mountain with the syncopated Latin music. Whishes flared out over the field. With each one Honcho hit the ground again, clutching and cushioning his knee, growling and spitting obscenities.

Deke'd found his missing cigar and crawled on the leaves with it in his teeth, singing and howling, groveling in the circle of burned-out flares. A beer in each hand, he rolled somersaults in the smoke. He arched on his head and feet, hunching the sky, singing into the trees: "*. . . We live in fame or go down in flames!*" he toasted. "*. . . for nothing can stop the Army Air Force . . .* you sons of bitches! . . . Go you fucking eagles!" He collapsed, moaning and rolling to his side, turned on his stomach with his face mashed into earth wiping, whimpering against it. Rolled over and sat up groggily guzzling his beers, flopped on his back again gazing at the mackerel sky puffing and glimmering flashes. Crawling to the cooler he flipped the lid and stuck his face in the ice water. The slick cans bumped him like miniature submarines. He bobbed to clamp one with his teeth. Giggling, he noticed a blurred flicker down in the trees. Oh shit, he thought, watching it to make sure it was real. It was licking up. He got up lugging the leaden cooler, staggering down the mountain shouting "Fire in the hole you motherfuckers! I told you not to do this shit! You stupid sons of bitches! I warned you, didn't I? Fire in the hole . . . *Fire in the fucking* . . ." He dumped the sloshing container in the middle of it and threw himself on top of it, rolling and wriggling like a scalded snake, yodeling and laughing hysterically on the hissing coals. He didn't know if he was burning or freezing or care as long as he kept rolling and snuffing it. He was fucking bullet-proof, he thought, elbowing and slapping the smoke and ashes, wallowing in them until he realized the ground was lukewarm. He lay there laughing on it, popping a few black-muddied beers that spumed down his stomach chilling his crotch. "*Ahhhhhh, yes*, he said, "Where'd they go . . . all those women . . . all those beautiful goddamn women . . . you too, little boy . . . goodnight, little boy . . ." he toasted the sky two-fisted, collapsing with his head in the simmering mud gazing cross-eyed at the stars blinking through the clouds. Smoke floated like the aftermath of a firefight. He shut his eyes to those grisly memories, murmuring quietly, half-singing to himself: "*Anchors . . . away, my boys . . . anchors . . . away . . .*"

Barrett left early in the morning before the heat set in, giving him extra time to reach Memphis with wet weather rolling east. Side winding through the mist-green-blanketing humidity, he floated like a ghost through the little flag-waving towns. The farther he got from the place the saner he felt, opening his valves to burn through any inertia dragging him back to it.

He felt like a new man after spilling it finally, a weight lifted. Regardless of what Deke and Jason believed they were carrying it with him now, and he was getting the hell out of there for a few days which felt like crawling out from under a rock. He didn't like being treated like some overdosing pothead making up shit, but he was used to that with Deke. It was trying to protect Deke and getting this for his trouble exasperated him. It was maddening trying to enlighten people who wouldn't acknowledge the other world if their lives depended on it, and Deke was the hardheadest son of a bitch he'd ever known. Jason was another story. The Reverend knew damn well something was going on there, but Jason wasn't running the show. Contemplating heading back to the farm in a few days, Barrett vowed to put this out of mind and give himself a break. He had a thing about keeping promises to his friends, especially when they were in a mess like this, but self-preservation had its merits too.

When he reached the interstate it was hazy-hot and drizzling. After eight months not hearing Marsha's voice he had butterflies ringing her up outside a Sizzlers. Her number was unlisted but he knew she was there, it wouldn't be hard tracking her down; they had mutual friends and he knew her haunts. He would've called earlier to let her know he was coming, but wasn't sure what kind of reception that would get. If she'd answered he would've said he had business in Memphis and was just checking in with her. Probably better anyway to show up before she had time to think about it.

He reached Red Seasons, The Shadowhauler's booking agent, who greeted him like the prodigal son. They'd been trying to get hold of him since New Years. The boys were on the road gigging from Texas to Washington State with long stretches in between, one of those hell trips he knew too well. They were ready to give him a raise and a perk or two if he came back with them, but he was taking a break from schedules, he said. The road was his bed and breakfast, he didn't know where he'd be. There was no way they could contact him really. He'd get in touch sooner or later. He sent his best to the boys.

Waiting out a downpour under an overpass he met Jimmy and Molly Hardegree, humping their BSA from Ashville to San Francisco to live with her parents. He was a steel walker, she a tattoo artist. Jim was on the GI bill studying architecture in night school. Did he want to ride with them as far as Memphis? They'd buy him a Shoney's burger buffet at the next exit. He'd eaten an hour ago, he said, and was pushing on. They tried to give him two or three joints of some very good Ouaxjacan. When he told them he was on leave from the stuff they looked at him dumbfounded. They were good-hearted, fresh-faced kids he said he'd do his best to run into down the road somewhere.

He sat out a squall near Sycamore Landing playing chess with Russ Highwater, owner of The Three Fingers Diner, listening to Indian stories of how his family'd escaped the reservation in the twenties and migrated from Montana to Tennessee. He'd been a medic in the 101st of all places. They'd spent a week in the same base together near Bong Son getting their asses shelled into the dirt. Probably sat in the same mess together, ducked under the same tables.

Near Brownville he caught up with Susie Hoffsteader, six months pregnant with her broken cat in a cardboard box. Wearing cutoffs and a white lace blouse, she was pushing her Nissan truck barefooted up the side of the interstate, trying to get over the hill to coast to the next station. Her fuel gauge was broken and she couldn't leave her cat she was bringing home from the hospital; she was afraid of motorcycles, so he siphoned gas from the Harley and rolled it into her truck. When they reached the station she tried to pay him but he wouldn't take it. Her husband who'd left her was doing seven to ten for armed robbery and grand larceny, she said, the sociopathic son-of-a-bitch. She gave Barrett her number and told him to call her on his way back for the best squash casserole in the state. The knife scar on her right cheek made his skin crawl. He couldn't stop thinking about it and that shimmer in her eyes, her face being like a physical contradiction telling you life was too beautiful for you to be looking at what you were seeing.

West of Yuma some boys in a lavender pickup covered with Confederate flags and stickers pitched firecrackers under his wheel, nearly running him off the road, swerving into him a couple of times. One with a crew cut shot him a bird as they weaved up ahead of him. He could see them laughing and jawing back, one of them waving a pistol in the window with a grin. He had the adrenaline jitters and pulled off for water. Good fun giving the nigger a heart attack. A few more gargoyles in his head. He was more concerned with what *he'd* do than with them if they fucked with him again. You had to shake off that nausea and do the cleansing mantra; you couldn't live in anyone else's hellhole. You said a little prayer and wiped the slate clean until the next time.

He wore his flight shades against the glare of cumulonimbus rumbling up ahead, his t-shirt billowing in the sun. A biker gang named the *Delicatos* thundered up, nodding for him to ride with them. They were husky, scruffy-looking guys with round-assed, longhaired women. The leader's girl kept giving him lingering, friendly smiles. He traveled with them as far as Jackson, all of them pumping their ritual farewell from the sky as they rolled up the exit ramp.

Ten minutes later traffic began to back up on the interstate and he saw emergency vehicles through the leaves behind a curve where two parts of the highway merged. Cruising the shoulder he came up on the sixteen vehicle smash-up strewn along the road, median and banks. A crumpled boat lay upended on the opposite side of the highway against the embankment, an eighteen wheeler lay on its side in the outside culvert leaking fuel, two more wrapped around each other on the inside shoulder. Mangled, upturned and twisted vehicles were scattered down the highway like a high speed demolition derby, people running around panic-ridden. A woman cried as she pounded an ambulance window. A group of women with heads in their hands cradled children on the hillside. There were a dozen ambulances and fire trucks, emergency crews scrambling up and down the glass-glittered wreckage, cars on fire. He recognized the lavender pickup in the culvert behind one of the semis, rocking on its nose, wheels turning. Rescue workers on their knees maneuvered someone out a window and were using the jaws-of-life to rip the roof away. He could see torsos and a bloody hand slugging cracked glass from inside. He asked a State Trooper if there were anything he could do, he'd been a medic in the army and could treat wounds, give CPR, whatever they needed. The chinless man stared at him behind his wire-rims and waved him on.

He passed a rodeo covered with flag-fliers and banners, a shining stream of black stretch-limos. A line of country singers in buses were headed over from Nashville for the Fourth of July shows. Traffic was piling in on the outskirts of the city. He checked into a Motel 6 near Summer Avenue, washed and shaved and cruised into town. He sat at the bar at *The Rendevous* and ordered a plate of ribs with a frosted draft. The place was roaring and filling up though it was early for the dinner crowd. He asked Sarah the bartender if she'd seen Marsha lately. She said the last time was two weeks ago when she'd come in with a well-dressed white gentleman and sat right where he was. They'd tipped vodka tonics and laughed a few hours. Where'd he been? She hadn't seen him in a season or two. Don't be so scarce, she said, drawing him a draft on her with a wink.

He sipped the icy foam, relishing the warm mind-numbness. As he watched the couples and parties drifting in, the women languorous and glazed from the heat on the sidewalks, he wondered what he was doing there. He was in Memphis and she was a couple óf miles away. She had no idea he was in town, and he was sitting at this bar drinking, thinking about her. Exquisite torture, he guessed; maybe it was the safest place to be. What the hell, enjoy it anyway, what's five more minutes. Sitting in the well-lit establishment with the piano clanking and crowds roiling over each other, the smell of perfume, rotisserie smoke, alcohol and cigars, an Independence Day parade on the bar televisions, he pictured the visitors at the Hawkins place and stared at the liquor bottles in front of the mirror. They glowed like the luminous figures in the fields. After a while he looked around, realizing where he was. How long had he been doing that? Damn it, he had to stop it. He was there to get away from all that, remember? Turn it *off* for God sakes.

He tipped Sarah, climbed on his bike and headed toward the river along Summer Avenue, the fragrant breeze of restaurant and shop smells intoxicating after the beers. Something big was going on at the Rhodes Coliseum, the place decked out with American flags, and there were a hundred buses in the parking lot. He cruised the lane of apartment buildings off Thomas Street and parked in front of the red-brick two story, glancing up the steps before cutting his engine. He sat a minute with his head down, getting ready for God knew what, pulled off his flight shades and walked up the cracked concrete steps. A sheltie lay at the side of the entrance panting in the heat, ignoring him with a smile looking down at the road. Fireworks were popping in the neighborhood and she jerked nervously. When he leaned to pet her she ducked and whined.

He went down the creaking old-smell of the hallway, reminding him of the night he'd met Marsha when she'd brought him there. He looked at the letters JRH carved halfway down the door-molding, grey-painted-over since he'd seen them last. They meant nothing except that they were on her door. Strange how insignificant things affected you. After eight months not seeing her he stood in the hall staring at a stranger's initials. Music played inside. He knocked and waited. A thin-faced, waifish blonde in a pink t-shirt opened the door a quarter way, shutting it with her straw-white fingers, dragging on a pencil-length cigarette.

"Something I can do for you?"

"Marsha here?"

"I don't know *Marsha*," she said in a languid-silky voice, flat-business-like.

"She used to live here. I'm—"

"How would you know that?"

He shifted. "Friend of hers."

"You from the club?"

He looked down the hall at the in slanting light. "No, which club's that?"

"How do you know her then?"

"What's it to you if you don't know her?"

The woman stared at him silently; she shut the door slowly.

"We went out, all right? She live here or not?"

She stared a few seconds through the narrowed crack.

"I'll give her your name. Got a number?"

He took out pen and paper and wrote his name, motel phone and room numbers.

"Tell her I'll be here a few days," he handed it to her, already figuring who he'd call next to find her. The door creaked open as she looked at him with a serious shyness, twisting her hair with a curling finger.

"She's working *The Love Machine* on Beale Street. You know where that is?"

"Imagine I can find it. Hey, I appreciate it," he said, padding down the hall.

"She's wondered about you. Thought you'd dropped off the planet. Girl can't be too careful in this business. You ought to understand."

He kept going out, noticing the sheltie gone by the door, on down the steps to his bike. Two boys were ogling it and wanted to know how fast it'd do. He told them and sat a minute, revving it for them. He said to be careful with those fireworks hanging from their pockets, showing them the scars on his cheek and temple, the big one on his side from the claymore, and roared off toward Beale Street.

He found *The Love Machine* with its gaudy ten foot neon naked woman wired with multicolored blinking sprockets, pulleys, pistons and tubes. She leaned over, wagging her breasts and bottom, stood up back-bowed tossing her tits around oooing and ahing. He was just in time for free oysters. He parked his bike at the side corner on the grass facing the adjacent sex-shop in case he needed to get out of there fast. He kept his shades on and strolled along the back wall, sitting out of light in a rear corner booth.

It was a typical sex-den with red vinyl and mirrors smoked-up from machines and too many cigarettes. Over "Sexual Healing" the black DJ was telling a loud bunch of cowboys at the end of the main platform to cough up cash for the ladies. A neckless giant staggered up and hunched the stage sending them all into stitches. A couple of nervous bouncers watched them from the shadows. There were gangster- and pimp-looking brothers scattered around the club, dancers and waitresses hovering like bees around a table of well-oiled businessmen. Some white mobster look-a-likes with slinky black prostitutes held court near the bar. A tall blonde in nothing but black stockings and heels did a table dance ten feet away. Other table dances were going on all over the club and naked dancers, mostly half-starved blondes, leaned and worked off mirrors, most of them entranced-looking, floating around the room like soulless sexual shells. Another day in paradise-hell, he thought, not spotting Marsha yet, feeling funny about taking too much of this in while he was waiting for her. The place was half-full of customers but heated up. A wild-eyed, wiry brother in dreadlocks was darting around talking excitedly to everybody as if he'd just discovered a cure for cancer or was a desperate morale booster in a depression ward. He was high as hell on something. He must have spread a lot of money around because everybody was humoring him. He sensed Barrett like a radar and jetted over to him, squeezing his hand and raving about seeing him at *Sliders* last night. The more Barrett said no the more agitated he got, insulted and frantic, looking around as if he were going to call in backup. When Barrett remembered it all suddenly, he nodded, rolled his yellow eyes to the next table and blew over to it, exclaiming and waving his hands in the air.

Barrett ordered a beer with his oysters and sat back surveying the place, trying to pick her out of a smoky corner or alcove. He'd done too much time in these places and hated them, but these women were stunning to look at. After his time in the woods with the guys it was like looking at some mythical superrace, which it sort of was anyway. Then it would sadden him because it was such a puppet show, and the woman he loved was part of it and he didn't want to be there. The DJ came on with a drum roll.

"At this time, ladies and gentlemen, give a warm and generous L-o-o-o-o-ve Machine welcome back to the main stage, to the ravishing, the delicious, the intoxicating Aleysha and Aristaphal!"

Two very good-looking dancers, one black, one white, jogged onto center stage with strobing lights to James Brown's "Sex Machine." The black one was Marsha. Wearing white-lace silk pajamas she covered the stage, hunching, kicking, doing splits, bending and shaking her shoulders, swinging her head and hips and knees, working her tail to the crowd. You asked for it, Barrett thought, as she bent over to shake her pants onto the stage with an undulating movement, splaying her palms on the floor. Under them were see-through bikini panties. She turned and fell in a spidery hover, shaking her pants in her teeth with her rear opened to the ceiling, her body rippling like an exotic centipede. She looked better than he remembered, as if that could've mattered. It was a relief to see her. Then he felt a little inappropriate. Maybe after the words they'd had eight months ago it wasn't the coolest thing in the world to be watching her get naked from the shadows.

She rose to her knees doing a willowy dance, undoing her white-lace bra working it slowly over her head as the cowboys in front screamed and pounded their beer mugs. The white dancer was working some crazies on the other side of the stage. She wore black lace and lots of beads under an unbuttoned man's pinstripe shirt. She was a pale, sinewy, black-haired beauty. As she strutted around Marsha who was still playing the floor, one of the drunks in front lunged for her high heels and she skipped back coquettishly, rubbing the naughty finger at him with come-on eyes. He was a huge, fat-faced man the size of a professional lineman, and his friends in western hats and boots weren't much smaller. He turned, guffawing to them, and a stout bouncer in a knit shirt tapped him on the shoulder telling him to cut it out. A minute later he was doing it again, both girls hurdling his lunges like a field game, flirting and trying not to alienate the rest of the crowd.

Barrett ordered another beer and tried to relax, cocking his head against the cushioned booth. He turned away when Marsha squatted and wagged her bottom at the cowboys. Her garters were feathered with bills. When she did movements with her abdomen the boys gawked stunned-like, then popped up like jumping jacks mimicking her, screaming and hooting.

Both women were down to their heels and garters. The DJ kept telling the crowd to put their money where their drooling mouths were, cajoling their manhood from their wallets. A billfold and a dick were the same thing in these places: you pleasured the women or you were an impotent loser. The dreadlocks brother was skating around the platform singing and pointing, his face oil-sheened with frenetic sweat. He dangled a C-note in the air the girls kept luring from him. He'd run off as if he'd forgotten something and reappear like some ecstatic marionette. He reminded Barrett of photographs of Salvador Dali. A voluptuous redhead leaned over Barrett shaking her pretty breasts in his face, asking if he wanted a table dance. For a few seconds he couldn't take his eyes off them. It's unkind, he thought. Unfair. Even with his woman up there they made him want to cry, to just lay his face in them and wallow. There were too many things going on here. Looking past her he flipped her a dollar and waved her away. She snatched it and stomped off pouting, her luscious thonged bottom smacking him in the face as she disappeared into the smoke.

Two of the raucous seven in front were getting table dances. One of the dancers was letting the recipient lick her stomach, navel, and thigh. The white dancer on stage was doing a slow, bobbing split, holding her breasts to the boys with both hands. Barrett saw the lunger get up and grab her string beads, jerking her face to the platform. Some of them snapped and baubles flew everywhere. He was unzipping his pants as a bouncer head locked him from behind. One of lunger's friends had the bouncer in a headlock himself, howling as they all swayed, rocking in a gripping, crab-like huddle, "Come on, it's his birthday! Let him have some fun! . . ."

Suddenly there were six men holding each other like a rugby scrummage, groaning and shouting as they fell over tables and beer pitchers backwards, the black-haired dancer sliding off the stage with them like a dog being collared from a platform. Lunger had her hair and beads and was choking her with one hand, pulling her toward his crotch with his friends holding off the four outnumbered bouncers. Barrett saw lunger's massive brick-head sweat-straining to stay on its feet as someone was squeezing his thighs and waist, a black bouncer on his knees in a grip of viselike arms. There were five scuffles going on. A Latino bartender and manager fought into the melee, all of them on the floor kicking tables and chairs, glasses shattering. Dreadlock brother was darting around gesticulating, screaming and grinning. Lunger erupted from all this again like some beleaguered Cyclops with his captive dancer writhing, clutching at her neck. Marsha leaned over him, pounding at his temples and face. Another bouncer had him by the forehead from behind, but lunger was necking down to look at his new flame on the floor.

Suddenly Barrett stood in the big man's face against the stage, straddling the gagging dancer with a six-inch blade at his throat. Through his shades Barrett scowled at him while he put a garroting choke on the back of his neck with his other hand.

"Release the girl and put it in your pants, or I'll make you a soprano and shove your dick down your throat, you got me?"

The man's eyes rolled to the knife with drunken bewilderment. He didn't understand his fun being interrupted. He waited to see if anybody was going to rescue him, dripping head twitching and gyrating in the stranglehold. No one was going to help him. Face blackening, turning several shades of purple, he dropped the girl finally who slid down Barrett's leg like a limp washcloth, gasping with her tongue on his shoe.

He sat with Marsha in the Beale Street Diner, watching panhandlers working the corner. A legless bearded man in a sleeveless military jacket propped on the curb peddling American flags on sticks as foot-traffic shuffled by. Firecrackers crackled with horns and sirens. There were more street people, beggars, crazies and drunks than he'd ever seen in this river town. The splendors of siphon-up economics, he guessed. Stevie Wonder played on the jukebox. A starved-looking couple with shaved heads except for a few pointed tufts sat in a booth gazing deadly out the windows. Some brothers in gold African robes and jewelry strolled in and sat at the end of the diner.

"I think George Clinton just walked in here," Marsha said.

"Looks like him. More coffee for Aleysha?"

"Very cool, Barrett, pulling a knife in my place of business. Lucky you're not in jail."

"I used to bounce skin-dens, remember? It's not like that never happens, Aleysha."

"Call me by my name, all right? It wasn't your job. You pulled a goddamn knife, Barrett."

"Your boys weren't handling it; they were about to get that girl killed. You get a good look at her neck?"

"Nobody asked you to be there, did they? What the hell were you doing?"

He watched them facing each other in the window.

"You said you were done with the clubs when you got that film part."

"One lousy role as a prostitute."

"You were good in that flick, baby."

"I couldn't get another one. There were bills to pay."

"I offered, remember?"

She stared at him, nodding: "For a price."

"You're payin' all right. When you've got no self-respect and another redneck rapes you in his truck, you'll be just about paid up."

She leaned across the table.

"You don't own me, Barrett, and I don't owe you shit. You left me here, remember? I don't even know why I'm sittin' with you."

"Yeah you do."

"Oh yeah? Where've you been? I haven't heard shit from you. I thought you were dead. I was fucking *worried*. None of the band knew where you were, what was I supposed to think? My mom passes on, I still don't hear from you. You show up tonight like some caped crusader; you're a hell of a note, Barrett."

"Sorry about your mama."

"She asked about you."

"I've been kind of preoccupied."

"Where've you been?"

He looked at them again in the glass, reflected with a drunken panhandler staggering on the other side. Lost souls picked up on wounds like hyenas sniffing blood. He stared at the man's demon; something fell out of him and he stumbled away.

In the glass she was willingly there for him, leaning into him, talking earnestly. What'd he want, to love her, run her or both?

"On a farm," he said, watching fireworks lofting across the rooftops.

"A farm?" she said, amused.

"Yeah."

"Whose?"

"Guy named Deke."

"That your Vietnam buddy?"

"Same guy."

"Imagine you're growin' potatoes out there. Kettle calls the teapot black, nothing's changed."

"He's losing his daddy's place."

"So you're going to jail for him."

"Fuck no. Give me some credit."

"Don't quote the Bible to me, not right here. You're one of the best singers in the world, Barrett. You and I know it, everybody says so, and you're out in the boonies growing that stuff? Why's that? I might have a shot as an actress if I work long and hard at it, but you can be ripping people's hearts out *tonight* with your pipes. Who'd that producer compare your voice to, Bobby Bland's? Otis Redding's?"

"They blow a lot of smoke."

"Well, I don't. It's your gift, honey. You're nuts to be doing anything else. You should be sitting in a recording studio right now, laying down everything you've got, playing the main arenas. You *know* you should. Why're you doing this?"

"It's a recreational break and an emergency situation for a blood brother, not a career choice. How long you been dancing, five, six years?"

"Don't change the subject."

"This *is* the subject. Stripping will kill your soul. I've seen it happen. One day you'll wake up strung-out, burnt-out and they won't even want to look at you. I know how it goes, so do you. Then what?"

"What I'm doin's legal."

"With whom? The state of Tennessee? The redneck board of adulterers?"

"Asshole."

"There's legal bad and illegal good, you know that, Aleysha. If I were croppin' tobacco that'd be one thing, I'd take a different view of myself. If I were pushing liquor across a bar I wouldn't feel too slick about it. This is different to me."

She lit a cigarette, shaking her head. "You're puttin' me down for my work and you're workin' a hooch farm? Who do you think you're kidding?"

"Cool your voice."

"Why should I? I may just turn you in."

"Why don't you get up on the counter and shake your pussy for everybody?"

"Fuck you, Barrett."

He leaned forward. "Yeah and who else? You got plenty of regulars at the Love Machine asking you to come over to cop a little personal show? Add a little . . . personal touch if there's a nice tip in it, huh? A little . . ."

"Shut up . . ."

". . . extra change for a hand job, and the high roller's lay-in' out, what, half a K for the private dance? That what it's going for now? You forgot what slavery is girl? You wonder why I couldn't hack it?"

"Is that right," she said, nodding.

"How many regulars you puttin' out to, approximately? Let's have a body count. Couple of execs? The mayor, a truck driver, couple cops. How many tricks you countin' on the side—"

"Fuck you!" she got up, twisting the table against him. "Do you hear me! I don't do anything but dance now. I don't see you most of a year and you come back in here laying this moral crap on me! I don't believe you!" Her face contorted, her wet eyes shimmering. "You asshole! I couldn't find you to tell you I was gonna have your child, to see what you wanted me to do about it, as if that mattered to you. Why should it? So I just did away with it so you wouldn't have anything else to hold against me, 'cause I knew you would, 'cause you always do. So now you'll probably hold that against me, won't you? Well, I don't give a damn anymore, Barrett. I'm saving my money and looking for a real life, see, away from here, away from this business, and I don't want you in it. So just fuck off back to your bosom buddy. Go fuck him on his goddamn farm and fuck yourself and stay the fuck away from me, all right!"

She slid out of the booth with her hand on her mouth, raking her cup to the floor splattering in the aisle. He heard a whimper as she pushed out the door, and watched her trot up the street with her hands on her face, running side to side in her short black skirt and blue stockings. He stirred his coffee as the waitress put the check on the table and cleaned the mess without looking at him. The couple across the aisle stared at him, amused by it, waiting to see what he'd do. He thought about it, thought better of it, drained his cup and slid a five on the table. He winked at them and strolled out into the stale, gun-powder-rich, garbage-humid noise on the street to his motorcycle.

He headed to the 51 and drove a hundred miles an hour toward the motor sport park, whipping through cars like they were standing still. He didn't know why they acted this way. Sometimes it seemed their little battle of wills meant more to them than each other. He had a soreness round his heart like he'd been kicked in the chest.

Seventy miles out his adrenaline deflated and he made a U-turn and started back to town. Cruising down Riverside Drive, he took the 55 over the river, watching the fireworks on the wide black water from the Arkansas side. He took the 40 bridge back across by the Great American Pyramid, passing the Fairgrounds where a music show was wrapping up. From the hilltop he watched a passel of kids playing together in a parking lot with yellow sparklers, the halo-like fires swirling round their faces. They seemed oblivious to anything but this blissful night, in their own perfect children's world. Watching them, it struck him how much justice there had to be beyond this life; behind what you could see in it. How many benefactors of the bloodiest sacrifices weren't even aware the sacrifices had been made. They didn't know how many fathers and brothers and sons had suffered and given their lives so they wouldn't have to endure anything but this perfect American night. He hoped the boys who'd made the sacrifices could see them down there and knew what they'd done for them, himself included. Singers and steel guitars twanged in the amphitheater. The crowd cheered a country singer coming onstage and everyone was singing "Oh, Beautiful For Spacious Skies." He started up and headed over to Mulberry Street on his way home.

He drove past the Lorraine Hotel and sat in the dark, looking at the balcony with the wreath on the railing where the shots had hit the great man, listening to the cracklings. He cruised through town, taking his time getting to his motel, he bought a quart of Budweiser, checked the desk for messages, went to his room and took a hot bath and cool shower. He sipped his beer while he read the Gideon's Bible, listening to a couple making love in the next room. Muffled moans rose and whimpered as their bed creaked in a steady two-part rhythm banging and tapping the wall occasionally. They'd stop and he'd hear playful murmurs, then they'd start up again. A few firecrackers rattled outside. The television droned with talk show laughter.

"*Judge not, lest you cut your own fucking throat, asshole,*" he muttered to himself, plopping the Bible on his chest. He stared at the ceiling, listening to the quiet voice-tones as he thought about her, his mom and pop, Deke and Jason, a sweet, pregnant Susie Hoffsteader with her broken cat in a cardboard box. After a while he shut his eyes with his arm over his face and dreamed about a blissful night in this town a few years ago.

In the morning he rode to a cafe on Union where they'd always had breakfast, hoping she'd get the same idea and wander in herself. From the night they'd met they'd shown up regularly at the same places without planning to, as if on some unconscious rendezvous schedule. But she didn't show this morning. She must've known he'd be there and really didn't want to see his face.

He ordered eggs, maple syrup sausages and coffee, feeling foolish, worse and sicker, then finally like some deluded idiot waiting for someone who was over him and wasn't coming. He could almost feel her ridiculing him. Maybe she was gone this time. Maybe she wasn't with him last night. She'd seemed to be with that beautiful pouting way she got pissed and fumed at him, but how could he tell? Maybe she was in love with some blazing new stud and tying up loose ends. Not able to read his mind all this time, she'd written him off and started over. It happened to the best and it happened to the rest. Aborting his baby had been the right place to do it. Goddamn, he was going to have a child with her and was too oblivious to realize it. He'd loved her on his terms and been too proud to check in on her. There was nothing sadder than believing, no, *knowing* a woman was with you and gloating over it long after she'd started pitying you. *Nothing.* He cringed as he watched the waking couples smiling at each other over coffee and clanking dishes. He felt the pang go all the way down, then started to climb back up. He wasn't going to apologize for trying to save her, hell no; he was doing the right thing here. Why was he getting so maudlin about it? Don't let your feelings cloud the truth, he thought. There were too many good women that weren't strippers he had to fight with over something like this, and her comparing stripping to what he was doing for his brothers irritated him. She didn't have any sense of charity, of putting your ass on the line for a buddy. That was part of him she didn't care about that he cared a lot wasn't in her. They were different in that way, always would be, and it'd always cause conflict. She cared about him, sure, but for herself, not for him. He knew that wasn't absolutely true, but it felt true enough, and in time would be enough to get over her.

He made the rounds of guitar shops he'd traded with for years, running into a few old friends and burned-out musical acquaintances. He found the Fender Stratocaster he'd been looking for at Hank's and Don's Vintage Guitars, a 1964 original that'd been handed around. He felt the juice in it when he picked it up, and when he played it through a '59 Fender twin-reverb the tone was velvet heaven. The scratch through the natural finish on the back made it sweeter, like the scar under Susie Hoffsteader's eye. The neck was sweet and fast as a young girl's hips. They wanted twice as much as he had with him, but offered to put it on layaway until Christmas and he could send the rest.

He dropped by three different studios to see what kind of deals he could get on time in February when he was ready to record. One thing Marsha had clenched for him last night was to do his own project now, to get up front with his voice. She was right: *it was time*. It'd been eating at him for years. Hell, all his life. He'd written some new tunes he was pleased with and what she'd said last night gave him no where to go but to do it, her parting gift. She'd always been wife-like in her instinctive way, they'd been each other's consciences whether they liked it or or not. It was fitting this was the last thing she did for him.

At Sun he wanted to talk to Sam Phillips to get in touch with session players he'd need when he came back to town. He found out which ones were with which bands and when they'd be around, taking down numbers. He'd use some of The Shadowhaulers, his bass man brother Midas Singleton for most of the tracks, but wanted two or three monster players to back up his first choices in case some were on the road or he couldn't find them when he got in the studio. He was going to do this right, and lay down some mind-boggling tracks, put his own distinct dent into the comatose blues world. When their crop was done he'd have plenty of time and money and stored up musical uranium to work with.

By the time he'd put together what he needed it was two in the afternoon. He ran to *The Run Boogie Cafe* for a steak and to check out the lunch band. Bored to death by a bunch of sterile white kids without a grain of

blues in their bodies, he was half-drunk on tequila Bloody Mary's before
he stumbled over to *Joyce Cobb's* club and met up with a crazy party of
Little Rock yahoo's. The women were lit and twice as loose as the men,
thin, short-haired, wild-headed blondes that kept manhandling him out of
his seat to dance, one of which named Dolores kept massaging him under
the table and wouldn't let him pay for a drink or finish one before another
appeared. He was good and soused before they stumbled and shouted down
the street to *The King's Palace Cafe*. By now they knew he could sing. One
of them had seen him play with The Shadowhaulers New Years before last.
They were calling him Big Bloody Bear as they fed him tequila shooters.
The women talked Little Boy Blues into letting him sit in and delivered
him staggering and laughing to the stage.

It was like a sweating, reeling hot-dream under the lights watching
all these hooting people's contorted faces waiting for him to perform.
Drunk enough to fall on his face, he somehow railed through a couple of
songs, "Baby Don't You Go Too Far" and a Nehemiah James tune, "Devil
Got My Woman," and people were applauding and whistling. The band
were giving go-ahead looks and some kids in front were either as drunk
as he was or thought he was somebody else. Suddenly he realized how
bad off he was and tried to leave the club. His friends insisted on getting
him to his motel. One of the men picked up his bike and tailed the rest
in an old Buick station wagon, all of them singing over a Johnny Shines
tape. They took a vote for bluesman of the year and Big Bloody Bear
won unanimously, the car rocking and shimmying as they jerked and
swayed and seesawed through traffic. His face against the cold glass in
the backseat, Dolores was massaging his temples. He could've sworn she
was scratching his gonads under his leg with her other hand. She was one
you'd like to have a case of stuck away for another time. Halfway through
the ride he realized her husband was riding behind them on his Harley.
The last thing he remembered was lying on his bed with the light slicing
from the bathroom, everyone patting, telling him goodnight and to meet
them tomorrow night at B.B.'s if he was up to it. He listened to the voices
filing out singing "Baby, Please Don't Go."

He woke with a massive headache seeing 8:41 on the sidetable clock.
It was too dark to be A.M. He'd gotten head-swimming drunk for some
reason; he felt like he'd been hit with a sledgehammer. Tell the truth, he
thought. Oh yeah, he'd felt so motherfucking lousy about Marsha and tried

to pretend it didn't matter. He'd stonewalled and the tsunami of alcohol had washed over his parapets. Faking would always get you, he thought. He felt like a soul sick piece of dogshit because he loved her so much. He did, their differences be damned, and he had to get like this to realize what really mattered.

His pride didn't matter. Fuck pride in the ass. Where the hell did pride get you? Could you take it with you? To hell you could. Pride was the enemy of the heart. Oh, wasn't that astute? You're damned eloquent when you're pie-eyed. It was true though, wasn't it? In the morning he'd bare his soul to her and not react to anything she threw back at him. He was a notarized witness to this. Don't get sober and try to squirm out of it, he thought. He'd feel clean about them when he left this town. Something had been nagging him to do that anyway. That was half of why he'd run over here, he realized, for some godforsaken reason. Which creeped him even as drunk as he was, but don't start on that now. Who else had he felt this way about? It didn't matter how she reacted or if she spit in his face, just tell her how you feel and leave it at that. He felt absolutely like hell.

He crawled to the window to see if he could spy his bike. It was parked by the door with a bottle in a paper bag bungeed to the back of the seat. He crawled to the john and sat on the floor throwing up, took a long shower sitting in the tub letting the lukewarm water trickle over him, taking small sips of Alka Seltzer. He dried off, sitting, crawled back out finding his wallet and keys on the dresser, realizing he hadn't spent a dime after running into his Arkansas friends. They were good people. Goddamit, they were. That goddamn Dolores had just about killed him. He crawled under the sheets and went to sleep.

The room was ice-chilled from the whining air. Sweating naked and twisted in sheets, he had a dream with some grotesque woman's face in it. He realized a woman was cackling outside his door. A drunken couple were rolling around in the courtyard by the pool. Rain whipped against the windows and the cackling ceased. He heard a key twisting in the door. Through the peephole he saw an older black couple dressed in dark suits and hats against the flashing downpour, cheek-to-cheek as if posing for a family portrait. They looked like refugees from the forties stepped off a train in some country little town.

"Yeah?" he said.

"226?"

"126."

"Excuse me," the man said, flustered, scooping up their luggage with embarrassment, scurrying off. He listened to their footsteps clicking down the corridor with water slapping from the eaves. He stood a while leaning on the door, swaying a bit. He took more aspirin, lay back down and shut his eyes. He couldn't stop seeing the old couple's faces staring through the peephole, the looks in their eyes peering in at him as if they knew him. As he drifted off they became mixed up with his dead parents. They'd come in the middle of the night to give him a message, he thought. What'd they want? He shouldn't have turned them away like that.

He sat up in bed. What are you doing? he thought. They were just an old couple looking for their room, they weren't your parents. They weren't some mystical messengers from them either: mom and pop by proxy. All right, all right, so this is working on you, eating at you from all sides. You thought you had a choice but you don't. There's no sense saying you don't feel worried about going back there, but you have to, the boys are counting on you. You don't know what's really going on and you don't want to be run out of there any more than they do. To hell with it. What if all this meant nothing? What if you were an alarmist and they forfeited the farm because of it? Whatever's going on there you belong to now, and no number of elderly black couples rapping on your door's going to change that.

He dozed off again; he was sleeping soundly. He heard clicking sounds outside. He was floating down a long, leaf-covered lane of drooping marijuana colas the size of baseball bats, turning to greet him like half-plant, half-human children. The light was soft-tinged: a rarefied protective glow. It was like heaven for plants: nothing could harm him here.

He felt someone sink to the bed, lifted his eyes and turned to see the eclipse-like outline of a woman. Too stunned to make a sound, he wasn't sure he was awake. *Who?* he thought. *What?* She wore a pale t-shirt, her hair pulled back in a soft braid; there was something familiar about her. For a few seconds he thought it was his mother's ghost, then he saw the flowered print on the curtains, car lights swinging around the walls.

"Barrett?"

"Yeah."

"You okay?"

"Uh huh."

"*Pedro?*"

"*Marsha?*"

"You're dreamin', honey, wake up."

A hand like radiating silk touched his forearm; he felt the hair rising under his goose bumps.

"What is it, baby?"

"It's . . . what?"

"Rest easy. Lay back, there you go."

He let out a relieved groan. "My God," he said, looking around the room. "How the—"

"I said I was your wife and wanted to surprise you on our anniversary. You're tremblin', baby."

"I didn't know what you were . . ."

"What?"

"Who. Where . . ."

". . . just us."

"Thank God. What time's it?"

"Late-thirty. You weren't expecting someone?"

"Hell no. Scared the living shit out of me."

"Maybe this isn't a great idea."

"No, no, I was going to find you tomorrow, today, to apologize—"

She sealed his lips with her fingers.

"I was kinda rough myself. We'll get over it. Want some company?"

"You kiddin'?"

She stood and pulled her t-shirt over her head and he saw the lines of her face in flutters, her deer-like hips against the curtains. He touched her liquid thigh as she loosened her hair and shook it down, her full copper breasts shining from the window. She crawled on the bed draping them up his legs, brush-rubbing them on his pelvis, pressing and moving her fur on his, kissing him gently with her open mouth.

"Oh Lord," he said. "Let me do something."

"Don't worry about that."

When she lifted and sat on him his voice cracked. She leaned against him, rolling her hips in a steady rhythm as he gnawed her wrists.

"Dance if you want," he said. "Save this for me."

She sighed and tossed her head, sat up and lifted and lowered herself on him with her hands on his chest. His fingers on her soft hips and buttocks, thumbs in the creases of her thighs, he moaned and begged like a man being tortured. He twisted her nipples in his fingers as she lowered one to his mouth, moving deeper and faster on him, saying *oh my God, you . . . you . . . yes, you . . . baby please . . .*

"Let's . . . children."

"Oh, Pedro . . . Say the word . . ."

"There's my word . . ."

"Oh, baby, that's all I want if that's what you want. I'm sorry . . ."

"Stop it."

"I didn't know . . ."

"*Marsha.*"

"What do you want?"

"You know . . ."

"Yeah," she cringed and groaned, her back bowing as she fell against him rocking and screaming. He pushed her off and lay behind her with the tops of his feet in the balls of hers, pinning her to the bed.

"Do you really want that?" she groaned.

"Do you?"

"I've always. I was foolish . . ."

"Don't . . . we'll bring it back right now . . . the itsy bitsy spider . . . up the spout . . . again . . ."

She laughed, seriously: "Listen to the rain, honey."

"Missed you so goddamn much, Marsha."

"Oooooh, baby . . ." she said.

He watched her heartbreaking seam rise in rumbling flutters with the air getting brain-lit. He felt them going, lifting and floating up into that open door where everything flooded in singing and laughing.

"Oh my God," she said to it. ". . . Pedro . . ."

". . . Marsh . . ."

"Oh my fucking *God*, yes."

". . . Lord God . . ."

"Heavens," she said, laughing uncontrollably, twitching with her back bowed letting out startled, rippling screams. It felt like they'd left their bodies and were attached in some radiant breeze. He kissed her shoulders making her shiver and buckle. "Oh my Lord in heaven . . . Oh my Lord . . ."

". . . darlin' . . ."

"Have you ever . . ."

". . . you kiddin' me . . ."

"You haven't left," she said.

"Give me a second," he giggled.

"Did you feel that?"

". . . it had me . . ."

". . . oh papa . . ."

". . . sweet Martian . . ."

"I'll stop dancing, Pedro. Whatever you want."

"They may want to watch a pregnant girl strip."

"You're a sick boy, Pedro."

Watching the shape of her lips was enough to urge him. He saw her feel him in her face, the affectionate tilt of her head on the pillow and her pleasured smile.

"You're putting me out of business, Mr. Barrett. Mas, Pedro? Hm? You're gonna have to sing for this from now on, you know. Oh God," she said, her voice weakening as she started to nod into it, ". . . That'll work too . . . that'll work . . ."

In the turquoise-paling room they slept on their sides away from the windows, Barrett spooning her with his right arm round her elbow. When he kissed her ear her head swiveled and she snuggled into him with a hoarse, childlike groan, her rear-end caressed against him.

He listened for a while to the sounds of feet beating through shallow water. Snatches of voices connected to running patterings seemed farther away. The steps were close enough to touch him, water being splashed and broken. He heard echoing exchanges and shouting coming in dribs as the hums turned to churning concussions sucking the air, thrumming at it. He watched the shallow green water rippling with rotorwashes as he listened to the continuous, plodding feet, a pair at a time, three or four pair, a few again.

His and Sixth Platoon were crossing a large paddy in thick fog. Everyone was in a panic to get across. Visibility was fifteen or twenty feet at best, dense as pea soup. With what was coming the visibility made everyone nervous as virgins in a brothel. He noticed the ghost-like figures of farmers as he listened to the running soldiers shouting and barking out orders. Gunships made crisscross patterns over the circling Hueys. The slicks were heading toward LZ Miranda just beyond the southern tree line.

Troops stumbled over Vietnamese women working in the paddy with their children, tripped soldiers wound up, trigger-happy, snapping and cursing. His captured AK swung down, he was running farmer-to-farmer yelling at them to get out of there, to follow the evacuating soldiers from this field. He gestured to the sky, telling them what was coming. They seemed uninterested. They didn't seem to be registering anything. Faces of young children looked at him with no comprehension.

"We're gonna burn this paddy!" he shouted. "Chung ta se dot khu Quan nay! American planes bringing fire. Nguri My du dinh den voi lua! You gotta get outta here! Take these kids and go!"

As he started pushing them they slapped back. A few at first, toppling over, getting up dripping, their faces red and furious. He couldn't believe this shit. He shot his AK in the air, waving and shouting at them. They yelled back, kids joining in, ranting, pushing against him. They closed round him slinging their arms in his face. More choppers popped and circled overhead, the water waving and riveting under them. Soldiers splashed by banging into him and a few of the farmers he was wrangling with.

He heard small-arms fire, bullets thunking the muckwater. There was mounting confusion as troops entered the field from a perpendicular flank. Where the hell were they coming from? He kept hearing footsteps from different directions, that constant, plodding, beating through water. He pushed through the mob to farmers who were still working, yanking their hands from the mud, yelling at them, "Leave it, for God sake! It's gonna burn! You gotta evacuate! Get the hell out of here, goddamit!" As he stumbled along dozens of bent-over women and children appeared and he was splashing through them, shouting, shrill, half-crazy that he couldn't get through to them. Some wouldn't look at him. He'd get under their faces on a knee, yelling up at them, slapping their sides. Unless he physically grabbed them they'd gaze into their hands as if he wasn't there.

Finally he started lifting children, dragging them squalling through the water chased by mothers who jumped on him like rabid monkeys, cursing and tearing at his face. He fell under a flailing tangle of them. He saw the RTO jogging by on a field phone. He jumped up and ran after him with irate mothers at his heels, a few hanging on, hurling them off as he yelled:

"We gotta get these people outta here before we burn this thing! There're hundreds of farmers out here! Tell them we need more time!"

"*. . . Tango, Charlie, Delta, November, Whiskey, Romeo . . ." the lieutenant spouted into his receiver. ". . . say back . . . repeat your ETA, Wild Fox, we're set for dinner here, over . . . "*

Barrett grabbed the RTO by the neck as he was being mauled and climbed on himself, shaking him frantically, digging fingers into his throat. "Tell them to delay the goddamn strike, I said. Tell them now! They're gonna fry these people! TELL THEM OR I'LL FRAG YOUR ASS. YOU HEAR ME!"

Jets roared overhead, drowning his voice. For a minute the noise was a whiteout as he struggled in a bound-up morass of octopus-like arms constricting his hands from inflicting pain on the RTO, tying him up, prying him away. He was bleary-eyed-crazy, helplessly laughing and crying at the stupidity of this. He was trying to help these people, save them. Why were they keeping him from it? For several seconds he was sure the RTO was controlling them like some voodoo zombie-master. He smiled the maddest smug smile at Barrett, a Svengalish screw-you-they're-mine smile, then pushed away. "Strike's in motion, sergeant," he said, back paddling. "This paddy's smoke in nine minutes. That's a Roger, Wild Fox, we will be clear, over . . . "

The lieutenant disappeared into the fog following the running steps. Barrett pried the furious women off and now they were like featherweights. He could pick off and throw them like withered paper bags. He stumbled across the paddy, crying hoarsely at farmers to get out of there or be incinerated, pleading with them. None of them looked at him. He pulled at them and they snatched free. Bullets skipped round his feet, stitching the shallow water.

He ran toward the coconut-palm tree line half a kilometer away. He saw it like an island now through the mist under the brilliant-orange sunrise. He was the only soldier left out here; and he was running. He listened to his feet beating across the slick-silver mirror, running on the silent lake past dozens of Vietnamese farmers squatting and bent-over as if hypnotized, like dumb statues. The trees were lined with green uniforms staring past him, watching the paddy as if they were in some kind of group trance. It seemed to take forever to get to them. They looked like spectators at a football game. Nobody noticed him splashing up to them.

He turned as the heavy planes rumbled down the field, more than a dozen lumbering like big dead birds in a slow motion death-glide over the glass-still marsh with a myriad of insect-like specks. He watched as something grey-white fell from the bottoms of the ships. He shook his head, waiting, getting ready to see the paddy turn into black-orange fire. "Beautiful, beautiful . . . " blared from a radio. More planes scooped in low behind the first wave, the same grey-white stuff piling out of their pregnant-looking bellies. There were no flames. He saw dot-like specks standing on the mirror, frozen-like. There was unearthly quiet, the strangest silence. A few mutters, laughter from some of the men around him. Blakely, his dead friend, was chewing gum beside him. Grinning like a bratty kid watching some weakling getting beat up after school. Was everyone out of their minds? he thought.

"What was it," he whispered. ". . . that wasn't . . . what'd you do . . ."

Suddenly there were blood-curdling screams from the paddy.

As he looked out the specks on it became twisting stick-figures.

He could see people stumbling and crawling toward him through the orange-sheened water from the sky, but there was no fire on it. He heard a radio transmission from a plane say: "Looks good down there, Jolly Roger, send me a postcard . . ." Most of the farmers coming toward him were collapsing before they reached him, writhing and splashing in the puddle-green water. Screaming into gargling sounds, sinking out of sight fifty meters away, they seemed to have something attached to them sucking them under the muck like a drain. One woman kept hobbling toward him carrying a small child, stumbling lower and lower to the water until she was half-walking on one arm, both of them squalling in some writhing death-dance. As she came closer he saw most of one of her legs removed, stripped to the bone. She collapsed ten feet ahead of him. He saw the child's feet eaten off and half his stomach gone.

He retched, recoiling inside. He couldn't go anywhere.

Looking up he saw dozens more of them flailing, half-crawling toward him, as if he could do anything for them, as if he were some kind of saviour or healer. What could he do for them? Why were they coming to him?

He felt his own feet stuck in mire as he felt the things raining around him, bouncing off his shoulders. Looking down he saw water rising with raining, splatting fish. He heard screams from the paddy, from the woman and child on the ground in front of him, the hot-buzzing radio in his ear: it was irrelevantly blaring. He felt and saw the piranhas working around him, their jagged teeth gashing and hanging from the arms, legs, faces and stomachs of the woman and child at his feet.

He was in the middle of this paddy alone suddenly. A few half-eaten limbs were sticking out of it like branches. He felt his feet, shins and ankles being churned by razors. He saw the bloody teeth of piranhas chewing his boots, socks and flesh as they bumped and grazed his shoulders.

White buildings stood across the glassy lake in the fog. He couldn't make them out at first, they were out of place reflected in the limb-broken water. He recognized the Hawkins farmhouse surrounded by tin roofs in the shadows of the pecan grove. He felt panic building but he couldn't move. He tried to scream but his voice was muffled. Looking down he saw flesh chewed loose from his calves, draped in flaps on the water, razor-sharp teeth hanging from his shins and ankles . . .

He leapt out of bed banging into the table under the window, clipping his head on the hanging lamp. Wheeling, he back-handed it and fell sideways over the table to his knees, clawing at his feet and ankles. He got up high-step-dancing, digging at his shins feeling skin and muscle, stopping to stare at his toes, patting his calves.

"Barrett?"

". . . can't do nothing for you . . ."

"For me? . . ."

"What can I do? . . ." He paced the room thinking *what am I doing?* Where am I? I'm not in-country. Hell no, I'm not. Coming across his pants, he wrestled them on leaning against the dresser with his heart squeezing like a fist.

"Tell me what's happening."

"What do you want . . ." he said, his face in his hands.

"What do I want?"

"No . . ."

"Who?"

"What do you need . . ."

". . . Your friends?"

". . . why me . . ."

"What're you . . ."

". . . what does this *mean* . . ." he laughed.

"*Barrett?*"

"Oh my God . . ." he panted.

"Let's have breakfast and talk."

"... not hungry..." he chuckled, flinging clothes on the bed. "... the hell you say... it's gotta be me, dudn't it?... it's me then... *always* fucking me..."

Stuffing his overnight bag, he went to the sink, splashing his face, looking at his eyes in the mirror.

"What's happening, Barrett? You're scaring me."

"Nothing..." he said, yanking on his boots, pulling on a black t-shirt yanking it around.

"Talk to me, Pedro. I'll buy breakfast."

"Next time."

"When?"

"I don't know."

"Are you serious?"

"Something's come up!"

"No shit! Why are you acting this way?"

Grabbing keys, change and wallet he started for the door, forgetting his bag, turning for it stumbling over a chair, kicking it under the table, looking up seeing her sitting there naked looking at him like he was some kind of mutant. What's *wrong* with her? he thought, completely disoriented. What'd he say? Did he *say* something? Oh my God, what was he doing, he didn't even remember. He didn't remember anything from the last five minutes except that ungodly dream, and now she's sitting there glowering at him like she'd just materialized in the room.

"What is it, Barrett?"

"Oh hell," he shook his head, gazing at the flowers on the bedspread.

"Don't keep me out of this, don't even try."

"Come on," he said, slumping beside her, pulling himself back into the room with everything he had. He still felt five feet under water. He was completely dazed, out of his mind. As if he could just turn this off by coming here. "Hey, stop it," he grinned, lifting her chin to him, but she wasn't buying it now. He sat a minute, turning back to her drinking that glass-clear loyalty from her eyes, drawing it as she ransacked his. He thought about it, then thought, hell no, you'll tell her nothing, not a damn thing; keep smiling, kiss her in a minute, and walk out of here like nothing's happened.

"Hey, listen," he said. "You know me. Always fretting over some crazy as hell bullshit."

"I know you," she nodded.

"Havin' dreams, Marsha, nothing to worry about."

"Sure about that?"

"Yeah, really. I gotta get back, darlin'."

"What's your hurry?"

"No hurry, a lot to do. Take care of what we made here," he patted her tummy. "Be back before you know it."

"Barrett?" she said flatly.

He kissed her and got up and she was staring at him with that fierce knowing silence, knowing damn well he was full of it. Knowing he knew she knew and was pretending he didn't.

"How many times we been together?" he said. "You really think anything can come between us?"

"Promise me. You have the gift, Barrett."

"Cross my heart," he said, ignoring what he knew she meant. "Wait 'till you hear this song I wrote you: 'This World's a Prison Without You.'"

"Need to record it, baby."

"Soon as I get back."

"I'll hold you to that."

"You're the only woman ever held my feet to the fire. Only woman ever really gave a damn about me."

"Daddy," she caught him before he shut the door. "Watch yourself, whatever it is. Don't orphan us off right away?"

"Ah naw," he shook his head, winking his wide-cheeked, crooked-eyed grin.

As she listened to his Harley rev up she noticed his clothes draped over chairs and dressers, socks and a leather bracelet on the floor. His shaving kit was by the sink, his muddy little dog-eared New Testament opened by it. She stared at the filtered light on the walls with a feeling so strong she couldn't move for a minute, listening to his cycle throttle up and echo away. It faded into the sound of the eaves dripping with a fast-running tapping.

Deke and Jason spent the day rebuilding dams washed out by all-night battering storms. In high-tops and cutoffs Deke waded thigh-deep in the muddy stream as Jason handed down the long pine braces. They dug and lodged them, stacking them into the banks behind the perforated plywood, tying the wall of trees with crosspieces and ten-inch nails. An engine purred down and they listened to Barrett's Harley barreling up the drive. Deke dragged to the bank hooking his claw hammer around saplings, lifting up with his face on fire.

"Can't believe the son of a bitch had the nerve to come back here," he said, tearing off his muddy shoes.

"What're you doing, Deke?"

"I'm gonna kill the motherfucker."

". . . Let's talk to him first . . . wait a minute . . ."

Through wrinkling heat waves Barrett crossed the fields past the Hawkins farmhouse, relieved to see the place wasn't burned to the ground. Hitting the foot of the mountain, he lost traction in mud patches, swinging along the high right edge of the drive, skirting a rotted spruce laying in pieces across it. He eased into the woods, picking his openings, rejoining the trail up to the cabin.

Under the grape arbor he peeled off gloves, helmet and glasses. Tecate cans dangled in a cockeyed pyramid on the arbor table. Shades of Deke Hawkins, he thought, seeing the jeep and truck parked under a kudzu-garage of twine-lashed posts. The boys'd been busy, he thought, as he was blindsided and thrown from his bike with the muscles in the back of his head throbbing. He landed on his shoulder with Deke on top of him, right arm pinned, feeling the burn on his cheekbone as Deke cuffed him.

"What the *fuck* . . . Hey! *Hey!*"

"You dirty motherfucker, I ought to waste you! You think I don't know what you're up to . . ."

"Deke, it's me!"

"I know it's you, cocksucker! Who else'd pull this crap . . ."

Stunned by flashes, Barrett fought off more slugs as he tried to grab Deke's chin, shoving him into the kudzu. He handcuffed a wrist and managed to partially hogtie him as they scuffled on their sides.

"What the fuck's wrong with you, you crazy son of a bitch!"

"You don't know anything about it, do you . . . *fucking liar* . . . some goddamn joke . . ."

"What joke . . ."

When Deke lifted his knee into Barrett's groin, Barrett thought, okay, that's it, just before the nausea hit raising up and coming down with a right and most of his weight into Deke's left jaw, following it with a horse-kick to the stomach.

"I told you, I don't know what the fuck you're talking about, asshole! *Son of a bitch*. Goddamit!"

Running up Jason saw Barrett shoving off his brother, Deke balled-up on his side coughing as Barrett held his own stomach, clinging to an arbor post. He stumbled away, leaning on a gnarled pine.

"What the fuck is this, little brother?"

"You don't know?"

"Hell no, except this asshole's trying to kill me."

"He's lyin'," Deke said, crackling his jaw.

"I don't get that, Deke . . ."

"About what!" Barrett turned, backsliding down the trunk, breathing against the nausea with his head between his legs.

"Somebody cut down our plants," Jason said.

"Oh shit. How many?"

"Thirty or so, but they didn't take them, left them with these weird photographs."

"Kind of photographs?"

Jason pried them from Deke's pocket, peeling them from a baggie, wiping and handing them to Barrett. There were twelve wrinkled black-and-whites of Vietnamese soldiers' decapitated heads lined-up on a wall. Cigarettes dangled from their slack mouths. Looking at the pictures Barrett got that old, surreal, dreadful malaise, feeling it permeating his already radical nausea. He felt wide-awake and bad-dreaming at the same time. This was a joke. They were getting him good with this one.

"You in on this?"

"What do you mean?" Jason said.

Barrett looked at them. If they were putting him on they were doing it all the way.

"You're not serious."

"Cut the crap," Deke growled, rolling to his elbow.

"Ever seen pictures like these?" Jason said.

". . . Oh hell yeah. In the good old war days . . . These boys got no ears, noticed? Somebody's wearin' 'em on a necklace or they were mailed home to sis. Lotta good came outta this . . ."

He dropped them on the straw, belly-laughing with his head against the tree. "Onward Christian soldiers . . . marching as to war . . . with the cross of *Jesus*! . . ."

"Some idea of a prank, asshole."

"I don't know who the joke's on," Barrett said, rubbing his eyes. "You tell me."

"You've got some goddamn nerve coming back here."

"You really think I did this? Why would I?"

"You're askin' me?"

"Yeah."

"To spook us out of here. Fuck you, Barrett."

"Come on, Deke, I was trying to tell you what I knew. I don't play psycho games like your big brother. If plants are down . . . shit, man, they're my *babies*."

"You were damned determined to flush us out of here before you left."

"Not like this, hell no. Give me a break."

"I believe him," Jason said. "Maybe *you're* smoking too much, Deke."

"Yeah," Deke said, lifting up slowly. "Everything's in the smoke now. How was Memphis, bro? Tell me about it."

"It was there and I was there."

"Marsha good?"

"You know she is."

"You've got to admit it's coincidental. Say you're seeing Vietnamese people out there, you disappear a couple of days and these pictures show up on our plants."

"I don't know," Barrett shook his head. "I don't see a lot going on here that *isn't* weird. Proves my point's what I see, but you don't want to look at that. I tell you something's coming down, next thing you're blaming me for it. I find that pretty weird. *Scary*."

Deke turned, blowing his nose in the straw.

"I don't believe this," Jason said. "You're blood brothers, for God sake, you've saved each others' lives. You told me Barrett was the only man you trusted outside this family."

"You don't get it, kid."

"Why would he come back if he'd done this?"

"So we wouldn't *think* he'd done it," Deke said, dead eyed. "He thinks he's doing us a favor hustling us out of here."

"I don't know which of us got it worse," Barrett said.

"I'm starting to wonder," Jason said. "But I don't believe he did it. It's . . . *ridiculous.*"

"Who then, the tooth fairy?"

"We don't know, but why blame him? I've had plenty of premonitions."

"About what?"

"About daddy dying a few months before it happened."

"Didn't tell me."

"What if I had beforehand? Would you've blamed me for it?"

"I blame you now," Deke smirked.

"Premonitions don't make things happen is what I'm saying; they're warnings, people have them."

"Only sane man left," Barrett said. "The truth'll come, give me the benefit; I fucking deserve it."

"Yeah, yeah . . ." Deke said, peeling off matted leaves. "I hope you're right, for your sake."

"And don't be threatening me either, bitch. I didn't come back here for your fucking suspicions. If you weren't my blood brother I'd've kicked your faithless ass and ridden out of here twenty minutes ago."

"That so?" Deke stepped into him. "Swear to me you didn't do this, on the blood of Saps, J.T., Dosier and Marcos—"

"Hell no I didn't do it! I almost wish I had because who the hell knows what we're dealing with here. On the blood of those boys, *hell no*! Now get out of my fucking face."

Deke turned and walked under the grape arbor.

"I don't get it," Jason said. "They didn't take anything. So what are these pictures about?"

Barrett shook his head with a sniffle. Deke gnawed his lips, staring into the shadows.

"Come on, guys, you've got all the answers, what do we do? Deke?"

"Show me where these plants were cut down," Barrett said, squinting at the cracked photos. "Got to be more out there than these lovely snapshots. We'll track this twisted bastard back to his front door if we have to. We'll get to the bottom of this shit, don't you worry, little brother."

Body-shadows rippled like stilt-figures on the bright sloped clearing. Barrett sat on his haunches turning and examining leaves as Deke stood with his hands on his knees, surveying the ruffled ground. Their boots lay in a pile at the clearing entrance. Twenty-seven plants lay raggedly-scattered on their sides where they'd been felled like Christmas trees. A whippoorwill droned in the churning shrillness.

"Same tiny prints at the other plants, but something new here," Barrett said. "Military issue. Give me that penlight, little brother. Sure you came in that corner barefoot and left by it?"

"Tracks are clean," Deke said. "It stormed last night."

"I see it did," Barrett said. "But these prints are decent."

From a squat he went to his knees, pivoting in the opposite direction, taking the penlight from Jason. He followed the boot prints toward the edge of the clearing, crawling to the woods moving the light print-to-print, paused, swung to his right twelve steps and stood hovering the beam around the muddy floor in a tight circle. He studied the cracked leaves and ground stirred-up and scarred.

"Two print-sets moved to here and mixed it up some. Sure did."

Deke and Jason peered over his shoulder, Barrett shining the light from the ground up two nearby trunks. He went to one and lifted a small tuft of fur from the bark at head-level, shining on the ground fresh-scattered bark pieces with wood-dust. He squatted, picking up a bloodstained chunk, peeling back leaves revealing earth, twigs and more leaves drenched in dried-black blood.

"*Hello*," Deke said.

"What is it?" Jason said.

"Looks like raccoon hair. Good bit of blood here."

"Wild animal?"

"Can't tell. May be."

"Let me see the beam a second," Deke said. "Looks like they cut this way maybe. I thought it was the way they'd come in, but it looks like they went in and out this way."

He shined down a trough-like trail as they moved carefully to it, Barrett duck walking, tracking the clearer-stamped imprints. Barrett stopped and made a circle palm-down over the leaves.

"Just the larger set here," he grunted. "One man. Someone left the ground here."

"Left the ground?" Jason said.

"You sure?" Deke said.

"Looks to me."

They pushed along the trail crossing a narrow ravine, in blazing moonlight following the wake of leaves to the crest of a hill. A shallow creek glittered like mercury through the trees. The dead stench hit them as they slid down to it.

"Snake shit," Deke said. "Where is it?"

"Up there."

Deke swung the beam along the opposite bank where chalk-white outlines overlapped. The hillside was smothered as far as they could see with rotted, skinny carcasses. Barrett paced up and down in the ankle-deep water checking the silty edges.

"Prints don't pick up on either side," he said. "Must've gone up or down from here. Let's try up first."

Sinking to their calves they waded up the creek, parting and ducking overhangs, Barrett clearing webs with a broom-branch.

Every ten yards they stopped and scanned the banks into the squatty, bare-washed trees. Snake skeletons littered the stream edges, broken, dangling headless in the eddies.

"Watch for snapped and bent twigs," Barrett said. "Logs or rocks they might have stepped out on."

"What makes you so sure they followed the creek?" Jason said.

"Believe me, little brother, I've got a feel for this."

Something crackled on the other side of the sandy ridge. Barrett lofted a hand size rock over the bank startling whatever it was rustling into the trees. They waded up on a shallow pool shimmering with gnats and mist. A dark-banded snake slithered across disappearing into a rotting stand of bamboo. Water trickled to the basin from a twelve-foot drop through a natural dam of fallen trees and mud cut with cave-like hollows and overhangs.

"How about it, straw boss?"

"Let's head down," Barrett said, fanning the light along the banks. He studied patches of moonlight in the center of the mist, the bright-colored stones at the middle of the pool. He brought the light close, flashing it around his feet. "Hold it," he said. "Be still, fellas."

He squatted, looking at some traces of animal hair. He took several strands on his fingertips, moved the light to the top of the pool and strode across it to where more hair glittered around rocks breaking the surface. He followed a trail of it under the overhang where water seeped through the drenched mud wall. Going to one knee, he shined the beam into one of the hollowed-out spaces. He held the light in his teeth and crawled up into it on his knees in shallow water, the beam flashing the clay walls. He crawled over something furry floating, half-submerged. Dead beaver or muskrat, he thought. Shed hair drifted around it. Something loomed to his left and he turned the light to a body-size bulk wrapped in camouflage laying on a narrow shelf, bobbing a little as part of it draped the water. He picked up the waterlogged coonskin hat, seeing what it was, tossing it behind him.

"Got something in here," he said.

"What's that?" Jason said.

"Oh hell," Deke said, flipping it inside out.

Barrett struggled to drag the covered bulk out with him on his knees, half-floating it. He straddled to unsnag it from rocks. One leg out, he handed the light to Deke who looked at the camouflage thing dangling with lines.

"Lend me a hand here, little brother."

Jason gripped the foot of the thick-wrapped bulk and lifted it with Barrett to the creek bank. It was tied in twenty places, Barrett clipped quickly with his Buck knife.

"We have a parachute," he said. "Pretty new one. Late army issue."

He yanked one end of the tightly-wound chute and a body rolled out on its stomach with something clanging next to it.

They turned the body over and it was Davey, his pale throat slit, trickled, dried blood on his neck and mouth. His eyes were swollen open in a startled expression. Deke fingered the coonskin cap. He looked at Davey's child size, unlaced boots.

"Who is it?" Jason said.

"Oh shit," Barrett said. "What's *he* doin' here?"

"You know this guy?" Jason said. "Who is he?"

"Called him Davey Crockett. Was in our company in Nam. Crazy little redneck motherfucker."

"Told you about that Memorial Day scene we had," Deke said. "This is him."

"You didn't tell him anything," Barrett said.

"'Course not. Always had an animal sense though, probably smelled it on me. He could scent a Cong at ten kilometers."

Deke picked up the machete that had fallen out of the chute, turning it in the moonlight. Plant residue splashed the blade but there was no visible blood.

"What's he doing here?" Jason said, his voice trembling. "Why would anyone want to kill him?"

"One with the larger tracks toted him here," Barrett said. "From the place where I said one left the ground."

"Davey wouldn't have brought anyone," Deke said. "He would've come by himself."

"Or when they found the shit the other guy figured he'd have it all. I don't understand chopping the plants now, they're worthless. Sure no other patches were tampered with?"

"Nothing touched. Checked them all."

"You never said there were going to be people killed, Deke. I can't believe this. There's a murderer out here. Is he going to try to kill us?"

"Take it easy, little brother. Ain't nobody harmin' you."

"We're involved with this man, Barrett! He was murdered on our property over our illegal plants! This is *serious* . . . my God, I can't believe this . . ."

"You and Deke and I are peaceful farmers, Reverend. We didn't have nothing to do with this. Somebody got greedy and bit it with his hand in the till, that ain't our fault. All we have to do's watch our backs, look after each other and guard our crop till we harvest and sell it. That's all we owe anybody. Ain't a bit different than if some thief killed another one rustlin' your daddy's cows."

"Daddy'd call the sheriff if that happened," Jason said. "That's what we've got to do."

Barrett hummed, glancing at Deke, stooping to fold the chute over Davey's depthless gaze. They listened to the choir of frogs upstream.

"We're not calling the sheriff," Deke said with his wrist on his mouth.

"What're you talking about?" Jason said.

"We're taking care of this ourselves."

"How are we doing that?"

Deke grinned at his dead friend. After all they'd been through he ends up here, he thought.

"Deke, we've got to get the sheriff out here right now."

"If we call the sheriff there'll be people swarming over this place, Jason. If they don't accuse us of murder outright, there's a damn good chance they'll snoop around until they find our crop, then they'll think we killed Davey *because* of the crop, to protect it. We'll be busted, charged with murder, lose the farm and be screwed every which way."

"What do you think we are now?"

"We're simple farmers, kid. We didn't kill this man. You and Barrett and I are *not* taking the blame for it."

"You think covering up a murder's blameless?"

"If we had nothing to do with it it is. If our survival's at stake, hell yes. We're not detectives, we're trying to save our asses, remember? I'll be damned if I'll play into the law's hands and get strung up because this crazy bastard came out here and got himself killed by some other loco yahoo, probably as needle-high as he was."

"What are you saying?"

"We're going to bury him in the woods."

"You *can't* be serious."

"There's nothing else to do."

"He's not livestock or a pet dog, Deke. This is a man. He's got family somewhere."

"He's not doing a hell of a lot for them like this now, is he?"

"But they have a right to know what happened to him."

"What if we hadn't found him? Would they still have that right?"

"But we did find him. And we know he's been murdered. We're obligated to come forward, right, Barrett?"

Barrett looked at Deke and dropped his eyes.

"Illegal plants are one thing, guys, but I'm drawing the line here."

"You draw whatever you want, kid."

"I won't do it."

"We'll do it," Deke said, stepping into him.

"I can't believe this. What are you going to do, kill me?"

"No, but I'll damn sure stop you from doing anything that jeopardizes us or this farm."

"It's wrong, Deke. On every level it's wrong. This isn't just about growing plants anymore."

"Oh, really? What else do we have? Those plants are the only thing between us and the street, Jason."

"And doing the right thing. If we don't no crop or anything else will save us."

"Listen, kid. There's wrong and there's stupid wrong. I didn't come this far to lose our heads now. I didn't trust this guy as far as I could throw him, see. He was a junkie and a liar and a goddamn thief, but I loved his crazy ass. You think it doesn't hurt me to find him out here? It still comes down to what I've got to do to save this place. If the situation were reversed I'd expect him to do the same damn thing, and he'd do it, if he had any sense."

"We better do as Deke says," Barrett said. "We turn into victims if he don't, Rev."

"Daddy would skin us alive!" Jason said, exploding fists in Deke's face and chest. "You're crazy! You got us into this life and now you want to hide a body on our farm! You've lost it, Deke . . . both of you . . ."

Deke held his arms, bear-hugging him. "Hey, hey, hey, come on Jason. We don't have any choice here! Think about it. Stop trying to hit me, goddamit!"

"We've got choices! Every second we've got choices! You like to rule out the ones that matter!"

"All right, are you ready to start a ministry getting buggered in prison for a murder you didn't commit! Do you want to lose Terrence and Irma's homestead over this mind-fucked war junkie laying here? Because I'm telling you, kid, as sure as we're standing here if we call the sheriff that's what's going to happen to us, you understand me? We're not out to get or defraud anyone. We're minding our own business. We pretend we never found him and we keep this fucking shit in perspective, goddamit . . . you've got to keep your head on, Jason."

"Perspective," Jason said, shivering-giggling, yanking free stepping back. "Hide a body and keep it in *perspective*. That's a good one, Deke," he said, thinking suddenly of bolting for the cabin, of just making a run for it in his jeep to the sheriff's office or a phone. Maybe he could do it. He had to save his brother; he had to save all of them. But he could do that any time now, couldn't he? Not just at this moment when there was a better chance they'd catch him, and they probably would, and then what? Deke planted just enough doubt to make him wait, just enough for him to consider what he knew to be insane. He'd been worried about Barrett for weeks until Barrett let them know what was going on with him, then he'd begun to worry in a different way, wondering what it meant. What Barrett'd told them was giving him nightmares now. He and Deke had argued about Barrett as he tried to keep the peace between them. He'd known there was something more than fantasy to Barrett's story, and now this. Deke and Barrett were of one mind again like a couple of twin criminals. He could feel himself getting sucked into more than he'd bargained for; he felt tainted and mired, stuck and half-considering this logic that twisted his spiritual world into moral dilution. Deke tempted him toward doing anything required to get justice and fairness in this material world, which Jason knew didn't exist. You got it through faith and doing the right thing, whatever the cost. He knew that and had always known it, so what was he doing? Even if they got away with this, how could he live with himself? No matter what Deke said, he couldn't. He was too weak to do anything, his spirit felt wizened and drained. Maybe it was not going to church, although he did have a kind of church with Janie, and occasionally with Deke and Barrett, but maybe it wasn't enough. He thought he was some spiritual rock who could save everybody, but who was saving him? Maybe breaking the law had eaten at his spirit so much he couldn't tell how much of it was gone. He didn't want to lose the farm any more than Deke did, or go to jail, and the things Deke said made too much sense at times, then he didn't know where he was. He'd lost his bearings. What now was he willing to sacrifice? More than ever in his life he'd pray for clarity, he thought, like he'd told Barrett to do. "God help us," he groaned, remembering Barrett'd said it just a few days ago after his warning to them. The Witch Doctor seemed to be ignoring his own premonitions, what was wrong with him? He was too loyal to Deke, that's what it was. Brothers in war stuff, look at them, they were like two peas in a pod again. "God help me the day I agreed to any of this," he said to them.

"He'll help us, little brother. We ain't that in the wrong here. This boy was dead a long time before he got here."

"Everything hidden will be revealed, Deke," Jason said, gazing at the covered body.

"I'm counting on it," Deke said. "Save your sermons for someone else, kid."

Deke squatted, lifting Davey onto the mud-crusted chute surprised at how heavy he was. He and Barrett went to opposite ends and began to roll the body up in it, folding and tucking the ends around Davey's head and feet.

"You've forgotten something kind of important," Jason said.

"What's that?"

"How do we know whoever killed Davey won't come after us?"

"I wouldn't fret about that," Barrett said, running the chute lines underneath, yanking them taut. "If he's got half a brain he's long-gone from here."

"What about those photographs? You think those heads smoking cigarettes were just for laughs?"

Deke and Barrett didn't look at him.

"We left playing cards on the bodies of the Cong for markers," Deke said. "A psych thing to rub in the enemy's faces. I don't get this."

"That's it?" Jason said with a laugh. "That's . . ."

"I don't get the photos and leaving the plants. Not really. We don't know if it was Davey or the other guy doing it, or both."

"A warning maybe," Barrett said, strapping the lines around Davey's feet, knees, middle, chest and head until he was mummy-shaped in his body-bag, his stunned face outlined against the thin fabric. "Maybe they figured we'd spook and leave the crop for them. We know damn well Davey was nuts, but who knows what this other guy was thinking."

Using the long-handled shovels they'd planted with, Deke and Barrett dug a narrow grave as Jason watched from the shadows. He hadn't spoken since they'd started down the creek, Barrett lugging Davey wrapped over his shoulder to this needle-carpeted plateau surrounded by thick brush. Now they stood over the open trench with the camouflaged body in it, Jason staring catatonically into the ground. Dripping mud, Barrett leaned on his shovel beside him; Deke sat on his knees sifting handfuls of dirt. They listened to the whippoorwill that had seemed to follow them from the same mournful distance since they'd left the clearing.

"He was a real little hell-fighter," Deke said. "Came back from 'Nam with a mean needle problem. Finally kicked it, I guess."

"Balsiest tunnel rat we had," Barrett said. "Slipped down an NVA tunnel that morning and never came out for three years. I'd have a habit myself if I'd seen the shit he has. Played the hell out of a mandolin, too. Made me laugh lot the time."

"Probably after our crop, but we don't have to worry about that anymore. Wish you'd tell us who did this, you crazy bastard."

"Just stay where you are, all right, buddy? Don't try 'an get up or nothing," Barrett said. "Say a prayer or something, Rev?"

Jason opened his mouth to speak but couldn't and nodded quickly no. His face quivered a little in the blue buzzing light. He watched them fill the hole with a dazed smile and dress it with straw until it was nearly not there anymore. Barrett covered and marked it with a large pine limb with antler-like fanning branches.

Deke stood against the sheer drapes of his mother's unlit room, the floor and ceiling crowded with Kleenex dolls, studying one of the soft figures in his hand, occasionally glancing at his mother's dozing profile. Her chin pointed to the ceiling as if she were listening to "Love Me Tender" droning over the racket of dinner trays being stacked in the hall. Faded roses lay on the sidetable by her water pitcher. He kept looking at the doll curiously. It wore a tiny, perfectly-shaped soldier's cap, high military boots and four penned stripes on each shoulder. In the window more soldiers floated and gyrated on monofilaments with roughly-sewn helicopters and planes. A two-seat AT-6 like his father had trained in dangled by the bed. He flinched at the sudden gruffness of her voice.

"Honcho? *Honcho?*"

"It's Deke, mama. This is Deke."

"Deke?" She rolled her eyes with a smile.

Here we go, he thought.

"Yeah, mama. It's me."

She faced the ceiling swallowing and choking, clawing for a Kleenex.

"Why you've been coming all along, haven't you?" she said in a caught voice. "Honcho hasn't come to see me. Would you ask him why that is?"

"'Course, mama."

"Thank you, Deke. Jason dropped by the other day and read to me. I don't understand why Honcho would be in town and not visit his mother. Do I deserve that?"

"'Course not, mama."

"Tell him to cut out this silly business and come see me."

"I don't think he's in town, Madge."

She looked at him.

"You boys aren't as sharp as you think you are, are you? You don't think I know when my own sons are around?"

"I guess—"

"I guess I do. You tell him to get his butt over here."

"Yeah, mama, sure I will. Anything else? Need fruit or chocolate? Toffee bars?"

"I don't need anything really. You're a good boy, Deke. You've always been a trustworthy son and I appreciate that."

Deke frowned and studied the doll in his hand as she reached for her water. Someone was playing Louie Prima down the hall.

"I could use a Snickers or two," she said, cough-chuckling.

They listened to Elvis' dying scene at the end of the movie.

"When I'm dead and gone I don't want any such mawkishness, you hear me?"

"You're not going anywhere, girl."

"No, I'm staying right here 'till I die."

"The hell with that, Madge. You're coming home like I promised."

"Stop it now," she said, shutting her eyes. "I know we've lost it all. Don't waste my energy, son."

"It ain't true, Madge. You think I'm gonna let that happen to us? Daddy always said nobody'd run us off our place and we're not gonna let it happen now. You're coming home Christmas and we'll catch a mess of bluegills and fry 'em up for breakfast, make hot fudge and sit out on the porch listening to the frogs down at the pond. We'll call your friends over, Mapsie and Choradine and Miss Jessie, Donald Greene, the Maple sisters, get your lunatic sisters to come stay with us and put on a wild feast for everybody. How's that sound, girl?" he said, but she was already dozing again, her eyes fluttering like moth's wings toward the ceiling. He sat a while watching her stern face that was like a proud Indian priestess', hawk like with a strong widow's peak, defiant but humble. He touched her sun worn farmer's hands rivered with wrinkles and tendons, feeling the virile, sleeping strength in them. He lay his chin on the sheet by her fingers, her right forefinger truncated beneath the first knuckle from a blade accident when she was twelve, listening to her raspy, snoring breathing.

Wearing handguns on holsters Deke and Barrett hauled eighty gallons of water to the top of a stony ridge. Deke stood on the ledge anchored to a safety harness studying the high, glossy vapor trails. Lines crisscrossed like drifting clouds on the fleckless sky. Hair red with rock dust and wearing a tattered army t-shirt for a sweat-bandanna, Barrett tied the full jerry cans to nylon ropes at the foot of the wall. He filled the cans in the shallow stream, dropping now and then to splash and drink from it. Another blistering day. The drought had returned with a vengeance and they'd been watering on rotating shifts to keep from burning out.

"Quit kicking that shit down here," Barrett said, wiping grit from his eye. "I'm sun-blind as it is."

"Wonder what they're doing up there," Deke said, studying the slow-crawling specks. "Hung over us all day."

Barrett snugged the can-knots, firming the lids.

"Routine exercise shit. These are ready, Tar Baby. Bombs away."

Tossing the glasses in the leaves, Deke stepped onto the ledge hoisting the cans.

Jason propped on his bunk reading the third book of *Leviticus*, mouthing the words silently. The walkie-talkie on the sidetable hissed with the scanner. Carpenter ants rustled in the trash over fresh peach seeds. At night the ants woke them, flitting over their lips and eyelids, invading with the kudzu that sprouted like a virus through the walls and floorboards.

Static breathed as Barrett's voice purred.

"Boogieman got you, little brother?"

"Cut it out, Br'er Rabbit. How much longer?"

"On our last laps here. Give us a couple more hours and call in the militia."

"Anything unusual?"

"Copasetic so far. Big ears talking to you?"

"A few flutters. Pretty quiet."

"Here too. Nothing but birds and crickets."

"Check in again if you're running late."

"Wouldn't it be funny if you just never heard from us again?"

"Hilarious, Bar . . . Br'er Rabbit. Check in, all right?"

"Lighten' up, little brother. You'd seen what I've seen you'd know to work on your sense of humor."

"Copy that, dark meat. You're the Boogieman's preference, you know."

"There you go, Rev. Ain't nothing the old Witch Doctor can do about that now, is there?"

Jason tossed his radio on the bed and thumbed through *Proverbs*.

Deke and Barrett dumped their last water on the tree-size bushes scattered over the mountaintop. Geese stretched long-necked across the fiery horizon. Deke clicked his penlight on a leafy branch glistening with tiny-white female hairs.

"This girl's a pound of flowers," he said.

Barrett snipped a few with his miniature scissors.

"Lord, this sends me. Ever smell anything this wonderful?"

"Matter of fact . . ."

". . . Besides that."

Barrett put his head back, inhaling it.

"If He had anything better than *this* He kept it for Himself too, didn't He?"

They started down the mountain feeling the temperature dropping in gradations; Deke palmed the light on the dark path.

"Sorry I jumped you, brother. I saw those goddamn photos—"

"Don't fret over that. We're all burned-edgy here. Little brother's quiet as a church mouse, you noticed?"

"Wasn't ready for this. Neither was I."

"You think he's all right? Will he do anything rash?"

"He swore he wouldn't go to the sheriff. He's got God, at least. Think it's hurting him though."

"*Let the dead past bury its dead* I told him the other day, and he looked at me like I was the devil."

They crunched along the trail overgrown with muscadine.

"Batteries weak?"

"No, I'm covering it." Neither of them spoke for a minute and Barrett could feel it coming. "Tell me you didn't see that shit, buddy."

"What shit?"

"*What* shit?"

"Don't start with me, Deke."

"Still seein' them?"

"You gonna believe what I tell you?"

"I want to know."

"Haven't seen them since I came back here. Pickled them out with tequila in Memphis, I hope. Haven't smoked one out here either."

"How long you expect that to last?"

"Until we get through this."

"So you're not smoking out here anymore?"

". . . wouldn't say that."

". . . So you don't hallucinate Vietnamese—"

"What do you know, Deke? What do you fucking really *know*?"

"I don't think you're lying to me."

"That's comforting."

"I'm worried about you, Hoss."

"Change the subject, kimasabe."

"You're freaking me out if you want to know the truth."

"Then shut the fuck up about it, goddamit."

"Tell me . . ."

"You're not going to believe anything I tell you. You've never believed a goddamn thing I tell you until we had our asses shot off or blown sky-high, so drop it . . ."

Something rustled in the brush and the penlight caught the whitish-grey tail of a possum, its marble-bright eyes shining like saucers.

"Wish we knew what this joker iced Davey had in mind," Deke said, beaming ahead.

"Like I told Jason, murder's not something to come snooping back around. He'd be foolish to stick around here."

"Unless he's got designs on our crop and planning more of the same. I don't want Jason worrying, but you know it's gonna come down to you and me staking out when these girls deliver."

A yodel-like trill drifted up through the trees.

"Whas' that?" Barrett pushed the light down.

"Owl or something."

Barrett snatched the penlight off.

"That was no fucking owl."

"Come on, you been taking hits from the Chaser down by the creek?"

"Seriously," Barrett whispered. "Sounded like human chords to me, coming from that patch down in the hollow."

They listened in the chiming blackness.

"We can check them," Deke said. "Couldn't hurt."

Reading Job with an eye on the clock, Jason was getting nervous after two hours not hearing from them. He listened to Barrett's whisper-growl with clicks of a gun being load-checked.

"Heard something down here, little brother. Probably nothing, but we're gonna take a look."

"Don't joke around please."

"Ain't jokin'. Holler back in a bit; sit tight."

"Be careful, will you? Barrett?"

"Relax little brother."

They left the water cans at the edge of the trail and felt down into the needle-briars ten yards apart with pistols drawn. They'd agreed no lights, but before going five steps Barrett realized he wasn't going to see a damn thing in this darkness. It was like those moonless nights in the Cambodian jungles: your vision didn't adjust to this shit. He was nervous about his eye getting poked again, recollecting that explosion when the thorn sparked his pupil making his skin crawl. Neither of them could see beyond arm's reach, tracking each other by faint crunches and gripping thorns. The yodel-like voice warbled again. What *was* that? Deke thought. Wounded animal? They sure didn't need to be sneaking up on a lame bear cub if its mother was around. He heard a harsh-irritated screeching fifty yards to his left. Barrett heard Deke's dry-crunching again as he ducked and squinted, shielding his eyes, creeping on at an agonizing pace blinking to make out what he thought was Deke's blackened bulk below him. He heard a rummaging in the leaves to his right and knew Deke wasn't over there. He felt a tingling body rush, believing he was seeing his luminous friends standing where the thrashing was coming from. Freezing he stared at it until he realized it was a static wall: the illusion of light that *is* darkness. Your imagination's fucking with you, he thought, get a grip. You haven't seen them without the Chaser, remember? But if he'd smoked the stuff they'd be there, wouldn't they? Then they were around him, standing next to him, right behind him. *Quit it, for God sakes.* What are you trying to do to yourself?

He'd decided not to tell Deke and Jason about his dream-visitations returning the first night back. He could deal with them as long as his head was clear the rest of the time. It was like something itching at the back of his head, but he wasn't losing his marbles like he had been, feeling he was being invaded and had no recourse. Tell me there isn't some weird shit going on here, he thought. He heard thrashing to his right and felt a hard lump underfoot, reaching down feeling a bat-width tree on its side; when he pressed it the top of it bumped and brushed the leaves twenty feet to his right. Goddamit, he said, shutting his eyes, plowing ahead groping-blind, twisting and thrashing. He couldn't see anything, but they couldn't see him either. He shoved down with his hands forward, crashing and tripping to his knees. He didn't hear Deke at all and kicked himself for getting this separated. As he started again he nearly tumbled over him, waiting on his haunches listening to Barrett barrel down through the woods like a freight train. Deke grabbed his pants to keep him from pitching into the briars.

"Not *too* goddamn obvious," he said. "Where the hell've you been?"

"It's goddamn *dark* out here. You know how I am about my eyes."

"I thought you wanted to do this."

"I do, but let's stay together so we don't shoot each other, how 'bout it."

They started down again, keeping lower several yards apart. They could feel the slope beginning to flatten as they bared down on the patch, listening to an airliner rumbling over the sizzling cicadas. There was no brush down here, just a thick-padded floor of pine and fir straw under a low umbrella of draping branches. The screeching circled with a distressed intensity like an invaded, ragged bitching. There was enough light to make out the patch softly glowing in the trees. Barrett crawled to it with gnats whining in his ears, dripping sweat from blind nerves. Deke worked around the other side of the clearing, squeezing his .45 with both hands. He stepped into the rear corner of the patch, squatting, smelling something acrid with a mealy-rotted odor. He cricket-whistled.

"Br'er Rabbit?"

"S'me," Barrett elbowed to him.

"See anything?"

"Nothing, you?"

"Nope. What's that smell?"

"I don't know. Don't like it."

Barrett sniffed a plant from his knees.

"It's here. Smell this."

Deke whiffed it, pulling back, clicking the penlight on withered branches, the leaves shriveled-brown.

"What the hell?"

"Check the rest."

Deke shined chest-high stepping through the patch. Every one of the thirty-odd plants were rust-colored and drooping.

"It's a morgue," Deke said.

"Somebody poisoned these girls."

"No shit. Can we salvage—"

"Cut the light," Barrett said, smothering it.

"What?"

"Heard something."

"This had to've happened days ago to look this bad."

"Swear I heard something over there. Here come the fucking flower police."

As they listened to the moaning patter of chopper blades there was a crack like a log splitting on the other side of the clearing, a tree snapping and a high-pitched, hysterical voice screamed out in Vietnamese. Deke squeezed Barrett's arm feeling his goose bumps, squatting next to him. They duck walked toward the voice with guns up, the choppers humming toward them, shuddering the ground. The voice screamed out again in a high-pitched, yodel-like rant.

"*Chung bay dang lam gi day, GI! Chung bay cu muon chet day o! Chung bay o cu tuong o quoc gid nay! Chung bay la uguri chet, GI!*"

Mouths on the ground breathing straw, they belly-crawled through the plants toward the solid black tree line. Suddenly Barrett was snatched headfirst twenty feet into the trees by something clamped-choking round his neck. Teeth grinding, he dropped his .38 and clutched furiously at his throat and the leaf-coated wire chopping his breath. He tried to swing and get hold of anything with his legs, kicking wildly in open air as searchlights knifed through the trees. His silhouette rocked over Deke who was on his knees screaming up at him and the still-ranting voice coming from the tree line.

"Barrett! Barrett! *Goddamit!* . . . Goddamit!"

One of the choppers swung around and hovered on top of them, pivoting slowly. Deke was blinded, squinting at Barrett's legs dangling and kicking in the glaring light.

"You motherfucker!" he said to the voice in the trees, stumbling toward it. "I'll kill you motherfucker!"

He was yanked himself by one leg as if catapulted by a slingshot, watching the white-lit floor and drooping plants fly away rocking-bouncing beneath him. He swung under the strobing searchlights vibrating through the leaves, feeling the downwash of rotorthuds like a warm blazing wind filled with flying debris. He saw Barrett eight or ten feet away, wincing, pulling up with both hands at the coarse-rusted wire constricting his throat. Deke twisted and wriggled like a fish, trying with both hands to reach his ankle as he held onto his .45. He could see the radio and Barrett's .38 a few feet apart on the ground, elongated shadows swinging against the floor as the choppers circled and popped overhead. He had to hold onto his weapon, find a way out of this son of a bitching maniac's sling, then he was going to kill somebody.

In the blacked-out cabin Jason peered through window cracks, trying to raise them on the radio. Searchlights flashed as he saw one of the choppers nose down toward the farmhouse; it vaulted back up the mountain, objects shimmying around him, slipping from shelves. The floor tremored as the aircraft rumbled overhead with radio transmissions and slapping blades crowding through the scanner.

"Deke! Barrett! Say something to me! Where are you! Br'er Rabbit, talk to me! . . ."

Feeling vibrations pulled into darkness, he pushed out and ducked by the kudzu. One of the choppers turned in his direction and he burrowed into the vines as the radiating light swung back across him. Ten inches from his face a chameleon eyed him sideways, rigidly bubbling out its lime-green neck, Jason thinking, at least you can disappear into this hairy maze. As the chopper pulled off he heard gunshots down the mountain.

Dangling upside down screaming with blood draining into his face, Deke emptied his .45 in the direction of the ranting voice; it fell silent. He could see in the revolving grey light Barrett clutching weakly, pulling his weight up on the line he dangled from. One of the choppers thrummed overhead with the sky flashing white as Deke struggled and wrestled up the wire on his ankle. He worked his Case knife from his pocket with both hands, trying to catch raining bullets as he held the .45 with his right thumb. He swung hard, rocking with the open blade over Barrett's head nicking and cutting the choking wire a few inches from Barrett's scalp. He pulled himself up a little more on his wire with his left hand, which held his gun now, accidentally dropping it, almost losing the knife, bobbling and catching it with his fingertips. "Hold onto the goddamn knife!" he shouted. "Hold onto it, motherfucker!" He gripped it like a vise and kept lunging at Barrett's wire with one arm, fighting to ignore the slicing pain in his right ankle. He saw Barrett's wire strands splintering as he watched Barrett's arms sinking to his side. "*No! No! No!* Come on you son of a bitch! Come on motherfucker!" he screamed, beet faced, making a wild desperate roundhouse lunge, chopping hard into the snapping metal fibers, dropping Barrett like a sack of bolts to the clearing floor. Crushing plants beneath him, flopping on his back with his arms to his sides like a dead puppet's, Barrett lay panting and limp.

Listening to the choppers pull away Deke sawed frantically at his own wire, wincing and grunting, moaning in agony and frustration. He fell in a fast crooked watermelon dive, managing to pitch the knife clear of both of them before landing hard on his left shoulder, feeling the stabbing pain in his left rotator cuff. The air singed grainy. He nearly passed out as he seemed to be floating up again just above the clearing. He patted the ground for the .45, found it and two bullets, dug one from his pocket and jammed them into the chamber. He yanked the tightened wire off his ankle and elbowed to Barrett.

"Okay buddy? Barrett. *Goddamit* . . ."

Barrett grimaced and nodded he was with his eyes shut. He'd loosened the wire on his neck but was too weak to get it off. Deke stretched and slid it off his head. Barrett's look with his narrowed eyes slits said, that was just about it. He kept trying to swallow with his tongue on his lips as he coughed and wheezed. Jason's voice sounded like a gnat ten feet away, Deke dragging himself to the radio, cursing, worrying about another spring trap as he covered the dark tree line.

"We're here," he grunted. ". . . take it easy . . ."

"Where?" Jason said. "What's going on? What were those gunshots?"

"Tell you in a minute. Stay at the cabin. Don't move."

"You're kidding. I'm on my way down."

"*Get back to the cabin, goddamit!* Don't come down here, Jason. Do what I tell you."

"You sure?"

"Yes, I'm sure. Nobody's shot," Deke coughed, half-blacking out again from pain. "We're okay . . . get back to the goddamn cabin and stay there . . . Do what I say."

"All right, I'm turning back, but keep talking to me . . . *Deke* . . ."

Leaning on his elbow, Deke held the radio trembling in his left hand, the .45 shaking wildly in the direction the voice had come from on his opposite thigh. They listened to the chopper blades fading in the ringing darkness. The hoarse-irritated screeching circling them restlessly in the trees.

In the twelve-by-ten shale-green room General Craig and Colonel Hood conferred privately before bringing in the Major. They kept him waiting in the hall as they cleared other unpressing business from the table. Craig held a flame over his pipe studying the marked aerial photos under suspended light.

"No doubt, sir," Hood said, using a pointer. "Here. Here and here," he switched photos, indicating: "Here. This one could've been taken from fifty yards. We see the same distinct figures in this one, three in this one. More of the same in these two." He shuffled a dozen plates, most of which contained one or two black-and-white pale human figures in negative skeleton skins.

The General smoked, his powder-white beak lifted toward the ceiling as he leaned back, cradling his pipe.

"Remarkable," he said. "Does the Major take us for third world idiots?"

"I doubt it, sir."

"Do you think he's directly involved?"

"Probably not; he's been out of the country, and he's taken a thousand photos like this himself. We're sure he's aware of it now from his proximity to this."

"We have a clear hand, don't we?"

"We have everything we need."

"How do you recommend we proceed, Colonel?"

"I'd go along with his transaction," Hood said, slipping the photos into a stiff black folder. "Promote him as requested, sign the papers for his land, proceed with further security at our own discretion, when all the chickens are in the coop."

"You're *sure* all the chickens will be in the coop, Colonel? I don't want any slip-ups this time."

"On two occasions they have been. Just a matter of time."

The General deliberated in a halo of smoke, his raised chin bobbing as if he balanced a tea cup on it.

"All right, I'll go along. Hot shot played into our hands, didn't he? Have his paperwork?"

"We're ready, sir. I think it'd be smart to seem skunked here, General. We're going along because we have to, make him feel he's got us."

"By the short hairs, exactly. I've had it with these parlor games, Hood, one thing I won't miss when I retire next summer. Bring the Machiavellian son of a bitch in and we'll give him what he's asking for. I'm playing golf with Admiral Presser at 1600 Hours."

Honcho stood twenty yards down the polished linoleum with his back against the wall. Under the hovering glare Craig and Hood switched from conspiratorial to business faces as he stepped into the room.

"Major, come in and have a seat," Hood said, grazing his papers with a sigh. Honcho stood a few seconds, statue-like in his Marine dress. He smelled something more than Prince Albert in the room but wasn't sure what it was. They were toying with him or more nervous than they seemed. Half-expecting not to make it back here, he was beginning to believe giving him what he wanted was a fair exchange. They were wise to see it as that and write it off, as they goddamn well should. Our hard-earned taxes at work, he thought, with bitter irony. His father would approve; despite his old man's love for the Air Force and meritorious service to it, Honcho felt him with them on this one. He'd get back for them what was theirs, but it'd be a pittance of what they'd stolen, the contritionless bastards. He mock-saluted, sitting rigidly across the table returning Craig's unnerving glare. Not a clue to what the old buzzard was hatching. He wasn't offering any chinks himself. Let them sweat their goddamn hearts out, he thought. Of course there was always torture, he thought, in a flash of startling clarity, smiling to himself as he returned their dead eyed gaze.

"Gentlemen," he said evenly. "General."

Jason begged Deke and Barrett to go to the sheriff now. There was a maniac out there who was going to kill them all, he said. What good was saving the farm if they ended up buried on it? They weren't peaceful farmers anymore. The warning Barrett had given them before he left for Memphis, why wasn't he talking about that anymore? The visitors from their seeds and what they'd been telling him? Unless he'd made all that up, because Jason believed it now. It was no less bizarre than what they could all see happening here: snakes, frogs and fish raining from the sky? Did they have to get hit over the head with a hammer to realize something worse was coming? After getting these signs for months, they find photos of decapitated heads in the woods, and some killer's screaming at them in Vietnamese, were they just going to sit around until he picked them off for a bunch of flowers? What if he set more traps, how could they defend against that? They should tell the sheriff whoever'd killed Davey was after them now, tell him everything exactly the way it'd happened, so they could get out of this mess. If they weren't going to bring in the authorities, they should grab whatever they needed and get out of here before they started finding each other strung up in the woods or with their throats slit like poor crazy Davey's.

Flicking pistachio shells on the floor, Barrett shrugged off his warnings. He'd overreacted, he said, smoked too much like Tar Baby said and lost his head for a minute. The Spiritchaser would fuck you up if you did too much of it. He'd seen some bizarre *merde* out there, but he didn't know what it meant, if anything, and didn't want them scuttling the operation over smoked-up mirages in *his* head. He wasn't ready to throw in the towel for some psycho thief prankster. Hotshot had slipped in with Davey thinking he'd unnerve them with his little Vietnamese mystery show. Screw the bastard. They'd fuck right back with his creepy ass. There were always hidden costs for bringing in the Green Lady, you never harvested a crop without paying one way or another. She tested to see if you were worthy of her wares, and if you stood the trials the Boogieman went away and she gave you the Sweet Kahuna. Have a little faith, Reverend, they'd deal with prankster like they'd dealt with the drought and bugs, the flower police, and all the fucking rest of it. They'd come out smelling like his mama's prize yellow roses by New Years, he could count on it.

What? Jason thought. Who *was* this? This wasn't the Barrett from a few weeks ago who'd come to them like some half-broken ghoul, sweating through a crackbrained story of crawling through the woods spying on Vietnamese soldiers. That Barrett would've screamed bloody murder about this, sworn it was what he'd warned them about. That Barrett'd believed every word of his cockamamie story, and after praying about it so had Jason. He'd had his own visions, he knew when someone else was having them. Now the day after nearly getting lynched in the woods, Barrett was blaming this on smoking too much marijuana? This was getting stranger by the minute, and of course that's exactly what Deke wanted to hear. But however much Barrett had been smoking didn't explain half of what was going on here, and they all knew it.

He's hiding from himself, Jason thought. Sticking his head in the sand, pretending it isn't real. He'd done it himself when he'd started speaking in tongues. He understood Barrett wanting to duck this, it was very weird stuff for sure, but turning it into some Green Lady's obstacle course was going to get them all killed. They were being warned. Jason wanted to grab Barrett and shake it out of him, get him to talk about it again so they could get it through Deke's wooden skull, but Barrett wouldn't even look him in the eye. He mumbled nonchalantly, flicking pistachio shells on the floor with his big toe. Maybe he has a death wish, Jason thought. Maybe they both did and here he was at the mercy of whatever kamikaze plans they cooked up together.

Deke let them speak as he fumbled around the cabin with a cheek-full of Skoal. Then he flew into a rage and swore if Jason said one more word about the sheriff or leaving or anything related to either one, he was kicking his whining ass off the farm. He'd had it with this ghost and voodoo shit, he wasn't listening to another word about visions and signs. It was hard enough fighting everyone else, wasn't it, without listening to this defeatist dribble from his own people? This wasn't vacation Bible school. It wasn't mom's and pop's store anymore—it was guerrilla warfare whether they liked it or not. He'd hoped for a peaceful season, but that wasn't happening. Like he'd told Barrett before he left for Memphis, Jason could leave any time he wanted to, just don't try to sell him some milk toast forfeiture of the project because it suddenly occurred to him someone could get hurt. Barrett and himself nearly getting stretched by the bastard who'd slit Davey's throat didn't exactly inspire handing the farm over to him. If he'd wanted them dead they'd be dead; he might've offed them while they were hanging out there in the trees. But who knew what would've happened had Deke not caught his knife when it slipped from his hand. Had he dropped it they might still be hanging out there.

At the poisoned patch they found three unsprung traps and a two-year-old doe swinging from another one. They tracked a set of rewalked prints three miles across Mosely's property to the highway. Since they could assume somebody capable of killing had a hard-on for their crop, they'd work only in daylight, in pairs or all together, each of them side armed and with radios, checking in with each other hourly. One would stand four-hour watches while the other two slept. It was going to be like that, if Jason wanted to stick around, and if any more plants were tampered with things were going to get very fucking ugly around there.

That's it, Jason thought, they were in for it now. He was sure Deke meant what he said about kicking him off the farm, and Barrett was in some traumatized denial. Neither of them were going to listen to him. The military was digging in. He was that close to walking out anyway, but knew he'd be unable to help them if things went badly, and he didn't want that. His main reason for being there was to counsel them, so what good was this? It felt like they were in some nightmarish movie being dragged down a river toward a blind precipice: it was just a matter of time before they went over the edge. If he couldn't help himself, how could he help them? He couldn't shake out of this foggy morass that wrapped around him like some paralyzing snake. He should've been able to pray his way out of this, get a clear message and rescue them, but it felt like the Holy Spirit wasn't giving him anything. God was waiting for him, of course; He was always waiting on *us*.

At Moody before hearing about his father's "accident" his path had seemed simple. *Everything worked together for good for those who loved God.* Anything could be overcome with God's help. He had an unshakeable faith and a clear spiritual calling. He'd build this ministry on God's love the way he'd known it as a child, lifting people up in their hearts, lighting it in their souls. If God had chosen him for this, what could hold him back?

When his father took his own life he had his answer. The shot blew a gaping hole through his family's universe, scattering their energies like his father's brain against the shedwall. He had no bearings suddenly, couldn't think straight. In times like these he knew God carried you: *He understood the grumblings of our hearts.* He tried to find solace in church, in the sermons and communion, but everything seemed hollow and stupid. He realized the myriad petty things people were doing to each other, as if something were peeled from his eyes, as if his father physically splintering himself from this world molecularly changed the way he saw it. What was anything worth? How to teach the blind to see when they had no knowledge of being blind? When they weren't even interested in knowing they were? A conundrum Christ must have faced himself. It seemed no one looked at themselves or gave a damn about anything but their own little selfish vanities. Mankind was a cesspool of vanity, judgment and hypocrisy. Human spirituality was a phony, delusional lip service.

Instead of going into church that Sunday he sat in his jeep reading his Bible. For him God was not in that building. He felt closer to Him riding Shawnee up the high mountain trails, listening to the wind in the trees, sitting by a trout stream watching an eagle drift through the clouds. God was dealing with him, he knew, breaking him down into what *He* wanted him to be: stripping his spiritual baby fat. He had to die himself before he could speak for Jesus Christ.

A week after they buried Davey's body in the woods he'd started to the sheriff's office one morning. He was convicted to go to the authorities, he thought. On the road he felt something resisting him; he kept trudging along and speeding up. He saw Deke and Barrett slaving out in the heat with their precious plants, thinking, he had to do this for them, for all of them. They'd think he was Judas but in time they'd understand. He kept saying as he drove, *keep going, don't let anything stop you.* He started to feel like he was driving through water or glue, like he had no control over his vehicle. Cars blew by, honking their horns. A slow-moving tractor rumbled by. He felt emotionally paralyzed. He couldn't make himself go. He crawled to a stop next to a withered cornfield. Willows swung along the seamless fence line, tentacle-like branches floating up in the wind as he stared straight ahead, listening to a fly in his jeep, remembering when Deke had gone missing in Vietnam. He'd gotten physically ill and cried every day for weeks; prayed on his knees his brother would come home alive, prayed until his temples burst, thinking he could change even that with prayer: disallow death, resurrect his brother. He remembered the call coming from Saigon and his mother screaming hysterically, waving that orange scarf at his father as she stumbled across the fields. He'd never forget them sitting at the dining room table, his father saying a prayer of thanks, his old man bawling like a child. It was a miracle. He'd promised never to take his brother for granted again if God would give him back, and that's what He'd done.

So here was Deke putting himself on the line again, risking his neck for his loved ones. Like Deke said, if they reported Davey's death they'd probably be charged with it, busted and lose it all, but Davey's death wasn't their fault. Was he going to turn his brother in like some common criminal? Deke wasn't a criminal, neither were he and Barrett. They were *growing plants* for Christ sake. He admired his brother, at times even wished he was more like him. Hardheaded as Deke was, he won your heart with his sacrificial willingness to take care of them. It was like some loyalty curse he put on you, exasperating and inspiring you at the same time. The farm wasn't just a piece of ground, it was his flesh and blood. As wrong as it was to bury Davey in the woods, it was more wrong for them to go to jail for a crime they didn't commit. Maybe it was his diehard wish Deke'd lead them through this mess like he said he would. Maybe it was his blood-loyalty to him, or the Holy Spirit, his father's spirit, the spirits of all their fathers'd intercepted him on the road to keep him from going to the authorities that day. Whatever it was he couldn't turn them in. He'd made a U-turn and driven back to the cabin, sure it was the right thing to do. And now Deke and Barrett had nearly been killed out there, so had he made the wrong choice? God only knew. It was too late to worry about it either way. He didn't have the strength to do anything even if he wanted to, and he wasn't even sure what was right anymore. All he could do was help them and leave the rest to God. The current was too strong here, and if they went over that precipice he went over it with them.

After a week with no surprises they relaxed a little. Deke and Barrett combed the woods for booby traps, all the hidden weapons Charlie had once laid for them in the bush, finding nothing but a few tracks around their patches. They had to think like this character to deal with him, stay in his head. They paced grids around the patches marking them with blue strips, and on water runs Deke and Barrett swept them for fresh signs, anything suspicious. Who knew what the boy was capable of? Explosives and automatic ambushes were their main concern, but they didn't mention that to Jason.

Shorter days triggered white-haired female blooms. By September the crop was rushing to full-flower before freezing weather killed it. They combed the plants for male pollen sacks as they'd done in the spring. A couple of randy females straining to be pollinated could turn hermaphrodite and produce enough male flowers to seed a slew of patches in the wind. The seedy tops would be smaller and wouldn't bring as much cash. If they found a male sack they yanked the whole plant, leaving the rest of the sexually aroused girls to produce flowers until they dragged on the ground under their own weight.

The worst heat lifted after dog days. They were still in a drought, but the humidity wasn't as stifling. Electrical storms Barrett called the dry heaves crackled nights, mornings they found hail-and animal-beaten plants with limbs broken, buckled on the ground. Conditions were prime for popcorn fires, the droughts having sapped so much water from the soil even the kudzu was wilting; hardwoods hung limp and dust coated everything. Wildfires burned close enough that they smelled smoke most of the time, a blue smoldering fog blanketing the trees and mountains.

As the plants flowered yellow leaves like tiny flags were easier to pick out from the sky. Colas stood like blackening phalluses in the sun. On TV national guard units chopped down fields of cannabis, grinning soldiers dragging dark-green bundles into bonfires. Those crusading boy scouts would be rolling a few fat ones at the end of the day, Barrett said. Whatever wasn't found by November would be hitting the streets in January, and they could feel that kind of heat bearing down on them as time grew short.

Choppers circled the farm half of one long grueling afternoon. They huddled in the dry-caked marsh on Mosely's property waiting to hear troop voices along the river road. When after a few days nothing came of it they figured nothing would, but they were getting edgy now. Every slow truck on the highway or droning plane pricked up their ears. When one left they listened for it to come back, and when another did they listened to make sure it wasn't the same one. A snapping branch or flock of startled geese could mean everything. When they sensed someone on the property, Deke and Barrett hustled out to investigate. If they caught a whiff of aftershave or cigarette from the highway they spent hours combing the woods to make sure that's all it was. A healthy amount of paranoia was built into this game, Barrett said. They were too close to bringing in the crop to lose it now not being paranoid enough.

With their new partner they had twice as much to think about. When the crop reached full-flower Deke and Barrett would begin night watches, but it was too risky until then to be running around in the woods in the dark. They played cards and watched the Braves on TBS or worked up more blues tunes. This was when you needed a woman to get your mind off things, Barrett said, but it always came down to you and this perishable gold mine sitting out there, the sun ticking across it like a slow secondhand, you couldn't speed up or quit obsessing over. The Green Lady's final test was a pressure-cooker, she squeezed every drop of nerve juice out of you and then squeezed some more. Jason noticed Deke and Barrett were getting drunk just about every night now.

A muddy white van showed up one morning with four scruffy-looking men sniffing around the front pasture near the farmhouse. Hearing the motor, Deke watched them from the top of Hawkins Mountain then ran down to see what they wanted. Barrett and Jason were to keep an eye out and if any trouble started get down there fast. It was some mangy surveying outfit from Madison, a tobacco-chewing, scraggily-bearded man named J.D. Prather and his three toothless, angry sons. Prather said he'd been hired to verify property lines along the highway. Every time Deke asked who'd sent him he'd turn his head and spit. From the lookout Barrett watched the four men hovering around him. From their body language he felt something was about to break. The old man kept wagging his finger in Deke's face, and he knew how that was going to fly with Tar Baby. The other three were leaning awfully close. When Deke told Prather he was calling his buddy Sheriff Tinsdale, Barrett saw the old man's body shrink. He watched Prather slump into his truck where he talked on his two-way as his boys huddled on the drive, came out and told them to pack up, they were headed to another job. Without a word they loaded their filthy Econoline and crawled out to the highway. The license plate was too muddied to read. When Deke tried to reach Prather's surveying company in Madison, there was no business by that name, no J.D. Prather either. It was one of those quaint little visits happened when a crop was short-timed,

Barrett said. People gravitated to you as if they were being led by some unconscious force. It wasn't a coincidence or accident. It was another little visit from the Green Lady's bag of dues.

Jason called Janie every day he couldn't see her. Sometimes he couldn't face her, and missed her more on those days. He knew she wondered what he was doing. He was sick of lying about it, it was like some diabolical joke he was playing on himself. She was the woman he loved and needed to be with; she fed his soul, cheered him up, made love to him, then he lied to her. A splendid arrangement. Some days he thought she'd be better off without him, that he should keep her away until all of this blew over, but the second he saw her again he knew he might as well put a gun to *his* head. Pushing her away wouldn't fix anything. She was the only sane person in his life right now, his humoring angel, making him laugh when it was the last thing he wanted to do. He was a basket case some days, God only knew what she was getting from him then. She had a purple birthmark like his father's Air Force wings on her rear thigh below her bottom. He'd seen it when they were swimming as kids, and it'd always seemed like a sign to him, some kind of promise. She had to have been hand-picked for him, who else would've put up with him in this pathetic state? It was like they'd been married all along. After working on her boat they'd hike out to a point on the other side of Martin's Lake with red wine and a sleeping bag, make love up in the trees listening to the water lap the shore, nearly getting caught by fishermen drifting to the banks casting. When she was quiet he felt God compelling him to spill it. He'd be about to blurt it out, and realize again she didn't have a clue what it was. For all she knew he was brooding about his father, which was true, but he'd use that to cover the other and feel guilty about it. Great husband-pal he was. They'd taken formal vows, his idea, but because of it he didn't feel like he was holding up his part of the bargain. If in the eyes of God they were married, surely she had the right to know what she was married to.

After the near-hanging incident he tried to go along with Deke's new rules. The one he couldn't handle was carrying a handgun. Deke made him practice with his father's service revolver, but he'd refuse to wear it. If Deke brought it to him he'd toss it on the ground. Guns were magnets for guns, he said, you didn't need them if you didn't carry them; nobody needed the murdering things. He was wearing something better for protection and a gun would only hinder it. Sure he was, Deke said, they all were, and jammed the loaded pistol in his brother's pocket.

While Deke and Barrett were working at the front of the farm one morning he slipped out to check on Shawnee. He knew they'd hear his jeep going back to the stables, so he radioed first and hiked as the crow flew, crossing the three unplanted corn fields, using Slater's Pass to keep from tracking near their patches. He jogged so he could get back before they did, but he was going to do this whether they liked it or not. He said the *Twenty-Third Psalm* until he reached the stables. He could feel the shadow of the valley of death that morning. The smell of it, of decaying flesh seemed everywhere. There was an early chill and crimson leaves rained down the mountains, rustling in the trees. Waves of starlings swirled around like panicking spirits. He'd never seen so many seagulls on the farm before. Maybe the word'd gotten out fish were raining from the sky. There wasn't much water to find, the creeks drying were up, the ponds were lower than they'd ever been. Another month of this and they'd have to pump water from underground. Anywhere they turned kettles of vultures circled in the sun.

He knew Deke'd have a fit if he found him back there, but he couldn't worry about that. He'd kept his promise not to go to the sheriff, and he wasn't bugging out on them. He wasn't living in a cage of fear either. He'd come and go when he felt like it, it was his as much as Deke's place, and he'd rather be dead than hiding from some stranger on it. He had to believe his faith would protect him from whatever was going on here or he might as well be dead anyway.

He found Shawnee in rough shape skittishly grazing the dry alfalfa field. Lifting his head the horse tucked his tail, backpedaling from him. At first he acted like he didn't know him. He'd never seen him this nervous before. Shuffling sideways, he swung his head and whinnied as if trying to sling something off him. Jason suspected rabies, but thank God he wasn't foaming. He went to him, coaxing and speaking quietly, approaching a few steps at a time, offering an apple. The horse snorted with a scared, startled look, his ribs blood-and mud-crusted. He'd run through heavy briars or gotten tangled in another fence line. His knees, forearms and hocks were stone-bruised worse than before. There was heat around his right front ankle. Finally he stood munching the apple, shuddering and twitching, shifting a little as Jason stroked him. When a vulture's shadow crossed them he swung his head, backpedaling again, whinnying with that terrified, unhinged look, galloping away favoring his hind leg. It looked like a sprain in his second thigh. Jason brought iodine spray from the medicine cabinet, cleaning the scratches and cuts, the horse huffing and sidling, flinching as he doctored him. He rubbed white liniment with aloe on his thigh and gave him Calm and Cool pellets to steady his nerves.

Every other day he slipped back to the stables to check on him. The horse seemed a little less jumpy but wouldn't give up his wariness. The morning he saw him galloping without favoring the leg, his cuts and abrasions healing, he fed him a handful of calming pellets, saddled up and trotted back toward the marshes. They rode their favorite trail up through the birch forest, Shawnee balking a few times like he'd seen or heard something. Once they were downwind from a stench of rotting animals and rode up on them strewn along the trail like handfuls of manure, hanging in crooks of trees, the big birds working over them on the yellow-leaved floor. The horse huffed and threw back his head, stomping and kicking, swiping the ground. He turned broadside to the trail, refusing to budge. When Jason prodded him he fought back, jerking cater cornered, wheeling and stalling until they crossed the ridge over the river with the view for miles of limbless trees over the dried wetlands. The gold-and wine-colored leaves of mountains were an eye-feast from up there.

He spotted something shining in the water's edge and walked Shawnee down to it. The river was shallow-clear, metallic-sheened in the sun, yellow, brown and black stones freckling the sandy bottom. A five-hundred pound bomb was planted tail-up in the muddy sand a few feet from shore, black-washed brush streaming off its fins. He let the horse drink, pulled up and started along the southern fence line, munching scuppernongs hanging from cottonwoods. Waves of geese honked over in lopsided V's. The horse balked a few times, tossing his head twisting and rearing. When it seemed like he'd bolt Jason leaned in his ear stroking and talking to him, distracting him with apples from the saddle satchel.

Halfway to the highway he turned and zigzagged along the narrow creek bed up into the thick pines to the place where they'd buried Davey. He hadn't been back there since that night, taking his time now climbing the slippery shelves, loose-footing pine straw, dismounting and walking the horse up to the antler-like markers. He'd remembered it as a flatter, wider place. It was sloped with a few pine stumps and clumps of briars. The tree-antlers Barrett had stuck over the grave were tilted sharply. Having wanted to come back and say a prayer he wasn't able to under the circumstances, he got on his knees now and prayed Davey's soul found peace in this place. He asked God to forgive them and protect them for the thousandth time. One day he promised to tell Davey's family where he was, to see he was properly buried. He asked Davey's forgiveness. When he opened his eyes Shawnee was standing off in the trees staring back at him shyly. His head bowed as if he understood why they were there.

Jason leaned to pick up a flat aspirin tin. It was open like a sliver of mirror under loose leaves. Three tablets were in it, six more spilled in the straw next to it. They were crisp-dry and fresh-looking like they'd been there a day or two.

In full moonlight Barrett sat on the side of a mountain in a muscadine blind canvassing the valley with binoculars. He held on the seven patches, studying the glistening tops nodding in the breeze, panning along the far edge of the tree line for any bulk or movement in the bright straw grass. From their plants set into a notch of trees directly across from him he scanned the shining side of the mountain where he could see the entire floor of leaves, rocks and trunks, dropped to two patches in the middle of the field, then slid to the others on his far left, one a stone's throw from the wrinkle-slitted creek bed. It was quiet except for an occasional howl out by the highway. A military jet purred a fine vapor trail at high altitude near the full moon. Since it had risen yellow and massive at the eastern edge of the field, he could make out and count practically every plant in every nest, and to pass the time calculated the general worth of each patch from their heights, widths and numbers of colas.

In gusts walnuts thumped the ground in the sagging trees. He thought about what he'd be seeing out here if he were smoking the stuff, then to not think about it thought about Marsha and the way she'd come back to him that night in the motel, what she'd said and been willing to do for him, and then to keep from missing her too much, went back to the plants and made another slow-raking pass with the glasses, cupping the lenses to cut reflections. Now and then he stood or shifted to ease the ache in his butt from sitting on this rock-hard ground.

Five-hundred yards away Deke perched on a ledge with a view of two other fields and the variegated-colored ridge separating them. With his naked eye he could make out parts of nine patches, lighter-colored than their surroundings, glowing in moonlight and the flag-yellow leaves of those beneath him. He set his coffee down and picked up his 30.06 rifle, citing through the scope a half-dozen heavily-budded bushes, lay it down, flipped the portable glasses and combed the woods tree by tree, catching a small buck stepping to a rock near a thread-tiny stream, three then four does stepping gingerly out of the shadows behind him.

Barrett's low growl came over his radio.

"What time's it, Tar Baby?"

Deke glanced at his watch and whispered with his mouth against the mike, watching the deer drinking.

"Two-thirtyish. Anything with you?"

"Quiet as shit. Wish prankster'd make his move tonight so we can get this over with."

Snugged half-asleep under his army blanket in the cabin, Jason blinked and rolled to his side.

"Don't think he'll chose tonight," Deke said. "That round flare in the sky. Might have half a brain and want to keep it."

"May be. Wouldn't count on it."

"Seven or eight deer in my crosshairs tonight. Good shots up here, buddy."

"Giving away military secrets."

"How long we been sitting out here, two, three weeks? If he's around he knows we are. Any deterrent's good with me."

"I'd rather he never knew what hit him. Been over the son of a bitch."

Jason gazed at the ceiling listening to the refrigerator humming, the kudzu stirring at the corners of the cabin. He shut his eyes and prayed his usual prayer and mantra.

"Gonna' take a look on the other side," Deke said, followed by garbled noise and breathing. "*My God, what was that? Did you see that?*"

"Sure as hell did. What was it?"

Jason opened his eyes, glaring in the dark.

"Meteor I guess," Deke said shakily. "Never seen anything like that. Lit up half the fucking sky. Did you see it?"

"I'm tellin' ya. That was some shit, wudn't it? That what it was?"

"Had to be. What else? Lord God."

"I'm waitin' for the earth to shimmy. Guess it burned out before it hit us."

"Hope so, shit," Deke said. "Ever see anything like that before?"

"Hell no, Kimasabe. Little brother, you see that fireball or whatever it was?"

"No," Jason said crankily. "I was asleep, guys. Going back, all right? Goodnight."

But he didn't sleep for a long time. He stared at the ceiling wide-awake listening, his eyes burning into the darkness.

Barrett snored heavily on his side using his knotted bag for a pillow.

"Br'er Rabbit?" Deke's voice crackled. Barrett lurched up disoriented, fumbling for his radio.

"Yeah, yeah, shit. Talk to me."

"Hanging it up here. Be light in an hour. Anything that side?"

"No, but dig it. I was dreamin' some shit, man. I'm not sure who she was, but damn she was delicious."

"Got to get you some bennies, Br'er Rabbit. Not supposed to have that kind of fun out here."

"I'm with you. Just let me get my eyes working in the same direction."

Barrett stretched up, holstered his .38 and leaned to pick up the rest of his gear. Opening his canteen he saw soft-yellow flickers on the leaved floor. The moon was behind the treetops on the far edge of the field. Light-fingers looked like those cast on night walls of the house he'd grown up in from gas radiant heaters. Sniffing something, he turned and saw a fire several-hundred yards to his left in the corner of the field beyond the creek bank. That can't be real, he thought. Can it? I haven't smoked anything. Am I awake here? he blinked, flexing his eyes. Raising binoculars he saw thirty plants lit up against the trees and smelled the burning incense, bristling tops strung together like flame-engulfed torches.

"Tar Baby! Goddamit! Whole nest in flames this side! Get over here!"

"You're kidding," Deke said, scanning the horizon. "Are you serious?"

He followed the dark mountain line with moonlight glistening along its silver rim, yellow light reflected from a dip in the trees behind a v-shaped ridge.

"Oh shit . . ." he said, standing and looking at it. ". . . motherfucking . . . *son* of a bitch . . ."

Beating across the high grass dragging his sleeping bag, Barrett tried to catch a glimpse of fire starter darting into the woods or hightailing it across the field. He tripped in a gully, tangling his feet in the slippery lining, digging up bunching it under his arm crossing the creek where he dunked it quickly, reached the patch and hurled it over a cluster of plants. Whiffing gasoline, he thought, you don't smell gasoline burning, where is it? He grabbed a log and started pounding and smashing plants to the ground. If he could get them out maybe they could salvage something. This was goddamn wonderful, he thought, as Jason stumbled up with his army blanket stomping flames in the grass.

"Soak it in the creek, little brother! Drag the edges!"

As Jason ran to the creek Barrett gave up on the plants and started beating back grassfires. If he didn't every patch and the whole fucking place would go up bone-dry as it was. He heard crashing through the woods, limbs cracking, and saw Deke half-running, stumbling down the narrow seam between the two mountains, his face distorted-yellow in the shimmering trees. He ran right at Barrett as if he would bowl him over, angling off at the last second barreling past him, hurtling the creek as Jason came out of it. They watched him sprinting across the field toward another fire trickling up in the opposite corner. Barrett smothered the flames at his feet, glancing at the new one, going oh shit, what the hell, watching it knife up through the grass.

"*Goddamit!*" he said, shuffling toward it. "Stay on this one, Reverend! Get the edges down then get over here!"

Deke swung his shirt at burning tops, ripping half-charred ones up, hurling them. He beat at catching tree-branches but flames had already risen into the limbs. He shinnied the tree, cursing and clawing, bouncing on limbs until they snapped, dangling by an arm, kicking them. Dropping to his knees, he dug back a clean perimeter of brush and leaves. On the other side Barrett lashed and tore at burning trunks with his smoldering bag, kicking them apart, slap-smothering them. Sweat dripping from his nose, he was getting high from the smoke; he sniffed gasoline again. He saw Deke leaning in some kind of trance through the burning plants, his face transfixed across the field.

"Deke! Are you okay!"

"You son of a bitch! . . . *motherfucker!* . . . I'll wax your fucking ass . . ."

Barrett turned to see the third fire, unsure for a moment he wasn't hallucinating it, gawking at it as he fought on in stupefied horror. What the hell? he thought, watching Deke battle the fire in front of him viciously, darting back and forth along the edges gnashing and yelling, batting and slashing plants with a branch showering embers in the leaves. His face looked buggy in the flame light. He's losing it, Barrett thought; come on, buddy, keep it together. Watching him break for the third fire he decided to stay where he was to keep this one from jumping back into the limbs. By the time Deke reached the new one Jason was on it with his blanket, smothering the edges, Deke staggering up shaking his head, giggling in disbelief. This isn't happening, he thought. It can't be happening. He looked at the perfect candelabra beauties he'd germinated and nurtured, sagging mature with weight now, thousands of dollars incinerating before his eyes, hurling into them slinging and swatting crazily in a whirlwind of sparks. When he stumbled to his knees Jason yanked him out by his waist belt.

"What are you doin', Deke! You're gonna burn yourself!"

"Where is the son of a bitch!" Deke said, squinting through smoke, opening his pocket glasses barely able to fix on anything with sweat fogging the lenses. His blood rose seeing a wild-headed, wet-shirtless man flailing in the flames across the field, realizing it was Barrett. Something caught his eye at the opposite corner where the first fire had started and he stood, breathlessly wobbling, pants smoking, watching another set of flames spiking up through the grass. *No, no, no,* he cried, gulping nausea, sweeping the field again for the son of of a bitch: *he would run him down and beat him mercilessly.* He was out there somewhere. Was he some goddamn fire ghost? Swinging back to the new fire lapping at the corner, he hurtled toward it through claw-briars, ahead of him Barrett galloping toward something else in the far corner at the same end. Yelling something he couldn't understand, Barrett was pointing to flickers of a fifth fire trickling up a hundred yards to his right. Seeing it Deke cackled, screaming hoarsely as he stumbled hand-over-handing through foreshadows. He'd lost his goddamn shirt. He couldn't find a goddamn log or rock to beat it with. *Son of a bitch*, he screamed, plowing through the patch like a charging bull with his head down, tumbling out the other side with embers on his back. Jason was over him, knocking him off, dousing him with his ragged blanket. Deke elbowed out and tunneled through the patch again, scattering sparks and cinders, laughing maniacally.

"What're you doing, Deke! Stop it dammit! Are you out of your mind!"

"The marijuana's burning!" Deke said, howling. "You're a dead motherfucker!" he cried into the woods, reeling and falling. "I hope it's worth it you son of a bitch . . . you're dead as hell sweetheart! . . ."

Barrett's boots felt hot enough to melt his feet. He hit the creek feeling the chilled, instant relief, dunking his smoldering bag in it, digging up jogging to the next fire. Reaching it careful not to stumble in his stoned exhaustion. Save the place and take care of the bastard, was all he could think. Why would anyone do this? What was the point? He heard yelling across the field and saw the twisted silhouettes of Deke and Jason stumbling back and forth in front of the flames like dancing Indians, crazed marionettes. One seemed to be running right through the fires—an illusion or he was batshit buggy himself. As he smothered the flames at his feet something yellow caught his eye on his periphery and he caught another whiff of high octane, in a blur seeing tops of flames knifing up in the middle of the field, hearing Deke's .45 ring out. He blinked and saw the palely-lit figures of farmers bent-over around him the length of the field. They were soft lace and smoke themselves, the color of moths dotting all over it, laboring methodically in the grass. Glassy-eyed, he blinked and watched them in the moonlight as he listened to Deke's gun resounding. He saw Deke shooting it, listening to him howling, Jason leaping up trying to wrest it from him. Barrett dropped his parched bag on the fire's edge and made meticulous, sweeping perimeters, dragging and stepping on it. Peering into the shriveling plants, hypnotized by sizzling sounds, the mixed concoction of burning marijuana, gas and straw grass, he turned and weaved to the next blaze and saw the seventh patch burning beyond it, Deke and Jason scuffling on their sides between the two fires, their faces blacker than his. Jason was spreading his tattered blanket on the fire's edge, running back to Deke who kept struggling to get to his feet, staggering and crouching with a happy-deranged look like a punch-drunk boxer's. Jason was wrestling him, Deke lunging up trying to charge the fire again, his brother pushing him down shouting at him; Deke rocking, sitting forward with his head swaying in his lap as he coughed and howled like he was high on laughing gas, fighting to get to his feet again.

Barrett unspooled wire around a ring of pines at knee-level, yanking it taut. He tied off where he'd started and strung another at waist-level, taping the grenade to the stoutest tree with good natural brush on it. Adding camouflage he tied off the two strands, delicately setting the pin. There was enough give in the wires for the trees to rock a little in the wind.

Deke strung wire low around strong saplings and thick briars in an open patch. He braced the line on three sides with massive rocks rolled up from the stream, wired the grenade pin on a small live oak covered with vines, and fluffed leaves around it. At the next patch he hammered waist-high two-by-fours ten yards apart, eight of them in a solid circle, tamping them, running two strands of wire. Before taping two claymores to the stakes, one on each strand opposite the other, he pulled up grass and vines concealing the lines and stakes. He mounted and set the claymores, covering his trails with a yard rake back to the trees. His right forearm and shoulder were slathered with petro carbo salve for second degree burns. He'd taken a nice scalding on his back and singed an eyebrow and half the hair off his head. He'd been stung by a brown recluse to boot, or something as venomous, swelling his big toe purple so that it felt broken and he hobbled on it.

Pain, fury and lack of sleep drove him at this point. Since first light he and Barrett had been wiring every flower they had left with automatic ambushes. Assuming their boy was laying low, or not within miles of the place knowing they'd be watching for him, they worked separately to rig all the patches by sundown. He was at least predictable in his guerrilla methods. They'd found one-gallon gas cans at each torched patch. The boot prints were the same ones that'd carried Davey's body from their chopped plants up the creek to stash him in a cave; the same ones they'd tracked to the highway from the poisoned patch where Deke and Barrett had been snatched into the trees. It was clear he intended to demoralize them. He'd sabotaged enough of their crop to prove he could get it all, but when he realized he couldn't spook them off it'd be them instead of their plants he'd begin to get rid of.

A year ago Barrett had traded an ordnance officer at Fort Gordon a half-pound of sensimilla for a dozen claymores and a case of grenades. Like any good boy scout he believed in being prepared. He preferred doing this the easy way where everyone lived in peace and harmony in the land of milk and honey, but that wasn't happening here; he wouldn't have an ounce of compunction if the trespassing son of a bitch stuck his nose out again and recycled himself. He should know better than to mess with a man's livelihood. Wasn't there anything they could do besides turning the place into an armed camp? Jason asked. Could they nail up notices? Reason with him somehow? Deke suggested Jason get away from the farm for a few days, which Jason knew was a warning to not even start with that now. He'd seen Deke come unglued and knew he was on a short fuse; a few choice words could detonate him, and once he blew he was stubborn as the hills. Nothing anyone could say would stop him anyway. They were edging closer to that precipice, only some divine intervention would keep them from going over it. He'd taken clothes and a toothbrush to the church where he'd prayed in his jeep most of the afternoon. At four he called Janie to see if he could spend a few days with her.

At dusk eleven patches remained to be rigged. Taking turns with the lantern and stringing wire, Deke and Barrett hustled to finish them together, leaving five claymores for replacements. Out of forty-six patches booby-trapped since morning, one or two might go off with a falling tree or heavy gust, but the loss of a few patches was negligible now. They had to freeze this bastard before he decimated their crop. As they armed the last of them, they watched hundreds of vultures drift under the blood-red sky near the stables. Squadrons of F-111's echoed down the valley, scattering them into the trees. They bumped back to the cabin in the dark, polishing off a gallon of Cuervo with raw steaks and Mexican eggs. Deke soaked his toe and redressed his jellied arm and shoulder in petro carbo salve, wrapping them in a creek-washed sheet. Barrett set the cabin perimeter wires tripped to a Corvette car alarm he'd picked up at an auto graveyard, and they slept for thirteen solid hours.

Janie breast-stroked under the lover's bridge where the creek funneled into her father's pond and stepped to the bank, peeling off her t-shirt. Picking up a towel, sitting naked on the blanket by the picnic basket, she watched Jason gnaw a stalk of clover gazing into the trees. She'd noticed his knuckles were bruised, patches of hair and flesh were missing from his forearms. When she asked about it he'd mumbled something about burning off insects, but she could see the emotion in his hands. She sipped wine from a mug as she wrapped her hair in a towel, wondering what it was. She'd seen him come out of that state she found him in at the church, and he'd told her she was the reason for it. In the last few weeks he'd plummeted into this inconsolable gloom making it impossible to talk to him, and she wondered if that was her fault too. Him getting worse puzzled her. If he couldn't find peace in the scriptures he read for her, what was she to believe? She didn't want to bother him with her insecurities, God knew she had plenty of those, but when he pulled back into that little room in his head she got very lonely.

"What a day," she said. "Aren't you going to swim, honey?"

"Ever read Job, Janie?"

"Bible talk's not exactly what I had in mind right now."

"He was a Godly man, see, who was prospering, so God tested his faith by putting on him about every misfortune you could think of. Loss of property, fire, pestilence, boils, family deaths, you name it."

"What'd he do?"

"Never lost faith. Hung in there and took it. Everybody thought he was cursed. Ever felt like everything and everybody were slipping away?"

"Not yet. You?"

She draped a towel round her neck and poured a cup of wine, lifting his head.

"I may be slipping, but it won't be from you."

"You don't know that," he said. "We could lose each other without meaning to."

She pulled on an orange Tennessee jersey, untangling her hair.

"You're scaring me, Jason."

"Losses and disasters are part of life. Everybody suffers, dies, so what?"

"You're not terminally ill, are you?"

"Think we all are."

"We still having babies and launching our floating missionary?"

She faced him cross-legged nibbling on an Oreo.

"What's going on? Is it me?"

"*No.* Everything's all right." He glanced at her. "What?"

"Something's going on out there. Your family?"

"Why you say that?"

"I don't know," she shrugged. "Wild guess."

Of course this was coming. He was so wrapped up in it he couldn't see it, like a child believing he was fooling his parents when they could see everything. How did you protect and lose someone at the same time? Every time he lied another little piece of his soul washed away, the pure thing they shared feeling more desecrated. He lay his head against hers looking up into the trees.

"You're responsible for what you know," he said.

"What's that mean?"

"It's not wise to know everything."

"And the truth will set you free, right? Remember what you told me, Jason Hawkins, about how we take on each others lives making love to each other?"

He cleared his throat.

"We hook up to each other, you said, like an umbilical cord, and everything one has, demons, sins, lies, the other does."

". . . I said that . . ."

"Yes you did. What am I getting from you, bud?"

"A half-crazy man."

"*Oh, yippee.* Come on, Mr. Hawkins, you can do better than that."

They watched martins swimming through wrinkles in the branches, black specks floating against the sun.

"Dad said yours got the suckiest deal with the IRS. Same thing nearly happened to him, you know."

"Glad it didn't."

"That what's eating you?"

"We're trying to hold onto the place, it ain't easy."

"You think I don't know that?"

"'Course you do . . ."

"Listen, sweetheart, I know losing your dad was unbearable, especially the way it happened, I couldn't have made it through that. Your mom's not well and you've nearly lost everything else, maybe you're still losing it. I just wish you'd talk about it, you've clammed up. What do you think I'm here for?"

"I'm lucky . . ."

"We're not separate anymore, we're each other now, remember? You need to trust God the way you tell me to, Minister Man."

He looked at her faith radiating back like a child's; she was handing it right back to him.

"I think you're coping okay under the circumstances."

"You think?" he laughed. "Then what're you worried about?"

"I get the feeling you're not telling me everything."

"I can't now."

"You're not in any *danger*," she squeezed his hand. "Promise you'll tell me if you are."

"Danger's not real in this world. The only real danger's losing your soul."

"Then why do I pick up so much nervousness from you? You losing your soul?"

"Keep your eyes peeled . . ."

"You act like a condemned man. You haven't done anything *wrong*, have you?"

He chuckled with his arm over his face.

"Sure you're not seeing someone?"

"Oh come on. It's got nothing to do with you. It's . . . This time of year makes me feel like my life's ending or something. It's worse this year because I ought to be in a church preaching, and I can't even walk into one. Do you know how strange that is? I've got to get back to seminary the second this business is settled. Hey, what're you doing?"

"Your promised wife's rescuing you."

"You call that rescuing?"

"Good thing, isn't it? I don't think your life's quite over, Mr. Hawkins. What I hold in my hand's firm testimony to it. *He's alive!*" she cried into the trees. "*The beastly boy lives!*"

He looked at her changed eyes as the breeze lifted her hair. His head swimming from his genitals and she was smiling that unconditional smile that redeemed him.

"This spiritual man I read about, Sri Yukteswar, called this 'the Root of the Tree of Life.' Maybe you were onto something climbing that swing pole."

"Think so?"

"I think we're growing healthy roots here."

"I think our tree's become a California Redwood."

"No thanks to the wife of your heart."

"With extra stories being added in top limbs."

"See how the fruit just grows in our hands when you relax?"

"Who's relaxing?" he laughed. "Speak for yourself."

"Just relax," she teased him, breathing softly in his ear. "Take it easy. No hurry now," she chuckled.

"Come here," he said, taking and kissing her.

"Let's toast to the good stuff: seminary, your first church, our charmed life together. Our baby choirboys, how many should we have?"

"What are you doing with me, Janie One?"

"I've always been with you, Mr. Hawkins. Can't remember when I wasn't, can you?"

"You're not slipping away?"

"Hardly."

"Sure about that?"

"You tell me, Mr. Big."

She fondled him with one hand as she rose to her knees lifting the bottle, sitting astride him. Filling her mouth with the warm wine, she kissed it into his, singing and moaning as he wrapped his hands round her waist. She leaned forward, rocking gently, the soft juice sluicing down their cheeks dripping on the blanket.

Barrett scooped the glistening blue crystals into jerry cans, stirring them fast with a stick. He trickled the sea-colored solution around the roots and dry leaf-mulch, shaking the cans to keep it mixed. Thunder grumbled under purple-grey clouds, wind curling the undersides of leaves sweeping them across the fields.

"Got any bloom juice left, little brother?"

"Little bit," Jason said, lifting it over.

Barrett rocked the can end-to-end, dripping it around the trunks.

"These are about right, Rev. This'll make the flowers go nuts, I guarantee it."

"How do you know they're ready?"

"Watch for the worm."

"The worm?"

"In the flower, yeah. Deke never told you about the worm in the flower?" Barrett took a foot-long cola sticking to his fingers, pressing the tops apart with his thumbs. "See these small white hairs and these purple ones here? Soon as all of 'em turn purple the stink'll be so skunk-sweet it'll give you a hard-on. From the looks of these, two, three weeks now. At the moment that purple reaches its peak, a worm'll show up in the flower the same color. Gotta look hard to find him 'cause he blends in, but that's when you grab 'em. Wait till these hairs turn brown you've already lost something. The worm in the flower, be there every time."

"What'd happen if we chopped them now?"

"Be a waste," Barrett said, tossing the cans over the wires. "Crop'd taste green. Couple of weeks is all the difference now, gettin' antsy?"

"Been antsy."

"I'm about to rewire this tree-mine, why don't you tote those jerries up to the truck in case I slip."

"I trust you, go ahead."

Barrett snugged the wires taut and retied the grenade pin with needle-nose pliers.

"I know this ain't easy for you, little brother."

"It's insanity."

"Yeah, well. If one of these blows and don't kill the bastard he'll think twice about what it's worth. Ain't no excuse for losses we been taking, come too far to let him run us out of here and steal us blind."

Deke's voice crackled through static.

"Everybody good over there?"

"So far, Tar Baby. What's cooking?"

"Feel a nice one coming; knee's painin' like a son of a bitch. Keep your ears and bowels open."

"Gotcha."

Barrett parked the truck under a corridor of trees by the brightened field and slid a half-dozen sloshing cans off the bed. He took a double-twisted joint from his vest pocket, cupping the lighter with his palm.

"Little ceremonial service, Rev. Know how long it's been since I smoked one out here? Want a taste?"

Jason looked at it, thinking, a taste was probably the last thing he needed right now. He was nervous enough being out here and sure didn't need to add to it. He loved the smell of it though, the intoxicating incense: step inside, it said, you might learn something. It was God's truth all right, you just never knew how much of it you were going to be ready for. He'd had some fun nights on it, gut-laughing so hard his stomach ached. Maybe he could use a taste, something to lighten him up out here. He took the joint before he could think about it, inhaling it watching the resin wrinkle up on the paper.

"All right, little brother, while you feed that patch down in the bamboo I'm gonna hit these two in the field. We won't be more than a hundred yards apart. Your brother told me to stick with you, so you tell me."

Jason felt the amplified rush as he took the joint again.

He watched trembling branches above his head thrashing like floating arms reaching down to him, the floor changing colors and flickering with leaves rippling across it. Everything lashed around as if the woods were in an emotional uproar, blackbirds flitting by close to the ground. He took another hit and handed it back.

"I'll be all right," he said. "You unwired it?"

"Every one in here. I'll reset after you feed 'em. Take this with you," Barrett handed him his nickel-plated .38.

"No thanks," Jason said, shouting above the wind. "Meet you back here, when?"

"Thirty minutes. Call if anything happens. Mix it exactly the way I showed you."

Jason nodded, jamming the bloom-builder into his shoulder pouch. He lifted two gurgling cans and crossed the padded trail, stumbling and steadying himself down a flat-narrow path toward the rocking bamboo. It creaked and swished as he crunched into it, slipping over stalks and vines, catching himself on a poplar, stopping to pull the cans close to his body where the path squeezed between trunks. A bobwhite sang somewhere in the wind. This stuff was making him nervous. It always intensified what was there, what made him think it would relax him? He glanced around, distracted by movements, shrieking sounds and snapping limbs. He could feel Barrett's presences or whatever they were as he watched the trees darken ahead and heard the rushing sound like a high-pitched waterfall. Leaves whipped in his face as he ducked and twisted, losing the path, finding it again as hail clacked like popcorn on the rustling bamboo.

Barrett slid his four cans under the barbed wire fence, humming as he carried two at a time into the high grass. The wind tossed, flattening and separating it like dozens of invisible feet. He set the last ones in the middle of the patch as golf ball-size hail began to batter his neck and shoulders. Pulling his cap down he squatted to a knee, through the split, pressed grass seeing the bent-over backs of Vietnamese farmers working ahead of him, chalklike arms reaching into the straw. Listening to thuds and clacks on the cans, he raised up slowly, shielding his eyes, watching them with that same bewildered-welcoming awe, squinting and seeing more behind him. Face down, their hands picked at the ground, none of them looking up or seeming aware of him. He watched their conical hats and down-turned heads bobbing as the larger hail thunked around him.

"What you want with me?" he said. "I can't do nothing for you. Just like you. What you need me for?"

He heard heavier thudding mixed with hail and saw finger-size fish falling and bouncing. They streamed into the field of humped-over figures like small silver daggers. He shook his head with a strained effort to comprehend this again, opened his palms watching the ice and shiny fish ricocheting off them.

As Jason came out of the bamboo it was hailing harder. He looked down to keep it from peppering his face. He padded the back of his neck with weeds, stepping into the marijuana patch dropping his cans making an awning from his forehead. Through the darkened trunks he noticed the bottom of a splintered post jammed in the mud on the other side of the clearing, squinting at it through flashes. It wasn't like them to leave anything like this.

He ducked toward it, protecting his eyes, feeling the sardine-size fish prickling his neck and shoulders, shaking them from his hair. Hail popped and leaped at his feet. Face down he elbowed to the other side, pushing out through the grown-together, swinging colas.

Rocking side to back in the wind was Davey's dug-up corpse, vine-lashed to a cross of trees. He was barely recognizable, maggots boiling on his forehead and feet, his wrinkled, decomposed face slung to one side. His slumped torso nodded in a bobbing circle with hail and fish slapping it.

Jason felt his heart implode. He started to laugh in a broken, barking way, his eyes on the rocking foot of the cross.

Mumbling he slid to his knees with his head down, looking at the dangling, decayed feet, speaking in a halting cadence behind the peleting objects and thunder.

"*. . . father . . . hallowed be . . . thy kingdom . . . thy will be . . . on earth . . . please heaven . . . this day . . . deliver us . . .*" He slid to his haunches, his legs bent beneath him, hands pressed to his face with fish buffeting his cheeks and shoulders. "My God . . ." he whimpered. ". . . What've we done . . . *why is this is happening to us! . . .*"

On an eighty foot bluff Deke clung to a flailing mimosa, radio in his other hand. Below him trees tossed like twigs in the wind, ropes and water cans rattling. The sky was moiling-purple as far as he could see.

"Br'er Rabbit, little brother, what's your twenty?"

He heard static with high squiggly noise.

"Here, Tar Baby," Barrett answered through wind and clipping chinks. "Seen or heard from Reverend?"

Deke felt his pulse start up.

"What're you talking about? Isn't he with you?"

"Supposed to meet me at the truck an hour ago, been huntin' him, shoutin' on the radio, hollerin' my fool lungs out. Didn't hear me?"

"Shit no, my radio was off." Deke tried to get a breath and control himself. "You were supposed to stay with him asshole! Why'd you let him out of your sight!"

"We were close enough to spit at, Tar Baby. Got a feelin' he might've run back to the cabin."

"Why's that? Why do you think that?"

Barrett kneeled in the middle of the patch where gusts swept flower-heavy bushes on their sides, holding a plant with one hand bracing it as he shouted.

"Found his tracks coming out of the nest he was workin'. Bad boy'd been there and left somebody for us. Must've upset Reverend pretty good."

"Somebody?"

"Brought Davey back to us. Sure was glad to see him again, buddy." Deke heard a peculiar giggle through crackling and clanks. "Looked a little peaked, Tar Baby."

Deke took a long panicked moment. Livid and scared senseless, he forced himself to think.

"Listen to me," he said. "I'm runnin' back to the cabin to see if he's there. Meet me in case he's not so we can hunt for him together, copy?"

Barrett held a plant and stake together, mashing the button as he tied.

"Bracin' up these legs while I'm out here. Got some wind damage and gonna get more. Call if he's not at the cabin and I'll hustle in to you."

"Meet me at the goddamn cabin asshole!" Deke exploded. "What am I gonna do if you disappear on me, wander around these fucking woods with my dick in my hand!"

"Take it easy, Tar Baby. Ain't comin' till I brace up these babies, keep your head on now. Jog back to the cabin and let me know what you find."

Deke took a moment to gather himself. "Yeah, all right, I'll do that. Will you watch yourself, goddamit? Shit. Shit!" He jammed the radio in his pocket, making sure his .45 was loaded. "Motherfuckers!" he erupted again, kicking the roped cans scattering off the cliff ledge, slipping and clawing for hand-holds in rocks, chuckling as he hung there by his fingers.

Jason throttled his jeep down the rutted drive. Hail and raining debris battered his windshield as he sideswiped small trees, bouncing off of them, pounding up hard, punching his headlights. A speck of light gleamed below as flutters lit the faces of trunks. He hit a three-foot ditch like he'd dipped off a wall, whipping him up onto his right two wheels leaning and skidding down into the woods on his right side. His right mirror shattered. The front right corner of his roof caved in as he ground to a halt, wobbling as if he were still rolling. Teetering on his right side, the engine running with a slow, loping jingle, he was lodged against a hickory trunk, limbs jutting through his passenger door and window. *Not now*, he thought. *Not now, come on, come on!* Burning rubber into the dry leaves, he opened his door rocking back and forth, swinging his weight up from the shallow ravine he was partially cradled in. The jeep creaked and righted. He rocked forward and back until he got enough traction to move, scratching onto the drive, jostling hard to the foot of the mountain with something dragging-scraping under his wheel, gathering speed through a groundswell of dust and ice as he bumped out of the woods. Corrugated tin flapped across the drive. He couldn't see twenty feet through flying dust, weaving in the wind with the radio on gazing at the outline of his father's house as he floated past it. It was like being in a sightseeing car driven by someone else, gusts half-lifting him in a whistling scream. He fishtailed onto the shoulder and stalled. The ignition turned but wouldn't fire. He pumped and kicked the accelerator, grit blowing in his eyes through the torn plastic. *This is it?* he thought, pressing the pedal, wrenching the key, swiping his face with his muddy wrists. *Help me*, he gulped. *You know where I'm going, why would you hold me back from it? Why would you!* he cried, holding his face as he stomped the floorboard. He let off the gas, turned it to clear it and it made a grogging sound. The battery was dead. *Perfect, that's your answer; I got it, thank you.* He waited and tried it and it nearly kicked over. He waited and tried it again, it made a sluggish, slurred sound and cranked. He tore across the centerline, weaving in the wind, crunching over things he couldn't see with what felt like a limb lodged in his roof dragging like a scratching rudder, his front right wheel bouncing like it was lumping apart.

Lucas March lowered his storm windows as Monk's "Epistrophy" jangled on his turntable. He and Rashan stopped to listen to the scraping noise with the racket of tires popping over limbs and ice, the old man making a curious nod as Jason swerved by, dragging a tree limb like a street-sweeping tail. Branches clapped and sliced his roof, Rashan clinging to his heels yelping. Funnels whorled in the yard as the old man hobbled to pull down window flaps with the hooked pole, scratching Rashan's head, speaking in a calming voice.

"Jus' the world, old boy, nothing to it. Listen to that piano, will ya: *that's* the stuff," he said, grunting the trickling notes, the dog's stomach pressed against his ankles.

Deke staggered into the cabin yard seeing Jason's jeep gone. Rubber legged from sprinting up Hawkins Mountain, he scoured the yard for signs of him. Bare footprints led to freshly-dug jeep tracks. They had to be Jason's. Of course they were, he thought, listening to the screen door slamming in the wind. He yelled out in every direction. Where the hell was he? He was in his jeep, wasn't he? Of course he was in his goddamn jeep, would you cut it out?

He flicked the light switch in the cabin: no electricity. Shining his penlight he saw what looked like a tornado had blown through, everything scattered, chairs upended as if somebody had bowled over them stumbling out the door. His heart fell when he saw Jason's muddy boots on the floor, wind spinning a ragged piece of paper on the carpet. He squatted, reading his brother's scribbled hand: "*Blessed are the merciful for they shall obtain mercy . . .*"

He tried reaching Barrett through thunder and the screen door banging.

"Br'er Rabbit, I'm at the briar patch. He's been here, his jeep's gone, what's your twenty?"

Barrett stood in the flashing marijuana patch surrounded by bent-over backs of Vietnamese farmers. He pivoted and stumbled, gazing at them glassy-eyed.

". . . 'preciate your company . . . gets lonesome out here . . . mother's here . . . it's right to have human companionship . . . wouldn't mind you stickin' till I get this crop in . . ."

He paused as Deke's voice broke through the static.

"Talk to me, Br'er Rabbit, you alive or what? Where the hell are you?"

". . . feels like monsoon season . . ." Barrett stammered. "Everything's backwards I 'spect . . . long as crops make what the hell . . . we'll get 'em in . . . you'll help me . . . gotta make it this year, brothers and sisters . . ."

"Barrett, are you listening to me? Where are you Witch Doctor? I'm at the briar patch, copy?"

Barrett stared at the figures doubled-over in the grass.

"I help you, you help me . . . we'll get some rain tonight . . . smell that wind . . . told you sky was fallin' . . . listen to me, people . . ."

A strong gust knocked him sideways. He slid to his knees, clinging to a twelve-foot marijuana bush bowed in the wind, the field lit-up with strobe like flashes.

"Hold on now . . . hold on, honeys . . . come on, babies . . . that's right, hold 'em right there . . . hold 'em, people . . ."

Under the rattling kudzu Deke watched the sky raining leaves. He propped the door with a two-by-four to keep it from slamming. Hail raked the roof in waves starting with a high hissing pouring out of the trees.

"Br'er Rabbit, what's your twenty? How the hell'm I gonna find you buddy? Talk to me."

He listened to the winding static.

"Push the fucking button and say something asshole! You on the west corner? Give me your fucking twenty, please."

A tree-sized limb hit the roof making him flinch. *Goddamit*, he said, whacking his knee with the radio; it felt like it was being bored by an electric drill.

"Man, if I find you messed up out there I'm gonna be pissed! I won't like it one goddamn bit! Got no fucking patience for this, Br'er Rabbit . . . talk to me, *pick it up* . . ."

He watched dust and leaves flying in the wind.

"All right, goddamit, listen to me . . . just . . ." He paused, scratching his face. "Br'er Rabbit, will you come back? You said to call when I got here, I'm here, goddamit, where the hell are you? What's your fuckin' twenty, Cisco? Talk to Pancho before I lose my fuckin' mind." He waited, digging his fist into the wall. "Witch Doctor, will you come back! If you hear me . . . just . . ." He clenched his eyes. "Where the fuck are you man! I know you hear me! Pick up the goddamn radio and say something!" He shook his head, tapping it on the doorjamb. "You're tryin' my patience, man. You really are, you son of a bitch. *Shit* . . . I don't know where Jason went . . . all right . . . all right, goddamit, listen to me . . . will you listen to me for one minute . . ." He waited. ". . . this is Tar Baby . . . if you . . . *Barrett* . . ." He waited again, starting to hallucinate, grinding his teeth. ". . . hey, listen . . . *Oh fuck it! Just shit on it goddamit!*" he shouted, kicking the screen door until it swung off its hinges flipping end-over-end into the yard. "Goddamit, son of a bitch!" he said, leaning toward the drive, the woods thrashing ahead of him with fish, gravel-sized hail and debris.

Shawnee backed wild-eyed toward a shelter of poplars at the edge of the field. Every time he thought about making for the stables the hissing started again. He listened to the clapping, sussurant scraping as falling things sliced through the limbs, a few grazing his back. He reared, circling a creaking pine trunk, tossing them from his hooves, swatting at them with his tail. Nuzzling them. Fish, frogs and lizards lay thick-still in the grass. He didn't want to cross this field unless he had to. He didn't like these wet things clinging to his back and haunches. He decided to wait it out here, at least for now where most of them were deflected or hung up in the branches. He could see the curved-blown, whip-like lines and hear them slap-raking the ground in waves.

There was an unsettling rhythm to it. Everything was still behind claps of thunder. A downpour came suddenly and ended as quickly, then that stillness again with a few leaves blowing over the raw-smelling grass. He shook his head, nodding and snorting, shuddered and rubbed against the rough tree bark gazing at the pale figures appearing again in his grazing. He knew none of them were his friend. They'd come like this spread out across the fields, after a while filing up into the trees in a tattered, single line. As he watched them it began to hail steadily harder. He stepped under a canopy of low limbs for shelter. There were so many he couldn't get out of them. He swung them off his head, rubbing into branches, looking curiously again at the motionless figures bent-over in the bright grass. There was an explosive burst of lightning he saw at the same time he felt it as a blue-swizzled line from the ground to treetop level. He felt it straight through his spine and was sure he'd been hit this time, bolting at an all-out sprint toward the stables. He felt the peppering mass objects slapping his back, hitting all over him, not caring about them as he ran, the building a beacon lit-up through his adrenaline. He galloped into the open-ended shelter where the noise was a high-pitched banging, spinning and tossing them off his back, neck and haunches. He backed into a corner stall, feeling ice pieces nicking his tail flicking through a corner-opening in the overhang. He strolled to the center of the stables and finally there was nothing but air touching him, unusually cool air chilling his flanks and belly. He watched the white line of flashes along the low roof crack, staring straight ahead listening to the drumming-whirring becoming a barreling solid groan.

Face lowered, shielding his head with his hands, Deke stumbled along the drive through blowing dust-pins and hail. Every few steps it felt like someone slapped him in the eyes with a handful of sand. Weaving side-to-side in the wind, he pulled his shirt over his head as ice tray-size cubes began to pummel him. Turning he tried to protect himself, but there was no way to keep from getting clobbered. He leaned from the waist jogging, able to make out a couple of steps ahead, his feet twisting on the blowing ice rocks. The wind chime jangled on the porch. It couldn't be that much farther to the gate, he thought, get *out* of this shit. In flashes he made out the corridor of fence lines but kept veering off into the ditches. Frogs tumbled across the drive. Squishing things as he ran, he slid on something loose, landing his elbow on something gurgling-fleshy, pushed up and with his face down ran as hard as he could until he saw the tire tracks through the open gate. He couldn't see the house at first; it lit up brilliantly. As he reached the screen porch the tin roof over his father's '48 Ford truck tore loose, sailing into the backyard wrenching around trees, lifted into the air and disappeared. Wind howled around the corners and eaves, tin strips clinging to sheds making sharp-banging rackets. The wind chime sang and froze making muffled dings as hail and solid chunks hammered the siding and shingles. He peeled off his shirt; steam poured from his breath and skin. Frogs dangled from awnings and gutters. The yard was white-speckled with fish, frogs, snakes, and those freakish-looking four-toed salamanders.

"What the hell is this?" he said, picking one out of his hair. "What the fuck's going on here?"

He stepped into the house, in the doorway listening to battering thumps on the walls and roof. The whole place shifted and creaked in gusts. He watched the living room's sheet-covered furniture flickering in the dark, chairs, tables, paintings and lamps, his grandfather's old bureau, his mother's black Indian chifferobe. The drapes swayed in drafts, flashes mirroring the hardwood floors. The old grandfather clock ticked quietly, then chimed seven times. He waited a minute, listening to it, and crunched to the center of the long green sofa in the middle of the living room, gazing into the yard, catching himself in the glass. He was a crazed scarecrow. He sunk to his father's molded seat, from the center of the wide picture windows watching the dark sky blink against the ragged tree line. Rain and hail bumped the windows.

"What is this, daddy?" he said, listening to the banging noises. "Tell me what's going on here; *I don't get this*. I'm hardheaded as hell, I know, but . . ." He paused, sniffling, listening to the clapping and thunder. "Did we deserve this? You or me or anyone in this family? Did we? Hell no we didn't," he said, peering around the ceiling. "I mean by now you gotta me on my side with this, don't you? You gotta be pullin' for me now, right? I know I'm an awful son and all, a terrible man, I planted this wicked seed here after all, and we know God didn't put His seeds on earth to grow or anything. Slipped up, did He? I didn't know He did that. So what was I supposed to do? Turn the other cheek? Bend over and let these people mash us like June bugs? Don't, daddy. You left us with this crazy shit, you can do better than that. I need something from you now, anything you can give me. You and Honcho and I didn't fight enough wars for these bastards to deserve fair shakes from them, did we? Did we? Oh God," he groaned, glancing through the porch windows. "They *raped* us, daddy; you know damn well they did. And this ain't gettin' any easier in case you hadn't noticed. I'm at a fucking loss here, like I've never been. I'm . . ." he snickered. "I don't even know who I'm fightin' anymore. You? God? The government? Nancy Reagan? Some psychotic bandit? Maybe all of you. So what was I supposed to do, give up the homestead? To hell with that. That's not the American way, is it? And don't tell me I should've planted a legal crop here cause you know damn well what *that* would've meant. Silos bulging with rotting grain the government wouldn't let us sell or make any money off of, the backstabbing bastards. Fuck that shit. *Fuck them.* If it were that easy you'd still be here, wouldn't you? Mama'd be in the kitchen cooking supper right now, we'd all be sittin' at the table with our heads bowed, sayin' grace 'for His bountiful goodness.' Wouldn't we! Where's our salvation, daddy? Where's *our* reward?" He glowered at the ceiling. "I need some answers now. You could always come up with 'em and I need 'em badly . . ." He broke a second, swallowing and chuckling, pulling back, covering his eyes with his palms. "I need to know what's going on here. Why everything's such a struggle and fucking freak show, you know? You know damn well what I'm talking about, so help me. We didn't deserve this shit," he said, listening to the house settling, whistling and creaking up again, moaning and vibrating. He sighed, rubbing his eyelids, staring into the yard.

Getting up slowly he listened to the grandfather clock ticking down the hall. It was the first time he'd heard it since his father pulled the trigger two years ago. Something'd jammed it that day, or it'd quit anyway, and it was ticking again. He went to the dining room and stared at the family photos reflected in white blocks on the walls, studying the head-up picture of his father snapping a football, the one of him grinning in front of his P-51 Mustang in leather flight-gear. Studying a photo of his father in overalls with Honcho and himself on a tractor, he took it from the wall.

"Give me a clue," he said. "I'm all ears. *Aw dammit* daddy . . ."

Glancing through the living room he caught a glimpse of the windmill on the yard fence freezing, spinning again fiercely. He'd heard something in the clattering noise as if someone had chortled out from the yard. Probably the wind howling around the north end of the house. It made a funny vibrating wortle from there, like a wind-flute, like someone singing or moaning. He felt his father's presence then and the hair rose on the back of his neck. He waited, frozen, feeling it with him in the room as if he'd just stepped through the door.

"Daddy?" he said, looking toward the kitchen where something was flapping lightly against the windows.

His front right tire flattened and wobbling, dragging the scraping limb he'd picked up in the woods, Jason turned onto Church Street and crawled up the last steep grade past the Firestone warehouses and Bill Roby's burned Shell station. Hail sprayed through his torn windows. There was a warbling screeching of metal on pavement as he shook up the hill, seeing the revolving blue light on the trees across the road as he bumped into the Holiness Lighthouse parking lot. Through delicate tappings he listened to the voices singing "Just As I Am" as he watched through the opened doors, hail slanting across the rotating beam catching his eyes each time it swung around. Except for a few flashes it was like he'd blacked out from the end of his drive to the bottom of the hill. He felt for his Bible on the seat. It wasn't there. He patted the backseat and floor for it. For a few seconds he was panicked, then he realized he didn't need it. Not really. Not this time.

He slid out and stumbled through the vehicles and trailers, steam rising on the pavement and the cranking light humming over his head. He leaned up the roped gangway hung with anchors, buoys and ropes, stepping through the double doors. Ushers Martin Jamison and Perry Stultz were singing with their backs to the doors, not expecting late arrivals. They didn't notice the barefooted man slumping down the center aisle. Carl Dresser, the musical director, led the congregation in "The Church

Is Our Foundation" behind the ship's wheel pulpit, his thick arms and shoulders flapping like wings. His oversized head oscillated like a floating doll's as he beamed and nodded. He kept leading as he glanced at Dr. Mashburn who leaned forward from his pastor's chair squinting through the floor lights. Looking at the man's clothes Mashburn figured him for a wino or miscreant. Ready to deliver his flagship sermon on promiscuity, homosexuality and racial intermingling, the last thing he needed was some vagrant wandering in off the street disrupting it. Where were his ushers? he thought, glaring through the lights with as benign a face as he could muster, realizing who it was as Jason reached the front of the aisle. He hadn't seen Jason Hawkins since his father passed. Maybe he should do something, he thought; or should have, noticing Jason's muddy clothes, streaks of blood on his face, neck and arms. Watching him turn and face the church under the pulpit the asthmatic widower stood. Dresser's arms dropped to his sides. The choir and congregation fell into coughs and whispers, Jason clearing his throat, feeling the stares, listening to the wind whistling through the double doors.

"Most of you know me," he started unsteadily, seeing the Higabothams, father, mother, two sons and a daughter sitting rigidly on the front pews. "Most of you know my family, and if you do you know we haven't been in here in a while," he swallowed, clearing the raspiness in his throat, feeling the critical eyes. "I've been confused about some things, angry and upset about them. You don't know how much I've wanted to come in here and tell you about them, but I couldn't get through those doors," he chuckled nervously. "I've been studying to be a preacher, see, before I even knew what that meant. You don't chose the ministry, it chooses you, they say, or He chooses it for you, and I thought He'd picked me, and I was ready to do whatever He said. Then some things happened to my family and I got side-tracked. I didn't know what to believe anymore, why things were the way they were, and I got eaten up inside. I got bitter, I mean. I was angry at you, at every one of you for looking in the wrong direction, for not looking at the things that were happening to all of us, not caring enough and not bein' able to do anything to help it. *For not being willing to*. For none of us helping each other enough in this tiny-minded, judgmental world we live in. Because it hit me we hardly ever do, and I couldn't face you this got so big. I thought I was someone who could set things right once I did, but I was too eaten-up inside to do it. I wanted to take you individually and shake you for being such self-centered assholes, for being so wrapped up in your separate little lives. I wanted to tell you to stop killing each other with your judgements and fears that cut us off from each other; because we're all the same Spirit, or supposed to be. I wanted to . . ." He swallowed. ". . . but I was too wrapped up in my own problems, like I said. I may've had some answers, maybe I did, but I was too Godforsaken angry to give them to you because of all the stuff that was happening to me and my family, which was what this whole thing was all about. I didn't have any charity, see, because I didn't think I was getting any. Isn't that funny? Isn't that hilarious? I mean, who was I to think that? I didn't have any mercy, I mean. I may've had plenty to tell you, plenty to fill you in on, but I'd lost all real mercy because I was so bitter and cynical, and I started to wonder if I was even supposed to preach to you; if any of you were worth it or would listen to anything I said." His voice wavered, and he swallowed taking in the hushed, transfixed room that was like an open-ended exhale, the wind whirring-crackling against the ceiling. "I got stupid, I guess, and selfish. Bitterly selfish, but I couldn't snap out of it. I couldn't do it. I kept praying, prayed everyday for months on end, but didn't think I was getting any answers. I didn't *think* I was getting them, right? Then it happened . . . something . . ." He stopped, stunned for a minute, listening to the breath like silence in the room, the quiet thumping. "It happened . . . tonight . . ." He felt his throat constrict, voice and jaw trembling as he tried to swallow. ". . . something happened to me . . . and I saw it . . . saw all of us here, all at once in here, you know . . . *together I mean* . . . and I . . . it hit me . . . it fell on me like a ton of bricks . . . a ton of tears, I think . . . and I was . . . we were . . ." He lost his voice for a few seconds, trying to clear it and swallow again. "I realized what was happening to us, you know? the main reason? The problem we all have, why we're suffering so much here, why things are so screwed up and getting worse. Why it seems like we're cursed with each other right now, with the way things are. It's not complicated really. Maybe it's not news to you but it was to me. *As a people we've lost mercy for one another.* Jesus said if we don't have mercy on each other, He won't have mercy on us, that's what He said, look it up. It's pretty important. That's *His* law. And we're merciless, people, which is why we're getting it right back in our faces. We're cursing ourselves, that's what we're doing. God doesn't abandon us, that's never happened. *We abandon Him by abandoning each other.* That's what it is. You don't have to be a prophet to see this. You don't have to . . ." Stumbling forward catching his toes on the carpet, all he could see was the room-glow of blurred faces floating in front of him, shadowed light swirling around them. "We're merciless for survival, though He's promised us that. For possessions, though He said He'd give us everything we need. When someone wrongs us we make them suffer. We put people to death, pull living fetuses out of mothers and kill them, molest and beat little children, hack up old folks, hate people for their color, religion, hair style, clothes, you name it. We sue each other out of greed and stomp on each other to feel strong ourselves. We lie and cheat and steal and hold grudges. We're merciless in our hearts. *In our hearts*, people, that's where it starts, the seed. You wonder why so many people are living in the streets, whole cities wandering around homeless now, farmers are losing their land, and our government's siphoning money out of us to fight more meaningless wars? It's not just the government doing it, because everything they do is us, right? It's *us* doing it. We the people. We're stepping over families sleeping in our streets, all of us together as a people, because we let our leaders lead us that way, they're what we are in our hearts. We're doing it ourselves, to ourselves. When we step over these people we step right in God's face. Sure we do. We're creating this monster whatever it is. It's *our* monster, it's us. We can do it differently if we want to. We can take care of each other if we want to, why don't we? What's holding us back? We're such good and moral people, right? *Aren't we?* We're more worried about homosexuals than starving children, and Jesus never said a word about homosexuals. He never stopped talking about helping the poor, the sick and hungry, the downtrodden, that's what his ministry was about. If that was his ministry, shouldn't it be ours? If we're really Christians, I mean, if we're really *God's* people. I'll tell you why. We're letting our leaders be merciless for us because that's what we are, that's what *we* want. We live on fear instead of faith. We feed off of fear. We're prideful and greedy and corrupt and their corruption's coming back on us. The less mercy we give each other, the less mercy we receive, which makes us more afraid and confused, fearful and insane, and we become less merciful, and God shows us less mercy, and it goes round and round and round. Don't you see it? This thing building inside us? Look where it's taking us. Where do you think we're headed? It's not that mysterious really . . ." he coughed, trying to swallow the constricting pressure in his throat. "I'm asking you to see what's happening to us, just look at it, please. That's why I drove here tonight, to ask you to do this, to beg you to if I have to. Don't be like I was because I had everything to tell you and not enough mercy to give it. Don't horde your mercy like fool's gold, please don't. Be merciful to each other and stop worrying about yourselves. What are you so worried about? Worry about each other and He'll take care of the rest. Do it without personal judgment. Stop stealing from each other's lives. Stop killing each other's hearts. Give up yourselves a little bit. Help each other for God sake. Love is the only thing you can take with you or leave behind, the only thing. Give the divine thing if you want any of it back. There's no such thing as winning in this world unless you give mercy, that's the simple truth. You think it's the other way around, that you have to beat each other down and take what you want from the other guy? Jesus Christ's law's the other way around, the opposite of that. We *know* too much, people. We know what He said and we're responsible for that, for each other. It's . . . impossible to . . ." He coughed again, catching the enigmatic eyes of Grace Pierpoint on the third row, the quizzical, kindly spinster who'd raised him in the nursery. "Every time you breathe, breathe mercy, that's what I'm asking of you; that's how you bless yourself. Even if you're right and know they're wrong, give mercy, give them a break or two. They're just human beings: you're just human beings, people. You didn't make yourselves, you can't take credit for it, why be so proud? Proud of what? If you want the one true secret, the one true lasting secret to save us all as a race, *it's mercy*. Give mercy and get mercy. Listen to me, I'm a . . . I'm nobody. I'm just like you, but listen," he said, his voice changing timbre, hoarsening-trembling. He staggered toward the center aisle, gazing under the balconies at the light diffusing on the blurred faces at the back of the room. Blinking he saw something there; grimacing, taking another step toward it, his lips moving silently. "Have mercy on them," he whispered. "Put mercy back in us, a merciful break's all we need, Lord. Give mercy to us, please," he said, feeling the spasming tightening in his throat as if something were slowly squeezing and transforming his vocal chords. He felt the familiar, flushed, feverish movement into his shoulders like some gigantic presence cramping his body, his eyes watering at the face at the rear-center of the room made up of rapt congregants. He shuddered and tried to swallow again as tears blurred his eyes. "Blessed are the merciful . . . for they shall obtain mercy . . ." he said, feeling the fluttering in his throat and shoulders with his voice breaking. ". . . blessed are the merciful! . . . for they shall obtain mercy!" he cried. ". . . blessed are the merciful for they shall obtain mercy! . . . *blessed are the merciful . . .*"

His eyes rolled up in his head and he felt the room hurtling, flickering with light. He lurched forward, feeling flutters like vomit welling up from his insides through his chest, vowels gargling out of some uncontrollable *Voice* that wasn't his. His body undulating in it, the room spinning and spewing upward with drum like filament-blurs, the strange *Voice* gurgling out of him. In the reeling light his arms were weightless as if a rope swung up through his throat to the ceiling where he saw his family flashing before him, suspended in that swimming, burdenless, orgasmic, unbearably perfect Holy laughter, trying to cry out but other sounds gargled out of him. Someone did cry out from the back of the church, a ragged, forlorn scream like a mother's in childbirth. In slurring syllables he felt the melding-together glow of filament-like bodies swirling round him, their faces washing through him, on his face and breathing through them; flashing through him as if he were transparent, feeling the face at the back of the room as he fell and stumbled toward it. The *Voice* sped up and he felt himself convulsing as if he were being driven upward through a fountain of splintered tongues and Holy voices speaking at once, floating him upwards on a guttural wave. He lurched and nodded, still gazing at the unflagging face, turning like a plane in a slow, vertical roll, pitching with his arms over his head; standing in that streaming light as if held up by it for a few seconds with his head and arms rolling, feeling his throat release, the sudden cold wetness on his cheeks, cramping in his shoulders, and collapsed hard to the carpet, convulsing on his right side. A muted voice groaned from the balcony. Light sung like static music in the sanctuary, the congregation frozen in it. Mashburn clamped the bridge of his nose with his fingers as he slumped forward, the familial tremor in his left hand shaking as he felt the low rumble in the floor. The congregation listened to the wind whip through the creaking doors. Jason twitched in a puddle of drool, his eyes turned inward, flicking a little.

Deke leaned forward on the living room sofa clutching the framed photo, listening to hail hitting the glass. Lightning struck the yard with an explosion that startled him, and he looked up through the wide picture window to see a giant pecan tree crumbling to the lawn. He stared at it lighting up the grass sprouting mothballs and flesh-limbs, getting up shoving his mother's push pedal Singer aside, studying the burning tree with fascination.

"Not bad," he whispered. "Hell yes," he said, watching the upright trunk-half implode in a mushroom of sparks. "Come on motherfuckers, gimme another one! What the fuck, bring it on in here!"

He looked around the yellow walls silhouetted with shadows, scooping the radio off the coffee table.

"Lancelot Leader, calling Sweetheart Maitre d', you're off-center with your first probing ordnance. Readjust fifty meters south——"

Lightning hit something behind the house, jarring it, rattling glass, setting the chandelier in the dining room jangling. He ran to the kitchen craning into the backyard over the sink. For ten seconds lightning was a sizzling, blue-static crackling on his radio as he watched the head-like gourds flopping in the wind.

"In my funny book I read: *Foxtrot Alpha November Tango Whiskey Echo X-Ray* . . . say back . . . you're fifty meters into the tree line——"

His voice was interrupted by another crash on the barn side. Running into the dining room he stripped the dust-covered blinds from the windows. Another leviathan pecan tree lay ripped in half caved through a tin roof, its black-mangled trunk flickering in the wind.

". . . *Heating up Maitre d'* . . . you're circling and closing . . . affirm new coordinates . . . I repeat, you're circling and closing . . ."

On his knees hugging the trunk of a thrashing marijuana plant, Barrett listened to Deke's voice barking out what sounded like a fire mission. He blinked at the shiny ground in flashes, snakes slithering between fish and belly-up frogs. He laughed over Deke's voice as he looked around, his arms wrapped around the trunk as if it were a swaying ship's mast.

". . . *Foxtrot Alpha Delta Victor Yankee November Bravo* . . . verify one adjustment . . . short of main structure . . . secondary structure damaged in tree line . . ."

Deke tore the drapes off the bedroom windows where lightning splashed on oval portraits of his grandparents. He peered through the slapping glass as sparks shot across the room making him jump and yelp. He whirled and howled in it, doing a buckdance, do-si-doing yelling out in the rocketing thunder.

". . . Sway your partner to and fro . . . lightning's like a mortar show . . . Heating up Maitre d'! You're hot, I repeat, felt the grease from that round up my goddamn testicles . . . continue range and bring it in here . . . *bring it on down you sons of bitches*! . . ."

He shadow-danced with the bedposts, hunching and circling the flowered draped lamps, cha-chaing back to the living room pressing his face into the blue panes, shimmying his breasts against them.

"Come on, Sweetheart! Bring it down you sons of bitches! . . . give it to me baby . . . where the hell are you . . ."

There was a flash synchronous with a crashing sound from the kitchen with shattering glass. Furniture tumbled against the wall with rolling dishes.

"Bingo! Yip yip yip yip yu-iiii!" he slid into the kitchen door. The round family table and lazy Susan lay splintered in the corner. Chairs were strewn over sprayed glass with five or six blackened frogs, fish heads and broken china. The drapes and table sheet cover were smoldering, hail like marbles popping through the vacated window.

"Fuck 'em where they breathe, Big Kahuna! I like it baby! Don't stop, good buddy, you're on a fucking roll magnificent fire! . . ."

In a patch several-hundred yards from where Barrett clung to his flailing bush snakes and branches sagged over grenade wires. A leaning walnut split in half collapsing across the clearing, blasting plants and trees into mud-raining fragments. Barrett spun nervously to the explosion, a minute later hearing another muffled boom as he peered into the grey-blue downpour, uncertain of where he was, transported to a war zone as he heard Deke hollering out coordinates on his radio:

". . . *Foxtrot Alpha Zulu Romeo Charlie Sierra Juliet Oscar* . . . make adjustments . . . where the hell are you! You're drifting, amigo! Come back to your last coordinates and nail it you stupid peashooters . . . breathe fire people—"

He stopped and listened to the wind. There was a slight rhythmical flutter and bottom-moan behind the rumbling whir. He listened to that shrill sound and splashed onto the porch. It was changing volume and pitch like some large, shrieking bird flapping through the trees. That's a voice, he thought, making out Vietnamese. He knew it was a single Huey from its drone-heft and bottom hum, the blades having that symmetrical patter one slick made. As it rumbled past the house he followed it, turning his

ears, thinking, who'd be crazy enough to fly into this dogshit, listening to
it circling Hawkins Mountain. It swung toward the highway on the south
side, banking across the field, and he jogged into the yard. The shrill voice
and thwacking blades ricocheted off the mountains. The storm had broken
but creatures splatted in light hail. Squinting into fog he felt things ooze
around his feet, bumping his shoulders; he couldn't see a damn thing.

Wait a second, he thought. The Vietnamese voice that'd snatched them
into the trees; the crazy cocksucker who'd been terrorizing their crop, who'd
likely slit Davey's throat; it'd be a hell of a coincidence if this were someone
else, wouldn't it? He followed the wailing staccato as he watched for a flash
of blades in the flickering clouds drifting to tree-level. It turned toward the
highway and he punched his radio:

"All right, you son of a bitch, who the fuck are you?"

Nothing. Even if he were on the right channel why would the psycho
say anything? The voice sounded like one of those demoralization tapes
they'd used against the Cong. Who was this? He flipped through frequencies
monitoring the swizzling, crackling hisses. On thirteen he picked up a
quick bleeding-in of the cockpit and the squawking voice. The pilot had
accidentally keyed his mike or he'd caught a fragment of transmission.

"Come on, you son of a bitch!" he called to him. "Say something, you
shitface coward."

Rocking and swaying through hail and slapping debris, Honcho heard
Deke's tinny voice break through the reel-to-reel blaring. Some genius had
replaced his headset with this handheld piece of junk. Starting his turn he
grabbed the mike, squeezing off a little salutation.

"*Hay la co hoi cuoi cuug cua May!*" he said. "*. . . Hay la co hoi cuoi cuug
cua May . . . Ray Suy ughi lai Di! . . . Ray Suy ughi!* . . ."

His systolic went mushy and he felt the Huey swimming up on its left
side, vibrating and wobbling, getting battered by wet debris. He dropped
the microphone, lodging it under his thigh, bumping it on and off as he
struggled to take control of his yawing machine. Deke heard whining
misflutters as he listened to the pilot coaching his chopper, unaware his
mike was hot.

"Straighten up baby . . . straighten up dammit . . . work for daddy . . .
come on girl . . . *hang straight goddamit!* . . ."

Who's that? Deke thought, following the flapping chopper around the farm. It sounded like . . . Yeah it did . . . someone sounded like him . . . A *lot* like him. Who the hell sounded like that?

". . . Honcho," he whispered. "*Honcho?*"

As the Huey banked overhead he caught a glimpse of skids shooting through the mist.

"*Honcho!* You crazy motherfucker! You insane . . . cocksucking! . . ."

On his knees hugging his whipping mast Barrett heard the chopper approaching again with its ricocheting, howling voice. He heard a claymore go off five-hundred yards away and clung tighter to his tree, watching the Vietnamese figures working around him in hurling vapor.

In his parent's bedroom Deke dug through the mothballed cedar trunk in the master closet. He tossed out his father's service uniforms, boots, plaques, a sheathed Korean sword, medals and manuals, uncovering the tarnished elephant rifle he'd wrapped in cheese cloth with a half-dozen ammunition boxes. Hands trembling, he dumped a box of .22 longs on the hardwood floor going *shit! shit! shit!* kicking them round the room. He fumbled a box of .45 loads, scattering them too, mumbling *Come on you fucking idiot*, tearing open the right ones, loading the cold brass shells, dropping two for every one he shoved in the chamber. Scooping loose shells he jammed them in his pockets, feeling the rotorthuds moaning past the house with the wailing scream. He stuffed the emergency flare gun in his thigh-pocket and clomped down the hall, sprinting off the porch into the yard hurdling scraps of dancing sheet metal, leaping the barbed wire fence into the field behind the sheds where the Huey was making another wide, popping turn. Stopping a hundred yards from the smokehouse in the dead corn, he shut his eyes firing five blind rounds toward the thwacking blades, hearing no interruption or change in them, his hands wobbling as he jammed in fresh shells. He watched the ground stirring as he listened to spit-splats and wiped the sticky stuff from his face.

"Honcho!" he yelled, his voice quavering. "Where are you goddamit! KIA travel bureau's got a ticket for you pal! *Hay lam lai Cuuc dor!*"

He fired up an emergency flare, orange magnesium dispersing into the dribbling sky, lightning fluttering round it with groans of thunder. He heard the detonation of a claymore on the near mountain flank as he watched the Huey reverse direction and shoot back across the field, running clockwise to the house in the churning, grey light. The ceiling had lifted enough that with the flare he could make out the chopper's Army star slipping in and out of the mist. As it passed within a couple-hundred yards he opened up on the rear stabilizer, leading each shot, the piercing voice screaming behind them like some giant bird being eviscerated. Come on, goddamit, you can do this. Hit something with this goddamn cannon: hydraulics, tail rotor, main blade, anything to disable it; he reloaded as he pressed the radio, dropping shells in the mud, stooping to wipe them on his cuffs.

"Land your fucking whirlybird or I'll land it for you, Honcho! Hear me! I'll drop you like a sack of shit, you crazy motherfucker!"

"Only we can prevent forests, boy wonder," he heard Honcho snigger. "Better blow this fuckin' hooch . . . Agent Orange's home to harvest . . ."

As the chopper swung across the house Deke followed it, pumping a set of rounds into the nose floor, dropping his muzzle by degrees as it shot away. It started to bank right, lifting fast toward Hawkins Mountain. He'd seen a flash of sparks near the tail rotor, the Huey swinging sideways, hesitating with an awkward lurch as if it were hung in a spongy net that wouldn't let it rise or move, reversing a quarter-turn. It hovered a few seconds, then started to sink and sling, pitching radically, wobbling and spinning like a drunken top.

Hearing the dings Honcho felt the sudden loss of airspeed as his craft swung around. As it started to shake vertically and laterally, his first thought was that his rear stabilizer was choked by these fleshy things glancing off his windshield, then he knew it was worse than that. Checking his altitude he started to auto rotate, fighting to keep from twisting to his side or upending. He was going down fast, another goddamn hard landing, bracing for it with his legs bent, clamping his teeth gritting and yelling. The craft's rotation picked up speed as it dropped, crashing into the muddy field flat on its skids. He felt the head ringing jolt up his spine, twisting pain in his left ankle, the chopper bucking wildly a few seconds bouncing-flapping trying to lift again; tilting still, the wailing voice ceasing, the Huey leaning on its nose smoking.

Deke was running toward it before it hit the ground. He fought the door open, tugging at it seeing Honcho trying to bar it shut, pried his belt off and dragged him into the muddy field. He slugged his grimacing brother who yanked away from him grunting, hobbling and knee walking toward the barns.

"You insane son of a bitch! What the hell are you doing!"

"S'gonna go!" he said. "Hurry up!"

"You're not going anywhere till I kick your fucking ass, you crazy motherfucker!"

"Chopper's gonna blow! You stupid little shit!"

Honcho squirmed out from under him, hopping on one leg. Deke saw the Huey's engine cowling billowing smoke and trotted faster, watching his brother half-limping and sliding ahead of him like a three-legged dog. They reached the barns as the Huey exploded, fragments and fiery debris clattering on the tin roofs. Honcho dragged himself against the planks, stiff-arming mud, blinking at snakes in the leaves and pecan husks.

"Destroying government property, boy wonder. Be frowned on, I promise you."

Deke grabbed him by his shoulders, slamming him against the wall.

"What the fuck's wrong with you, you crazy bastard! You nearly killed us! Who the fuck do you think you are!"

"*Executor*, corporal," Honcho swayed with a punch-drunk smirk. "Made deal to save us. Think my goddamn ankle's broken . . ."

"What kinda deal!" Deke said, squeezing him. "What the fuck are you talkin about?"

"Can't stop 'em . . . gonna get our land . . . they're juggernaut, Deke . . ."

"Who is?"

"Military boys. Whole fucking valley's turning into Air Force playground, research installation, God knows what . . . It's underway."

"You sold out to them?"

"Double the market rate, kid."

"You had no right!"

"I'm the one who had the right, boy scout! I'm the executor of this spread, remember? Who the fuck are you to plant a pot crop on it? They find one plant out here they'll confiscate the whole goddamn place and we won't get a dime, is that what you want?"

Deke straddled his legs, giggling-livid, clutching wads of his shirt.

"Daddy blew his head off because they were running him out of here, where were you then, Honcho? You didn't even come to his goddamn funeral. You slip in here like some black ops weasel, selling us out to the bastards who pushed him over the edge? What the fuck's wrong with you!"

"Isn't like that . . ."

"What's it like!" Deke said, shaking him. "What the fuck's it like!"

". . . tryin' to tell you—"

"You sabotaged everything we were doing to save ourselves. I ought . . ."

"*He was dying of cancer, Deke.* He didn't have six months to live . . ."

"What? . . . you expect me to . . ."

"I'm serious. He wrote me and said he had lung cancer, wasn't going to waste away in any goddamn veteran's hospital. If I'd known what that meant don't you think I'd've been here? You're goddamn *right* I would've. Who do you think flew his salute that day? I couldn't stand on the ground and salute anything else, I knew too goddamn much. I couldn't look anybody in the eye . . . I would've fucking lost it . . . I could've blown my own fucking brains out, hell, I almost did . . . closer than you know . . . the cocksuckers . . . shit, man . . ." he bit his tongue, squeezing his ankle. "He was *my* king, all right? . . . I got as close as I could, you don't know shit, hot shot," he shoved Deke. "You don't know what I've been through, so get the fuck off me! Hell yeah they killed him, they took away his reason to live, but he was dying anyway, there's nothing we could've done . . ."

Deke swallowed and tried to get this.

"You told mother you were on a mission . . ."

"Exactly . . ."

"Making deals with these vultures was your goddamn mission?"

"I had to verify what I knew while it carried weight. Had to take care of business, son. Double market rate, do you know what that means? You should be kissing my ass, little brother, because without this deal no amount of hooch money would've kept them from picking our bones clean."

Deke squeezed him.

"Let's say that's true, you nearly killed my partner and me, what was that for? You slit a man's throat, Honcho."

"Crazy pissant was trying to hack me up with a machete, what would you've done, kissed him?"

"What about the rest? Why the head games? Why didn't you tell us what you were doing instead of burning our plants, yanking us into goddamn trees, playing goddamn pranks!"

"You wouldn't've bought it, slick! You know damn well you wouldn't've! You're the hardheadest man in the world and don't know when to stop, you never have. You always said they'd have to drag your lifeless body off of this place, and that was in the works, believe me. You'd've thrown a shitfit into things and we couldn't've risked it. I *had* to flush you out of here. These are goddamn serious people, Deke, not some real estate agents putting up a shopping center. They're the grand scheme of things, see, and they could care less about a bunch of Tennessee dirt farmers. They're ruthless, under the map, and if I hadn't caught wind of this they'd've smoked us out of here, rigged another deal at the banks, come up with another tax ambush, done anything they could to eliminate us without drawing attention to themselves. They shoved daddy over the edge and I wanted them to pay a little, is that all right with you? Now if you don't get off my fucking leg I'm gonna fuck you up even with this mucked-fucking ankle . . . *swear to God . . .*"

Deke nodded, chuckling, his mind racing. Even Honcho couldn't make this up. Laughing out loud he sat on his heels, his adrenaline still flowing.

"They schooled you well, didn't they? What'd they fucking *do* to you?"

"I had to do this, Deke. What else was I gonna do?"

". . . talked to me . . ."

"Get off it. You wouldn't have left and you know it. I just wanted to rattle you a little."

"A little? You went too goddamn far!"

"Maybe . . ."

"What, as a jolly fucking favor?"

". . . Maybe I got carried away."

". . . You think . . ."

"I just wanted you and Jason clear of this place so you wouldn't get hurt."

"Oh my God, am I supposed to thank you now?"

"As a matter of fact . . ."

"You're out of your fucking mind, Honcho. You're nuttier than a goddamn fruitcake. What the hell's wrong with everybody?"

He let go of Honcho's shirt and fell back against the planks, giggling at the fizzling chopper. He started to laugh hysterically, blinking tears up into the trees, slinging his arms at his sides.

"We'll have enough to buy half the fucking state by Christmas," Honcho said, taking a warped cigar from his pocket. "Move mama to a new house, set up Jason, us; shit, could be worse."

"Could it?" Deke said, scratching his face, giggling. "I don't know. I just . . ." He paused, struggling to find the words. "*Goddamit! Goddamn the sons of bitches*! If they just hadn't treated daddy like some used fucking tampon. He was an American war hero, and they betrayed him. They betrayed all those old warriors, all those loyal old World War II veterans by grabbing their children and feeding them into that Indochinese bullshit, swearing it was a war we had to fight, using their loyalty and patriotism against them. And now look what they've done to him. Can you imagine how he felt when he realized they were stonewalling him? He didn't know why they were doing it. He'd sent you and me into hell for the bastards, would've gone back to the front lines tomorrow if they'd asked him to on their word, and they hand him this? This screw-you-jack piece of paper, saying you don't qualify as an active farmer anymore? You gotta cough up nine-hundred-thousand dollars or clear off your great grandfather's land you've been farming for fifty years? No credit, no reprieve, no VA loans, nothing. Get out, pal. That's what killed him, Honcho. The faceless bastards he trusted, his beloved countrymen, yanking his goddamn heart out." Deke nodded to the fields, chewing his tongue. Debris skittered across the dead corn stalks. "If they'd squared with him, told him they needed the land and why, he'd've fucking given it to them. If they'd told him the truth he'd've gotten treatment and maybe be alive right now, even cured. Am I right, Honcho? Tell me."

"Maybe he'd've gotten treatment if they hadn't blindsided him, I don't know Deke. Be damned if we ever will."

"Was it in his lungs?"

"And lymph glands, don't know for how long, he wouldn't say. His last letter didn't sound too promising; said it could come quicker than anyone figured. Said I was the only one he wanted to know for certain practical reasons. You know how daddy hated pity. Shit . . ." Honcho said, slapping his thighs. "He was dead by the time I got it . . ."

Deke rocked from his waist, his face in his hands. Honcho reached over, ruffling his hair.

"Oh well, boy scout," he sighed, licking his crooked stogie. "Been eating at me a long time now, but this was the kicker. I ain't staying in this warhorse mob any longer. Getting a promotion late-January and I'm outta here, outta the goddamn military."

"Never thought I'd see it."

"Yeah, well, I'm sick of being a hit man for these gangster bureaucrats. All be living in streets and military bunkers, spending every dime on weapons if our sleeping zombie-warrior can arrange it. Rattling through brass about secret arms deals, shadow governments, splinter CIA shit that'd curl your brain. We'll be fighting in the Mideast till the world ends to keep the oil families happy. Funny how the poor keep fighting the poor to make the rich richer."

"Somebody better." Honcho shifted to ease the pain up his spine, sliding out of his jacket, wincing. He wrapped it around his ankle with his chin out.

"Figured you for a lifetime member of that club, brother."

"Yeah, well. We hadn't talked in a while."

"Must be the water."

"What's that?"

"This Tennessee mountain spring water; *clarity* Jason'd call it."

"Always was the purest water," Honcho smiled. "Truth serum?"

"Could be."

"It's why Tennessee whiskey's so damn good. I could use a shot of that right now, maybe there's a bottle in the house."

"What you gonna do now?"

Honcho teethed his cigar.

"Farm a little. Thinking about it."

"You're kidding."

"You know the Indians farmed this land before we got here. We kicked them off it and dragged the black man over here to farm it for us, then they send us black and red and white farm boys over to Vietnam to kill a bunch of yellow farm boys minding their own business, four million or so of 'em. *Ha*," Honcho shook his head spitting cigar skin. "I'll be damned if they'll run us off this land so they can build some giant farm conglomerates and farm us with food like they do with oil now. What you think, little brother, give it a shot with me? We know this business better than anybody. Hell, what don't we know?"

Deke put his face in his hands.

"Come on, son. We'll buy a spread twice this size, get scientific with it. Thinking of pumpkins maybe. Ostriches are big-time now. Got any ideas?"

"I don't know," Deke chuckled. "Give me a couple of years to get over this. You give a whole new meaning to Big Brother."

"I was looking after you, Hoss. Doing my job keeping you outta trouble. You were too goddamned hardheaded for your own good. Imagine we put all that into a real farm, shit son, we're unstoppable." Honcho gazed at the speckled ground, lifting a striped snake with his boot toe. "What's this all about?"

"God's warning. Honcho's in town."

"Look at this stuff."

"Creature storms . . ."

"*What*?"

"They're raining here."

"What do you mean?"

"For months now."

"You're shittin' me. You've seen that?"

"You just flew through it. Jason and Barrett think it's a sign."

"Are you serious?"

"Haven't seen them in the woods?"

"Frogs and snakes, but not these fish. Could be an omen . . ."

"Oh God . . ."

"You know . . ."

"Hey, there's a shitload of money in cannabis," Deke said, holding a frog up by its hind legs. "Kept us afloat a year and a half, really saved our asses."

"Yeah, but it's too dangerous. It's just giving them an excuse. I got nothing against it, hell, you know the father of our country old George Washington grew marijuana. Now they've got a special agency to keep people from growing it, wonder what old George'd think of that? See brother, if you go after those evil drug dealers," Honcho said in a confiding voice, "those pernicious growers of that iniquitous devil's weed, then maybe nobody'll notice when you lie about trading arms for hostages, or fight secret illegal wars, or ignore masses of starving people living in cardboard boxes. If you put on a show of combating some goddamn flower for the do-gooders they'll believe you're doing *Gawd's work*. We're doing it all for

Gawd, see. If you only knew," Honcho laughed, shaking his head, looking at his hands;

Deke watched his eyes shining into the trees.

"If I only knew what?"

"Ha," Honcho turned away, looking at his fingers. "You see these hearings going on? You ain't seeing the tip of the iceberg, son."

"You know about this?"

"Covert operations are funded by black money, right? Funds not allocated or accounted for. Hidden money from unknown sources. The 'War on Drugs' is just a front, a big fucking diversion. If you make a lot of noise and denounce those evil drugs, act like you're doing everything on earth to stomp them out, who'd imagine *you're* the one bringing them in? Mulling in hard drugs by the planeload to finance your illegal little wars? Who'd ever think it, you know? Our righteous government's been secretly trading a shitload of weapons and drugs to pay for wars that aren't on the books, that aren't supposed to be going on, and guess who's been piloting in some of their dirty little cargo?" Honcho giggled, bristling and spitting, snapping his knuckles. "Life's awfully fucking strange, isn't it? I'm ashamed to admit it, goddamit. I wasn't sure I'd ever tell anyone but what the hell, you're my brother, what the fuck. It was supposed to be such a goddamn honor to fly these secret missions, 'the Core of the Corp' and all that pompous crap, but you know what? These people've desecrated this country and our service to it. I joined the army to fight some joke of a war in Vietnam, and end my career as a goddamn drug mule for Olie and his invisible shits. Isn't that priceless? Yeah. There're more lies than truths being told by these spooks. Nobody gives a damn. The country doesn't want to know. It's easier that way, you know? My knowledge of their drug business combined with what I discovered they're doing in this valley made a certain General and Colonel in the Pentagon particularly nervous though, I can tell you that; rather agitated them. Didn't hurt our bargaining clout either. When I verified I'd actually flown in some of those Panama shipments, I thought they were going to shit all over themselves. You should've seen their fucking faces."

"Ah God, Honcho."

"Hey, fuck it. We've done our share, there isn't a hell of a lot more they can do to us."

"Don't say that."

"Let 'em take a flying leap in a rolling doughnut. I'm ready to get back to the land and be a humble dirt farmer again. Take care of things the way daddy would've wanted."

They sat a minute in silence.

"Hear about the farmer accused of child abuse?" Deke said, knocking mud off his boots.

"Left his son the farm in his will?" Honcho said, spitting; they smiled across the field where debris and corrugated tin blew past the flickering chopper.

"Made a deal, huh?"

"Signed and sealed."

"Think they'll pay?"

"They'll pay. They've got too much on the line. They fucked with the wrong farm boys this time," Honcho grinned, shifting again. "Damn, I jammed the hell out of my spine on that soft landing. Son of a bitch," he groaned, lifting up. "Lucky one-shot . . ."

"My ass."

"What were you shooting at me?"

"Daddy's old elephant gun, the Manlicher. Dropped it by the slick."

"Son of a bitch; *Old Tembo.* Surprised it fires."

"So am I."

"We used to have real pellet fights, remember?"

"I've still got the scars."

"You never shot that well before."

"Shot a lot better."

"Fort Gordon?"

"Long before that. You don't remember?"

"You twenty-twenty?"

"Close to it."

"How close?"

"Pick out the color in a teal's eye at a hundred yards."

"Seriously. My right one's been off since a Plexiglas shard caught it on my first tour. Scammed a few exams to stay in the air."

"Doesn't hurt your performance?"

"It's light-sensitive sometimes. Hey, how'm I supposed to explain ditching this Huey in my backyard?"

"Tell them you flew through a snake storm," Deke snickered. "Fish, frogs and four-toed lizards."

"Fat chance," Honcho winced, twisting to his side. "They'll put me in the psych ward."

"You belong there anyway."

"What're you spyin' over there?"

"Is that Rigel or Betelgeuse at the edge of those peaks?"

"Both. Two brightest stars in the constellation Orion."

"That's right."

"Remember daddy teaching us stars when we were kids? Used to navigate by them on night missions in his P-51."

"I remember walking into this field after church on clear nights, and he'd say, 'All right, Dekester, get us home, the squadron's counting on you, give me some stars to reckon by.'"

"'The war's on your shoulders tonight, Jimmy,' he'd say. 'God's roadmap's above you.'"

"You'd think, man, I've got to do this now. Their shit'll be hanging in the wind if I don't chart this right."

"The fate of humanity and all that," Honcho laughed. "We got a dose of it, didn't we? What the hell else were we gonna do?"

"Ain't that right?" Deke said.

He felt it again then as if his father had spoken out loud; it was stronger this time and for a moment he couldn't move or speak. Finally he turned, half-expecting to see him walking up behind them in the trees. He watched the shifting shadows on the porch door.

"What is it?"

"Ever feel him around you?"

"Who?"

"Who do you think?"

Honcho nodded. "All the time," he said in a changed voice.

"More at times than others," Deke said, feeling the brush-like breeze on his arm.

"Yep," Honcho swallowed.

They watched the lace-like clouds drifting over Traggert's Mountain. Behind light hail and thunder there was a faint muffled drone. Honcho leaned up, listening to it. It was a low-pitched groan like some distant heavy machinery. In a few seconds it sounded like a bottom-heavy ship's horn, one low solid note. A cricket chirped in the yard. Honcho listened to the other sound with his ear tilted, his brow furrowed. When Deke started to speak he stopped him, adjusting his ears, squinting into the mud.

"What is it?" Deke said.

Honcho looked up with a soured expression.

"Can't be," he said.

"*Can't be?*"

"Come on," Honcho whispered. "You gotta be kiddin'."

They watched in the direction of the grinding noise gaining bottom. The wind chime tinkled on the porch in feathery gusts; jingles like icicles jangling and freezing. On the other side of the house the rooster crowed once, throaty and raw-nervous. Sprinkles pattered round them in the trees.

"What is it?" Deke said.

"Not yet," Honcho said, struggling to his good leg with a bent pecan cane. "*Not fucking yet.*"

"What not yet?"

"Only we can prevent . . . yeah . . ."

". . . prevent what?"

". . . Forests . . ."

"What . . ."

". . . *Forests* . . . only we can prevent . . . *forests* . . . remember? . . . the napalm slogan . . . good for you you lying pieces of shit . . . goddamn you . . ."

They listened to the planes rumbling behind the mountains, the ground starting to shiver with a thin, buzzing vibration. The weight of it built steadily until it had a leaden heaviness. They felt planks rattling and shimmying.

"What the hell . . ." Deke said.

Objects clanged in the sheds, janglings from tools and implements slipping from walls. Bark rained with tree dust as pecans clattered like shots on the tin roofs. The rumbling mounted like an oncoming train charging the air, changing it in their ears. They felt the thundering vibrations in their faces and legs.

Deke watched his brother hobble into the field dragging his coat knotted around his ankle. He was yelling something, swinging his arms at the sky, snarling at it with his fists. He couldn't make out what he was saying. His voice was a garbled moan under the mounting waves of noise. After a minute he couldn't tell he was making any sound at all; he watched his mouth moving as in some slow-motion dream without sound, his crimson face grimacing and contorted. Honcho hurled his fists, slashing the limb in the air, mud flying off of it. Deke read his brother's lips when he turned to him: ". . . Isn't it fucking *perfect*, brother! Isn't it fucking *beautiful*! . . ." The rumbling kept building with erupting undertones until it was deafening.

Barrett rose to the hum in a patch of arching plants, with Vietnamese farmers doubled-over around him in fog and wavering lightning. He felt the electric skidding in his fingers through his feet. Tremors mounted into his knees and backbone. Prop planes, he thought, big boys; *plenty* of them. The air seemed to quake and radiate with them. He listened to the booming that was like an unearthly storm surge rumbling closer. He looked at the drooping bushes, watching the noise vibrate the leaves and colas as he felt the whistling drumming up his spine.

"I'm just like you . . ." he said to the pale figures around him. ". . . see me . . ." he said, looking through them to the brightening trees.

The pitch of planes became a slow-leaden hum as he heard the mixed gabble of voices in his ears. In his head he saw the panicking, sweating faces crawling over each other across a shallow field. He heard the massive metal door slam and in his head he was sailing over a horizonless paddy where Vietnamese farmers scrambled on foot like a herd of driven water buffalo, splashing, wallowing through mud. He saw orange fire streaming out of the clouds like an umbilical cord swimming toward him. You don't see that every day, he thought, chuckling, watching the orange-yellow wind piling out of the trunks black-lined, soundlessly rolling toward him, the bent-over figures oblivious to it. Justice, he thought: it ain't here: it ain't in this Godforsaken place.

"Forgive me, Marsha," he said.

Lucas March woke to the building roar on his cot. He heard knickknacks, records and books tumbling from his shelves. An oil lamp on his Frigidaire shattered to the floor. His dog lay in his lap as he sat up, the room brightening as he looked to the yellowed window, covering and shading his eyes.

"Rashan, whas' that . . ." he whispered.

Hay and dust dripped from the high stable-loft. Shawnee backed against the shuddering wall beneath it, feeling the ground getting looser underneath him. The rumbling noise rolled in his ears. He swung his head to get it out, wheeling, lowering and nodding his brow, whinnying. He reared in panic, running from one side of the stables to the other, nostrils flared, screaming, freezing, darting again. He slipped to his right front knee feeling the white-brittle pain as it twisted beneath him, limping up in terror. Feeling the direction of the sounds, he started out of the stables away from them, crossing the shallow creek bed into the field, slipping on the pea-size creek stones, struggling up the short bank. He galloped through the yellow-wrinkling grass and the crouched and bent-over figures that didn't look up, unimpeding as shadows as he sprinted through them toward the north woods and trail. Expecting the fleshy things to be pummeling his back and haunches as he ran, he felt only the machine-like lumbering noise bearing down on him. The yellow-skied weight of it lowering like a ceiling of mashing thunder, his shadow running ahead of him into the shriveling field and trees.

Deke and Honcho squinted into the yellow light, watching raining objects under the outlines of planes frozen in fire. *Deke saw his family on the porch steps in their finest Sunday clothes. His father in uniform, high boots and staff with the American flag by his P-51. His mother's illuminated portrait of Jesus beside the dining room table. Light shining on dismantled silver bombs in the shed room. His father punting a football into a green silage field. His mother bringing him sandwiches under the trees. The faces of his family slinging mud at each other on the big twelve-hundred. Barrett shambling toward him with his bowlegged walk and wide-cheeked iridescent grin. His own right thigh feathering apart from the blast of a claymore mine. Jason sloshing down the drive to him in short pants and galoshes. Honcho's yellowed face snarling-red, muddy fist plunging the air at the ghostlike river of fire purled above them against the sky.*

The black and white Sylvania buzzed in early dusk light. Madge flipped to the evening news on Channel Seven, watching planes drop flame retardants on burning mountainsides.

> Forest fires ravaged parts of eastern Tennessee again yesterday destroying thousands of acres of woods and farmland. Rangers blamed the fires on parched conditions after months of some

of the worst drought in the state's history followed by violent electrical storms. Firefighting units from Jasper Air Force Base chipped in to bring the blazes under control, but a number of farms were destroyed. At least thirteen people are reported dead or missing . . . Despite President Reagan's denial yesterday of arms-for-hostages trading with Iran, a Los Angeles Times survey shows only 14 percent of Americans accept the President's version as accurate . . .

"How's your appetite, Mrs. Hawkins?" the grey-haired black man said sidling into the room with a foil-covered tray, flicking the overhead.

"I'm a touch hungry," Madge said, elevating her bed. "I hope you remembered my sweetener, Charlie."

"Got it, Mrs. Hawkins, and warm peach cobbler to go with your chicken pie, butter beans and okra," he said, rolling the high tray up to her. "I'm obliged for those Kleenex dolls you sent my grandyounguns. They cotton to anything having to do with soldiering."

"My oldest ones were like that," Madge said, uncovering her plates as Charlie peeled the foil from her iced tea. "As boys they were crazy with flying. Had mock air battles all over our farm. They'd come in black as you are from launching bicycles off hillsides."

"In a boy's blood, ain't it?"

"It was in mine," she laughed. "My husband, Jim, now, received a commendation from the President during the Korea Conflict, did I tell you that?"

"You did, Mrs. Hawkins. Saved a man's life had his arm chopped by a propeller?"

"Oh, he was handsome, Charlie. Still the handsomest man. Raised our boys like little soldiers."

"I know you must be proud, Ma'am. I'd like to meet your oldest son. Not many men gets to pilot jets *and* helicopters in the service."

"I told Jason last night, I wanted all four of 'em to come see me together," she giggled, munching her cobbler. "All four at once now, I said. He's been under the weather. Said he'd come by his self in the morning and give me the latest. They're so busy this time of year harvesting and haying, I expect they'll come by Thanksgiving."

"If humanly possible."

"Deke said he was carrying me home Christmas. I'm looking forward to getting back to my roses and ceramics, my baking. I haven't seen Jim in a month of Sundays, but I know he hasn't had a spare minute since I've been in here."

"Farm work's time-consuming."

"That's all I'm gonna eat now, Charlie. You can take the rest. There's nothing to watch on this old tube but these Iran-Contra Hearings," she said, snapping it off, reaching for her hand lotion. "That nice Col. North seems like such a *good* man."

"Hard to tell these days, Ma'am."

"They should leave the President and his people alone. They're just trying to protect us."

"Those fires they're showing are devastatin', Ma'am. My cousin Levele said he could see smoke clean across three counties."

"They're just killin' insects, Charlie. Running 'em from the fields into the woods to burn 'em out. Every year you've got to do it or they'll get out of hand. I'm gonna get some rest now so I can be up early for my youngest," she said, clicking her hands in white liniment. "He'll give me the latest on Jim and the boys. Jason's studying to be a preacher, did I tell you that?"

"Ain't that a blessing?" Charlie said, walking the tray into the corner lined with Kleenex dolls and flowers. "God's blessed you more ways than one."

"Would you turn out that light on your way out, see I'm not disturbed this evening. Unless it's my husband, of course, or one of my boys. I want to be rested up for in the morning."

"Yes'em, Mrs. Hawkins," Charlie said, flicking the switch.

"You bring those grandsons in to see me one of these days," she said. "I want to meet your precious little soldier boys."

"I'll do it, Mrs. Hawkins. They're like pig iron, every one of 'em. Hardheaded as can be."

"Goodnight, Charlie."

"Goodnight, Mrs. Hawkins. Hope the sandman pays you a visit directly."

THE END

CPSIA information can be obtained at www.ICGtesting.com
Printed in the USA
LVOW121332120912

298522LV00002B/38/P